Y0-BSL-209

Praise for Situation Normal

A triumph: madcap and trenchant, dancing on the precise meridian between funny and weird, with a wild, imaginative boldness that reinvents space-opera from the gravity well up.

— Cory Doctorow, author of *Little Brother,*
co-editor of *Boing Boing*, IP activist

A fast-paced romp reminiscent of Kurt Vonnegut channeled through the wild inventiveness of Charles Stross and the irreverent political attitude of Cory Doctorow.

— Don Vicha, *Booklist* (starred review)

Also by Leonard Richardson:

Constellation Games

Richardson, Leonard, 1979-author.
Situation normal

2020
33305249358528
mi   12/21/20

SITUATION NORMAL

Leonard Richardson

Candlemark & Gleam

First edition published 2020

Copyright @ 2020 by Leonard Richardson

All rights reserved.
Except as permitted under the U.S. Copyright act of 1976,
no part of this book may be reproduced, distributed or transmitted
in any form or by any means, or stored in a database or retrieval system,
without the prior written permission of the editor and publisher.

Please respect authors' rights: don't pirate.

This is a work of fiction. Names, characters, places and incidents either
are the product of the author's imagination or are used fictitiously.
Any resemblance to actual events, locales or persons,
living or dead, is entirely coincidental.

For information, address
Athena Andreadis
Candlemark & Gleam LLC,
38 Rice Street #2, Cambridge, MA 02140
eloi@candlemarkandgleam.com

Library of Congress Cataloguing-in-Publication Data
In Progress

ISBN: 978-1-936460-99-1
eISBN: 978-1-936460-98-4

Cover art by Brittany Hague
Book design and composition by Athena Andreadis

Editor: Athena Andreadis

www.candlemarkandgleam.com

For Mirabai, a connoisseur.

Content Note

Though far from realistic, this adventure story dramatizes many of the terrible features of real war: pain, torture, and death. Its focus on civilians and petty criminals means that the horrors of war, when they arrive, are visited disproportionately on people who would have rather stayed home. In particular, readers who think chapter 24 gets a little heavy should feel free to mentally 'fade to black' and skip to the start of chapter 25.

Humanoid sexuality is another pervasive theme. There is no sexual violence in this story, but readers should be prepared for what are euphemistically called 'adult themes'.

Situation Normal uses the standards for English punctuation set by the Galactic Siblinghood for Interlingual Precision (GSIP). Punctuation appears inside quotation marks when it is part of the quoted dialogue, and outside quotation marks when it is meant as a general pause signal. Example: "The manifest says 'medical chambers', but the container is actually full of 'weapons'."

Species names like 'egenu' and native terms like 'kelexn' are rendered using the GSIP anglicization. Timespans are given in imperial (days, years) or metric (shifts, kiloshifts) depending on the speaker's point of reference. Brand names such as sturdi and Hestin Compliance Systems are mentioned under the principle of fair use.

God speaks to con artists because God is a con artist.

—Egenu saying

The Main Players

The Terran Outreach

Rebecca Twice, a security guard
Myrusit Wectusessin, a woodworker's apprentice
Denweld Xepperxelt, another
Arun Sliver, a hitman

The Outreach Navy

Warrant Officer Hiroko Ingridsdotter
Commander Hetselter Churryhoof
Second Lieutenant Dwap-Jac-Dac
Specialist Chudwhalt Tellpesh
Mrs. Chen, a spy
First Lieutenant Texchiffu Rebtet

The Fist of Joy

The Chief, a smuggler
Kol, a system administrator
Styrqot, a trader
Thaddeus G. Starbottle, a scientist
The Errand Boy, an errand boy

Unaligned

Yip-Goru, a pilot
Tia, a priest
Qued Ethiret, a cosplayer

Part One

Cedar Commons

Chapter 1

Opt Out

Rebecca Twice
Steward station

"Wake up, poundcake," said Hiroko. "We got a bogey."

Becky rolled away from the senior steward, her nightshirt pressing against the crinkly layers of duct tape that divided the queen-size bed into her side (45%) and Hiroko's (the rest). "Can it wait until tomorrow?" she said.

"It is tomorrow," said Hiroko. "Bogey came in on the day side, betting we'd be asleep. Classic poacher move." Hiroko yanked the covers off the bed. "Up!"

Becky pulled the nightshirt down her legs and followed Hiroko into the lit-up common room, her bare feet searing cold on the stone floor. Hiroko pushed the 3-globe of Cedar Commons across the dining table, and Becky sat down in front of it. Blinking hurt her eyes.

A tiny green light pearled on the 3-globe's night side. That light was the location of the city-dock, the stewards' outpost, Becky and Hiroko, and the 3-globe itself with its tiny green light. On the exact opposite point on the globe, the dotted red curve of a trajectory stuck out from the freshwater ocean like a stray hair. Something small had just landed on Cedar Commons. Or impacted, or taken off. You couldn't tell from a static map, but Hiroko was confident about "landed".

"Get in the hovercar and intercept," said Hiroko. Her finger traced the trajectory from orbit into the ocean. "Wave the shotgun and they'll scatter. Do not try to upsell them. I don't want the paperwork. Get them off planet and we'll forget the whole thing."

"Why does it have to be me?" said Becky.

"Because I got a manicure yesterday," said Hiroko. She flared her nails like a lizard's frill. "And I'm the senior steward, and I don't want to." She stood up and rummaged around in the refrigerator like she wanted to hide in it. "Well, don't be a baby about it! I'll be on comm. My sleep's ruined, too, like you care."

"When I'm the senior steward," said Becky, "I'm going to be nice to my junior."

"That's what I said," said Hiroko. "And then you showed up."

Becky wanted to punch the refrigerator door closed on Hiroko's head. Instead she opened her locker and pulled out her Trellis On-Site Security branded jumpsuit. "What if it's not wood poachers?" she said. "What if it's a ring fragment?" She zipped the jumpsuit over her nightshirt.

Hiroko took a neutral Pepsi out of the fridge and cracked the bottle. "It's not a ring fragment," she said. "This same thing happened five months ago. Something came down in the middle of the night, exactly where my lazy-ass senior didn't want to check it out. It knows where we are and what a pain it'll be to get over there. So it's poachers."

"What if it is a ring fragment?" Becky dropped to one knee to lace up her Proudhon action sneaker. "How do I handle it?"

"You better hope it's not," said Hiroko. "We'll be putting out forest fires for a week, *and* housing the crew we gotta call to fix the defense grid." She slapped her Pepsi onto the planetary comm console. "Yeah, you think the bed's crowded now? Wait until you're sharing it with a fat guy and two rre." Hiroko's eyes glazed over as she coupled her capital terminal to the comm.

Becky's shoes were sealed. She grabbed a sweater and turned to leave the steward station. "I hope it's a ring fragment," she snarled.

"I hope it's an asteroid made of triple-crème Brie!"

Midnight on Cedar Commons was warm and windy, and it wasn't far to the garage where the two Tata Devout hovercars were parked. Becky skirted the edge of the concrete city-dock. After three months on Cedar Commons, Becky was sick of trees, but she'd have the rest of her life to appreciate concrete.

Drizzling light through the oak branches were the bright planetary rings, and three of the moons that kept the ring system stable. Becky was a city girl, raised on Earth, and this combination of the familiar and the otherworldly was infuriatingly romantic. A picture similar to this had been on Trellis's site, and below it had been a very promising bullet point saying

• *5-month placements with sexually compatible partners*

But Trellis On-Site Security was a rre brand, and to its sentient resources department, sex was a perk offered to the humanoid employees. They did not understand that although she and Hiroko had checked the same box on a form, Becky was *not* sexually compatible with the femmiest, most obnoxious lesbian in the universe.

Becky's sneakers pressed acorns into the dirt all the way to the garage. Goddamn Hiroko with her manicure machine and her Bible thumping and her pretentious jazz and her repetitive Navy stories. Becky entertained herself with a little fantasy about the fallen ring fragment she was about to discover, and the lanky satellite repairwoman who would drop out of orbit and ring Becky's doorbell once they called it in.

Myrus
Jaketown

Myrus should have been asleep, but Dad was meeting with the mayor in the living room, with Myrus not supposed to be listening, and who can resist that challenge? Unfortunately Mr. Nzeme was saying things he said a lot, "Hard truths", "We need your vote on this", "The party has to stick together", so Myrus had gone back to his book and was thinking about legitimately going to sleep, but then Mr. Nzeme said "They'll take your son." And *wait, what?*

"They'll take my twins," the mayor continued. "Every teenager on this ship. They'll take the *ship*. They'll train Myrus to be a killer and they'll put him in a uniform so he'll look handsome when he comes back in a bag."

"I fought in the last war, Jiankang," Dad said with quiet anger. "I was proud to wear that uniform."

"Sure, sure," said the human. "And what do we think about that war, now? Was it so wonderful that we need to do it again? What will we say about *this* war in fifteen years?"

"That war you're dismissing ended slavery in the Fist."

"Oh, don't you bloody start with me, Kem," said the mayor. Dad was silent and *Jaketown*'s fusion generators filled the space, throbbing far below decks. It wasn't Myrus's imagination. That sound had definitely gotten louder since yesterday. "Uhaltihaxl aren't warriors by nature," said Mr. Nzeme, trying a different approach.

"We are when we have to be," said Dad.

"Your son doesn't have to be," said the human.

"One ship can't opt out of a war!" said Dad. "It goes against the principles of representative government."

The heavy sound of a wooden chair scooting across the wooden floor. "It will not be a ship if we land it," the human said to Dad, and Myrus had to strain to hear him. "It will be a city, with very different legal obligations."

Landing! Landing meant an end to school, but it meant the beginning of work, which meant finally leaving the men's deck. On their last planetfall Myrus's whole body had quivered whenever he'd been in the same room with a girl; basically just Den, the one girl Dad didn't force Myrus to avoid.

Sometimes the men's deck made Myrus so frustrated he thought about sneaking up to the women's deck and...what? What did he think would happen? He'd never actually gone into love; he just *wanted* to, really bad. His body wouldn't cooperate with his mind.

He had told Dad about this hormonal problem—big mistake. Dad had put his head in his hands and said "You're barely fifteen, Myrus! Don't rush it! Your body's just...considering all the options, you know?" What was Myrus supposed to say to that? His body *had* considered the options and had definitely picked one, and he'd had to sit there—oh, crap.

"—ship in pursuit." Mr. Nzeme had just said "—decisive action because there's a ship in pursuit." Someone was chasing *Jaketown*. Someone wanted to kill them.

"The Fist of Joy," said Dad. Just the name took him back to the previous war.

"Nuh-uh. An Outreach Light Combat Platform. *Brown v. Board of Education of Topeka.*"

"That's us, Jiankang," said Dad. "They're the good guys. Why are we running? This is insane."

"Who knows what they want," said the mayor in a tone that was either flat or full of adult emotions Myrus didn't understand. "They've been sending us urgent messages, but the Navy drafted our comm tech last month, so we're not that good at decrypting."

"Who made this decision?" said Dad. "Why wasn't the council consulted before we committed *treason*?"

"The skipper's priority is protecting the brand's investment in the ship," said Mr. Nzeme. "If we want the city council to make these decisions, we need to stop being a spaceship and start being a city. That starts tomorrow, with your vote on planetfall."

The living room was silent for so long that Myrus wondered if Dad and Mr. Nzeme had fallen asleep themselves. The engines surged beneath Myrus's bed and his stomach jumped. The ship was skipping almost every hour, now.

"Do we have a candidate planet?" Dad said, finally.

"Cedar Commons," said the mayor. "Old-growth forest projected onto native biomes, leased by Eserion. It's exactly the same as the last ten planets we landed on, except the forest's only twenty years old."

"That'll affect the quality of the furniture," said Dad.

"Do you know what else will affect the quality of the furniture?" said Mr. Nzeme. "When *Jaketown* gets seized to run cargo for the navy, and your tools get jettisoned into space. And then we all die in a Fist of Joy minefield."

The chair scooted again. "The skipper's timing it so we land twenty minutes after the vote," said Mr. Nzeme. "If Tip-Iye-Nett-Zig decides thon's gonna make a big speech in opposition, we call it ten. This is going through with or without your vote, so you should stand with the party."

"I'll see you tomorrow," said Dad, not agreeing to anything.

The chair scooted again. "0600," said Mr. Nzeme. The front door slid open; Myrus pictured his big human thumb in the grasp. "War is insanity, Councilman Wectusessin," said the mayor of *Jaketown*, in a sweet and gentle tone he never ever used. "Keep your boy out of it." The door slid closed.

Myrus's sweaty ear was pressed against the nice wood paneling of the bedroom. He slid his finger down the grain like the flow of a nosebleed. "Nice wood paneling" was what Dad called it, but nice to Dad just meant "made out of wood".

Myrus had always thought the woodworking tools were nicer than the wood they shaped or the furniture that came out. The worst thing Mr. Nzeme had said, worse than "they'll take your son", was the thing about the Navy shooting those tools into space.

In the cafeteria—not the school cafeteria with its generic neutral food, but the uhaltihaxl place he and Dad and Den went to when they were working—was a corkboard covered in old government posters. Most people ignored them but Myrus had read them all: they were a glimpse of the universe outside *Jaketown*. Most memorable was a poster from the Outreach Navy. It showed an uhaltihaxl and a human and a rre in Navy uniforms, all looking in the same direction, and below it in letters that looked carved from stone it said: "SEND US YOUR BOYS*. WE'LL GIVE YOU MEN†."

Tonight was Myrusit Wectusessin's first inkling that the Navy of the Terran Outreach might not always deliver on their end of that promise.

A few minutes later Dad quietly opened the bedroom door and looked into the top bunk where Myrus was sound asleep, his nubby teenage horns pressed into the pillow, his breathing smooth and quiet, because Dad had enough to worry about without also having to worry about his son.

Churryhoof
Brown v. Board of Education of Topeka

The message came encoded in four-character blocks. Commander Hetselter Churryhoof tapped the decryption pencil against her metal desk and sounded out the terse official English.

WARD ECLA RED�

WAR DECLARED

Tucked beneath *Brown v. Board of Education of Topeka*'s one-time pad was an envelope of paper orders to be opened only once WARD ECLA was officially RED. The seal on the envelope was already frayed. Churryhoof had read the orders four days ago, as soon as *Brown* had left spacedock to draft civilian ships for the buildup.

In wartime *Brown* was to escort the fully crewed city-ship *Jaketown* towards a secret fleet rendezvous point. Little problem, though: *Jaketown* had guessed those orders and didn't like them. She'd been ignoring hails, skipping away from *Brown* as fast as she could on a trajectory that took her deep into the galaxy, away from the big Outreach colonies, into the disputed territories, towards the neutral systems and the Fist of Joy itself.

Civilians don't want to fight; that's understandable. Civilians run from a draft; that's illegal. Civilians flee *towards the enemy;* that looks like treason. The war was eight minutes old, and Churryhoof was contemplating having to execute Outreach citizens.

"Commander," said Lieutenant Dwap-Jac-Dac in her terminal. "I'm outside. May I come in, ma'am?"

"Come," said Churryhoof.

The door to Churryhoof's office slid open and a biped shape stepped in and stood silent as a statue. In fact the exobody *was* a statue: a suit of crystalline metamaterial crafted into a human form and given human features. Kilo for kilo, the most useless piece of gear in the service.

"Ma'am," said the lieutenant.

By the end of the war, Churryhoof would have given a kill order and seen how Dwap-Jac-Dac carried it out. If they survived, their camaraderie would be unshakeable. If they died, they would die together. But this was now, the war was a newborn, and Dwap-Jac-Dac was an inscrutable rre: a few tangled centimeters of fleshy tubes floating in a cloud of artificial blood, encased in a human form to make the colony more relatable to bipeds.

"We're at war, lieutenant," said Churryhoof. She held up the decrypted cable.

"Yes, ma'am," said Dwap-Jac-Dac. Thon already knew; everyone knew; it was just a matter of getting the signatures on the paperwork. "We've triangulated *Jaketown*'s course corrections."

"Good work," said Churryhoof, because that's what a commander says.

"They're not headed for Fist space."

"Then where?" said Churryhoof.

"EGS-RC121," said Dwap-Jac-Dac. "Near the border, but definitely ours. There's an uninhabited agriculture planet in-system. The leasing brand calls it Cedar Commons." Just... standing there, no body language at all, like a lucite award honoring twenty years' service. Dwap-Jac-Dac was a bottle of liquor with a worm in the middle, and Churryhoof had no way of knowing how strong the liquor was.

Churryhoof tapped her pencil against the desk again. "Lieutenant."

"Ma'am."

"A ship this small doesn't rate an executive officer, so when there's a problem, I like to talk things out with my Master of Drone. Do you want in on this, or would you rather just execute orders?"

Churryhoof thought she could see the bodies of the rre colony twisting around inside the suit with less than military precision. Maybe it was just the way light passed through the metamaterial.

"I'll serve as needed, ma'am," said Dwap-Jac-Dac. "Back at sector HQ I frequently offered suggestions."

Churryhoof held out one hand at the padded couch pushed against one wall of her tiny office. "Take a seat."

The servos of Dwap-Jac-Dac's suit hissed in the silence of the commander's office. The joints bent, the knees shifted forward, the hips extended back over the couch. Every movement was a deliberate decision for the lieutenant. The half-ton suit halted in an awkward squat, the crystalline buttocks poised just over the surface of the couch so as not to pull the upholstery or scratch the metal frame.

"The couch is to put you at ease," said Churryhoof. "If it doesn't put you at ease, there's no point sitting down."

"It's all the same to me, ma'am," said Dwap-Jac-Dac. "I'm just fine. Whatever works for you."

"Then stand up. I don't want you breaking the couch."

"Yes, ma'am." Lieutenant Dwap-Jac-Dac stood and kept perfectly still once again.

Churryhoof missed Lieutenant Lakshmi Prasad. Her old Master of Drone had put her full weight on that couch and liked it. Prasad could be as aggravating as any other human, but at least she was a normal biped *person*, with a face, and different expressions for happy and sad. She was quick with a joke and could give Churryhoof self-deprecating explanations of the insanities that periodically consumed *Brown*'s human crew members.

Prasad had been promoted during the buildup; she was now comm officer on *None of the Above*, coordinating half a battle wing. No promotion had been more richly deserved, but it meant Churryhoof was going into a war backed by a Master of Drone whose emotions she literally couldn't read.

"Well, let's get started," said Churryhoof, already feeling like this was a waste of time. "Do you have any clue why they're going hot for this particular planet?"

"If I recall my Terran biology, cedar is a kind of tree," said Dwap-Jac-Dac. "*Jaketown* is a furniture ship. I think they're pretending there's no war. They'll dock at Cedar Commons and carry out their normal manufacturing business. When we confront them, they'll say they didn't get the draft order."

Churryhoof's horns went up. "That's the stupidest fucking plan I've ever heard of."

"Not the plan I would have devised, ma'am."

Oh, great. "What plan would you have devised, Lieutenant?"

"Compliance with the draft order, ma'am." It was conceivably a joke. Even if not, it caught Churryhoof off guard in the right way.

"Now that we've triangulated," said Churryhoof, "can we get to Cedar Commons before *Jaketown* docks?"

"I couldn't say, ma'am. It's going to be close."

A new lieutenant, like any source of telemetry, needed calibration. "*You* can't say; what does the projection say?"

"It says we'll miss them by ninety minutes."

Tap tap tap. "I hope they enjoy those ninety minutes," said Commander Churryhoof, "because they are not going to like what happens afterward."

"Probably not, ma'am."

Chapter 2

The Upsell

Rebecca Twice
The bogey

Hovering above the shallow ocean in the Tata Devout, Becky could make out the impact site clearly enough. It was a blemish through the water, a cloud of mud and dead carp. The cloud extended a long murky finger that pointed towards the shore. "That doesn't look like a ring fragment," she admitted.

"Ya think?" said Hiroko over the comm.

"Okay, so," said Becky. "I run it to ground, wave the shotgun, they take off, I put out the fire."

"I've hit the panic button," said Hiroko. "But I think we're on our own. The midnight news packet just came in. We are at war."

Becky swallowed hard. "War" was just a word—a few years back she'd lost a cousin in a border skirmish that had been forgotten in a week—but it was a word with a lot of stopping power.

"Look on the bright side," said Hiroko, who'd misunderstood Becky's silence. "I'll get called up and they'll send some other asshole to keep you company."

"Moving to intercept," said Becky. She eased the hovercar towards the shore, staying well to the side of the wake. The ship that had made the blemish came into view, a lump of space-filthy metal buried under a hasty camouflage of oak branches and mud.

"That's not good," said Becky. "Cover means they plan to stay a while, right?"

"Oh my God," said Hiroko. "That's a Fist of Joy ship."

"Are you sure?" said Becky. This didn't seem like a good topic to joke about.

"The Navy's pretty insistent we learn this shit," said Hiroko. "Yeah, it's a rasme thau design. I could fly it if I had to."

"Who's rasme thau?" whispered Becky. She needed some booze.

"They're a minor Fist power," said Hiroko. "They have these big cranial fronds. Lots of independent traders, a.k.a. smugglers."

"What do we do?" said Becky.

"Well don't panic, poundcake," said Hiroko. "Pick up the shotgun and get closer. They've already seen you."

"I'm not a soldier!"

"You're private security, and you're paid to deal with this shit. Send 'em back home. You'll be doing them a favor."

"I'm gonna try the upsell," said Becky. "If they're Fist spies, I play stupid."

"If they're spies, you're already dead." Hiroko was still being cruel, but she'd stopped enjoying it.

Becky slowly moved the hovercar down below the treetops, forward towards the hill of metal built by a civilization that wanted her dead. From forty meters away she made out orange script below the mud on the hull.

"That's a Trade Standard, right?" said Becky. "What's it say?"

"It's D," said Hiroko. "Something 'bad'. Maybe 'bad sugar'. You want to get closer?"

"No, I'll do the upsell in D." Becky dropped the megaphone down from the hovercar chassis and dialed up a sales pitch in her terminal. "I'll need you to translate the response."

"I got your back," said Hiroko. It was the nicest thing she'd ever said to Becky.

The pitch was available in Trade Standard D, D-plus-B, and

eight human languages. It sounded the same in all of them, down to the cadence and the order of the words. Becky flipped it on in her terminal and there it was, the voice of the brand, coming down from on high. She easily followed along with sounds she'd never heard and couldn't understand.

Eserion Natural Resources thanked the intruder for an interest in its products. In hopes of keeping the intruder as a valued long-term customer, Eserion was excited to announce exclusive rates on a one-time, low-volume purchase. To ensure the lowest possible prices, the negotiation would be conducted through Eserion's partner, Trellis On-Site Security. A Trellis representative was on the scene and ready to explain Eserion's rates, at the intruder's convenience.

Becky's employer boasted the lowest shrinkage losses of any Outreach security company because it simply did not believe in theft. What the law labeled robbery, Trellis considered a sale which the customer service representative had been unable to close. Or did not want to, in this case. Becky greatly preferred the idea of hiding under the bed back at the steward station. She sweated out the recorded sales pitch, hoping to be ignored.

No such luck. A man climbed out a hatch in the top of the ship, standing just a little lower than Becky in her hovercar. A *human* man with shaggy hair: an Indian guy wearing antique-looking 2-glasses. He waved at Becky and made a dial-twisting motion.

"The hell?" said Hiroko. Becky turned off the recorded message.

The man cupped his hands to his mouth and shouted "Gnar-harna-harna-harna!" at Becky. Something like that.

"He's asking if you speak Trade Standard D," Hiroko translated.

"Uh, do you speak English?" said Becky into the hovercraft's mic, through the screechy megaphone.

"Oh, raw-ther," said the human in a toffy British accent.

"...Is this your ship?"

"Quite, quite," said the man. "Poaching a bit of wood, don't you know. Kids' playhouse blew away in a storm. I shan't be long. Your rates are reasonable."

"What the hell is a human doing with a Fist of Joy ship?" said Hiroko over the comm. "Ask to see his crew."

Becky leaned into the mic again but she ended up saying nothing because the man down below was pointing an illegal singularity pistol at her. "You must switch off that comm, mum," he said, his accent instantly shedding six tax brackets and a university degree. "Otherwise it will be difficult to negotiate a deal that leaves you alive."

The shotgun was lying on the passenger's seat. Becky could probably lift it and get a sight before the human down below vaporized her and the hovercar. But he wouldn't shoot her, right?

"Oh, before you switch off the comm, which you must do now," said the man down below, "tell your colleagues not to come after you."

He would shoot her. Becky had to move first. She inched one hand towards the gun. "Don't be a hero," she told Hiroko, loudly.

"No risk of that," said Hiroko.

"The unbearable slowness of your strategy, Mr. Arun Sliver!" shouted a woman's voice from...up in the trees?

The human looked up and to the side. "Chief, please let me handle this! Mum, disengage your terminal and land the car."

"The obvious expedient!"

"Chief, please stay where you are."

"Yaiyaiyaiyai!" came down out of the trees, a battle cry from a purple blur which halted its fall by grabbing onto the footrail of the hovercar. The vehicle tilted sharply to port, and Becky was thrown against her safety harness. The shotgun slapped against her side.

"Chief, you're spoiling my shot!" said the human.

"No such shot! Our need for the vehicle!"

This was the best opening Becky was likely to get. She grabbed the shotgun, ducked down as far as she could and fired blindly over the swaying metal horizon at where she guessed the man with the pistol was.

The mass-energy recoil sent the car spinning around the

motivator bar that ran from nose to tail. Becky went upside down and the shotgun slipped from her grasp. The trigger caught briefly on her index finger and the gun dropped to the forest floor. Becky dangled in the safety straps she had fortunately not unbuckled, her computer-set braids spilling outwards. In her peripheral vision Becky saw a purple squirming, someone trying to hold on to the footrail as the hovercar rocked back and forth. Becky turned her head, prepared to slap ineffectually at this new threat.

Dangling right-side-up from the hovercar's footrail was a woman with olive-green skin. She was wearing a purple cocktail dress. Her eyes and her nose were a weird shape, not that Becky would say that out loud, and instead of hair on her head there were these...cartilage things...

The cartilage things were cranial fronds. The woman was rasme thau. The human had called her "chief". This death machine was her ship.

"Pardon my reach," said the rasme thau woman. It sounded like she'd learned the phrase from human waiters. She reached across Becky's chest, muscles straining in the arm that held her five meters above the ground, and shut off the hardware switch that connected Becky to Hiroko with a precise, deadly *click*.

"I'm going to throw up," Becky said quietly. Being upside down was a reminder of the nauseous moment right before a spaceship skips, when they turn off the gravity.

"Mr. Arun Sliver!" the rasme thau called out. "Gnar harna 'frowup' harna?"

"Harna harna harna," said the human down below. He'd climbed down the ship's ramp to the ground and was collecting Becky's shotgun.

"*Not* to frowup," the rasme thau told Becky quietly, effortlessly shifting her grip on the footrail. "The motivator, your hand touching it. Our motion downwards, together. Your safety, my promise." Becky nodded and put her hand on the motivator and gently lowered the hovercar until the rasme thau woman stepped off the footrail into the mud and Becky's braids dragged spirals in a puddle.

"Your exit," said the rasme thau. Becky unfastened the safety straps and did a backflip into the mud and wriggled out from beneath the hovercar. Filthy water soaked through her wool sweater and the paper-cotton of the Trellis jumpsuit. She knelt in the puddle and glanced up, unsure if she was allowed to stand.

The human, presumably Mr. Arun Sliver, stood next to the rasme thau woman and held Becky's shotgun. The 'chief' was looking Becky over with a playful cat-and-mouse look, charging and decharging a little home-defense zapper by rubbing it up and down her muddy bare leg. She had caught a stick of oak in her dress on the way down through the trees, and it was tugging her scooped neckline *Jesus, Becky, can we get through one life-threatening situation without thinking about tits?*

The rasme thau noticed where Becky was looking and pulled the stick out of her dress. "Kol!" she barked, as if into a comm, though she wasn't holding anything but the stick and the zapper. "Gnar harna harna!"

The Indian guy with the various accents yanked Becky to her feet and held her arms behind her back. A man with glistening blue skin climbed down from the ship's hatch. No, the skin was scales; the man was egenu. Another Fist of Joy race.

Becky had only seen egenu on news shows yelling about treaties, or whacking mooks in Fist crime dramas. This guy was in-person, wearing cargo shorts and an unbuttoned dress shirt and a water bottle, carrying two laser cutters and a duffel bag that gave off a foul fishy smell.

"Harna," said the egenu. He set down the stuff he was holding, sucked at the valve of his water bottle and cast what he probably thought was an inconspicuous glance at Becky. "Harna gnar?"

There was a little more harna-ing and the upshot was that the egenu and the rasme thau should brace themselves in the muddy ground and try to tip Becky's floating hovercar right-side-up. The short woman squatted and her legs tensed up and her tennis shoes slipped backwards in the mud and *Oh my God, Becky, look at her butt.*

For someone who'd been stuck on a planet for three months with Hiroko's bony ass, this was like an alarm clock going off. The shifting fabric of the smuggler chief's cocktail dress allowed Becky to form not only a detailed topographic map but a density profile revealing an alien but aesthetically pleasing distribution of muscle and fat. The chief combined raw strength with a total lack of self-consciousness in a way that melted Becky. The only drawback was that this woman was likely to murder her; something Hiroko had only threatened playfully.

All too soon the hovercar growled and shifted around its motivator and tipped over. In that last push, Becky caught a tantalizing glimpse of black panty underneath the chief's dress. The machine splashed into the mud puddle Becky had fallen into, rocking back and forth in mid-air, tossing spray around. Becky tried to dodge but Arun just tightened his don't-go-anywhere grip.

The chief wiped her hands on her increasingly dirty cocktail dress. The egenu slid open the hovercar's cargo hold and dropped in the laser cutters and the duffel bag. He got into the passenger seat. The chief strapped herself into the driver's seat, settling that wonderful ass into the warmth Becky had left on the plastic seat cover.

"Our journey into the woods," the chief told Becky. "Its duration, measured in decishifts. Your sojourn in my ship. Our return, your anticipation." In other words, *Get in the ship, hostage.*

"Mr. Arun Sliver," said the chief, still in English for Becky's benefit. "Your hospitality towards our guest! The clothes you lend her. The tea you brew her."

"Fresh out of tea, I'm afraid," said the human. "I don't like to whinge, but..."

"The yriek bush in my quarters," said the rasme thau, losing some patience.

"I wasn't counting the yriek bush," said Arun Sliver, "because it's toxic to humans."

"The exaggerated reports of its toxicity!" said the chief.

"I will make her some tea," said Arun through gritted teeth.

"My satisfaction," said the rasme thau, and nodded at Becky. "Your name," she said. "Ma'am?" A bit of exaggerated politeness, from someone raised on Fist propaganda about humans and their intensely honor-based culture.

"Becky," said Becky, shivering from the wet and the cold and Arun's unwelcome grip. "Becky Twice."

"My anticipation of our next meeting, Miss Becky Twice," said the rasme thau in a way that sounded flirty if you were not thinking straight and hadn't gotten laid in four months. The Trellis hovercar shot back into the air and headed north, cropping the treetops. North meant they weren't off to kill Hiroko, thank God. So where *were* they going? The steward station was the only interesting thing on this planet.

"Into the ship, mum," said Arun, gesturing with the singularity pistol in a mixture of politeness and threat. He'd settled on a middle-income, technical college sort of accent. "You may borrow m'bathrobe."

Becky sloshed through the mud at gunpoint towards the promise of dry and warm. The events of the day had come from a completely different genre of lesbian porn than the one she'd been fantasizing about. Instead of the corny satellite repairwoman scenario, she'd been kidnapped by an alien butch in a cocktail dress who'd stolen her car. Some part of Becky wanted to follow this scene through to completion. In the chief's quarters next to the yriek bush, bound to the poached-wood bedposts while the rasme thau straddled Becky's chest and smothered her with those big green tits. But, realistically, Becky was willing to settle for getting off this planet alive. That was fantasy enough.

The smuggler ship had a horrible spacebound smell which the crew were trying to dispel by blasting the airlock vents. Arun Sliver escorted Becky to the kitchen area, where she sat on a plastic chair and rested her elbows on a plastic dinner table. Arun unhooked a coffee mug from the restraints that held it during skips, and opened a cupboard where six tea bags dangled from hooks like Victorian criminals.

"Fifth time around for these bags, I'm afraid," he said.

"It's okay," said Becky. "I'm not really in the mood for tea." What with the nauseating smell and the kidnapping.

Arun misunderstood. "American-descended, are you?" He slid the coffee mug into a cavity in the sink and Becky heard the hissing of superheated steam.

"I'm real American," said Becky. "I'm from Los Angeles. And I don't like tea."

"Apologies in advance, but the chief has told me to make you tea, and tea you shall have. You don't have to drink it."

"Are you gonna kill me?" said Becky.

"Oh," said Arun, grimacing, as though Becky had farted, or mentioned money. "Not unless you come after me, or Yip-Goru." He pointed through the kitchen into the bridge, where a rre in a squat suit resembling a Dalek or a municipal garbage can sat at a console.

"I'm not gonna rush a fuckin' rre," said Becky.

"Very wise," said Arun. "Please keep in mind I am a much tougher customer than this particular rre."

"Shut up," said Yip-Goru, without moving.

"Guys, we're at war," said Becky. "Clearly y'all haven't heard, because your boss just left a human and a rre with the keys to her ship. I don't know what your criminal records look like, but if you brought back a Fist of Joy cargo ship, that seems like something we could use."

"We know there's a war!" said Yip-Goru. "I predicted the war!"

"We watched it start," Arun told Becky. "Nukes deployed in orbit over Quennet. Professional noncombatants that we are—"

"He means 'cowards'," said Yip-Goru.

"Speak for yourself. We decided to retire for the duration to a quiet forest planet. Where you, the bloody tree coppers, had the poor taste to snitch on your new neighbors. So, please, don't incite us to mutiny, mum. You've done quite enough." Arun pulled the coffee mug out of the sink and presented it to Becky. The tea inside was the color of piss.

"Miss Becky Twice," he said in the posh voice he'd used when he first encountered her, "I offer you tea."

"I don't want your damn tea," said Becky.

"Ta very much," said Arun. He sat down and drew the mug towards himself. Printed on the mug was a drawing of an egenu woman holding a colorful human beachball. There was text on the mug, and the text used English words, but the words just didn't make any sense. The mug said "THE IF AND!"

"We don't keep hostages for long in this line of work," said Arun. "If you're still alive when the chief comes back, she'll probably invite you to join the crew."

"Why the hell would she do that?" said Becky.

"The chief likes to keep a bed-warmer," said Arun. No, that was Becky's imagination running off again. He actually said: "We're four at the moment. Our engineer was killed in an accident about twenty shifts ago."

Becky swallowed. "Can I have some water?"

"Of course," said Arun. He scooted back his plastic chair and unhooked another cup from beside the sink.

"I'm not an engineer," said Becky. She didn't even know how long a Fist 'shift' was. Their sitcoms ran five centishifts, so ten hours maybe? "I studied marketing."

Arun ran the faucet. "Nonetheless, four is an inconvenient number. We always end up at five."

"How hard is it to smuggle shit?" said Becky. "You need a pilot, you need a...hidey guy."

Arun handed Becky the cup of water without ceremony. It was a big enameled metal thing with a grip like brass knuckles, not designed for human fingers. Becky drank. "Greatly as I respect your knowledge of our field," said Arun, "you should know that our chief is a bit eccentric. Do you ever watch crime shows on the 3-tube?"

"Yeeeeah," Becky wiped her mouth. "Me and Hiroko watch *Undeclared* and *The Down Under Crew*."

"How many characters make up the titular Down Under Crew?" said Arun. "I'll save you the trouble: it's not four. Four characters sort into stable alliances of two. The drama becomes stale. With five characters you get shifting alliances, or you get two stable alliances with the chief acting as tiebreaker."

"But you guys do real crimes, right?" said Becky. "You're not reenacting a 3-show."

"You're looking at it as a binary, yeh?" said Arun. "The chief's not like that; she takes a holistic view of the matter. We're not your orthodox grey-market shipping company, but I can promise you good pay, fair treatment, and the excitement which has clearly been missing from your life. We often run restricted foodstuffs and recreational drugs, and if you see anything you like, you're free to skim a little off the top."

Fair treatment? This guy sounded like a Navy recruiter. *Speaking of which...* "I don't want excitement," Becky said. "I want to keep my head down 'til this war blows over. I work for a security brand, for Christ's sake. I'm not gonna join a smuggling ring run by the enemy."

"You *worked* for a security brand," said Arun. "Until this afternoon, when you left work and never came back. That won't reflect well on...Trellis, was it?"

"You kidnapped me!" said Becky. "I'm the victim here!"

"By law, perhaps," said Arun, as if this were an open question. "But from the brand's perspective, all you've done is become a liability."

"Oh, Jesus," said Becky. "I can't get fired! Do you know how hard it is to come back from an employment gap?"

"As a matter of fact, I do," said Arun. "Fortunately for the both of us, criminals don't check that paperwork."

Becky gulped down another slosh of water. She needed something stronger. Trellis had trained her to face down death. Not very effectively, but at least she'd had the training. Nobody trained you how to face unemployment.

"That's her cup, by the way," said Arun.

"Whose cup?" said Becky.

"Our late engineer's," said Arun. "You may keep it."

Becky set down the dead woman's cup and let go of the handle. "That's a hell of a signing bonus."

"We wash our own dishes on this crew," said Arun, as if he hadn't just said what he'd just said. "All personal items must be strapped down during maneuvers."

"I haven't taken the job yet."

"But the initial screening is going quite well," said Arun. "You haven't tried anything and I haven't killed you. Now, while we wait for the chief's return, I suggest you gather your thoughts and try to remember everything you can about *The Down Under Crew*."

"Do you have it on card or something?" said Becky. "All my stuff is back at the steward station."

"It's not that complicated, yeah?" said Arun. "The Crew have some mad plan, it all goes wrong, so they come up with an even madder plan to get out of it. That covers most of it."

"Arun!" Yip-Goru called out.

"Yeh, mate?" said Arun. He jumped out of his chair and leaned into the bridge.

This was Becky's big chance. She could brain Arun with the dead engineer's cup and...get torn apart by the rre. *Back to the drawing board, Becky.*

"Something enormous just skipped into orbit," said Yip-Goru.

The hatch was open. Becky could make a run for it. Cedar Commons wasn't designed for human habitation, but neither was it a hostile planet. Wouldn't get far on foot, though.

"Who's driving?" said the human.

"No one's driving," said Yip-Goru. "They're going for a powered crash. They don't care who sees them."

"Well, it's not mutual, mate."

"Indeed," said Yip-Goru. "Motivators are standby, everything else needs to go dark. How long until the chief gets back?"

"I don't know where they went!" Arun dashed back into the kitchen and flipped switches. The water heater belched, the electrical lights snapped off.

"O-kay, motivators go dark as well," said Yip-Goru. Lights danced in the darkness: instrument panel displays from the bridge, refracted through Yip-Goru's metamaterial suit. Then those lights switched off, and there was nothing.

The cargo hold, the crew quarters. The ship wasn't huge, but it was more than a kitchen and a bridge. She could hide in the darkness and find a weapon. Becky scooted beneath the table and a hand grabbed her shoulder. "Sit tight, mum," Arun said.

"Where is it?" she said. "Is it gonna hit us?"

"Yeh, what's its trajectory?" Arun asked.

"As a matter of fact, it's about to hit your house, Becky," said Yip-Goru. Becky heard a shuffling sound; the rre was joining them in the dark kitchen. "Good thing you moved to the exact opposite side of the planet, huh?"

"We have to warn Hiroko," said Becky. "Please, oh my God."

"I'm afraid that falls under the broad category of 'squealing to the fuzz'," said Arun. "Which we don't do."

"You're just going to let her die?" said Becky. She huddled beneath the kitchen table like a kid in an earthquake.

"She's not going to die, yaar," said Arun. "If she's any kind of copper, she's already headed over to rescue her partner. So, we'll... sort it out when she gets here."

Becky unsuccessfully looked up at her invisible captor. "You know we're not really cops, right?"

Chapter 3

Fancy Chemicals

Kol
The Tata Devout

Kol had a custom hotwire kit for stealing Outreach-make vehicles, but this one was easy: the hovercar's previous owner hadn't shut off the engine. He squeezed himself into the front passenger's seat and the Chief brought the craft up. They smashed through stiff tree fronds and saw the flat green roofs of the forest and the sea.

"We need to leave the planet," said Kol, once they were out of earshot. He didn't want the rest of the crew to hear him disagreeing with the Chief. "We can't spend the war here."

"And we'll leave," said the Chief, "once we pick up the Evidence." She gunned the hovercraft and sent them hurtling across the forest.

"I mean now," said Kol. "Miss Becky Twice blew our cover."

"We're broke, Kol!" said the Chief. "We need to take on some cargo. Do you want to cut down three hundred trees, or do you want to dig up a couple bags of fancy chemicals?"

Kol had made that decision long ago. He went quiet for a while. "Humans call this model of hovercraft the Tata Yudhisthira," he said at last. "It has a habit of suddenly losing altitude."

"Heh heh heh," said the Chief. "Those wacky humans."

"Bring us up," said Kol. "You'll have time to react if she stalls." The Chief increased their altitude by about her own height and sent the Tata through the thermals as fast as it would go.

Despite his best efforts, Kol started to like this. Speeding across an abandoned planet choked with mysterious alien plant life, the Chief handling the hover controls with the recklessness that made her uninsurable as a commercial pilot. Calling it 'romantic' was asking for trouble, but it was exciting in a controlled, probably-safe way that Kol almost never experienced.

A quarter-shift out from *Sour Candy*, oak trees below abruptly gave way to pine, more or less as Kol remembered. The sharp dividing line between biomes quickly vanished behind them, and then it was just that smell, like the stuff the Outreach used to clean bathrooms.

"Can you believe the size of these things?" said Kol. "They're not even full grown."

"I've always wanted a desk made from a tree," said the Chief. (Ms. Riana Sulwath, the human crime boss on the 3-show *The Down Under Crew*, had a desk made from a tree.) "Or carved out of a big rock!" (Kol combed his memory and decided this was the Chief's original, impractical idea.)

Town-sized clumps of trees had been lost to fire or disease. Kol looked down into a dead patch and saw small trees growing through the corpses of their predecessors. If they were lucky, those trees would survive long enough to be targeted by a harvester drone and made into cabinets.

"Kol," said the Chief, worried.

Kol brought his gaze back into the car. "Yeah." He'd been fiddling with the valve on his water bottle.

"You're holding cargo. Drop it."

"I am terrified," said Kol, "of what's in those containers we buried."

"We assume the big jug is Evidence," said the Chief. "The little vial...it could be anything. I admit that's a little worrying."

"I don't want it to be Evidence," said Kol. "Evidence only affects humans."

"So what?"

"So why were we running it for the Fist of Joy before humans had ever heard of it?"

The Chief took her hands off the controls and cracked her knuckles. "We discovered it," she said. "This stuff goes both ways. No-Ode was originally an uhaltihaxl painkiller."

"You don't 'discover' Evidence," said Kol. "It's a designer drug. And it hits the street right when the build-up to war starts? It's like two products they launch at the same time. I am having trouble sleeping, Chief. I have been moving illegal merchandise for twelve kiloshifts, and this is the one that's getting to me."

"Have you considered taking some drugs?" said the Chief, and giggled at this for a while. "Kol, Evidence is harmless. It's just a good time. Hey, I tried it. You know I wouldn't do anything risky."

Kol knew the opposite. "You tried it?" he said.

"Off of a tab, at an Outreach station. I was curious."

"What was it like?"

The Chief pushed one arm out the window into the hovercraft's pressure envelope, like an adolescent girl on a joyride. "Minor nausea," she said. "Like you said, it only affects humans. But you don't know unless you try it, is my point! It makes people happy; people who don't have a lot of options. They do some Evidence and it gives them some hope. You should be proud, man."

"Chief," said Kol, "When you see a computer, you see a computer."

"Oh, yes, that's very true," said the Chief.

"You're a user. You see a nice system where everything works. But I'm a sysadmin. When I see a system, I see all the mistakes that went into it. I see how the designers fixed those mistakes. I can sense the problems they couldn't fix, hidden underneath the parts they got to work.

So we designed Evidence. Who did we *test* it on? Some poor human who defected thinking he'd finally get treated like a person? 'Oops, his brainstem detached. Let's add another ethyl group.'"

The Chief looked at Kol as though she were afraid *his* brainstem was going to detach. "I'm sure they just simulated the chemical reaction," she said. The sunset had run down the horizon as they travelled north, and now the sun was gone. The Chief was flying on instruments and—per usual—her own gut reactions.

"We can't simulate an entire brain," said Kol. "They can, but we can't. And you know what happens when you simulate a brain? You have a brain! Trapped inside a computer! You want to give some drugs to *that* brain? Yes, please! Put it out of its misery!"

"Let's verify what we have," said the Chief. "Before we start feeling the stabby-stabs of conscience." The instrument panel illuminated her face. And then the sky got light again, just for a moment. The Chief frowned and looked up at the bright streak cutting through the sky. "Hmm," she said, the way someone else might scream.

"Maybe it's a ring fragment?" said Kol.

"The trajectory's wrong," said the Chief. She sighed. "I do believe the war has come to Cedar Commons."

"Damn private security!" said Kol. "They called us in. They think we're a Fist invasion force."

"Maybe *this* is the Fist invasion force," said the Chief, staying positive. "Come to occupy the planet."

"Oh, yeah," said Kol. "We put up such a fight last time. Occupying planets up and down."

"This time will be different," said the Chief. "This time Evidence is fighting for us."

The shooting star disappeared over the horizon. Kol let the afterimage sit in his eyes. He just wanted the Fist to win one lousy war. Get the humans to stop fucking with his country. But if Evidence was *how* the Fist was going to win...

"We need to find out what's in the little vial," said Kol, "because I have a feeling it's even worse than Evidence."

The Chief docked the hovercar just above the grass, leaving the headlights on to illuminate the burial site. Kol stepped out into the mud. The cavity they'd dug and undug so many shifts ago was gone beneath new grass and old pine leaves.

The planet's ring system was visible in the clear sky. Terran vermin hidden in the trees and under rocks sang out with creepy, piercing calls. Kol retrieved the laser cutters from the storage compartment and tossed one to the Chief. She caught it in one hand, looking up at the night.

"*Que ha menu b'foeha b'nu,*" she quoted.

"Is that the poet Ereru?" said Kol.

"Very close!" said the Chief. "It's the poet Bakh. 'At night the whole universe is one park in one city.'"

This is your last chance, Kol thought. *You're here alone. As soon as we get back to the ship she'll go after the human woman. War has come, and who knows how that will end? Do the mammal mouth thing, the kissing.* But the part of Kol that made him Kol instead of making him someone else, was thinking: *She didn't come here with you. You came with her. Let her make the move if she's going to. Otherwise the human can have her.*

"The poet Bakh clearly didn't grow up in a ternary star system," Kol said. He turned on the laser cutter and its beam sizzled into the mud. Skinny pointy pine leaves caught fire and were instantly carbonized.

Kol and the Chief lifted chunks from the earth and tipped them on their sides to make replacement easier. The buried treasure of *Sour Candy* wasn't buried very deep. Anyone willing to come all this way wouldn't be stopped by having to dig an inconveniently large hole.

The treasure was a little metal vial, and a food-safe jug that had originally held a shelf-stable neutral protein slurry. Now the jug was empty except for a little bit of clear liquid. Kol had wrapped everything in a plastic tarp before burying it. The Chief, in the little pit, peeled open the tarp, clipped the vial onto a metal chain around her neck, and held the large condensation-speckled container to her chest.

She wiped the top with a rag, unscrewed the cap and gave it a quick sniff. Fresh Evidence smelled like sour kine milk. When those enormous molecules started breaking down, it smelled even worse. "It's still good," said the Chief.

"Oh," said Kol, as though the girl he'd accidentally fertilized had accepted his offer of marriage instead of saying that was sweet but she knew of a simpler solution.

The Chief held the jug out, handing it to Kol. "Pour it out," she said.

"What?"

"Pour it out. If you want. We'll figure something out. We always get by." Kol hadn't taken the jug, so the Chief set it down on the muddy ground by his feet. She held out the cap. "You're worth more to me than the money. I don't want you to hate yourself."

Kol looked down at the jug, and then took the cap from the Chief's hand. "We already stole it," he said. "We might as well get paid." He picked up the jug and screwed the cap back on.

The Chief pulled up the plastic tarp and Kol filled in the hole, moving the dirt clumps with his hands, brushing it off on his shorts. They scattered sticks and pine leaves, then climbed into the hovercar and reached down with a rag to smudge those last four footprints. Within a dozen shifts, their second visit would be just as invisible as their first.

On the way back they unwrapped foil packets and ate the bland animals they'd roasted on reentry. "These 'fish' things are neutral," the Chief said, a few bites in. "Cocaine works on everybody. Caffeine works. Why doesn't Evidence work?"

"Chief, you ever hear of Multivax?"

"No," said the Chief immediately. She'd only heard of drugs with a street value.

"I was looking up what chemical could possibly be so heavy," said Kol. "And I discovered Multivax, which is the new INA-112 vaccine."

"I never even heard of INA-112."

"It's a human virus that causes liver failure," said Kol. "Very serious, but they had a vaccine. Except then the virus spread to uhaltihaxl, and they discovered the vaccine only works on humans."

"Uh-oh." One of the Chief's best traits, as far as Kol was concerned, was that she put no restrictions on what you could talk about while she was eating.

"So everyone panicked for a bit, until this pharma brand came out with a drug that simulates a chunk of the human immune system *inside* an uhalti. Can you believe that?"

"That sounds dangerous," said the Chief. Despite himself, another thing Kol liked about the Chief was the little cackle in her voice whenever she heard about something dangerous.

"According to the latest research, it's more dangerous to have your liver explode. So you take the Multivax and you have two immune systems for a while. Now the vaccine works on both species. And I'm sure they're doing that with other drugs; who knows? But the molecular weight of Multivax is way up there. So I thought we might have something similar in the little vial."

"An uhaltihaxl version of Evidence!" said the Chief. "That would be worth a fortune! Unless there's a reason why it never hit the street."

"It never hit the street because that's not what we have," said Kol. "The thing in the vial is twice as heavy as Multivax. But that's the kind of work you'd have to do, to get Evidence to work on uhalti."

"Oh, oh!" said the Chief. She touched the chain around her neck. "What if this is neutral Evidence? What if it works on *anyone*?"

"It never hit the street," Kol repeated. "How can we sell this? Nobody knows what it is, so it has no price. The Evidence, we don't even know what it's programmed for. It could be blank."

"I think you've forgotten," said the Chief, "that we just acquired a test subject."

"No," said Kol.

"What if she agrees?" said the Chief.

"Why would she agree?"

"The same reason she agreed to sit on an uninhabited planet and watch trees grow," said the Chief. "She really likes money."

Chapter 4

Brand Ambassador

Hiroko Ingridsdotter
Steward station

I t's another great day on Cedar Commons!" said Hiroko in her rusty Trade Language D. "You've reached Eserion, now a Trellis On-Site Security gold-star partner. My name is Hi-Ro-Ko, and can I get your Eserion customer ID, please?"

The brick in orbit gave no response. Hiroko's shaking finger traced the customer service flowchart in the printed operations binder they'd been using to prop up the game table. The operations binder, that sacred brand artifact that nonviolently transformed poaching and piracy into win-win sales opportunities. Too valuable to be copied into a contract employee's terminal. And useless, completely useless.

This wasn't poaching; this was an invasion. The monster in orbit was the mommy Fist of Joy ship, come to pick up its offspring, and Hiroko was a bug to be squashed, just like Becky had been. This was how she would die: not as a spaceman but as a rent-a-cop, caught in the bow shock of a Fist invasion. Hiroko's only hope was that somewhere down this flowchart she'd find the launch codes for Trellis's secret bank of missiles.

Someone was talking on the comm in English, but not to

her. "It's a trade language," said the voice. "I am positive it's a trade language. It's that 'harna harna' pigshit. Page someone from Marketing."

"I speak English," said Hiroko, except it came out "I can help you in English today!"

"Oh, great," said the man at the comm. "This is the light industrial city-ship *Jaketown,* about to commence atmospheric insertion. We expect to hit your dock in seven minutes twenty. You must evac immediately."

Jaketown was a human name. Were they impersonating friendlies? Hiroko queried the local database and let her brain respond from the operations binder.

"Okay, that's great to hear!" she said. "What I need first is just your Eserion customer number, so I can draw up the agreement." It was so easy, letting the brand speak through her. Trellis On-Site Security accepted the deadly terror of the situation onto its shoulders and left its avatar, Hiroko, with a trigger-finger calm. If they had brands in the Navy, there'd be no war right now; the Outreach would have won the last one properly.

"Bloody balls, she's doing the brand. Listen to me! Not the brand, *you*, the person on the comm. You need to evac! We can work out an agreement after we land."

Not Hiroko's problem. "Sir, I can't help you without a customer number." The database popped into Hiroko's terminal saying that *Jaketown* was a real city-ship run by Strigl Modern Design, an Eserion customer of long standing specializing in luxury furniture and bulk wood paneling.

The operations binder didn't explain why *Jaketown* might want to harvest an immature forest, but it did tell her what to say if someone tried. "Now, keep in mind that Cedar Commons is one of our younger forests," said Hiroko. "But because of that I am authorized to put down some surprisingly deep discounts for y'all. So why don't we just get the process started right now, okay?"

"No!" said the English speaker on the ship, but he wasn't talking to Trellis, or to Hiroko. "There is no time for this! They are going to die! I swear I will—" The chaos and static of the bridge was quashed and a drawling Scandinavian-sounding voice came on the channel.

"This is Strigl Modern Design," said the voice. "I understand and honor your core values, Trellis On-Site Security, and those of your partner, Eserion Natural Resources."

Well, this wasn't a Fist ship. The Fist of Joy hated brands, and even if they tried to fake it as a wartime tactic, they'd never get someone as competent as this fella. Hiroko had spent her whole life engaging with brands, but the first time she had to enact one, she'd made Trellis sound like a frightened kid. Strigl had a sophisticated voice that put you at ease and made you think about upgrading your dinette.

Hiroko's brand voice caught. The operations binder was very clear that stewards were not supposed to try to represent Trellis to another brand. She was to hit the panic button and wait for help. But Hiroko had hit that button hours ago, and no help was forthcoming.

"I want you to know, Trellis," said Strigl Modern Design in its smooth genderless voice, "and I want to make sure Eserion Natural Resources knows, that it will be compensated for the damage to its structures and its...admirably devoted personnel."

"What are you talking about?" said Hiroko in her own voice. When a brand started flattering you, it was trouble. "What damage?"

"My skipper was asking your brand ambassador to evacuate," said Strigl Modern Design, "because your city-dock has an A390 interface, and *Jaketown* is coming in still tooled for A550."

Hiroko's mad dash for the exit was cut short by a loose shoelace. Hiroko sprawled horizontal and hit her shoulder against the sliding door, which hadn't opened fast enough. Her Pepsi bottle toppled and bounced across the floor. Hiroko scampered to her feet and ran for the garage and the remaining hovercar, skimming the unguarded rim of the city-dock's vast pit.

Hiroko mentally abandoned the personal items she'd brought to Cedar Commons. The steward station would be obliterated in the shockwave when *Jaketown*, or whoever this was, mated with a dock that couldn't accommodate it. She was in the garage; she was in the Tata Devout. She never stopped moving. Hiroko peeled out of the garage and took the Tata up as fast as it would go.

She'd made it ten clicks out when the squealing started. Something was coming in behind her, compressing an atmosphere-sized volume of gas. Hiroko picked it up on radar. *Jaketown* or not, this mother was the size of a city. In the rear monitor she saw it dropping in an arc, deploying a glittering space elevator behind it like a spider's thread. It was an Outreach ship, not a hostile, but it was still dangerous.

The sonic booms hit first, invisible kisses that rattled the Tata's frame. Then the city landed, and from that came the shockwave. The hovercar tilted and spiraled end over end. Its motivator had confused the shockwave and the ground. It couldn't decide which one to cancel out. Hiroko called back her most recent round of reserve pilot training. She wiggled one hand on the joystick, the other on the motivator, trying to feel out what the computer was doing so she could cancel out the part that was wrong.

Down below, the seismic waves arrived, ripping out flaming trees by the roots and tossing them around like broccoli. The shockwave passed, the confused motivator stalled, and the Tata dropped.

Military vehicles don't stall, but even when they do, a Navy woman doesn't panic. Hiroko took the action necessary to maximize the chances of survival. She killed the engines, deployed the parachute, and restarted. The motivator seized and died. The Tata was junk. Hiroko launched the vehicle's entire stock of fire-suppression bombs beneath her. An ocean of foam bloomed beneath her, and the fire gasped for breath and died.

For a few moments there was nothing to do but fall. Hiroko studied the metal face of the driver's-side glove compartment, where there was supposed to be a safety knife for cutting off a stuck harness. A safety knife that, with a little work from a rock or something, could be turned into a knife that wasn't safe at all.

The situation didn't look good, but Hiroko wasn't much worse off than before. She had already experienced the worst thing that could happen: her comrade had been taken by the enemy. If she survived the crash and the fire and the rest of it, Hiroko was honor-bound to avenge that motherfucker Becky Twice.

Chapter 5

Work and Money

Myrus
Jaketown

Myrus felt the engines revving up for the final skip even before 0600, the time Mr. Nzeme had set for the council meeting. Myrus woke up early because he wanted to be awake when Dad came back.

While Myrus slept Dad had taken all the pictures down from the bedroom wall, and hung up the sturdi webbing they used during landings. Now Myrus knelt down and opened the solid wooden chest at the foot of Dad's bed. There were the wooden frames, stacked up and padded with spare blankets.

The picture on top was of Dad at a party with an uhalti woman who Myrus had always suspected was his mother. "Nobody you know," Dad had said. "Don't worry about it." But there was an equally unexplained picture of Dad with Maskitenny Xepperxelt, who was *Jaketown*'s head of marketing and Den's mother. Dad had a little trophy wall going.

Myrus slid the chest closed and went out to sit on the couch. Everything was quiet, like the opposite of a birthday. When Myrus's terminal was sending a big orange **0615** into his optic nerve, Dad came in the front door holding the sash that said he was on the city council. He balled up the sash and threw it in the corner of the living room and wouldn't look at it. His chin was wrinkled and his mouth moved silently. Something was inside him that he didn't want Myrus to see.

"We'll be landing soon," said Dad, even though it had already started. "Let's get in the web." They went into the bedroom and got in the webbing together, sandwiched in the sturdi envelope with their backs flat against the wood paneling. Myrus closed his eyes and Dad held him tight with one arm. "Once we land, we'll need to go out and build some desks," said Dad. "They don't have to be great. They're warm-up desks. We need to make them quick, okay?"

"Dad, I'm scared."

"Gonna be fine," said Dad. "Gonna be fine." He let go of Myrus and grabbed onto the sturdi. Myrus did the same and squeezed until his fingers went pale.

This was the bumpiest landing Myrus had ever been through. The engines groaned and whistled, the ship lurched from side to side. Myrus heard neighbors' babies crying from all directions. After a huge jolt something in the living room broke free from its restraints, and as *Jaketown* pitched through the atmosphere, that thing smashed into everything else in the living room, back and forth, like a hammer on a filebell.

Then the gravity went off. It wasn't quite free-fall, but the brakes weren't nearly enough. There was a CRASH that jolted Myrus and Dad upwards in the sturdi envelope. Then a strange kind of quiet: Myrus could hear explosions and groaning metal, but it was very far away. He felt natural gravity, weaker than the ship's. His clock said 0620, but that time was wrong now. The time was whatever time it was on this part of Cedar Commons.

Dad untangled himself from the webbing. "Do you need the bathroom?" he said. "Do you have pain debt?"

Myrus's leg had fallen asleep. He pinched his arm and it didn't hurt. He waved his hand and the arm flopped uselessly. "Dad, I'm, yeah, yeah, it's pain debt. Help help." He yanked the tuft of hair between his horns and felt nothing but a faraway tingle.

"You'll be fine," said Dad. He looked Myrus over and grabbed him in a hug. "Nothing's broken. Just too much excitement. I'll help you up."

"I'm okay," said Myrus, breathing hard. His legs were shaking.

"Let's go," said Dad. "Be careful."

The loose thing in the living room had been a chair; now it was a splintered mess. Dad kicked one of its legs out of the way and opened the door. The decking outside had only partially expanded after landing, and the safety railings at the edges had never popped up. There was a thin strip of metal walkway in front of the door, like the frosting on a cake, and past that it was just a hundred-meter drop to the public deck. All the way down, on every deck, Myrus saw people running around. Their faraway voices echoed through the vast space of the city-ship.

They headed towards the lift. Myrus hugged the wall, scraping in and out of other peoples' doorways. "Watch your head," said Dad. Myrus looked up and saw why there were so many echoes: the hull hadn't opened. There were big cracks in the roof, lit by spotlights. Myrus saw a piece of the roof fall in, and heard people scream and scatter.

The lift doors were stuck open onto an empty shaft. Orange sparks dropped down from above. Dad took one look and kept walking; they joined a crowd on the stairway.

The monotony of climbing the stairs had convinced Myrus's body that he was out of danger, and it started letting the saved-up pain into his blood and his joints. It was a stretching and a jolting kind of pain, the pain of being thrown against Dad and against the wall when *Jaketown* crashed. When they got to the top deck, Dad was out of breath and wheezing from the climb, and Myrus was knuckle-cracking sore from the pain debt. His scalp burned where he'd stupidly yanked his hair.

Myrus stumbled and nearly stepped in a trickle of brown liquid leaking out from inside the workshop. Dad unlocked the door with his terminal and they saw it was stain. A canister had cracked open in the crash and covered the floor with Rhennish Umber #26. The smell filled the room.

"I'll get the solvent," said Myrus.

"Cleanup can wait," said Dad. "Put on a respirator and get out the tools."

Myrus risked it. "Dad, what's going on?"

"Denweld will be here soon. We have seventy minutes to build as many desks as we can." And that was that. Myrus knew why, but he didn't. It had to do with the Navy ship chasing them, but why did it matter if they built two desks or three, or none at all?

Myrus pulled a respirator over his face and the smell of the stain went away. Dad was booting up the shaping machine, programming it for OCOLI, the simplest Strigl desk. His dress shoes left sticky dark footprints on the floor.

Myrus undid a cloth tie and rolled Dad's planes and chisels out onto his work area. He unzipped a plastic bag and pulled out his gloves, then Den's. The sandpaper gloves that, according to Dad, made uhaltihaxl the best woodworkers in the galaxy. He tugged one glove onto his hand.

"How's the fit?" said Dad.

"They're a little tight."

"You're still growing," said Dad. "We'll get you some new ones when things settle down."

Someone hammered on the workshop door. "Come in!" said Dad. The door slid open a crack, then all the way, and now there was natural light outside, the kind of light Myrus always associated with Den. And there was Den herself, a shadow in the doorway. A very, very tall shadow.

"The hull got stuck in the landing," said Den. She gracefully slid her respirator off its hook and checked the filter. "They fixed it."

Den had grown up. In the three months she'd spent on the women's deck, eating whatever they fed the girls, Den had grown and grown. Myrus would never catch up. She was taller than Dad. She was as tall as a human. This was infuriating because Myrus and Den had the same father—this was why she'd had been apprenticed to Dad in the first place. Dad wasn't short, so what was the problem?

"Hello, Den," said Dad. "Prop the door open, would you?"

"Hello, Mr. Wectusessin," said Den. "Hi, Myrus. How are you?"

"Hi," said Myrus, but it was hopeless. To Den, the one woman in the universe he might have a chance with, he was now a little kid.

"Apparently there's forest fires," said Den. "But they sent the harvesters out, so—" she was interrupted by the clunk-clunk-clunk of freshly sawed planks dropping into the input chute. "Yeah, guess so."

"Are you excited, Den?" said Dad. He and Myrus lifted the big plank and slowly guided it through the shaper to become the top of a desk. The wood wasn't totally dry; this desk was going to warp.

"Excited for what?" said Den. She picked up one of the smaller planks and followed behind them to shape one of the sides. In the next workshop over, Myrus could hear Violet Sun and her apprentices putting together the drawers that went with this desk.

"A new planet," said Dad. "Getting back to work." He and Myrus set the top of the desk down onto the sanding bench. The wood was warm from the shaper.

"Nobody knows what's going on," said Den. "Are we even going to be able to take off?"

"That's not a question we can answer," said Dad. "Providence controls the future. The best thing is to do our jobs and let the crew do theirs."

Myrus pulled on his tight sandpaper gloves. He liked smoothing wood with Den. They made it a game, like 2-hockey. Den picked up her glove and wedged three fingers into it. "Crap, Mr. Wectusessin," she said, "the gloves don't fit."

"Growth spurts, huh?" said Dad. "Well, don't worry about it. Come here and help with the detail. Myrus, can you handle the sanding? Just take off the rough edges. It doesn't have to be perfect."

This was unfair. Myrus and Den shared half their genes. Myrus's mother must be incredibly small, a little doll person. Myrus looked down at his tiny uhalti hands on the rough wood. He gritted his teeth, grabbed one edge of the desk and slapped his palm down and sanded the desk by himself.

He missed huge chunks of the surface, leaving it raw and rough; he saw opportunities to bring out the material's natural glow and he passed them up out of spite. As he handed the pieces over, Dad gave them a glance and didn't say anything, even though it was obvious Myrus had done a crap job.

Dad and Myrus held the pieces of the desk together, then Myrus held it on his own, while Den's long fingers twisted the fasteners together and tucked them invisible into the wood. Dad stood by with the airbrush and sprayed on the stain as soon as Myrus and Den stood away from the completed assembly.

Dad looked at his watch. "A twenty-one-minute desk," he said. "Not bad at all. Myrus, help me lift." Myrus lifted one end of the desk and Dad picked up the other. They hustled it to the workshop wall and pushed it into the deployment chute. The stain was still sticky, and it came off on Myrus's hands to match the stuff on his shoes.

The desk and its drawers would be packed into a container and lifted into a parking orbit. A twenty-one-minute desk from untreated wood was shoddy work, but maybe it would end up in a poor kid's bedroom. Some kid halfway across the Outreach, on a planet Myrus had never heard of, would set up his 3-tank on the desk Myrus had made. He and that kid would be connected by an invisible thread of work and money.

What do you call that feeling? It was as slippery as a dream and Myrus had no time to name it. Dad and Den were already guiding the second desk through the shaper.

Chapter 6

A Constant Source of Novel Ideas

Churryhoof
Brown v. Board of Education of Topeka

They wrecked it!" said Commander Churryhoof. "They wrecked their own damn city-ship!"

"Yes, ma'am," said Lieutenant Dwap-Jac-Dac, just in case this was an order to be acknowledged.

The 3-tank in the center of the bridge showed a composite map of Cedar Commons and everything known to orbit it. The ring system and the planet's surface were constantly redrafted, the pixelated areas and gaps filling in with new telemetry from the survey drones. One whole quarter of the planet was blocky and unimportant. Beneath *Brown*'s geosynchronous orbit, visible in as much detail as anyone cared to zoom on, was the scene of the crime.

Smoke from the forest fires hurt site visibility, but a proper landing doesn't *cause* forest fires. *Jaketown* had cracked her hull and spread the pulverized city-dock over a three-kilometer radius. She was a shipwreck. Yet on her hurried descent she'd been careful to deploy a space elevator up to a commercial orbit beneath the ring system. That way her citizens could keep shipping wood paneling out to fancy office buildings, while Outreach spacemen died because the Navy's supply chain was short a class zero cargo vessel.

"They're hailing us," said Spaceman Wang.

"I'm sure they are. Tank it."

The map of Cedar Commons became a 2-image of a human who hid his mouth behind prominent facial hair. He looked into the planetside 2-cam with a vacant, meaningless smile, as though ordered to stand at attention but unable to stop from thinking of his sweetheart. As soon as his call was picked up, his face brightened, right on cue.

"Captain!" said the human. "Thank God you're here. This has been a hell of a day."

"Are you the skipper?" said Commander Churryhoof.

"The mayor of *Jaketown*, ma'am. Mr. Nzeme, at your service."

"A spacecraft does not have a mayor," said Churryhoof. "I want to speak with the skipper."

"The skipper is under investigation," said Nzeme. "We had a very rough landing that caused structural damage to municipal buildings."

"Mr. Nzeme," said Churryhoof, "I don't know if you're aware, but there's a war on."

"A war!" said the human, and fortunately the hair on his face masked his simulation of surprise. "We'd heard rumors, but...my goodness."

This was worse than Churryhoof could have possibly imagined. They thought they could get away with this. *Jaketown* was operated by a brand called Strigl Modern Design. By the brand's logic, the rational countermove for *Brown* was to write *Jaketown* off as a sunk cost. The most effective way for Churryhoof to help the war effort was to leave right now and deal with the next-biggest problem. *Jaketown* had recruited the sleaziest of her citizens to lie and stall until Churryhoof made that call.

But Churryhoof practiced military logic, which shared the razor-in-the-handshake bastardry of commercial logic, but which also demanded that honor be satisfied. Or, failing that, justice.

"Of course," said Mr. Nzeme, "as loyal Outreach citizens, the people of Cedar Commons stand ready to assist the effort in any way possible."

"I'm glad to hear that, sir," said Churryhoof. "As the ranking officer in-system, I am declaring martial law."

"If you think that's right," said Mr. Nzeme. "Of course, we'll have to run it past the council."

"No, I don't think so," said Churryhoof. "Martial law is, by definition, the suspension of civilian authority."

The human flinched and glanced at something outside the 3-tank. "I...I appreciate that, Captain, but we have procedures we must follow, just as you do. Everything must go through the council."

"Ma'am, bogey coming up the elevator," said Wang.

"Details!" said Dwap-Jac-Dac. Light flickered out from thons exobody against the metal walls of the bridge as thon tapped into the ship's tactical context.

"Civilian class eight shipping container. Self-tagged as furniture. We have visual from halo three-one Bravo. Shall I tank it?"

"Dwap-Jac-Dac, have Spaceman Wang build a firing context and destroy that container." She cocked her head at the image of Mr. Nzeme, her horns arched back. His jaw was set.

"Yes, ma'am," said Dwap-Jac-Dac, who was standing directly between her and Wang. "Spaceman, destroy that container."

"Yessaer," said Wang. One breath later: "Kill confirmed."

"Kill confirmed, ma'am," said Dwap-Jac-Dac.

Sadly, this display of military prowess did nothing to deflate the human's ego. "I hardly need to remind you, captain," he said, "that deploying military drones against Outreach citizens is illegal."

"On the other hand," said Churryhoof, "using drones to clean up orbital debris is a public service. Do not put things in my space, *Jaketown*. It makes me jumpy."

"Captain, we're making the best of a bad situation. We are stranded, our ship is ruined. If we're ever going to get off this planet, we'll need to pay our way. That means doing what we do best. If—if there's a war, as you say, at least let us put stock in orbit until things cool down."

"Lieutenant, in my office." Churryhoof turned away from the human on the surface and stormed away with an anger that was finally being let out a bit. Behind her, Specialist Entwetterwick had replaced Mr. Nzeme's video feed with a hold screen showing the Great Logo of the Terran Outreach. *Universi sumus una hac in re*, asshole. Think about that one for a while.

Dwap-Jac-Dac's exobody followed Churryhoof into the commander's office. There was no pretending to sit on the sofa this time. Churryhoof would be getting rid of that sofa at their next station stop.

"Can you believe that smug bastard?" said Churryhoof. Her metal chair squeaked.

"Yes, ma'am."

"I don't suppose you have a miracle plan for getting *Jaketown* back to the fight?"

"We can get her into an orbit," said Dwap-Jac-Dac immediately, as if thon had crammed all night hoping to be called on in class. "She dropped plenty of potential into her elevator; we can use it as a winch. But that won't make her spaceworthy. She won't hold atmosphere, and we'd have to fill her with skip-drones to move her FTL."

Space elevator as a winch? Using skip overlap to move a city-ship? Did Dwap-Jac-Dac get all thons ideas from cheesy heist dramas? A line from the lieutenant's personnel report came into sharp, horrifying focus: *a constant source of novel ideas.* Churryhoof would not have dreamed of writing "a constant source of novel ideas" in Lakshmi Prasad's personnel report. That was something you wrote for an officer you hated.

"So to sum up," said Churryhoof, "you don't have a miracle plan."

"Not as such, ma'am. In terms of the war effort, *Jaketown* is a total loss. Unless we decided to turn Cedar Commons into a Forward Operating Base." Dwap-Jac-Dac sensed trouble and changed course at the last moment. "But we wouldn't want to do that, is my point."

"Merciful Providence," said Churryhoof. "We are in *trouble.*"

"I don't think one ship is going to cost us the war, ma'am. The enemy barely have a military."

"The Outreach will survive," said Churryhoof. "You and I are fucked."

"The fellas did their best," said Dwap-Jac-Dac, sticking up for the enlisted beings. "Earth should have sent a ship closer to *Jaketown*. It's just math."

"Earth doesn't care about math! Earth sees a bunch of draft dodgers outrunning a Light Combat Platform. Earth sees we lost a city-ship before the war even started, because I wasn't fast enough. Good beings are going to die because we don't have *Jaketown* in the fight. Do you see what this means, for your career and mine? How many craft in the service are there with no human officers?"

"I don't have the exact number."

"If a human fucks up an assignment, the human looks bad. If one of us fucks up, everyone takes the hit. You and I are in this together."

"Yes, ma'am."

"We need to set a deterrent," said Churryhoof. "We have to be tougher than humans. Send a message. You can't crash a city-ship and get away with it."

Dwap-Jac-Dac's crystal fingers tilted and tapped together, throwing off glints of light like a holographic print. Thon was finally copying biped body language. "Traditionally," thon said, "the War Duties Board handles these situations."

"We need to bring back a *solution*, Lieutenant. Not more work for people. We need to bring back a solution and pray that it's enough."

"I don't know if this is what you're looking for," said Dwap-Jac-Dac.

"No, no, please," said Churryhoof, waving a generous hand. Time for another fucking episode of *The Down Under Crew*.

"We could declare *Jaketown* a munitions factory," said Dwap-Jac-Dac. "Ma'am."

Churryhoof rolled her tongue around her mouth for a bit, behind tightly pursed lips. "Clarify?" she said diplomatically.

"Your authority under martial law is very broad," said Dwap-Jac-Dac. "In particular, I'm thinking of your ability to commandeer production facilities for defense purposes. You can give *Jaketown* production orders and we can head back to the fight."

No one could say this officer lacked imagination. In fact, Churryhoof planned to say the opposite, in thons personnel report, assuming she survived ninety days of war with this lunatic as her Master of Drone.

"Production orders?" said Churryhoof. "What kind of munitions can a bunch of carpenters make?"

"It doesn't matter," said Dwap-Jac-Dac. "Boomerangs or something. We will make them suffer *hless* throughout the war. The shame of useless work, ma'am."

"Shall we send down a Jalian monk as well, to teach them about *hless*? These people turn living things into furniture! I don't think useless work holds any shame for them."

"Alternatively, ma'am, we can draft her crew," said Dwap-Jac-Dac. "That's what they were trying to avoid, after all. There's plenty of useless work in the service."

Oh, wow. "Is there, now," said Churryhoof.

"Absolutely, ma'am," said Dwap-Jac-Dac, casually skipping across the thinnest of ice like a rwit on rollerblades. "Monitoring the raw event feed from the drones, for instance. A lot of outfits don't even bother."

"But *we* have someone monitoring *our* event feed," said Churryhoof carefully. "Don't we?"

"Oh, certainly, yes," said Dwap-Jac-Dac, covering thons sparkling ass. "Specialist Park is sitting before the shithose at the moment."

"And what did Specialist Park do to deserve this?" said Churryhoof.

"He used a racial epithet to describe Specialist Entwetterwick," said Dwap-Jac-Dac.

Hetselter Churryhoof, an ambitious uhalti officer in what was still largely considered a human's navy, had in her time been described by a number of racial epithets. She gave as good as she got, and had made it as far as she did without needing an overzealous superior to swoop in and save her from some nasty words. But after the munitions factory idea, Churryhoof was relieved to learn that Dwap-Jac-Dac had disciplined a crew member for *anything*. And thons draft-and-leave idea combined military and commercial logic in a way that could conceivably keep Churryhoof from being kicked out of the service altogether.

Churryhoof looked something up in her terminal and tapped one hand against her head. "Let's say we draft the crew. How many on *Jaketown* are 'crew'?"

"Fifty-one," said Dwap-Jac-Dac. *Brown* crewed seven. "Obviously they won't all fit. But only nine would be officers in a military context. If we drop both scoops we can pick up the big shots in one go."

"Big shots," said Churryhoof thoughtfully. *Everything goes through the council.*

"Ma'am?"

"We're thinking about this wrong," said Churryhoof. "The crew didn't scuttle *Jaketown*; her city council did. Did you see the way that 'mayor' was strutting? That guy thinks he has power. He's the problem. *He's* the one we should draft."

"I don't know how much it would help the war effort to draft middle-aged politicians," said Dwap-Jac-Dac. As if thon had the standing to criticize anyone else's plans.

"No," said Churryhoof, the idea blossoming, "but middle-aged politicians tend to have teenaged children." Dwap-Jac-Dac was silent. Commander Churryhoof dipped into her terminal to run another query.

"Are you sure this is a good idea, ma'am?" said Dwap-Jac-Dac, god-emperor of bad ideas.

"The 'mayor' has two children of draft age. Twins. Six other council members, one of 'em's rre. There are six kids total. Lieutenant, put together an away team. Land a scoop, bring back the six kids. And, uh, get Dr. Joshi as well. The service needs dentists."

"Honestly, ma'am, I don't like this plan."

"Do you like following your C.O.'s orders?" said Churryhoof.

"Yes, ma'am."

"Then it's unanimous. Oh, for the away team, get Tellpesh and Heiss. I want this to look like a nice multi-ethnic op. Not a rre ordering humans around. You got that?"

"Yes, ma'am," said Dwap-Jac-Dac with all the enthusiasm of a recording. Thon rotated the big useless exobody thon lived in, turning to leave the commander's office. "I get it."

Dwap-Jac-Dac
Brown v. Board of Education of Topeka

Everybody loves Lieutenant Jac. Thon's not a stick-up-the-ass like your rre drill sergeant was, or a humorless swot like the guy who took your promotion. Thon makes sure the work gets done, but thon's also made it clear that thon only cares about the *important* work. If you play ball with thon, Jac is happy to let the shithose monitor itself. Thon's even been known to wink at a little off-duty hooch.

Yep, everyone loves Lieutenant Jac. Until thon orders you to dress up like shock troops and take a bunch of kids away from their parents. Dwap-Jac-Dac could imagine Spaceman Heiss and Specialist Tellpesh whispering to each other as thon left the bridge for the launch bay. *Jac doesn't know what this means. Rre don't know what it's like to have kids. What the fuck are we doing, man? I didn't sign up for this.*

Nobody signs up for this, but this is what happens in war, and soldiers are the ones who make it happen. Maybe we should put it in the oath of citizenship, just to make it real clear. Add it to the instruction block of all triplicate government forms. Carve it into the Great Logo of the Terran Outreach. *Universi sumus una hac in re hand over your children.*

Dwap-Jac-Dac's job was to move the drafted kids, plus a dentist, from the bottom of a gravity well to the top. If it cost the respect of thons fellas, well, worse things happen. Worse things were happening right now, and *Brown* needed to get to where they were happening ASAP so it could make the situation even worse.

The away team filed into the launch bay, faces hidden behind the reflective visors of the hardsuits they hadn't worn since basic training. Dwap-Jac-Dac had gotten there first because thon didn't need to change. Taking thons hardsuit *off* would have been a surgical procedure.

"Multi-ethnic op" sounded good in the commander's office, but there was no uhalti face in this group, just a short dark mirror-smooth shape with TELLPESH on its lapel, standing next to the taller shape labeled HEISS. That uhalti name on that badge wasn't going to make Councilman Wectusessin any happier about losing his kids.

Heiss piloted scoop Bravo down. Apart from his regulation chatter with *Brown*, he was silent. By the tilt of Tellpesh's head thon could see she was staring out a porthole, down at the planet or over at the space elevator.

Why didn't thon stand up to the commander? Thon doesn't know what thon's asking. I'm willing to die for the Outreach but I don't know if I can do this.

Pull it together, soldier.

The only comfort was that Dwap-Jac-Dac didn't have to tell the people down below what they were coming to do. The commander was taking care of that right now.

Scoop Bravo landed with a shudder. "Weapons down," said Dwap-Jac-Dac, both vocally and over the comm. "Weapons off. Weapons *stay* off."

"Yes, aer," said Tellpesh and Heiss in relieved unison.

"Let's go."

The scoop steps opened down onto a shouting mob, but when Dwap-Jac-Dac and the other hardsuits stepped out, the mob became a shocked and cowed group of civilians. The only hostile movement was a rre, thons bodies invisible beneath a flashy black suit of obsidian and pearl, pushing through the crowd towards the scoop.

"Who is in charge here?" the rre vocalized loudly. "Who is

in charge?" Heiss and Tellpesh tilted their heads imperceptibly towards their LT.

"Move out," said the lieutenant. "Check the draftees against the photo records. I wouldn't be surprised if some of these hot-shots are paying some other family to send a kid in their place." Thon silently turned to the other rre. *Does that answer your question?*

Tip-Iye-Nett-Zig, said the rre, in native-voice. *Jaketown city council.* Of course they'd sent the rre, the one with no children to lose. Lieutenant, let me remind you that it's your duty to resist an illegal order. This is collective punishment. It is *beyond* illegal.

Perhaps you should file a complaint with the War Duties Board, said Dwap-Jac-Dac. The WDB knew a thing or two about collective punishment.

The politician thrust a finger at the chest of Dwap-Jac-Dac's suit, possibly aimed at Dwap-Jac-Dac thonself. Don't threaten me, Lieutenant, thon said. I'm a member of the bar.

Dwap-Jac-Dac didn't move a servo. Listen, you little shit, thon said. If it were up to me, your ship would be a radioactive hole in the ground right now. Better beings than you are going to die because we don't have *Jaketown* in the fight. The only reason you're alive right now is, my C.O. is a sentimental flower-kisser who thinks we should save our nukes for enemies with the stones to paint the Fist of Joy on their ships.

This is conduct unbecoming, said Tip-Iye-Nett-Zig. I'm going to take this directly to your commander.

If you're smart you'll keep your vocalizer cold, said Dwap-Jac-Dac. My commander's the only friend you have this side of the border. If you start pissing into the comm with your shyster justifications for aiding the enemy, you're liable to knock some sense into her.

Tip-Iye-Nett-Zig ostentatiously dropped the native-voice, spun around and stormed off to whine at Commander Churryhoof about her loose-cannon lieutenant. Tellpesh and Heiss crept through the dispersing crowd like demons, converging on the five other council members who stood together in shocked solidarity, a parody of a receiving line for visiting dignitaries.

What kept them here, in their places of importance? They had a whole planet to hide on, covered with unscannable foliage. Dwap-Jac-Dac, in their position, would have headed into the forest with children in tow. Was it denial? A bureaucrat's sense of duty? Some residual faith in the government they'd betrayed?

Or maybe rre just don't know what it's like to have kids.

Dwap-Jac-Dac walked through the crowd calling out "Where is Dr. Joshi?" No one volunteered this information. The idea of hunting down the only dentist in a city of identical civilians was absurd. Tracking an individual through their capital terminal would require access to *Jaketown*'s disposition context, which the local authorities would not be granting.

"Aer, there's a trouble with one of the councilmen." It was Heiss. He'd popped up the visor on his hardsuit and his mustache was slimy with nervous sweat.

Dwap-Jac-Dac rotated thons suit to face the human. "What's the trouble, Heiss?"

"Well, aer, the manifest says the councilman has both a son and a daughter, but the gentleman insists he has a son only."

"Let me guess," said Dwap-Jac-Dac. "It's the uhalti. Councilman Wectusessin."

"Uh, yessaer."

Heiss guided the lieutenant towards the only uhaltihaxl in the huddle of terrified council members. "Good morning, sir," thon said to the uhalti man.

"I don't have a daughter," said Councilman Wectusessin. His son, his acknowledged son, clung to his shoulder, crying. "I told your man, I don't have a daughter."

"I'll handle this," Dwap-Jac-Dac told Heiss. "Call Tellpesh over. She can explain it in Narathippin."

"I speak English," said Wectusessin quietly. *"I don't have a daughter.* Maskitenny Xepperxelt has a daughter. Leave them out of this."

Sir, my uhaltihaxl C.O. specifically ordered me to take both of your children. Under Outreach law, Maskitenny Xepperxelt's daughter is your daughter. No, this was it; Dwap-Jac-Dac had found thons limit.

Thon couldn't draft two kids from the same family, even if the "family" didn't recognize itself as such.

"Lieutenant, aer, please understand," the uhalti man said. "I voted against this." He was sobbing now, worse than his son. "They tried to force me; I voted to stay loyal. I went against my party's instructions. Please!"

Dwap-Jac-Dac moved the head of thons suit to face the politician. "We all have our instructions, sir," thon said. "Your daughter can stay with her mother."

Dwap-Jac-Dac opened a comm connection to Tellpesh. "Take Li Nzeme off," thon said. "She won't be joining us. Wei Nzeme stays." Thon moved the suit's head down to look at the kid. "Myrusit," thon said. "Can I call you Myrus?"

The kid said nothing. "It's time to earn your horns, son," said Dwap-Jac-Dac. "Go ahead and get in the ship. It's going to be okay. I'll look after you." Dwap-Jac-Dac moved one arm onto the kid's shoulder and guided him towards the scoop, disentangling him from a tall uhalti girl who ran up and hugged him briefly.

"Lieutenant, aer!" It was a human woman, limping in from the wreckage and the fire at the edge of the city. Her mouth was covered with a wet cloth, her face smeared with mud in a best-effort at camouflage.

"Are you Dr. Joshi?" said Dwap-Jac-Dac.

The human tugged down her mask, stood at attention and gave a crisp salute. "Aer!" she said. "Hiroko Ingridsdotter, Reserve Warrant Officer, Class Two, reporting for duty, aer!"

"At ease, spaceman," said Dwap-Jac-Dac. "You're not on *Jaketown*'s manifest. What brings you to Cedar Commons?"

"I work here. Aer, there's an enemy vessel on this planet. Rasme thau cargo craft, crew of about five. They got my buddy Becky. Using 'buddy' in the military sense, aer; I actually can't stand her."

"Do you have coordinates?"

"Directly antipodal to...this li'l pig-fucking party right here, aer. Pardon my Trade Standard F. Oh, at least one of the enemy crew is human. Seemed a little odd."

"How's your leg?"

"Just a sprain, aer. I'm not out of the fight."

"Get in the scoop. We'll patch you up on *Brown*."

"Yessaer." The human saluted again and limped double-time into Scoop Bravo.

Dwap-Jac-Dac opened the comm to *Brown*. "Commander, some interesting developments down here."

"I'm busy," said Churryhoof. "Give me the five-second version."

"The good news is, I've found you a reservist."

"Bad news?"

"She's spotted the enemy, and/or she's a spy."

Chapter 7

The Fun Part

Rebecca Twice
Sour Candy

just realized," said Kol the egenu, "that your name makes sense in English. 'Miss Becky Twice.'" He brushed some crumbs off the kitchen table. "As in, 'You may miss Becky twice, but you only have to hit her once.'"

Becky checked her side of the table for crumbs. The Chief sat between them, looking real butch in a jacket and black trousers. *I wouldn't say no to her fist of joy, hur hur hur.*

"Why were you wearing a cocktail dress?" Becky asked her. "Did I interrupt a party?" She laughed. That was so funny and Becky was going to die.

The Chief (apparently this was actually her name) frowned at this and tried to put it into words. "My..." she said, and gave up and harna-ed at Kol for a bit.

"She says she's a girl," said Kol, "and she's allowed to wear a dress once in a while, if that's all right with you." Becky shrugged.

"So, we have a problem, Miss Becky Twice," said Kol. "You're trained in Outreach security techniques. We'd like you to advise us."

"Where's Arun?" said Becky. "Why don't you ask him?"

"We want your opinion," said Kol. So this was the final part of the interview. Becky tugged at the neck of her Trellis jumpsuit, freshly washed but not completely dried.

Kol whacked a 3-tank in the middle of the table and it sent up a globe of Cedar Commons. This was a different user interface from the tank at the steward station, but the map was the one Hiroko had shown her...was it only earlier that same day?

Kol pointed out relevant orbits and protrusions as he spoke. "There's an Outreach military ship in orbit," he said. "They've docked some kind of structure at the steward station. Probably a forward operating base; you see here that the two are connected by a space elevator. To avoid an embarrassing and potentially fatal misunderstanding, we will be leaving the planet before your partner and her buddies find us."

"Maybe I want them to find you," said Becky.

"Forget what you maybe want, because they will not find us," said Kol. "Our question for you is, what will happen instead?"

This was a test of Becky's criminal instincts. They wanted to see if she was flexible enough to make the face-heel turn. They probably also wanted her on record proposing something illegal.

"Can we skip from orbit?" said Becky.

"We can, but this volume is now full of your Navy's drones. When we skip, they'll sight the stars on the other side of the bubble. They'll know exactly where we went, and they'll follow us."

Becky knew this one from *The Down Under Crew*. "Flashbang," she said. "Blinds the sensors so they can't sight through the skip bubble."

The Chief's eyes were closed, her hands folded on her cute pudgy tummy. Becky didn't know how much of the English conversation she was following. One of her fingers bobbled back and forth as Kol and Becky spoke. Hiroko did that; she'd listen to a song and pretend to conduct the band.

"A flashbang is good against underpaid cops who don't care," said Kol, "but it's not enough against a military adversary with mass spectrometers."

"What's a mass spectrometer got to do with it? You're gone, they didn't see you leave."

Becky had apparently failed the mass spectrometer test, because the Chief grunted and Kol went down to kindergarten level. "What happens when you skip, Miss Becky Twice?" he asked.

"You switch places with an equal volume of empty space," said Becky.

"The fullness of space!" said the Chief.

"Space isn't empty," said Kol. "It's full of gas and dust and pollutants. If you have spectrometer drones, you can swoop in, take a sample, and cross-reference against a survey. Your Navy admits their survey's accurate to within three-cubes of a sector, which means it's at least twice that good.

"Even that would be plenty of space if we were running from underpaid cops who don't care, but..." He gave a shrug like the statue of Providence in a Hasithenk shrine, the shrug that says "I guess you're fucked."

"Who does a survey of empty space?"

"Your government does them," said Kol. "All the time. And my government just finished theirs, so that we could have our little war."

"This is idiotic," said Becky. "Gas and dust? That shit is free. We can just drop a load along with the flashbang and flood the zone." The Chief opened her eyes and smiled, and Becky knew that she'd passed her test. At the time she thought she'd passed it with "flood the zone" but not much later she realized the magic word had been "we".

"Your position on this crew, Miss Becky Twice," said the Chief. "Your inclination or your reluctance."

"She's asking if you want in," said Kol. "The terms are the ones Mr. Arun Sliver gave you. We all do the work and we share the profits."

Becky tried to shrug nonchalantly. "*Universi sumus*," she said. "I'm in."

Kol sat up straight. "What did you say?"

"Just a joke. It's the Outreach motto."

"I know what it is," said Kol. "*Universi sumus* means 'The universe is ours.'"

"Where'd you get that?" said Becky. "*Universi sumus una hac in re.* 'We're all in this together.' They make you say it in school."

"The pointlessness of argument on this topic," said the Chief. "Our departure! Kol, a briefing on Charlie's capabilities."

"Gnaharna-harna *universi sumus*?" said Kol.

"Kol!" said the Chief.

"Who's Charlie?" said Becky. Was there another human on this ship?

Kol stood up and straddled a bidirectional utility ladder. "Come with me to the cargo hold, Miss Becky Twice," he said. The Chief stayed seated at the kitchen table with her hands on her stomach. As Becky swung around to step down the ladder, she glanced back and she swore she caught the rasme thau running her eyes down the backside of Becky's damp Trellis jumpsuit.

The cargo hold was a mess and Yip-Goru was in the middle of it, connected by a wire to an Outreach military drone folded up and hidden in a dummy plastic crate.

"Where the hell did you get that?" said Becky. The drone was off-white through a layer of grime and had "CHARLIE" stenciled in military lettering on the dorsal.

"Payment in kind," said Kol.

"You guys run weapons?" said Becky. "'Cause I didn't sign up for that. Arun made it sound like you were all about the raw milk cheese." The hair on her arms prickled in the wine-cellar cold of the cargo hold.

"Charlie here is a pacifist," said Kol. "He's been running interference for us."

"And like a good pacifist," said Yip-Goru, "he's about to get killed because he can't defend himself."

Kol picked up a filthy plastic grocery bag and emptied it into the drone's sample hatch: dirt and leaves from Cedar Commons, bound together with a black slime that looked like what would show up on your sponge if you wiped Charlie down.

"After we skip," said Kol, "Charlie sticks around and drops the chaff. Then—this is the fun part—he creates a *second* skip bubble that overlaps the volume of our original bubble. Charlie skips to a completely different location and never comes back. I don't care what kind of tech you have; you're not tracking us through that." Kol closed the hatch. "The molecular deck is shuffled."

"Goodbye, old but stupid friend." Yip-Goru patted Charlie on its side, like a horse, leaving a grasper-shaped smudge in the grime.

"When you say this is the fun part..." said Becky.

"It's the part we've never tested," said Kol.

"Yeah, I see a problem," said Becky. "How's a drone supposed to make a skip bubble that big? You'd need an engine as big as the ship's."

"Incorrect," said Yip-Goru. "Charlie needs to eat a big-boy breakfast, but he doesn't have to cook it himself."

Kol picked up a little transparent-metal jug from the floor near the ladder and walked towards the far edge of the cargo bay. "Miss Becky Twice," he said, gesturing Becky over with a sloshing hand. "I need to talk to you without the Chief overhearing."

Becky looked up the ladder expecting the Chief to be up there, poking her nose through the hatch. She followed Kol out of curiosity. "What's going on?"

"You've been...looking at her," Kol murmured. He opened a fifty-gallon type drum and twisted the cap tight on the small metal jug.

"Yeah, I have," said Becky, "and unless I'm mistaken, she's been looking at me. What's your problem?"

"You're crew now," said Kol. "Your problems are my problems." Kol set the metal jug down into the drum with a little splash. "You're headed for a lot of pain, Miss Becky Twice." It was like Kol wanted Becky to act as a witness to him hiding the jug. The drum had been full of liquid, and it now nearly overflowed.

"What, is she straight? She has someone already? Do rasme thau have poisonous spikes on their vulvas?"

Kol glanced at Yip-Goru, who could certainly hear this whole thing, but who had no reason to give a shit. "The Chief is a neophile," Kol said. "Right now you're the new thing for her. It's magic. You're going to have the best fifty shifts of your life, and then it's going to stop." Kol clapped his cerulean palms together. "Someone else will catch her eye, or she'll get bored with you. You were the guest star in her life, and now the episode's over."

"The voice of experience, huh?" said Becky.

"There's a war on. We can't be swapping out crew." Kol picked up the drum's metal lid and screwed it back on. "If you want to go ahead with this, prepare to be living in a tin can taking orders from your ex. Or, the simpler option: keep it in your pants to begin with."

"What if we get killed in the war?" said Becky. "I don't want to miss the best fifty shifts of my life."

"We won't get killed," said Kol. "We always make it."

"What about your engineer?" said Becky. "I've got her coffee mug. She didn't make it." Kol just let out his breath in one sad giving-up sigh.

"I would like to mark this moment," he said, "with a special word, the name of a memorable animal or flower, so that in fifty shifts when the Chief moves you from one list to the other, I can say that word, and you'll remember the advice that I gave you just now."

"Yeah, don't bother," said Becky.

Sour Candy lifted off in darkness. Gravity and light, two of the universe's fundamental forces, were unaffordable luxuries to a ship trying to evade the Outreach Navy. Floating in the kitchen, Becky saw nothing but the glow of instrument readouts, felt only an infinitesimal tug in one direction or another as *Sour Candy* tumbled through the rings above Cedar Commons.

"We are now a ring fragment," said Yip-Goru. "A very large ring fragment with abnormal orbital velocity. In about three centishifts we'll be on the far side, where we'll rendezvous with Charlie and skip."

"Um, I have a question," said Becky. "As a, as a crew member. Why are we going to the far side? Where the Navy is?"

"The Navy's everywhere at the moment," said Arun. "They saw us take off. We need Charlie, and he's at the space elevator by now."

"Omigod!" said Becky. Despite her imminent death she felt a little fannish thrill. "That's how you're charging the skip generator! We're stealing potential from the top of a space elevator, like on fuckin' *Undeclared*. I can't believe that really works."

"The original provenance of that tactic!" said the Chief.

"As always, there's a catch," said Arun Sliver. "You'd have to be mad to dock with a military space elevator. But apparently we're all mad here."

"Charlie's a pretty convincing drone," said Yip-Goru.

"I'm sure *other drones* find him *very* convincing," said Arun.

Not much time left. Becky swallowed hard and pushed off the hull towards the Chief's voice. "Chief," she whispered.

"Mmm-hmm?"

"I don't..." said Becky. "I don't know if this is the right thing, and I don't know how you're going to take this, but I'm really scared right now and if we die I don't want to die knowing I didn't have the courage to..."

Becky found the Chief's face with her hands, she found the lips, she found that the Chief was smiling. Becky pulled the Chief to her, setting both of them slowly rotating through the kitchen, and she went in for a basic entry-level kiss.

The Chief's lips gave way a little, and Becky found the pushback and pressed her advantage. The Chief took the kiss willingly, pulled it into herself and when she did Becky found some of the calmness the Chief must feel throughout her life of constant danger, the unflappability she'd shown dangling one-handed from Becky's hovercar.

"*Not* to be scared," said the Chief.

"This is helping," said Becky. "I wasn't expecting that but it is actually helping."

"Hoo boy," said Yip-Goru.

The Chief giggled. "The proper technique," she said. She cocked her head a little and stretched her alien mouth to match Becky's, and whaddaya know, this *was* the proper technique.

Light sparked and spread across the aft portholes. *Sour Candy* was crossing Cedar Commons's terminator, passing from dusk into sunset. The Chief's face was half-illuminated by starlight reflected off the planet and those romantic ring fragments, and then *Sour Candy* spun around and the light shone on Becky's face instead.

The rest of the crew were visible now. Yip-Goru glittered from the bridge. Kol was very quiet, looking unhappily out a porthole and drinking from his water bottle. Arun Sliver lay strapped to the kitchen ceiling, working on a crossword puzzle.

The Chief's cranial fronds wriggled like anemones. Her arms opened gracefully and closed around Becky's back. Becky tried for the tongue and the Chief pushed it around a bit with her own before accepting it. Her mouth tasted like sweet fennel.

Below them sunset became evening, and evening became late afternoon. The local time at the steward station was about noon. Becky had five minutes to spend six hours in the Chief's arms, and she wasn't going to waste any of it.

Chapter 8

Skip Overlap

Churryhoof
Brown v. Board of Education of Topeka

This is unconscionable, commander." The rre in the obsidian suit actually grabbed thons 2-camera and shook it. "We are defenseless!"

In addition to grabby manipulators, this rre had balls the size of Precision Hyperkinetics' new Ophidia mapping drones, because after sabotaging a city-ship so it couldn't be used for the common defense, thon wanted *Brown* to personally stick around Cedar Commons and protect them from the big bad Fist of Joy.

"You'll probably be fine," said Commander Churryhoof. "You're a good fifteen light-years from the border. In fact, if you set up an antenna you should be able to pick up some enemy broadcasts from the last war. That should put your mind at ease. According to their propaganda, the Fist of Joy is a merciful conqueror."

"Commander," said Spaceman Wang. "Another bogey coming up...from the far side, ma'am."

Churryhoof's curiosity tamped down her rage. "What's on the far side?"

"Nothing, as far as we know, but we don't have good coverage."

"Break off swarm zero niner and converge on the bogey."

Churryhoof looked back into the tank. "What's going on, Tip-Iye-Nett-Zig? You sneaking the kids out the back door?"

"I have no idea what you're talking about," said the rre in the obsidian suit. "Can you explain it without the military jargon?"

"Commander, some interesting developments down here," said Lieutenant Dwap-Jac-Dac, the less annoying of the two rre on the comm.

"I'm busy. Give me the five-second version."

"The good news is, I've found you a reservist."

"Bad news?"

"She's spotted the enemy, and/or she's a spy. She says she saw a small cargo ship parked antipodal to *Jaketown.*"

"We just saw that ship take off," said Churryhoof.

"She claims one of the crew is human. We may have stumbled on an infiltration mission."

The party line in Churryhoof's ear got an in-person caller from Specialist Entwetterwick here on the bridge. "Commander, we've lost bogey in the ring system," she said.

"Search from the point of last contact," said Churryhoof. "Lieutenant, wrap it up. I can't guarantee we'll still be here in ten minutes."

"Yes, ma'am. We're having a little difficulty locating Dr. Joshi. The natives are being most uncooperative."

"Get *up* here, Lieutenant. Up here where we have bigger problems."

"Roger, we can lift immediate."

"Tear the damn ring system apart!" Churryhoof ordered. She paced around the 3-map, running her hands through billions of holographic rocks as if the bogey would sting her if she touched it. "Lieutenant, do you have *anything* else from your eyewitness?"

Dwap-Jac-Dac's vocal was blurred as Scoop Bravo flung itself through the atmosphere of Cedar Commons. "She says the name of the ship is *Bad Sugar.* She didn't actually see the Fist on it, but it was a rasme thau design."

"Oh, excellent," said Churryhoof. "Now of the thousands of ships hiding in the ring system, we can easily pick out the one we're looking for."

"Commander?" Park was well aware this was a bad time but he was more afraid of something else.

"What do you have, mister?"

"Well, ma'am, the LT put me on the sh—the event feed, but I'm using that to help Entwetterwick, and I noticed a drone that's not sending events."

"So on top of everything else, we have a crap drone?"

Entwetterwick butted in. "Not sure, ma'am. It's like it was never initialized. It's reading quad-zero Charlie."

"Where's this drone?"

"Um, it's kinda nearby, ma'am." She highlighted it on the 3-map, ten clicks beneath *Brown*, clinging to the space elevator like a limpet mine.

"Shit! Wang, take us to a higher orbit. Is that our mystery guest, or did *Jaketown* send it up their elevator?"

"Mystery guest was much larger, ma'am."

"Scoop Bravo, be apprised of potential hostile in your path. Tellpesh, prepare a malware check."

Wang: "Ma'am, quad-zero Charlie just detached from the lift on unknown orders. Accelerating into the ring system."

"Entwetterwick, focus your search on Charlie's projection. I bet our mystery guest is along that orbit."

"Commander," said Heiss on the scoop, "I actually have visual on quad-zero Charlie. Request permission to intercept."

"You got permission to destroy," said Churryhoof.

"Roger."

"Bogey just lit up," said Wang. The evil red dot tore through the ring system, heading for quad-zero Charlie, the green dot that ought to be red.

"I don't feel like this excellent crew needs to hear me give this order," said Churryhoof, "but I want all this shit blown up ASAP."

"I can't build a firing context," said Heiss. "Computer thinks Charlie's a friendly."

"Override!" Churryhoof and Dwap-Jac-Dac shouted in unison.

"Flashbang!" said Heiss and Entwetterwick and Wang. "That was our mystery guest," Wang added.

"Quad-zero Charlie may be running chaff for it," said Churryhoof.

"I'm right on its tail," said Heiss. "Firing co—"

"Flashbang!" said Entwetterwick and Wang. Two dots on the 3-map merged and vanished.

"Heiss," said Churryhoof. "Heiss!"

"Oh, good God," said Spaceman Wang. "Skip overlap took them. They're gone."

Chapter 9

Space and Death

Myrus
The scary shuttle

Women like a man who puts things together." This was
the foundation of Dad's advice on girls. It was also the
entirety of his sex ed pep talk, which was good because
it was squirmy enough listening to a guest teacher from the
girls' school talking about vaginal hoods and trush and perineal
orgasm. Myrus sweated in a cramped Navy shuttle, waiting for his
red uniform, his training into a killer, and the other horrors Mr.
Nzeme had told Dad to vote to avoid. The thought in his mind
was not Dad's crying; not Den's desperate hug and what she had
whispered into his ear; but this phrase, which came from a much
earlier Dad moment.

A couple years back, after dinner on a different forest planet,
Dad had sat on the chair that would shatter in the Cedar Commons
landing. His hands had shaped excited curves as he'd leaned
forward and told Myrus the truth about women, the secret that
for generations had given the Wectusessin bloodline easy access to
eager pussy: "Women like a man who puts things together."

The goal of this advice was to keep Myrus happy as a
woodworker, someone who would stay on *Jaketown* with Den

instead of going off to uni and becoming an accountant. But Dad really believed this. To him, skill at putting things together was the defining feature of uhaltihaxl manhood. Even when two men went into love for each other, they *both* had to be real putting-things-together type guys, or Dad would grumble about the decline of civilization.

Myrus was thinking about that moment and that phrase because of the human woman sitting across from him in the shuttle. He'd overheard her name: Warrant Officer Ingridsdotter. She was a commando, with a secret mission on Cedar Commons during the buildup to war.

Warrant Officer Ingridsdotter was covered in dried mud and smelled like burned oak. The nails on her fingers were carved into ten sharp weapons and painted red: the color of the uniform Myrus was about to be issued, the color of war and human blood. She had hair to her shoulders, like the warrior queens of antiquity, but her hair was deep black, a color much darker than you'd ever see on an uhalti. The color of space and death.

It didn't matter that she was human or that her clothes looked like a ripped-up janitor's jumpsuit. She was an elite soldier and Myrus sat as helpless before her as women supposedly were with Dad. One glance at this woman and Myrus saw that Dad's phrase had an obvious partner: *Men like a woman who takes things apart.*

Myrus had finally gone into love.

"Hey," said the human woman, to Myrus, amazingly enough. The shuttlecraft's engines screamed and it lurched off the ground. The soldiers in the front were chattering and arguing, including the rre in the creepy human-suit who'd taken Myrus away from Dad.

"Hi!" said Myrus, over the noise. He'd found himself with an uncomfortable erection.

"You got varnish all over your arms," said the woman, once the takeoff noise died down a little.

"It's stain," said Myrus. "Varnish is clear. I, uh, you got mud. All over."

"Yeah," said the woman, and grinned. Myrus fantasized

her yelling at him in boot camp, turning him into a killer. "You worked on the furniture ship? You're a carpenter?"

"Woodworker, yeah."

"I never met a carpenter before. You know who else was a carpenter?"

Myrus knew a lot of carpenters but it seemed like she was thinking of someone famous. "Uh, the fella in the English story?" he ventured a guess. "*Alice in Wonderland*."

"No!" said the woman. "I'm talking about Jesus."

"Jesus?" said Myrus. This guy must have a woodworking 3-show or something, unless... "Is that the rre's name? Je-Zus?" Myrus was now pretty sure his erection wasn't necessary, but it was sticking around just in case.

"No!" said the woman. "He's not rre or human or anything, he's the son of God. He came to Earth as a carpenter, during the Roman Empire. He died for our sins, and three days later he was resurrected. You never heard about this?" The woman reached into her jumpsuit and took out a little gold sculpture on a chain. "This doesn't mean anything to you?"

The human was mentally ill. Myrus shifted back from her and his erection went *zing* against his trousers and right then Myrus learned another lesson they don't teach in sex ed. Once you go into love, your dick doesn't care if the woman is crazy. It isn't even a factor.

The soldiers in the cockpit got loud whenever the flight got bumpy, and when it became smooth sailing they quieted down. Myrus couldn't understand most of what they were saying, but at least they weren't lying to him, the way Dad had been with his pig-crap about making desks. If they were yelling, Myrus knew he should be scared. If they calmed down, things were probably going okay.

The yelling periods got longer and louder as the ship went up into space. Myrus's heart pounded and his dick went mercifully soft. The human woman was glancing sideways into the cockpit with an annoyed look. Probably Jesus the unkillable carpenter would have done things differently back in the days of the Roman Empire.

Then there was a bright flash of light and the nausea of a skip. The stars shifted and the adults in front went very quiet. Myrus sighed in relief but then it became obvious that no one had calmed down at all. The people on the comm weren't there anymore, and the adults in the cockpit were now too frightened to yell.

Through a tiny porthole, Myrus saw a white shape in a cloud of dust spinning away from the shuttle and into the darkness. It looked like a harvester drone, but what would a drone be doing in space?

Warrant Officer Ingridsdotter stood up and climbed into the cockpit, initiating an argument like the one between Dad and Jiankang Nzeme that had started this whole thing. *Wei* Nzeme, who was like his dad in every way that Myrus didn't like, then began a separate argument with Sanjit Mathis and Teresa Inez over which of the kids should go into the cockpit and find out what was going on.

Myrus pulled his shirt over his head and hid inside. His breath warmed the fabric. He thought about Den, how she had hugged him and whispered: "I'm going to get you out of this." Which was nice, more than Dad had done, but realistically? That was their last hug.

The inside of the shirt smelled like furniture stain and Myrus was getting lightheaded, so he pulled the shirt back down and saw someone standing in the doorway between the cockpit and the passenger hold.

It was the scary rre in the human-suit. "Hi, kids," said the rre. Thon squatted down smoothly so thons fake head was pretending to look Myrus and the other kids in the eyes. It was like a clown with a hand puppet wanting you to talk to the puppet.

"My name is Dwap-Jac-Dac; you can call me Jac. I'm in charge on this ship, so it's my job to tell you that we've accidentally been skipped into Fist of Joy space. We don't have a good way back right now."

"But they're gonna rescue us, right?" said Teresa Inez.

"Maybe," said Jac. Dad used that "maybe" when Myrus asked for a human-style dartboard or to skip a form in school. "We're going to stay here as long as we can, to improve the odds, but pretty soon the only way to survive will be to call the Fist and surrender."

"Are we still drafted?" said Myrus.

"Absolutely not," said the rre. "The Fist isn't very nice to Outreach soldiers, and you'll be more useful to the war effort as civilians."

"Useful how, aer?" said Wei. "What's our success metric?"

"Since you're civilians, I can't give you orders," said Jac. "But I suspect you kids know a lot more about politics than the average teenager. So, instead of spending a couple years in a prison camp, I wonder if you'd like to help out the Outreach by having an adventure."

"Oooh!" said Wei and Teresa and Sanjit. Myrus just wanted to pull his shirt back over his head and breathe until he passed out from the fumes.

Part Two

Heavy Evidence

Chapter 10

Classic Coke

Rebecca Twice
Sour Candy, **en route to Spark Station**

T here has been some grumbling among this crew about a lack of money," said Kol.

"And there will be more," said Yip-Goru. The five crew members were seated around the kitchen table, the default place to hang out while waiting for the engines to build potential for a skip. Becky sat in the dead engineer's chair, which was designed for a species with a different attitude towards vertebrae.

"Kol, the dramatic reveal!" said the Chief. She snapped her fingers right in Kol's ear pocket. The egenu lifted up a clear metal jug, the one Becky had seen him stow in the fifty-gallon drum, and thumped it down on the table.

"This is seven hundred doses of evidence," he said.

"O-*kay!*" said Yip-Goru. Arun Sliver, leaning back in the chair next to Becky, was so amazed his eyes widened slightly and he set down his coffee mug full of teabags. Becky raised a wavering hand.

"Evidence of what?" she said.

"You've got to be taking the piss," said Arun. "Have you been living under a rock?"

"Actually, I have. So, uh, sorry I'm not impressed. What is this stuff? It looks like uhalti spooge."

"Evidence is a hallucinogen," said Kol. "You ever trip on Quantumm or Protein Cycle? O-Series?"

"God, no," said Becky.

"Why not?"

Because I'm a nice middle-class girl who doesn't belong here. "I guess wine and pot are enough for me."

"Yeah, you don't *want* your mind expanded," said Kol. "You're scared of what you'll find in there. Most people are like that. When you went under that rock of yours, hallucinogens were an art form for Cametreans and rich hippies. Now they're a market, and Evidence is the product.

"Evidence is an *objective* hallucinogen. It doesn't unlock your mind; the magic is programmed into the drug. It only works on humans, but every dose affects every human the same way every time. It's reliable, it's repeatable, and there's no risk of a bad trip.

"The best part is that your government, in its infinite wisdom, has put Evidence on General Prohibition. It's illegal to synthesize, possess or distribute. Even a brand can't handle it. You can imagine what that does to the street price."

Maybe it was his residual unhappiness from Becky's daring makeout with the Chief, but Kol didn't seem real happy about Evidence. He talked about it like *Sour Candy* would be fencing a beautiful sculpture made out of deer intestines. But Becky hadn't had anything nice for three months. Trellis employees weren't supposed to drink or get high on duty, and "duty" for a forest steward didn't end until they left the planet.

Becky had smuggled two joints onto Cedar Commons in a sock, hoping they might break the ice with her 'sexually compatible partner'. The partner had turned out to be Hiroko, and Becky had smoked both joints alone in the forest. Now here was the real shit, and Arun had told her she could boost a bit of anything that looked good.

"I hate to be the sparrow crapping on this garden party," said Yip-Goru, "but we just fled the country where Evidence is illegal and everyone wants it. Now we're in the country where it's legal and nobody cares."

"The human inhabitants of the Fist," said the Chief. "Black markets on the flexible borders of war!"

"What's it do?" said Becky. The liquid in the clear metal jug glistened in a way that made it seem alive, or at least recently alive.

"I'll defer to our resident human," said Kol.

"What's it do?" said Arun, spreading his hands apart as if setting up a long and complicated joke. "One may pick one's poison. There's a flavor of Evidence to match any fantasy a human might have. Power, sex, wealth, a quiet life in the country. Dear old Pater in the library saying he's proud of the way you've become your own man."

"Um," said Becky. "So which flavor we got?"

"We don't know," said Kol. "It's probably a prototype, because we were running it before Evidence actually hit the street. About four hundred shifts ago."

"That's about five months," Arun said to Becky.

"Four hundred shifts, dammit!" said Kol. "If Miss Becky Twice wants to be part of this crew, she must learn to use standard units of measurement."

"Can we use months," said Becky, "if I say it's okay to stop calling me 'Miss Becky Twice' all the time?"

Kol angrily slapped the metal jug. The liquid inside was so viscous it barely sloshed. "Four hundred shifts ago. Nobody'd heard of Evidence; this was just a really heavy molecule. A thousand times heavier than Hiprox antifungal, which is what the manifest said."

"Is that an Outreach thousand or a Fist of Joy thousand?" said Becky.

"Yes, wonderful, welcome to the crew," said Kol. "Let me try to finish this story without using any more numbers. The Chief and I boosted...a small amount of the mystery molecule."

"This specific amount!" said the Chief, taking her turn to slap the jug.

"We took a quick side trip and buried the molecule in the middle of nowhere, on an uninhabited planet where the Outreach grows trees. We figured we'd pick it up once we knew how much we could get for it."

"And how much is that?" said Arun.

"No more numbers!" said Kol. "I'll say it's enough to get us back in operation. It'd be more in the Outreach, and it'd be a lot more if we could tell the buyer what flavor they're getting, but I don't want to ask either of you to test a prototype."

"Do we know which brand invented it?" said Becky.

"Not a brand," said Kol. "The Fist invented it."

"How'd you do that?"

"We invent things, too!" said Kol.

"But you'd have to test it on humans, right?"

Kol picked up the metal jug in both hands. "I'm going to put this away," he said, with a significant glance at Becky, "where it won't tempt anybody. We'll fence it when we get to Spark Station, and then we can stock up on luxuries, such as tea."

"About bloody time," said Arun. His mug was empty and he was just as cranky as before.

"Hey, Arun," Becky whispered, once the meeting had dispersed.

"Yeah, mum."

"How do you take Evidence? Injection?" It would be nice to get some help her first time out.

"Under the tongue," said Arun, "as with many famous hallucinogens."

"What's the dosage?"

"Kol said seven hundred hits," said Arun. He was not interested in either helping her or stopping her. "Do the maths."

The bed in Becky's new quarters was bigger than what she got on Cedar Commons, but the room itself wasn't much bigger than the bed. The mattress was convex, with a reinforced hump running down the middle. This had probably been very comfortable for the dead alien who had previously bunked here.

The Chief's bed was the real goal, but the Chief was surprisingly a "not on the first date" kind of girl, so Becky was spending her first sleep shift horny and bored in the quarters of the woman she'd replaced. A idea went bonk-bonk in her head like a running shoe on a treadmill. The more she didn't sleep, the more detailed the idea got, and after about thirty minutes Becky decided to see how far she could get with it.

There was no doctor on *Sour Candy* but they did have a medical chamber, the kind that Fist charities brought in to disaster areas for propaganda purposes. Becky had already been inside the chamber, to have her capital terminal pulled out from behind her eyeball so the Outreach police couldn't track her.

A medical chamber was overkill for scratches and headaches, so there were first aid kits stowed *near* the medical chamber, and the first aid kits probably contained syringes or eyedroppers. Something Becky could use to measure out a dose of Evidence.

Becky slipped on her Trellis jumpsuit and her socks (thick and fuzzy, borrowed from the Chief). She snuck out of her quarters and tiptoed into the access hallway, feeling like a kid trying to catch Santa Claus in the act.

Becky pocketed a syringe from the first-aid kit. On her way to the cargo bay she saw a glint of light in the half-darkness: Yip-Goru, the pilot, still sitting on the bridge, plugged in to the ship.

"Hey," Becky whispered.

Yip-Goru said nothing and then said, "Hello." Now Becky felt bad; she'd woken thon up.

"Can't sleep," Becky explained.

"Go lie down, at least," said Yip-Goru. "One more skip and we're there. You'll have to work."

"Okay," said Becky. She went into the hallway and waited until Yip-Goru had probably gone back to sleep. A few minutes, anyway. Then it was back down the ladder to the cargo bay, where Becky's predecessor had been killed in an accident, or maybe an 'accident'.

The metal jug of Evidence was still in the screw-top drum where Kol had put it, clearly visible through the hopefully sterile liquid. He'd hidden it right in front of her, deliberately, so this was okay. Becky rolled up her sleeve and reached in and lifted out the heavy container.

The next problem: there were no real numbers on the syringe. There were little red Trade Standard D chicken scratches, but Becky couldn't even tell what quantity they were measuring. She pulled some Evidence into the syringe and decided to take it one drop at a time until something happened.

Back in her bedroom Becky steadied herself against the hull and prepared to have her mind expanded. The first drop did nothing. Becky waited thirty seconds and carefully squeezed the syringe again. The next two drops hung out under her tongue along with the first and did nothing. Becky had decided to give up at six drops, but the fourth drop, or the time between the first drop and the fourth, smacked Becky's head on the porthole and sent the syringe rolling to the floor.

The Evidence said that Becky was a soldier sitting on dusty stone stairs leading down to a dirt road. She wore a metal helmet and a leather skirt, but not the fun kind. She was sweating in her armor, propping herself up with a hand on her spear. The dry air smelled like human shit. Across a baked city she saw a sun that had done its damage for the day and was about to set.

Standing on the road near Becky was Jesus Christ, the Son of God. He had the beard, robes, sandals and everything. He was walking down the road, trying to get somewhere by the end of the day. Becky had seen him and thought *Oh my God that's Jesus*, and right then his eyes had caught Becky's and he'd seen that thought inside her.

Becky hadn't actually experienced the moment of recognition; the Evidence filled in that memory for her. But now Jesus walked to Becky in his sandals and looked her over with tired, complicated eyes. "*Scis me?*" he said. Apparently Becky now understood Latin. *Do you know who I am?*

Becky nodded. Her mental image of Jesus was Black Jesus, because that was how He was depicted in the antique oil painting in the Echo Park Baptist Fellowship when Becky was a kid. But she recognized Traditional Jewish Jesus when she saw him.

"Legionary, who do you serve?" said Jesus. He sat down on the steps beside her, on the side opposite her spear.

"I serve Caesar Tiberius," said Becky, who didn't even know who Caesar Tiberius was. But being near Jesus filled Becky's kindergarten heart with blissful peace, and she let the Evidence speak for her.

"Why has Caesar sent you here to Judaea, so far from your home?"

"They say there's going to be a war," said Becky. She thumped her spear on the stone step. "I have to fight."

"Aye, Caesar Tiberius will have his wars," said Jesus. "And Caesar Caligula who follows will have his. Caesar will always have his war and his triumph. You have your duty, and I have mine. My duty is to put an end to war."

The Sunday school at Echo Park had used a variety of inconsistent depictions of Jesus. Young Becky had found this very confusing, but in retrospect it showed that the adults weren't being dogmatic about it. Traditional Jewish Jesus was the timeless original, like classic Coke. Black Jesus got Becky comfortable with the guy, made Him feel like a family member and less like a schoolteacher. Korean Jesus and Indian Jesus did the same for the Korean and the Indian kids. Blonde WASP Jesus and Female Jesus were grudgingly tolerated. Even Uhaltihaxl Jesus had his place in iconography.

Jesus loved you. He didn't care what color you were or what planet you came from. That was his whole shtick. But no matter how you depicted him, Jesus was, well, Jesus. *Indian Jesus was not Krishna.* Full stop. They were different guys.

The part of Becky's lapsed-Baptist mind left unanesthetized by the Evidence had grabbed a sledgehammer and was ringing alarm bells hard enough to break an eardrum, because despite the sword-and-sandal setting of this hallucination, this Jesus was acting suspiciously Krishna-ish. He was talking in terms of war and duty, not love and forgiveness. The Gita, not the Gospels.

"I don't know how I can carry out this duty," said Jesus. "It seems hopeless. In the future I see an eternal Caesar and war without end. It might be better if I gave up."

"Don't say that!" said Becky. Not Rebeccus Publius Secundus or whatever, here on the porch, but Becky Twice in the Fist of Joy spaceship, lying spaced out on a dead woman's mattress. Jesus shouldn't say shit like that. Jesus never gave up. "What if you... talked to Caesar? Made him understand."

"Aye, talk to Caesar! What then, when Caesar hears me? When I speak to Caesar Constantine and he hears me say 'conquer in my name'? Then I will *become* Caesar, legionary. My name will be on the coins that pay the soldiers. Yeshua Caesar, Christus Rex. Millions will die in the name of the Emperor Joshua." Jesus shaded his eyes and shook his head. "I see it so clearly, but I can't see how to stop it. What can I do, so long as Caesar has men like you, who serve him so faithfully?"

"I'm not a man," said Becky. "I'm not a soldier. I'm barely a Christian."

Jesus captured Becky's gaze and turned on the full Jesus eyes. "My son," he said.

"I'm not a man!" said Becky.

"My son, promise me..."

"You don't know me! You're just pretending! I'm not your fucking son!"

Ancient Israel blew a fuse and Becky Twice sat slumped in her humid quarters, tears running down her cheeks. The Chief was shining a light in her eyes; Kol was standing next to her with his arms crossed.

"Becky, your safety," said the Chief. "It's okay."

"Jesus lied to me!" Becky wailed. "He didn't recognize me and he thought I was a man!"

"Well, now we know what flavor it is," said Kol.

Chapter 11

Against the Rules

Dwap-Jac-Dac
The prison cell

Dwap-Jac-Dac's suit hadn't moved for about a day. The sensors had been deactivated as part of the plan, and the first thing the Fist soldiers had done upon boarding Scoop Bravo was to lock down the servos. This was humiliating in the extreme, but now there was nowhere to go. Dwap-Jac-Dac was alone in a cell in a military prison.

Captured human and uhalti officers got communal quarters, mess halls, exercise rooms; but rre had to be kept confined. Rre were killers.

Dwap-Jac-Dac could move around *inside* the suit. The Fist of Joy could do nothing about that. The capital terminal still worked, although Dwap-Jac-Dac was limited to locally installed software. Apart from having lost control over thons life, this wasn't much different from being off-duty in quarters.

During the prisoner transport Dwap-Jac-Dac had performed a Jalian meditation exercise that heightened the body's unaugmented senses. Now that thon had arrived in solitary confinement, heightened senses were a liability. After forty-six minutes of tedium by the clock, Dwap-Jac-Dac heard a door slide open and the dull thump of flesh against metamaterial. A corestin man was knocking on the sculpted features of Dwap-Jac-Dac's dead combat suit.

"Have you been helped?" said Dwap-Jac-Dac.

The corestin glanced at a handheld terminal. He was tall with a flabby face, a prominent but receding fringe of orange heth running up to the tips of his perked-up, on-alert ears. He wore a white linen atmosphere suit with the hood unsealed and the respirator dangling from his neck.

"Congratulations, Lieutenant," he said, in English. "The war is over."

"Really?" said Dwap-Jac-Dac.

"Don't get too excited," said the corestin. "It's over *for you.* Outside this room, it's still going on." The corestin held his arms out in a friendly way. "But inside these walls, you and I, the Terran Outreach and the Fist of Joy...we're at peace. We have our differences, but we settle them without resorting to violence."

"I want to talk to a representative of the Red Cross."

"That's going to take a while," said the corestin. "You are the first officer in this prison. We're still setting up."

"I want to talk to a Jalian priest."

"I'm trained as a psychiatrist," said the corestin. "Sort of a secular priest, heh heh. In fact, I did what you'd call a postdoc in the Outreach. University of New North New South Northampton." He briefly adopted an American accent. "'Go Manta Rays!' You want to talk to me, or no?" Dwap-Jac-Dac said nothing. "I guess you're a 'name, rank, and serial number' sort of fella. That's okay, I'll do the talking. We can do a lot with name, rank, and serial number.

"Name: Dwap-Jac-Dac. Obviously you're a colony of three inside that suit. Now, 'Jac' has become a very popular name, because it sounds like a human name. Whereas 'Dwap' and 'Dac' aren't so popular anymore. My guess is that your middle died and you brought in young blood to keep the colony together.

"Rank: Lieutenant. Not too special, if you don't mind me saying so. The Navy of the Terran Outreach must have a half-million lieutenants. Which takes us to your serial number. I noticed it's a PI5 series, which tells me you trained at Camp Mayxenner. Not exactly West Point, is it, heh heh?

"So you didn't start out a lieutenant. You're not some privileged grub fresh out of university, treats a battle like a term paper. Your predecessor was a grunt. Probably fought in the last war. Maybe you got a field promotion; maybe when Jac joined the colony you wised up and went through Officer Candidate School. My point is, you worked for those bars.

"See? It all fits together. Name, rank, and serial number. You've been around, you're smart, and you don't make mistakes. So how in heck did you get outmaneuvered by a bunch of teenagers?" Dwap-Jac-Dac said nothing. "I wouldn't wanna talk about it either," said the psychiatrist. "We'll, uh, we'll come back to it, okay?"

"What's *your* name?" said Dwap-Jac-Dac.

"Hmm?" The psychiatrist had to check his terminal again for some reason. "Bolupeth Vo," he said. "No rank, no serial number, no 'Doctor', just Bolupeth Vo."

"Are you a slave?" said Dwap-Jac-Dac.

Bolupeth Vo gave a disgusted look. "Really, Lieutenant?" he said. "I told you, there's no war in this room. You can keep the cheap propaganda in your suit."

"I was just curious," said Dwap-Jac-Dac. "I've never met a Fist doctor before."

"Do I look old enough to be a slave?" said Bolupeth Vo. "I'm a psychiatrist. You wouldn't keep a slave as your analyst. It would be a conflict of interest, heh heh."

"You haven't answered the question," said Dwap-Jac-Dac.

"You have no standing to ask that question," said Bolupeth Vo, but he didn't seem displeased. He thought Dwap-Jac-Dac was finally opening up. "Every soldier is a slave, wouldn't you say?"

"To the state, you mean."

"To duty, Lieutenant. Your duty is to get out of this cell and back home. Mine is to get the truth about what happened on that Outreach scoop. Now, I don't see any obvious conflict between your duty and mine. Do you?"

Dwap-Jac-Dac said nothing. "Did you ever hear of a 2-show, Lieutenant, called *Home Front Heroes*?" Still nothing. "They ran it during the last war. One of those low-budget reality things, you know? I was just a kid, but my demi-uncle, Aebit, he had this idea: he really wanted to be on *Home Front Heroes*. They'd show someone who'd turned a park into a garden, or built their own early warning satellite, and he'd say, 'I could do that. That's nothing. I'm gonna be on that show, you'll see.'"

The psychiatrist glanced around the room, looking for something to sit on, but chairs and bunks are for humanoids, and he couldn't very well sit on the prisoner. "He'd been giving blood," said Bolupeth Vo. "For transfusions, you know? Every few days he'd go to a different donation site and give blood. They'd ask him if he'd given before and he'd lie. He gave blood *sixty-five times.* He was going to write to *Home Front Heroes* once he got up to a hundred. He would have died, if the war hadn't ended."

"I'm very sorry that your demi-uncle Aebit was an idiot," said Dwap-Jac-Dac.

"Idiots are one thing," said Bolupeth Vo. "Society has a place for idiots. Do you know what's worse than an idiot? Someone who can't tell the difference between real life and something you'd see in the damn 3-tank.

"They're bringing back *Home Front Heroes*, Lieutenant. It's called *Real Heroes* now. Those daring teenage defectors of yours, you bet they're real heroes. They're going to be famous. They're going to tell everyone how they hijacked an Outreach scoop ship and disabled a rre's combat suit and hacked a drone to skip themselves into Fist space. It's perfect propaganda. It's too good not to use.

"Problem is, other kids are going to believe that story. Egenu kids, hopore kids, corestin kids like my demi-nieces. They all want to be heroes. Our kids are going to imitate those defectors of yours. They're going to steal things and hack weapons and get themselves killed. Do you want those kids on your conscience, Lieutenant? Or do you want to tell me what really happened on that scoop?"

"That's ridiculous," said Dwap-Jac-Dac. *"Real Heroes.* That show will never go out. The war's over. You said so yourself."

"Lieutenant..."

"Those meddling kids can grab vacuum," said Dwap-Jac-Dac. "All of them. The whole bloody Fist of Joy can grab vacuum."

Bolupeth Vo grimaced, turned to the cell door and rapped on the wall. The door slid open and a humanoid in a fully-assembled atmosphere suit pushed a medical supply cart into Dwap-Jac-Dac's cell. The top of the cart was padded like a hospital bed, with a raised metal lip.

"This fella had better be with the Red Cross," said Dwap-Jac-Dac.

"No, not exactly," said Bolupeth Vo, "but he is a very good doctor. Don't worry." The psychiatrist winked at Dwap-Jac-Dac. "Private practice. Not a slave." A wink looked bad enough on a human; on a corestin face it was hideous.

Dwap-Jac-Dac heard a hissing sound, indicative of poison gas being pumped into the cell, as if poison gas could do anything to an exobody. The gas was there: Bolupeth Vo waved it away as he slid his respirator over his frizzy heth. But Dwap-Jac-Dac thonself couldn't see it. It was a gas invisible to rre.

Bolupeth Vo attached the hood of his atmosphere suit to the respirator and sealed it tight. "It's a waste, an unbearable waste," he said, his voice now hollow and faraway. "The only known non-biped intelligent life in the galaxy, and what do the humans do?" He rapped on Dwap-Jac-Dac's metamaterial suit; the doctor waved him away. "They make you look human! They extract the parasite from thons host and dress thon up in a suit. Like a dog wearing a hat."

Once the propaganda came, Dwap-Jac-Dac was expecting it to be laughable, amateur stuff, like every other time the Fist tried to be creative. Something about how just as rre had once been parasites inside rwit, so was the Outreach a parasite eating away at galactic peace from within. But that was the kind of melodramatic monologue you'd get from someone like, well, Dwap-Jac-Dac.

Bolupeth Vo's duty was to get information out of his prisoners.

Slandering the Outreach would get him nowhere, but he might have luck playing one race against the others. There was just enough truth in what the shrink was saying that Dwap-Jac-Dac didn't trust thonself to respond.

"And what do you do, once they put you in those suits?" said Bolupeth Vo. "You collaborate! You join the Navy of the Terran Outreach!"

"Nobody calls it the 'Terran Outreach'," said Dwap-Jac-Dac. On the cart, among the scalpels and clamps, thon noticed a plastic copy of a classified Navy multiratchet.

"It says 'Terran Outreach' on your medals," said Bolupeth Vo. "You serve on a ship named after a human, Brown; and a Terran city, Topeka! Yes, we know who you are, Lieutenant Dwap-Jac-Dac. We determined which ship your shuttle comes from. And we found this, in your skip residue."

Bolupeth Vo unzipped a pocket on his atmosphere suit and pulled out a small plastic bag. He dangled it in front of Dwap-Jac-Dac's conjoined bodies. There was a bit of a plant in the bag: yellow and brittle, freeze-dried by space.

"The mystery deepens, Lieutenant!" said Bolupeth Vo. "This is an oak leaf, from a Terran plant. Oak doesn't grow in space. How the heck did this get into your residue? What were those kids doing?"

"I've never seen that leaf before in my life," said Dwap-Jac-Dac.

"I understand how it is," said Bolupeth Vo. "You're not in the mood to talk. We've been bad hosts, heh heh. Get it? 'Hosts'?"

Neither the other doctor nor Dwap-Jac-Dac found this funny. Bolupeth Vo groaned, unappreciated. "Let's get you out of this suit. You'll be able to move around, and we can provide you with facilities befitting an officer."

The "poison" gas was aerosolized mkire, the chemical soup that keeps rre alive by simulating the interior of a rwit. It wasn't invisible at all. Dwap-Jac-Dac couldn't see it because thon was already submerged in it.

"I'd just as soon stay in here," said Dwap-Jac-Dac. The doctor picked up the bootleg multiratchet and slid one head into the disassembly bolt hidden in the ear canal of Dwap-Jac-Dac's humanoid exobody. A few spins and the bolt unlocked and popped out. The doctor moved around to the other ear.

"You know we can't allow that," said Bolupeth Vo. "It wouldn't be fair. The other prisoners don't get to keep their weapons." The doctor stabbed the sharp end of the multiratchet into the top of the exobody's head and pried it open. Crumbs of accumulated grime showered from the seams of the suit onto Dwap-Jac-Dac's unprotected bodies. Liters of Navy mkire gushed from the split sides of the humanoid exobody and dribbled down the legs. Dwap-Jac-Dac sat naked to the mist, atrophied muscles quivering.

"But, Lieutenant, you'll be happy to learn that I have not been idle on your behalf." Bolupeth Vo slid a metal case out from a rack on the medical cart. It was a bulky thing with its own refrigeration unit, liberally decorated with the international biohazard symbol: a comforting bit of serrated roundness among the ovals and diamonds of Fist design. Bolupeth Vo set the case on the wet cell floor, reached into it and carefully lifted out a *person*. A small person; a rre singleton twenty centimeters long.

"We *do* have a Jalian priest for you," he said. "Precedent Tia here made some powerful enemies in the Outreach, trying to 'liberate' the brands. We offered thon political asylum." Bolupeth Vo lay the rre singleton out on the padded top of the cart. "Now thon's active in the disarmament movement. Not my thing or yours, but a worthy goal, I'm sure you'll agree. Jalir is the religion of peace, after all."

Dwap-Jac-Dac couldn't run, even a token distance to the far end of the cell. It had been almost a year since thons last suitless training; thon couldn't even lift thons own insignificant weight.

"Periodically," said Bolupeth Vo, "Precedent Tia volunteers part of thonself for medical purposes. Just like my demi-uncle with his blood. Quite the...I believe the English word is 'humanitarian', unless they've updated that one. Anyhow, it's clear that Dwap-Jac-Dac is not happy here, but I think Dwap-Jac-Dac-Tia will have a much more positive attitude, and a concept of duty less focused on fantasies of escape."

Dwap-Jac-Dac pressed against the manual vocalizer switch. "Bolupeth Vo," thon said, "forced grafting is torture, and that's against the rules."

"Torture?" said Bolupeth Vo. "Torture would be about me: how do I force you to confess to some imaginary crime. This is a medical procedure. It's about your well-being. It's *like* a *kind* of torture, I suppose, but I promise you there will be no pain."

The doctor lifted Dwap-Jac-Dac out of the cavity of the military exobody, and thons physical connection with the vocalizer was broken. Thon could no longer speak. Dwap-Jac-Dac called out to Tia in native-voice, but the singleton was unconscious. The doctor set Dwap-Jac-Dac down on the padded cart, a tangle of flesh next to the calligraphic straight line of the anesthetized priest.

"I personally recommended that Tia be featured on an episode of *Real Heroes*," said Bolupeth Vo. "But I don't think it will happen. Thons work is politically sensitive, and many in the Fist of Joy still suffer from racial prejudice against rre. I don't claim that my civilization is perfect, Lieutenant. But we are working to solve the very real problems that face us."

The doctor dipped a squeencloth in anesthetic and wiped down the tissue where Dwap, Jac and Dac intersected to form a colony. Numbness flowed along the bloodstream through the three bodies. Dwap-Jac-Dac's claws twitched and thons flesh went dead. Thon scrambled for consciousness.

"If there's nothing else," Bolupeth Vo told the doctor, "I'll clean up the mess, and let you work."

Chapter 12

Flattering Facts

Myrus
In the studio, under the lights

"Helloooo, all you wonderful viewers!" The hopore woman had a huge origami hairdo that dangled with cameras. "Welcome to the all-new *Real Heroes*, the uplifting show that teaches us that peace doesn't just come from superior weapons and tactics—it comes from the quiet courage and hard work of people just like you! I'm Merikp Hute Roques, your star-trotting optimist, and you may be wondering why I'm speaking in boring old Trade Standard D. Well, gentlebeings, this fourshift our traveling studio has been invaded by the Terran Outreach!"

Half of the cameras snaking out from the hopore's helmet of hair swiveled on their stems and focused on the kids on stage. The rest of the cameras drooped down and pointed inward, at Merikp Hute Roques herself. Myrus wasn't sure what her cameras were even for, because the stage was surrounded by people running traditional 3-cameras.

"Ha ha, no, don't call for help just yet!" said Merikp Hute Roques. She clicked her beak in a playful way. "I'm joined by a cosmopolitan group of young adventurers, an uhaltihaxl and three humans who've fled the Outreach's coercive military conscription and made a daring escape to the space of freedom!" Most of the time she spoke normal D but on the word "uhaltihaxl" she adopted a terrible Narathippin accent: "ooh-walty-wackel".

"Now let's meet these brave boys and girl, a reminder of a better time to come when we can all be friends again!" Myrus supposed this beat boot camp. The food was okay, for neutral stuff, and no one was trying to turn him into a killer.

The kids and the Navy soldiers had been yanked out of that cramped shuttle by Fist of Joy soldiers: weird soldiers who didn't wear proper uniforms. Myrus and the others had been passed along from one interviewer to another, like trees pulled out of the ground by a harvester drone and sent down an assembly line to become furniture. Lieutenant Jac, the rre in the scary suit, was picked off immediately, like a tree with root rot. The next people in the processing chain had assumed that the lower-ranking soldiers were in charge of the kids. But Warrant Officer Ingridsdotter had badmouthed Myrus and the other kids so badly that they were sent to another room to spare their tender ears. They didn't see the adults again after that.

With Myrus and the other kids identified as civilians and isolated from the soldiers, the Fist of Joy folks had to decide who was in charge of the council kids. They made the stupid assumption that Myrus was responsible for making sure everyone took their vitamins and went to bed on time.

Myrus wasn't good at lying and just didn't want to be in charge, so he did his best to get out of this duty by acting like a normal grumpy teenager. This was helped out by his dawning realization that he was probably never going to see Warrant Officer Ingridsdotter again. He should have asked the beautiful human on a date when they were the shuttle. Dad would have moved decisively; Myrus had screwed it up.

For the first time in history, Wei Nzeme helped Myrus out. Wei was a kiss-up son of a mayor. He wanted to be in charge, and he hated how the adults were paying attention to Myrus instead of to him. So he sprang into action. When he was learning to read he must have memorized an A-Z book about the Fist of Joy, because he knew all the races by sight and had a couple flattering facts ready to go whenever they were led into a new office with a new interviewer.

For instance: "Wow, you must be from Wirch! What an experience, to finally meet a daughter of the Great Ocean! You know, the drama and emotion of wirchak opera is famous even in the Outreach! And, gee, the gang and I were just talking about how we'd love to explore the Lukewarm Fire Caves! With the proper safety equipment, of course!"

Myrus winced as Wei did this, but it got the people in the offices smiling and shifting their attention away from Myrus. Wei Nzeme and his buddies were really good not just at lying, but at telling the specific, detailed lies that would get them sent to the next office.

It had taken an entire day, but Myrus and the human kids had gone through the processing chain and they were furniture. Now it was time for them to repeat their adventurous lies for the 3-cameras, to make people in the Fist of Joy feel better about the war.

Myrus hadn't liked this idea at all. It seemed unpatriotic. But Dwap-Jac-Dac, the rre in the suit, had sent them in this direction, and you couldn't call thon unpatriotic. Thon was probably being tortured in a prison camp right now, and Myrus would be getting the same treatment in the cell next door if it hadn't been for this pig-crap cover story and the incredible ability of the children of politicians to tell adults what they want to hear.

Now Merikp Hute Roques was looking directly at Myrus, who had to be punished for the sin of not wanting to talk in the 3-tank. "Now, I'm told by our wonderful backstage crew," she said, "that you four were *captured*, by a rre in a jolly dreadful combat suit! That must have been frightening, Myrusit. I would have pissed my pants, I assure you!"

"Uh, yes, it, it was scary, but, y'know, you keep a positive mental attitude?"

"But tell me, Myrus, how did you manage to disable that suit? It seems impossible!"

In fact "we outsmarted a rre and disabled thons suit" was the weak point in this thrilling story. The rre had told the kids that the longer they kept the Fist of Joy occupied with vague explanations, the more chaos they could sow behind enemy lines. But Myrus got the feeling the adults who'd captured them were now seriously considering the nonsensical but true explanation that the rre had disabled thons own suit. Now was the time to act.

"Well, uh, Merikp Hute Roques," said Myrus.

"Please, just call me Hute."

"Myrus..." said Wei in a warning way. He had no idea what Myrus was about to say, and disliked not being in control.

"Shut up!" said Myrus. "We have to tell them eventually. Do you know about trees, ma'am?"

When the show was broadcast there would be a 3-picture of a tree stuck in there for someone who didn't know what they were. But 'Hute' knew about trees. She made a yes-click and said, "Ah, yes, one of the great natural wonders of Terra."

"Well, we, that is, humans, cut down trees and, and, cut them up and make them into furniture." Myrus patted the metal chair he sat on. "A human might have a chair like this, only it's made from part of a tree."

The hopore woman shook her head. "What a tragic disregard for nature."

"It's not really that bad," said Myrus. Teresa Inez subtly hit him with her elbow. *Do it right, idiot.*

"Well, we were exploring on this forest planet. That's a whole planet of trees. And we found, um, ah..." This was the big lie, and Myrus found he couldn't go through with it.

"Shut off the cameras," said 'Hute', very calmly, to the crew. "He's the shy one." The cameras surrounding her face went stiff on their stems and slipped back into her hairdo, clicking like insects. She switched from Trade Standard D to her horribly accented Narathippin. "What did you find, Myrusit?"

In her eager look and in that little bit of his native language, Myrus discovered why everyone in the Fist went to him before the human kids. They thought he was the one they could get. They assumed any uhalti was doing what some human had told him, and if the Fist were just nicer, the uhalti would switch sides. The idea that Myrus might *actually want* the Outreach to win the war didn't compute for them.

"A, a mutant," said Myrus, in English. Wei and Teresa and Sanjit looked at each other with fake worry and real confusion. "A mutant kind of tree. It evolved a defense mechanism, like poison oak, so it wouldn't get cut down. It gives off an energy field that, um, stops machines from working." Myrus took a deep breath. It was over. "And that's how we disabled the suit. We used stuff from that tree, and the suit stopped working."

"Myrus!" said Wei Nzeme, suppressing a smile. "You're not supposed to tell them about that!"

Merikp Hute Roques was sitting back in her chair with her beak wide open. After a moment she blinked and crossed her legs and leaned forward again. "Myrus, what's the name of the forest planet you were exploring?"

"I probably shouldn't tell," said Myrus. Yes, 'Cedar Commons' was the worst thing Myrus could say right now. Those two words would get Dad and Den and everyone else on *Jaketown* killed.

The hopore nodded at someone Myrus couldn't see. "Let's talk about this later," she said. "This doesn't need to go over the air; people won't be interested. Why don't we film a little more to wrap the segment, and then we can all go out to eat?"

Chapter 13

Unreliable Officer

Churryhoof
Brown v. Board of Education of Topeka

C hurryhoof ordered Entwetterwick, Wang and Park to stand watch and leave her undisturbed in her office for one hour. Quite a motley crew she was left with. Entwetterwick a near-washout, Wang an ass-kisser, Park with his not-so-secret Evidence addiction. She'd used her two best fellas, Heiss and Tellpesh, on the kiddy-snatching mission, and now they were gone.

For a few minutes Churryhoof sat in her office combing through papers and terminal records, looking for some obscure regulation or exculpatory fact, but this was a cover for the real work she had to do. She needed time to accept that her career, and her usefulness to the war effort, were over.

She had punitively drafted the children of civilian officials. This fell into the broad category of 'illegal, but'. Lots of kids were being drafted, and the brass wouldn't second-guess a field commander unless forced—say, by a hearing regarding the loss of a scoop and four spacemen. The Navy could tolerate cruelty and forgive failure, but never both at once. Not for an uhaltihaxl woman, anyway.

One hour; then she would leave her office and give her final orders. Hide the queen and her drones in Cedar Commons's ring system, task it with protecting the furniture-makers from whatever the war might bring, then take her doomed crew home.

Twenty minutes into the hour, Spaceman Wang knocked on the office door. Churryhoof was staring at the blank reverse side of her printed orders, trying to remember how crying worked. In this emotional mood she considered yelling at Wang, but he probably had a reason.

"Ma'am, sorry, but a ship just skipped in."

Churryhoof was on her feet, glad not to have yelled. "Whose?"

"Ours," said Wang. Churryhoof was through the door, brushing past him. "Civil service." Churryhoof was on the bridge. "Ministry of Agriculture." Churryhoof stopped walking.

"Why?"

"No idea, ma'am. Single-crew ship with a Min-Ag call sign. They want to talk."

Investigating *Jaketown* did not seem like Min-Ag's responsibility just because the crash had happened on a resource planet. Didn't they have war work to do? And—

"How'd they get here so fast, ma'am?" said Wang.

"They were already en route," said Churryhoof. Nothing else made sense.

A flat image unrolled in the bridge's 3-tank. In keeping with the pointless thrift that kept the Outreach civil service hungry, the Min-Ag ship communicated over a grainy 2-screen. The crew comprised an elderly human woman wearing a Navy uniform with commander's insignia but no service ribbons whatsoever. Her hair, much longer than regulations allowed, floated around her head. Apparently artificial gravity on civil service ships was also a waste of taxpayer money.

"Churryhoof, right?" said the human. Like all spacemen, she wore a unit patch on each shoulder, but the patches were blank.

"You have the advantage, Commander...?"

"Just Mrs. Chen is fine," said the human. She tugged at the lapel of her uniform as though it were too tight. "I don't usually wear the monkey suit, but first impressions..." she didn't bother to complete the cliché. She clapped her hands. "Have you seen a rasme thau cargo ship with aftermarket motivators?"

"Is the ship called *Bad Sugar* and is she a huge pain in the ass?"

"Her name is *Sweet-and-Sour*. I don't suppose you destroyed her?" Chen seemed hopeful.

"I wish I had, Commander. She just skipped out and took one of my scoops in the overlap."

"I asked you to call me 'Missus'." The alleged commander peered at Churryhoof through her 2-screen. "But that's all right. You've got a problem too heavy to hold. Maybe we can make each others' problems go away."

Once the Min-Ag ship got close enough to *Brown*, a burst of automatic protocols negotiated rank and clearance between Churryhoof's capital terminal and "Mrs." Chen's. All relevant details of Churryhoof's recent tactical and moral failure were synced to someone she'd never met. That was military life, it was how the Navy maintained operational context across a galaxy of empty space, but it stung that Churryhoof got nothing in return. Chen's security clearance was very high, and she was able to hide everything but namerankserialnumber and a service record spanning forty years but light on detail.

Mrs. Chen's ship squeezed with hull-scraping tightness into the space left by the lost Scoop Bravo. Chen popped out the exit hatch, ignoring the nervous salutes of Entwetterwick and Wang and Park. Churryhoof motioned Chen to her office; she followed with long human strides. Her time in free-fall hadn't affected her at all.

The final line of Chen's taciturn service record: assigned for twenty years to Echo Division, the Navy's PSYOP unit. When it came to wastes of taxpayer money, Churryhoof considered Echo Division the tops. It was a bunch of literature majors who couldn't cut it in the signal corps. The Outreach hadn't won two wars with propaganda and publicity stunts. We'd hit the Fist of Joy harder and sooner than vice versa.

Nobody spends twenty years in Echo Division. Mummy pulls strings to get you in because a brief Navy stint will look good when you stand for Parliament.

Churryhoof's office door hissed closed and she turned on the human. "I don't think you're in PSYOP," she said. "You feel like a spy."

"One can be both," said Mrs. Chen. She vaulted onto Churryhoof's couch and stretched as though posing nude. Churryhoof already missed Dwap-Jac-Dac. "Case in point: you just got fucked over by the Fist of Joy."

"You think that was enemy action?" It was a tempting thought: defeat was bad, but there was honor in it. "*Sweet-and-Sour* is an unarmed smuggler ship. They probably don't even know we're at war."

Chen snorted, as if Churryhoof had inexplicably declined a chance to punch a defenseless child. "Maybe you can tell me what a Fist smuggler was doing on an Outreach resource planet?"

"At a guess, smuggling?"

"I understand your skepticism," said Mrs. Chen. "It took me a while to see the pattern." Information finally began to dribble out from Mrs. Chen's terminal, but she was controlling the flow. "The *Sweet-and-Sour* crew are my opposite number."

Chen sent over Outreach and Fist mug shots of that crew: a rasme thau, an egenu, a human, and a transparent domed blob that was either a working-class rre or some kind of experimental Fist cyborg. In both mug shots, the rasme thau woman was blowing a flirty kiss to the police photographer.

"They look like small-timers. The pissants we use as tracers to see what the big fish are up to. And yet they keep getting involved in...incidents. This is the first crew to 'smuggle' Evidence into Outreach space. They 'accidentally' destroyed a classified reskipper during a convenience store shootout. They 'unknowingly' produced the anti-Outreach propaganda that has done such a splendid job of keeping Quennet neutral and out of the war."

Chen punctuated each example with an incident report stamped SECRET. "These are the big fish. They have spent seven years *in peacetime* spreading chaos and confusion, and they... always...make it look...like an accident. Now it's war, and I shudder to think what they might do. If you want to stay in the fight, you'll come with me and hunt them down."

"Why do you need me?"

"PSYOP is storytelling, Commander. I can't take a civil service craft into Fist space. The story wouldn't make sense."

"Also you would be killed."

"Mmm." Chen politely acknowledged this opinion. "But here is poor Hetselter Churryhoof, with a combat ship under her command and disgrace awaiting her back home. Maybe she goes rogue. A suicide mission to avenge the spacemen she left to starve or suffocate.

"Because maybe something important happens out there, and when Churryhoof comes home covered in glory, the Navy decides to overlook one little mistake in an otherwise outstanding career. Do you think that's a plausible story?"

Mrs. Chen, so experienced in psychological warfare, was manipulating Churryhoof in the most obvious way possible. This was how brands spoke to spacemen. It worked because there was no need to create complicated new consumer desires that only a brand could fulfill. Spacemen needed what soldiers have always needed: alcohol, better gear, sex, a good night's sleep. A way to pretend the horrible thing wasn't happening, or wouldn't happen to you. It was working.

"What was *Sweet-and-Sour* doing here?" said Churryhoof. "Since you know them so well."

"I don't know that," said Mrs. Chen, "but they really like it here. This is their second visit."

"Really?" Churryhoof couldn't imagine anyone wanting to come to Cedar Commons *once.*

"Six months ago, they spent seventy hours in this star system. We don't know what they were doing, but their next stop was an Outreach station where they sold forty kilograms of Evidence to an undercover cop."

"We need to get down there," said Churryhoof. "Find out why they came back."

"Yes," said Chen, and Churryhoof hated that she was smiling, "we do." She sat up.

"Your kids..." Chen parodied Park's nervous salute, one hand up and the other on the holster of his service weapon. "Are they any good?"

"They're spacemen," said Churryhoof, defensive and nearly parental. "But they signed up for a normal war, not...whatever this is going to be."

"Send them back in the Min-Ag ship," said Chen. "They can report their C.O. talked to a crazy woman and went crazy. That will validate our story, and they'll get reassigned to something normal."

"Stay in here," said Churryhoof. This was her way of telling Chen that her office contained nothing of value. The door closed behind her. Entwetterwick and Wang stood on the bridge. They'd been talking, but they immediately stopped, looked embarrassed, and said "Ma'am." Then Wang repeated it: "Ma'am ma'am." They'd had an hour to whisper-debate how much of the coming shitstorm would land on their heads.

"Stand down the queen and bring the drones in," said Churryhoof.

"We're leaving, ma'am?" said Wang.

"You are leaving," said Churryhoof, trying to make it sound like the better option.

Uhaltihaxl need seven hours of sleep a night. The service gives you six, you get five if you're lucky. Churryhoof had slept for three hours when a blinking green light in her quarters woke her up. She rolled over inside her sleeping bag, fished out a hand and opened the document safe.

The Navy had, at great expense, skipped a tiny chunk of encrypted matter to a pinned location in space. Decrypted and exposed to room temperature, a microscopic piece of ferroplastic had exploded into something less loseable: a wrinkled ball the size and shape of an axule blossom. Churryhoof rolled the document out of the safe with one finger and copied it into her terminal.

The document safe was rarely used in peacetime, but the fact that it worked was great news. Churryhoof was still the ranking officer in-system, and the Navy still trusted her with classified intelligence. Mrs. Chen hadn't snitched on her as she slept.

The *contents* of the intelligence were another matter. The Fist of Joy had somehow gotten the impression that Cedar Commons hosted a secret research station. Depending on how everyone was feeling today, the enemy would respond with something between a single uncrewed spy ship and a full invasion fleet.

The Fist's threat to the wreck of *Jaketown* was still a probability distribution, but safety through obscurity was no longer an option. Deploying *Brown*'s queen to manage a few nuke-tips would protect *Jaketown* from the most likely threats. Mrs. Chen wouldn't like this, but Churryhoof was the ranking officer. The queen would obey her.

Churryhoof opened the connection. "Barhukad, this is your deployment officer."

"Hello, Commander," said a chirpy synthesized voice in Churryhoof's terminal. "This is Barhukad." Churryhoof had served with countless queens named Lizzie and Manikarnika, but on her own ship they were naming the queen after an uhalti woman, damn it. She pictured Barhukad snuggled in *Brown*'s drone bay, surrounded by sensors and missiles. Like Barhukad of old in her floating palace: so powerful, but too proud to listen to advice.

"Funny story," Churryhoof told Barhukad, "but I need you to redeploy some of our drone complement."

A queen wasn't smart enough to understand the semantics of phrases like "funny story," but it did know that sentient beings said that sort of thing in a jokey sort of tone when they were under a normal amount of stress. Hopefully this would convince Barhukad that everything was fine.

"That's an unusual order!" said Barhukad. No such luck; the dance had begun. "I was given an order to bring in my drones thirteen hours ago, in preparation for breaking orbit. What has changed?"

"The Fist is sending an invasion force to Cedar Commons." Churryhoof copied the queen on the report the Navy had skipped her. Queens couldn't understand intelligence reports, but they could check provenance and scan for keywords, and this document had all the right keywords.

"I understand! What should be deployed?" Good: obedient, trusting. Churryhoof tried to game out the likely size of the force headed for Cedar Commons, as opposed to the unknowns they'd encounter hunting down *Sweet-and-Sour.* "Three nuke-tips," she said. "Sixty reconnaissance. Hide the missiles in the ring system and scatter the recon for maximum coverage."

A long silence. Barhukad was weighing its inputs—Churryhoof's words, her tone of voice, keywords from the intelligence report—and deciding whether its deployment officer was compromised. If so, it would stick to its old orders, issued by a presumably non-compromised Churryhoof thirteen hours prior.

What was going on? Barhukad had never been so suspicious before. "Deploying now," it said at last.

"I commend your thoroughness," said Churryhoof. She cleared her throat. "You may be getting more unusual orders in the near future."

Barhukad was not impressed. "I evaluate all orders using the same algorithm."

"Please remember that your top priority is protecting Cedar Commons from the Fist of Joy." Churryhoof tried to think of all the ways Chen could twist this unambiguous order. "Do not pull back except on my direct instruction. I hate to say this, but I don't think Mrs—Commander Chen is a reliable officer."

"Commander Chen told me that she did not consider you a reliable officer," said Barhukad flatly.

"That's exactly what an unreliable officer would tell you," Churryhoof pointed out.

"I agree!" said Barhukad. Churryhoof closed the connection and breathed in and out. Far away she could hear grinding: the drone bay opening, Barhukad deploying herself.

Churryhoof splashed cold water on her face, then ran hot

water over the classified document until it melted down the drain. She opened the door between her quarters and her office, and saw the back of Mrs. Chen's head.

Chen was sitting in Churryhoof's chair and had littered her desk with empty ruxlt squeezes and exploded blue popcorn-documents, skipped directly into *Brown* without going through the safe. While Churryhoof slept, this human had cost the Navy nearly a million credits and bent its regulations on secure document delivery to the point of stress fracture.

"Good morning," said Chen without looking back.

"Are you mad?" said Churryhoof. "What are these...?"

"Oh, relax!" Chen held one up and set it down. "They're consumer data profiles. Not classified. We get them from the brands. I found out why *Sweet-and-Sour* came to Cedar Commons."

"You did?" said Churryhoof.

Chen picked out one of the blue plastic wads and tossed it over her shoulder at Churryhoof. "See what jumps out at you about Rebecca Laverne Twice."

Churryhoof caught the document and dipped her terminal into a stagnant pool of consumer data: the accumulation of a million tiny decisions. Nearly everything Rebecca Laverne Twice had ever done had been written to her disposition context, the shared record from which a brand could predict her desires, and therefore her future.

The data formats were unfamiliar, but perhaps Churryhoof could apply the same tricks used to make sense of drone telemetry. She set up some basic classifiers and ran learning passes, and a human life began to take shape. Did everyone look like this? Is this what a brand saw when it looked at Hetselter Churryhoof, her hopes and dreams?

"Nothing stands out," said Churryhoof. "She is totally unremarkable."

"Nothing?" said Chen, as though this were Churryhoof's fault. "Really? Look closer."

Another learning pass threw the dunes of this desert into relief. "Rebecca Laverne Twice is dishwater. She has no passions, no ambitions, no political opinions. Her strongest brand loyalty is to Crest toothpaste. Six months ago she didn't have a passport. She has an associate's degree in marketing, but she's never held a marketing job."

"Ah!" said Mrs. Chen.

"Ah?"

"Rebecca Twice is the only person unaccounted for in this clusterfuck," said Mrs. Chen. "But we know she was near *Sweet-and-Sour.* Remember what Warrant Officer Ingridsdotter told your LT? 'They got my buddy Becky.'"

"I see," said Churryhoof. "'Becky' is one of your hilarious human nicknames. Like the guy in the officers' club who tried to get me to call him 'Dick'."

"Rebecca Twice is a defector in waiting," said Mrs. Chen. "She looks dull to the disposition context because she's not interested in what the Outreach has to offer. She gets her marketing degree, she gets her passport, and she takes a job that will bring her to a quiet place near the border, where she can be picked up by the Fist. And then the real work of her life begins."

"And that work is what?"

"Marketing," said Mrs. Chen. "It's the Fist's biggest weakness. They've created the most addictive drug in history, absolute genius, and they let it spread via word of mouth. Idiots. Now they're trying to force it on us in combat. Morons! We'd beg them for it if they knew how to sell. When the war doesn't go their way, they'll finally try a professional marketing campaign. And that, Commander, is when we all get fucked with Becky Twice's dick."

"See, that's why I didn't believe him," said Churryhoof. "How can your name literally be 'Dick'? I'm sorry, what was your problem? Secret Agent PSYOP is worried about a community college marketing major single-handedly destroying the Outreach?"

"Marketing *is* PSYOP. It is deadly. That's why the brands have safeguards. They don't assassinate people to sell frozen custard. But now the science of marketing is being recruited into the endless war where there are no rules. The hell I have been subjected to throughout my career is about to be unleashed on the civilian population."

"Wow, I feel silly," said Churryhoof. She forwarded the report she'd received in the document safe. "Because all I got is this secret research station thing."

Chen skimmed the report. "This makes no sense," she said. "Unless the furniture-makers *are* the base, and your draft order was a snafu." She retreated into her terminal and re-sorted the pile of consumer profiles in this new light.

"They look like normal people," she said. "But these things are easy to fake. I'm a professional chef!"

"There's no research station," said Churryhoof. "The snafu is on the Fist side. The problem is, *we* have to deal with whatever the Fist sends to investigate."

"Hmm, research station or defector...?" Mrs. Chen stood from the uhalti-sized chair and cracked her back. "We can see who's right. I'll go down to *Jaketown* and do some interviews. Spot checks. You take the scoop to *Sweet-and-Sour*'s landing site and scan for Becky Twice's capital terminal."

"Just the terminal?"

"First thing defectors do is surgically remove the terminal," said Chen. "It gets you off the disposition context. The brands track what goes on in the Fist as best they can, poor dears."

Churryhoof tried to imagine life without her capital terminal. Then she tried to imagine being a *civilian* without one. Without the safeguards that protected Churryhoof from full-brain ads at inconvenient times, defecting might just be worth it.

"And if Ms. Twice is just a regular security guard..." she ventured.

"You'll find her body. Microscopic black hole through the back of the head. *Sweet-and-Sour* does not play games." Chen walked onto the bridge without making a token gesture to clean up the food pouches and data litter.

Churryhoof rifled through the trash on her desk and located an unopened pouch of ruxlt. She sucked on the valve and let the caffeine boil into her system. She sat in the human-warm chair and dropped Cedar Commons into her private 3-tank.

The planet was a mess. The chairmakers were still sending up shipping containers of merchandise (or was it?) to clutter the higher orbits. A forest fire raged on the far side, where Rebecca Twice's corpse and/or capital terminal might be found. Scattered through the ring system were sixty-four comforting green dots corresponding to Barhukad and the drones under her command.

Cedar Commons did look like a secret research station, albeit one where things had started to go a bit wrong. It had the appropriate defense context: sensors hidden in the ring system, nuke-tips coordinated by a queen. Enough firepower to deal with minor trouble but not enough to attract attention.

It wasn't true. Churryhoof had set these defenses herself, ten minutes ago. But alone in space with a mindfucker like Mrs. Chen, you started seeing things that weren't there.

Chapter 14

User Experience

Rebecca Twice
Spark Station, Fist of Joy space

B ecky followed Arun down the ladder and assumed she would keep following him out of *Sour Candy*, but at the last moment he jumped off the ladder and pulled out a chair from the kitchen table. "Becky," he said, "please sit a moment before we disembark."

Becky laughed. "You know I'm gay, right?"

Arun made an impossible British face. "I am also gay," he said. "But I don't make a public display of it. You need a human to give you the food talk."

Kol gave the two a grumpy look and passed them on the ladder, climbing down through the cargo bay and into Spark Station's docking strip. Becky stood across from Arun, her hands in fists and her knuckles on the table. Sitting down would make Kol think Becky was slacking off, instead of having the important food talk.

"Do you have a dairy or nut allergy?" said Arun.

"I'm allergic to mosquito bites."

"Good news: nothing out here wants your blood." Arun unhooked a multitool from inside the breast pocket of his shirt and clicked at it until it became a mechanical pencil. He drafted some Trade Standard D squiggles on the back of a flyer which was itself written in Trade Standard D. Having no capital terminals, the Fist used a lot of paper.

Arun rotated the flyer 180 degrees and pushed it across the table towards Becky. "This says *inrahi*," he said. "It literally means 'neutral'. Food certified *inrahi* is safe for any humanoid species. Dairy or nut allergy? Some restrictions apply. You'll be fine.

"When we're in Fist space, you only handle food from containers that have this word on. Then you double-check: you go to whoever's in charge, so they see you're a human, and you show them the food and say *Inrahi? Inrahi?* like an idiot. If they start making excuses, you put it back. If they say *inrahi* or *taw*, you open it up and smell it. If it smells like eggs or fresh tofu, you can eat it. If it smells like something else, bring it to me and I'll help you."

"I get to buy my own food?" said Becky.

"You're crew now," said Arun. "You're not a hostage. When we don't need your labor, your time is your own."

"That means I can leave, right?" said Becky. "I can quit."

"If you'd rather beg for *inrahi* on Spark Station than snuggle with the Chief, I won't stop you."

Becky tried to memorize the squiggles. "What if I eat something that's not neutral?" she said.

"Best case, it'll go through you in fifteen minutes and push out everything in your digestive system ahead of it. Worst case, it'll push out your digestive system. The whole thing." Becky felt food being pushed through her digestive system in *both* directions. Arun stood up and clapped her on the shoulder. "Cheer up, mate. Some of it tastes good."

Down through the airlock, in Spark Station proper, Kol was waiting for Becky with the transparent canister of Jesus-flavored Evidence. Then Kol slipped a chain around Becky's neck, attached to which was something metal: a very heavy bullet or a very small vibrator.

"Go with the Chief," said Kol. "Do as she says. The buyer might ask you to demonstrate the drug. If that happens, put your teeth together and take another hit. I'm sorry, but that's the business."

The Chief was down the hall, talking to a mehi-peri man using a hep-pep language Becky had never heard before. Becky tucked the bullet inside her jumpsuit. "What's this fun little guy?" she said.

"An unknown chemical," said Kol. "We're selling it on a 'take it or leave it' basis. My advice is, don't put it in your mouth. But I gave you similar advice regarding the Chief's tongue, which you ignored." Kol turned to leave.

"You're not coming with?" Becky asked.

"No," said Kol. He passed the Chief with a nod and disappeared into the station.

"Our sales pitch!" said the Chief, waving Becky over. The mehi-peri man was heading down the hall towards a big open area that buzzed with the noise of commerce. "Crazy Rooroo, the buyer. Our departure, our wealthy return!"

Arun double-checked his singularity pistol. "Crazy Bloody Rooroo," he said. The Chief beckoned and the two humans followed her towards Spark Station's commercial district. Crazy Rooroo had probably not chosen that name to advertise his 'crazy good deals' on illegal drugs, but following three paces behind the Chief's sexy black ass-trousers (Arun's recommendation, to make her look like a big shot) made Becky feel like everything would work out.

The docking strip had an eerie air about it. It was a quiet place that wasn't quiet at all. Even docked ships ran their engines to keep the batteries charged; the food cold; and, in *Sour Candy*'s case, to support the rre pilot who apparently never left the ship. All those idling machines harmonized in a low-frequency hum that you didn't notice until you tried to talk.

Something about the quiet place that wasn't quiet made Becky acutely aware that she was a human walking onto a Fist of Joy space station during a war. As they approached the gateway to the commercial district, Becky encountered something just as creepy: a noisy place that wasn't noisy.

There were definitely decibels. The commercial district was probably louder than the equivalent deck on an Outreach space station. It was full of bars, and people spilling out of the bars; arguing, haggling, singing, flirting, fighting, and probably, off in the shadows, fucking. But something felt off. Apart from the singing, there was no music. Certain frequencies and certain sounds were missing, in a way that *reminded* Becky of quiet places.

Then Becky looked up at the signage on the bars, and even through the language barrier, she saw what the problem was. There were no brands living on Spark Station.

Becky knew the Fist of Joy didn't have brands. She'd assumed it was just a naming thing. The Fist didn't technically have a "military", but it did have plenty of people in spaceships who were keen to nuke the Navy's spaceships. This was different; there were no brands here.

In a world without brands, there could be no brand engagement. Fist of Joy merchants had to engage consumers one-on-one. Their marketing strategies were no more sophisticated than those of the Roman shopkeepers Becky had seen as extras on the periphery of her Evidence trip. The resulting cacophony sounded completely different from the well-executed campaigns that filled life in the Outreach.

The eye seeks out familiar patterns, and Becky's jumped to one 3-sign in particular. It caught her attention partly because she could make out *inrahi* in the middle of the squiggles of Trade Standard D; partly because beneath the D there was English: "Safe Eats! Splendid Veg+Nveg!"; but mainly because whoever had made the sign had at least *seen* what Outreach brands were capable of. None of the signage were professional jobs, but this sign signaled to Becky with calm, clean lines that here was a place she could eat without worrying about her pancreas dissolving.

An excitement was building up in Becky Twice that had very little to do with the Chief's ass. Becky had taken the Cedar Commons gig after learning the hard way that the Outreach produced a lot more marketing majors than it had jobs for. But here was a whole civilization that had barely *heard* of marketing.

A smart girl like Becky could clean up just by helping restaurants with their...whatever branding had been called before there were brands.

Without ever looking back, the Chief had been slowing her pace, slowly dropping back so that she could walk next to Becky and brush the back of her hand against Becky's. Well, Becky just about dropped the canister when that happened. Arun Sliver stayed three paces behind them both, watching the crowd for trouble.

The Chief's fingers intertwined with Becky's, and now she was holding Becky's hand under the guise of helping her with the metal canister. Becky projected this trajectory through the rest of the shift and liked where it was heading.

"My civilization," the Chief said in Becky's ear, in a whisper that had to be louder than a whisper to be heard. She meant the Fist of Joy; not the spaceships-with-nukes part but this chaotic, primitive mess. She'd seen the Outreach, and somehow she was still proud of this, wanted to show it off to her girl.

Maybe she wasn't wrong. The Fist wasn't as technologically advanced as the Outreach, but they had more people, and whenever it was time to have a war, they put up a good fight. They were doing all right. But these people still had *slavery*, for God's sake. Becky wasn't a hardcore patriot, but at least the Outreach had gotten that one right.

Hand in hand Becky and the Chief passed a burbling fountain, a bit of white noise to cancel out all the arguing, haggling, singing, etc. A hologram projector had been set up to create a 3-tank inside the water. You could see at a glance what sort of thing had come in on the latest news skip, but it was tough to make out details, so no point loitering at the fountain. Becky's pattern-seeking eye saw something familiar in the bubbling water: a human face, and then another. The faces of teenagers, inaudible but speaking excitedly about something.

"Hey, Arun!" said Becky. She pointed into the fountain. "Do you see that? There's humans in the tank. Human kids, right? What's going on? Do they show Outreach programs here?"

"Plenty of humans in the Fist of Joy, old man," said Arun. The 3-tank was the one place on the station he wasn't looking. "Been here three generations, some of 'em. They don't teach you that in school, do they?"

"Crazy Rooroo," said the Chief. "The fountain, a right turn. A short distance." The *Sour Candy* sales team veered off to the right, leaving the kids in the fountain behind.

They passed a restaurant that smelled Szechuan in a way that incited Becky's stomach to unreasonable demands. In the alleyway next to the restaurant was an anonymous door that required two hands on two doorknobs to open. The Chief jacked the door open and stepped up a stair onto dirty linoleum. Becky went in behind the Chief. Arun took one more paranoid look around and followed her inside with nonchalant hands in his pockets.

The door led into a narrow hallway lit by staggered glowing linoleum squares. A corestin man sat blocking the hallway in a shitty white metal lawn chair, reading something out of his 3-goggles. He reminded Becky of the lady who sits outside the bathroom in a hotel lobby and wants you to tip her when you come out.

The Chief hep-pepped at the corestin man. He stood up, not removing his goggles, and motioned for the three of them to follow him down the hallway. He opened one of the two-handed doors, which led into a sort of airlock, and then into an enormous refrigerated room filled with the skinned and dangling corpses of alien animals.

"Um," said Becky. Arun put a hand on the small of her back and pushed her forward, towards a clanging and shouting noise that fortunately proved to be the kitchen in the restaurant next door.

The corestin man took them through the chaotic kitchen, never glancing backwards or removing his 3-goggles. The cooks and dishwashers ignored them. Becky walked through the thud of knives and the sputtering foreign chatter of the diners. She took big eyewatering huffs of the aerosolized spices, hoping that none of them were toxic. They descended into the kitchen basement, through a freezer even colder and more grotesque than the refrigerator had been, and then into an Outreach-style office.

The workers were all of one particular species Becky didn't recognize. Each sat in a cubicle, as Becky had done at her stupid temp jobs before signing on with Trellis. The air conditioning was warmth compared to the freezer next door. The temp workers all wore 3-goggles, and their job involved a lot of subvocalizing. The only sound in the office was the sound of everyone's lips moving and the hiss of their breathing.

The corestin man picked a path through the cubes, zigzagging and looping around. Becky whispered back to Arun Sliver: "Shouldn't they blindfold us or something? This is a crappy maze."

Arun indicated their escort's 3-goggles. "We *are* blindfolded," he said.

The corestin man took them down one more hallway, an unfinished thing with bare plaster walls, and opened the door to a private office. Inside, they were right where they started, with a guy sitting in a chair. Only this chair was a fancy carved wooden one, and the man sitting there was most likely Crazy Rooroo.

His face was gaunt, cheeks sunken, tiny white lips peeled back to reveal plank-chewing herbivore teeth. He looked to be the same species as the temp workers outside, but his long stringy grey hair reminded Becky of those Ice Age humans they'd found mummified in the glaciers. He stared at the new arrivals through an enormous pair of 3-goggles that outweighed his head. The goggles thing was very rude by human standards, but Becky didn't mind because it meant she didn't have to see what Crazy Rooroo's eyes looked like.

The drug boss's neck constricted constantly, as if he were swallowing nutrients through an invisible tube. A repetitive mechanical sound, muffled by flesh, came from inside his fancy ribbon suit: *hiss-pop, hiss-pop.* Somewhere in the universe a precisely calibrated skip engine was pumping something into, or out of, his body.

The Chief stepped up and started going back and forth with Rooroo in the hep-pep language, which Becky had even less chance of understanding than the harna-harna of Trade Standard D. But you didn't need to understand the words to see the Chief doing some major league code switching:

                    THE CHIEF
              Double R, m'man!

The man in the chair stopped sucking on his invisible
milkshake long enough to say:

                  CRAZY ROOROO
       It is a pleasure always to renew our
              acquaintance, Chief.

Rooroo's voice was the blustery gruffness of a talking elephant
on a kids' 3-show. It sounded like a teenage boy pretending to be
a crime lord. This guy was just daring you to laugh at him so he
could cut your face off.

              THE CHIEF [indicating BECKY]
       My fine lady here carryin' some quality
       E. Prototype, limited edition. Hopin'
              you can front it for us.

                  CRAZY ROOROO
       I must congratulate you, Chief. Your
       skill in acquiring primo human shit is
       equaled only by your exquisite taste
              in the creatures themselves.

                    THE CHIEF
       Well said, sir, but do keep your eyes
       on the merchandise. The woman is
              private stock, capiche?

                  CRAZY ROOROO
       Then may I turn the conversation to
       my second-favorite topic: exotic
                    chemistry.

Something like that. The Chief's fake-tough tone and sassy body language paid respect to Rooroo by carefully making herself the butt of every joke. They danced between two equally incomprehensible languages: hep-pep for gangster trash talk, Trade Standard D for low-affect technical terms. Becky faded out of the conversation and had started admiring the Chief's rear view again when she was surprised to hear Rooroo suddenly speak to her, in English.

"Sorry?" said Becky.

"Your attention," the Chief murmured, a little pissed off.

"The drug, American girl!" said Rooroo. "Your boss says you took of it. Describe the story within."

"Uh, it's a period piece. You're back in ancient times, on Earth, and you're talking to Jesus. Do you know Jesus?"

"Only of his reputation," said Rooroo. "A most holy gentleman."

"Well, he...talks to you. He just looks you deep in the eyes and talks, and it's the most incredible feeling of peace." Becky felt a primitive echo of that feeling, and saw what addiction felt like: a heedless yearning for something you knew was no good. If she could get just the first minute of that drug, before Jesus screwed the pronoun pooch...

"He talks of you," said Rooroo, unimpressed.

"It doesn't sound that great when I explain it, but...I think you have to be a Christian. Uh, and you gotta know there's a bug in the program. It only works on men. I mean, Jesus talked to me like I was a man."

Rooroo chewed on this and shifted his head slightly to "look" at Arun behind Becky. "Arun," he said, "I'm surprised you didn't take of it?"

"I do as my Chief wishes," said Arun.

THE CHIEF
My man takes the drug right now if
it'll close this sale.

CRAZY ROOROO
I am known as Crazy Rooroo, not Stupid
Rooroo. Your fellas can drink sugar
water and say it was great. I need
independent verification from a trusted
third party.
[In a major feat of pneumatics, he
turns his head to the side.]
Jeong!

Jeong was Crazy Rooroo's human. He came in through a door in the back, wearing a large leather backpack that he flipped over his shoulders onto telescoping metal legs. He was a tall Korean muscle man with a snake tattoo coiled around his bald head.

As soon as the metal legs hit the ground, Jeong unzipped the backpack to reveal a miniaturized chemistry lab. He stood behind it, hands behind his back, like at the signal he was going to reach into a freezer and hand out strawberry paletas.

CRAZY ROOROO
My good man, please take a snort of a
completely unknown drug.

JEONG
Yessir!

"The large container," said the Chief to Becky. Becky handed the metal can to Jeong. The Korean guy set the canister on the floor, unscrewed the lid and extracted a few drops of Evidence with a pipette that looked like the beak of a human-sized hummingbird. He dripped the Evidence into a tiny glass vial, held it down to the light, and shook it vigorously, expecting it to change color or explode. When that didn't happen, Jeong put the vial in his mouth and crunched down on the glass.

Jeong then sat down in front of Rooroo, knees to his chest. The glowing floor tiles threw inconsistent shadows of his body onto the ceiling. Jeong's eyes glazed over and his face twitched. His blinking was as rapid as someone dreaming, but they were deep eye-creasing blinks, as though he were trying to talk to Becky in code. His lips quivered. He was subvocalizing, like the temp workers outside in the cube farm.

The Chief watched Jeong's lips move for a minute or so and got bored. She turned to Becky and said: "The small container." Becky reached into her sweater for the heavy bullet, and the Chief started in on a pitch which Rooroo cut off with a gesture. He was scanning Jeong through his goggles, up and down.

Was this what Becky had looked like, slumped against *Sour Candy*'s bulkhead, her eyes fluttering, her lips moving? How long did the trip go on? When would Jesus call Jeong "my son"? What would it feel like, to hear him say that and be able to take it? What happened after that, what if Jesus hugged you? Didn't Becky deserve that hug, too? What kind of idiot releases a product with such a bad user experience?

Jeong's blinks became wet. Tears streamed down his artificially tanned face. His jaw was slack, his mouth hanging open like a fish's. A wet spot spread across the crotch of his fake-cotton trousers.

Becky cast a glance back at Arun, who'd fixed his gaze on Rooroo with an expression of mild concern: the British equivalent of white-hot rage. This wasn't good from a bodyguard perspective. If someone killed them, it would be a surprise sniper, not the guy who couldn't get up from his chair without getting sliced open by skip overlap.

Finally Jeong opened his eyes. He stretched out one arm and slowly rolled onto his knees, looking up at his boss.

"Hep-jep Jeong prepep," Rooroo croaked, holding out one hand in a token effort to help his henchman up. The Korean knelt at Rooroo's side and whispered something into his boss's ear. Becky saw the Chief clenching her fists.

Then Jeong climbed to his feet and walked out the door. The front door, not the one he'd come in through. Becky caught a whiff of urine as he passed her. He stumbled past bewildered Arun, out into the cube farm. Jeong's face: well, he'd just had a one-on-one with the Son of God. That kind of face.

Rooroo's head fell to his chest. He looked sad, as if whatever Jeong had whispered in his ear had infected him with the melancholy Jeong had taken out of the Evidence. "Gnaharnahoo," he said at last, like it was the name of a pet who'd died.

"Narharnahoo," said the Chief immediately. They'd switched to D to talk numbers.

"Heynarahoognar.".

"Pephep repey!" said the Chief. She darted to Becky, kissed her on the cheek and whispered, "We're rich!"

"Before the sale!" said Rooroo, "I speak a moment of the American girl. Chief, wait in outside, please."

The Chief turned back to the old man.

THE CHIEF
Bitch, you crazy!

"Please!" Rooroo squeaked, sounding like the frog who gets boiled to death. "I speak of the American girl, please."

The Chief looked worried, but not worried enough to call off the sale. She squeezed Becky's arm and said, "My presence outside," and she walked out the front door.

Arun followed the Chief. If he had to choose between protecting her or Becky, he'd choose the Chief. Becky couldn't blame him. However much *heynarahoognar* was, it would be more if *Sour Candy* only had to split it four ways.

Rooroo took a few deep huffs. "American girl," he said, finally.

"Yeah," said Becky.

"Of Americans I have a most admiration. I think I am American, too, of my soul. Americans and I have a most admiration of two things: of freedom, and of pharmaceuticals."

"We got the Corn Palace, too," said Becky. Aliens always went gaga for the Corn Palace.

"So I tell you, American girl," said Rooroo, "and maybe you understand my feeling. Fourteen kiloshifts Jeong works of me. I like of him, he likes of me. He has never complain. I think he is my son!"

Becky flinched. Rooroo's English wasn't great; he probably meant Jeong was *like* a son. But if you hadn't been psychologically prepped by all those temp workers, you could conceivably think that Rooroo's body had once been a human body.

"My son, Jeong today, he takes of your Jesus Evidence, this weapon you found, I do not ask how, and sudden he is quits. Nobody is quits for Crazy Rooroo!" The man's head drooped and he muttered to himself. "I of no contingency plan when one is quits. Likely I have Jeong killed, and then support of his family."

"M-maybe you could *not* have him killed?" said Becky.

Rooroo's head snapped back up. "Your input of this matter is not required," he said. "Instead, Rooroo presents you something to consider. You are human, like Jeong. You took my drug, same of him. Your chief is a criminal, same of him. You don't work her for fourteen kiloshifts, because I don't see you before. But you take of the drug, you talk of the Jesus, he says of you the things he says of Jeong. And but, *you* don't quits of *her*."

The drug crashed. I didn't finish the trip. Becky didn't say any of that.

"I see your chief," Rooroo continued. "Many times, I know she has of good supply. Now I know she has also of her fellas' respect. She succeeds where Rooroo is fail." His heavy head fell again, and in that moment Crazy Rooroo was a pathetic man who'd ruined countless lives and had nothing to show for it but a lot of money and some kind of medical condition.

"Think about that, American girl," the drug lord said to his chest. He sounded like he was crying behind the goggles. "Please take of unsold merchandise on your neck, and now leave."

Becky lifted the heavy little vial and stopped before sliding it back under her sweater. "Can I ask you something?" she said. "What's in here? Do you know?" It was the first brave thing she'd ever done.

"Workbench," said Rooroo. He waggled a hand dismissively. "Helper. Utility drug." Stabbing at the English until he got to words Becky could understand. "To create Evidence in new tastes."

"Why didn't you buy it?" said Becky.

Rooroo stifled a laugh that might have been a sob. "I have not *that* crazy!" he said.

The Chief and Arun stood waiting for her out in the office that rustled with the sound of the temps subvocalizing. Hundreds of them, a sound like a ghost screaming at you from another dimension. The Chief squeezed Becky's hand, like your mom does when you're done with the doctor.

"What did he want?" said Arun, possibly feeling a twinge of guilt about leaving Becky unguarded.

"He asked if I'd ever seen the Corn Palace," said Becky.

Arun scoffed. "Bloody Corn Palace!"

"I know, right?"

"New clothes," said the Chief in despair. She tore a strip of tough meat off a skewer and chewed at it. When she was done chewing no one else had said anything, so she said "new clothes" again. She and Becky both sighed. Of course Becky realized she couldn't walk around the Fist in the increasingly-dirty jumpsuit of an Outreach security brand, but was *clothes shopping* really the answer? Hadn't she been through enough?

"For God's sake," said Arun Sliver, further down the bench. "You just negotiated a major drug deal. Go to the bloody tourist shop and buy her a jetk muumuu." He picked his teeth with his empty skewer.

"Ugly clothes!" the Chief chided.

"This is why we have brand loyalty," said Becky. The Chief was leaning back against her and her cranial fronds were tickling her arm in a way that raised goosebumps.

"No brands in the Fist, mate," said Arun.

"You have the *concept*," said Becky. "You can go to a store you went to earlier. Chief, where do you get your jackets?"

"An Outreach brand," the Chief admitted. "Jayspray Petrowear."

"She thinks they make her look like Captain Jagadeesh from *Nightside*," said Arun. The Chief made a chuff-chuff noise at him.

Becky shifted her weight and slid an arm across the Chief's collarbone, pulling her towards her. *Smooth move, dude.* "What about that purple dress?" Becky could get into wearing dresses if it meant not shopping.

"An heirloom," said the Chief. She tilted her head up and looked into Becky's eyes upside-down. "The dress my mother was married in."

"It's pretty..." *trashy* "...simple for a wedding dress."

"*Not* to be a wedding dress!" the Chief insisted. "The dress she happened to be wearing!"

"Okay!" said Becky. "Geez." The commercial district sprawled all around them, a multi-level mall. Half the stores were selling clothes—more than half, since every Fist race had its own sartorial quirks. "We can do this. Have you ever been to *any* of these stores?"

"Not to have been."

"In English, we just say 'yes' and 'no'."

"No," said the Chief.

"Arun, have you... Where's Arun?"

The Chief dislodged herself from Becky's affectionate headlock and cast a glance at the empty bench. "Ignorance."

Becky leapt to her feet. "Jesus, where'd he go? He's your bodyguard!"

"Miss Becky Twice..." The Chief didn't know how to put this and she gestured all around her. "Stores for clothing. Stores for food. Safety!"

"We are at war!" said Becky. Maybe that explained the low foot traffic. A lot of the stores were closed and the only people window-shopping were...oh, it was Arun, coming over with some wirchak lady.

"Where the hell did you go?" said Becky.

"Oh, hullo," said Arun. "I took a *fucking millishift* out of my day to find this nice woman who wants to sell you some clothes. Now I am going to go drink beer and complain about my boss." Arun fled the scene.

"Gaharnanu!" hooted the wirchak woman. She wore a big flowy skirt and a topologically impossible blouse, but Arun had gotten one thing right: for a reptile-type humanoid, her build was similar to Becky's.

"Hey," said Becky.

"Narg," said the Chief, resigning herself to their shared fate.

The wirchak turned to Becky. "Harna?"

"No habla Trade Standard D," said Becky.

The wirchak woman looked at the Chief's coat. "Hoom!" she said. Her talons were dipped in different colors of resin and she ran one flat edge down the Chief's arm. "Jayspray!"

The Chief shook her head in agreement. "Jayspray, Jayspray."

The wirchak swept her arms up in a billow of fabric and screeched "Gaharnahernhungee!"

"Our journey to her store," the Chief translated.

"Bou-*tique*!" said the wirchak. This would prove to be the only English she knew.

The bou-tique was a mess. The shopkeeper was moving out in advance of the war, and all her good merchandise was in plastic boxes. At least Becky hoped so, because the clearance tables were dismal. The wirchak stopped dead in the center of the store and screamed "Hargar!" Becky looked around for a henchman named Hargar until the Chief translated: "Stillness, Miss Becky Twice."

Becky stood still. The wirchak circled her and, with great dignity, let rip with "Cragarhan!"

"Your posture," said the Chief. Becky stood up straight like some douchebag from Orange County.

The shopkeeper's hands hovered around Becky's body like parentheses, as she tried to visualize how her designs could meet the previously unknown challenge of containing a pair of tits. A puff of mist diffused from her jacket and surrounded her lizard head in scented moisturizing vapor. Finally the wirchak slit open a box with her cutting talon and pulled out the dress you might wear if you'd waited until you were sixty years old to have your quinceañera.

"Gahoor?" she asked Becky.

"Yuck," said Becky.

"The same opinion!" said the Chief. She stretched an elastic necklace of glittering beads on one finger and fired it across the store to nail a mannequin right between the eyes.

The shopkeeper's second try was a sequined tracksuit, a choice clearly inspired by what Becky was already wearing. "Yuck?" said the wirchak.

"Let's start with that and go studlier," said Becky.

"Hargnarna!" said the Chief, slapping the lapels of her vinyl jacket. She did kind of look like a girl-alien version of Captain Jagadeesh.

"Yes, like that," said Becky.

The wirchak led Becky and the Chief a merry chase through her shop, slicing open boxes with her right hand and loading her left with a disturbingly high pile of clothes, chattering nonstop in Trade Standard D, stopping only to bask in the moisturizing clouds that occasionally materialized from her jacket. Becky drifted off into the shadowy netherworld of the Nordstrom her gramma had taken her to for school clothes every year, so she wasn't prepared for the wirchak suddenly ambushing Becky with the pile o' clothes and shoving her into the dressing room.

"Ugh," said Becky. Time to face the music. The dressing room had a bench but no mirror. She set the laundry pile on the bench and unzipped her jumpsuit.

"War sale, Miss Becky Twice!" said the Chief from the other side of the curtain. "Goods that would be abandoned! A bargain!" And then she wasn't on the other side of the curtain anymore. She was inside the dressing room, eyeing Becky mischievously.

"Hey!" said Becky, covering her naked shoulders like a pinup. "Private room!"

"Private rooooom," said the Chief, in a parody of a sexy voice.

"Turn around," said Becky chastely. The Chief folded her arms and obeyed. Becky took off the stinky Trellis jumpsuit and tossed it through the curtain. Now she was committed. The heavy metal vial of workbench drug bopped around in her cleavage.

"Here we go," she said. She stepped into a skirt and pulled it up her hips. She fastened the skirt with its little plastic wingnuts and picked through the tops, looking for something that wouldn't make her look like she ran a bed-and-breakfast.

"Chiri!" the Chief called out, and Becky turned to see if she was cheating, but no, arms still folded, facing away. Somewhere outside, the wirchak woman said "Gor!"

"Gna harhai nara *inrahi* hoo!" the Chief called out.

"What the—now she knows you're in here!" said Becky. She quickly grabbed a top and tried to figure out how to operate it.

"Private rooooom!" said the Chief. Becky gave up on the wirchak top and took something that was frillier but which operated on human principles. It barely fit around her sports bra.

"I'm decent," she said optimistically.

The Chief turned and put her hand on Becky's hip in a way that sent shivers in all directions. She leaned into Becky's chest and smelled her sweat and murmured something in an alien language, not the snarling hoots of Trade Standard D but the Chief's native language, a language too beautiful to ever be written down.

"Aww, you like it?" said Becky. She put her arms around the Chief's vinyl jacket.

"Yes," said the Chief into Becky's cleavage, and then something she'd memorized: "I...like...you." Becky heard a thump and a tinkle outside the dressing room, and a taloned hand pushed an open wine bottle and two martini glasses through the curtain. Becky blushed.

"Rooooom service!" said the Chief. She drank pirate style, from the bottle, ignoring the glasses. She passed the bottle to Becky. The label was in French, with a little blurt of D in the bottom right. Champagne. *Inrahi.*

Becky drank. The Chief was swishing her champagne like mouthwash, but that was what you got when you hooked up with an alien smuggler. Becky made a big show of swallowing her wine like a civilized person, but the Chief didn't take the hint. She was moving in for a full-gravity kiss and her tongue swatted away anything Becky might want to say.

The champagne *was* mouthwash. The captain had used it to get rid of whatever chemicals from her dried-meat lunch were dangerous to humans. Becky was bigger than the rasme thau and could easily have pushed her away, but she went ahead and sent the kiss back into the alien's mouth.

Between six and two hundred kisses later, Becky remembered that the Chief had a really nice ass, and she reached around feeling for it. It wasn't hard to find. Becky's style was to start by dragging her thumb along inside the other girl's waistband, but the Chief's black trousers were so tight, there was no way in.

"The benefit of a skirt," said the Chief. She grabbed Becky's butt with one hand and used that for leverage to put her other hand right between Becky's legs.

Becky was four months worth of wet. "Do you know how a human...?" she squeaked.

"Yes," said the Chief. With a double-jointed motion her thumb pulled Becky's panties out and away. Two fingers gently squeezed Becky's vulva around her clit, and a third went right up her cunt to stroke from the inside.

"Hanh," said Becky. The Chief body-checked her against the wall of the dressing room. Becky lifted one leg against the Chief's hip so she could go deeper, but the Chief didn't want to go deeper. She wanted to cup Becky's cunt in her hand and squeeze and tickle it in ways that defied Euclidean geometry.

"Wha vu vu," said Becky, and gave up on words. The Chief's palm and six fingers were everywhere, wringing Becky's nerve endings with the power and precision she brought to stevedoring cargo and dangling from disabled hovercraft. A knot went out of Becky's stomach and she went limp against the dressing room wall. She grunted, her lip quivering.

"Much practice!" said the Chief. "Much practice with helpless humans!" She leaned up to take another kiss, and she must have read what was about to happen because she hissed "Patience, Miss Becky Twice! Not yet!"

"F-f-f-fuck you!" said Becky. For four months she had rubbed herself to quiet, tidy orgasms on her 45 percent of a bed, pointedly ignoring the hum of Hiroko's milspec vibrator. Now she was finally getting the handjob she deserved, and it was someone else's turn to ignore some noisy shit.

Becky squeezed hard and came all over the Chief's already-squishy hand. As soon as it started, the rasme thau pushed two fingers inside Becky and finally started fucking her properly, digging for every bit of quivering she could pull from Becky's body.

Becky's mind was swimming with rusty emotions: relief at getting her ashes hauled, a meta-relief that her dry spell was broken, and concern that the Chief would pull some stupid kink "punishment" on her for coming without permission. But the Chief had moved on entirely. She'd pulled a plain brown dress off the spilled pile of clothing, and was measuring its sleeve against her arm.

Becky took a few deep breaths and reached for the champagne bottle. "I...I can go again," she said. She *needed* to go again.

"My turn," said the Chief. She shrugged her vinyl jacket off her shoulders, then changed her mind and coyly shrugged it back on. She twirled one glistening hand around in the air. "Turn around, Miss Becky Twice," she said. "My change of clothes."

"You can keep the jacket," said Becky, now quite warm to the idea of fingerbanging Captain Jagadeesh.

"Turn *around*, Becky."

So Becky did.

Kol
Spark Station

Kol got drunk in a lot of sysadmin bars and often capped off the shift by starting a fight. Throwing a punch in a bar makes good sense; it's a tradition, like the birthday song. You're *supposed* to do it.

But today the little puke mouthing off at Kol was just a kid, a fuzzy mehi-peri younger than the scar on Kol's knee. Reality was about to hit him a lot harder than Kol ever could. And they weren't even arguing about computers.

"And, and, they took over Hairt's Pocket," said the mehi-peri. He drew strategic diagrams in the condensation on the cold bartop. "Just came in and took the whole system. They got these bombs that make perfectly square craters, so after they drop one, they can just ship in the Starbucks and the Big Deal and Lxatit Original Steakhouse and all the other shit *brands!*"

Kol was riding the crest of luxury atop the wave of an oncoming war, that precious moment where the basics are out of stock and luxuries are cheap. Today this took the form of the largest glass of trute Kol had ever drunk, or seen. A critical mass of trute that would take a decashift to sweat out as intoxicating mucus. He sipped. Trute was his antidote to the kid.

"Have you *been* to Hairt?" he asked the kid. "The whole system's one big hydrogen mine. A Starbucks would be the best thing that ever happened to that place." Kol loved Starbucks. He loved the variety. They would not put trute in your coffee, but if you brought your own, they couldn't stop you.

"Three hundred thousand miners," said the mehi-peri. His proboscis dribbled mucus from cocaine he couldn't normally afford. "Under military occupation, union leaders tortured, everyone denied their basic freedoms! What are *you* going to do, man?"

Kol had only come to the bar because you can't drop in on your girlfriend in the middle of a shift. Now he was being called to defend the freedom of all sentient beings, as if anybody cared what he thought. Every war in history there's some joker tying it to freedom, and even when it's true, it's a lie.

The problem was bigger than one kid. The kid was surrounded by old-timers, or at least what passes for old-timers in the high-risk world of spacefaring computer management. People Kol respected were stenciling the Fist on their ships, or quitting their berths on commercial vessels to support the assault force. The worst part was, they thought they understood Kol. Nobody would pressure him. They got it. The kid was out of line. The kid was still *talking.*

"Guys like you know all the systems. You probably know more about mehi-peri computers than I do. Any ship in the Fist would be glad to have someone like you."

Kol decided to throw that punch after all. "Guys like me. You mean former slaves?"

"That's," the kid stammered. "That's not what I meant. I just, you of all people, must..." And now Kol had to keep hitting a kid because he wouldn't. Shut. Up.

Kol took a breath, drawing back, and Big Hishinte rescued him. She'd come out of the pisser adjusting her belt. She scowled and slapped a thick hand on the kid's shoulder and yanked him away from Kol.

"Thank you," Kol murmured. Big Hishinte honked an acknowledgment through her proboscis. She was the kid's mentor, a former slave herself. She'd been a better sysadmin, on egenu systems, than Kol. Now she was a mehi-peri training a mehi-peri to maintain mehi-peri computers on a ship full of mehi-peri.

That was the new, post-slavery Fist of Joy. Twenty-six little civilizations with nothing in common, slowly spinning apart now that the pin had been removed.

Fuck it. Kol unscrewed the cap of his water bottle and poured the trute into it, ice and all. He stood up.

"Hey, keep your eyes open," he called out to the kid. He slid a very valuable gift certificate code to the bartender. "I'm getting old. We need people to not fight the next war."

After the empty shelves in the bar, and the abandoned shops on the way to Long Term Memory House, it was odd to step into the brothel and see the lobby completely unaffected by the war. But the important thing is to get the staff out in time. The decor was replaceable: fake marble columns. Ancient-Terra stuff. Long Term Memory had probably developed a standardized package, like the drop-in Starbucks that offended the kid so much.

A pretty female-presenting jetk sat behind a curved stone desk. "Is Dura Turwale here?" Kol asked her.

The jetk smiled. "You're cutting it close."

"When do you all leave?" He thought about offering them

passage on *Sour Candy*. What a stupid idea. They had their own ship, and somewhere to go.

"You will be Dura Turwale's last shift," said the jetk girlish. "Password, please."

Kol tweezered two fingers into his boot and pulled out a small sheet of plastic. He unfolded it and a little patch of color brightened the monochrome white of the lobby. The password represented the entire history of his relationship with "Dura Turwale". Sometimes he'd take the password out at night and look at it, try to find flowering shapes in the random lines. The jetk girlish scanned the password with a handheld 3-terminal and kept it.

"You've got a bit of a tab," she said. "Can we...?"

"Yeah, clear it out," said Kol. *Use my share of the drug money.* "I brought some lemon pickle. Is that okay?" Kol couldn't remember if this Turwale liked lemon pickle.

"Oh, I remember you," said the jetk. "All kinds of human stuff. You brought her the little tree."

"The bonsai," said Kol.

"Turwale loves lemon pickle," said the jetk. "It's going to be about a decishift. If you want to explore the station, I can call you."

"Everything's closed," said Kol. "I'll wait here."

Kol sat on the floor, back against the wall, and retrieved his own 3-terminal from its waterproof pouch. He had to find *Sour Candy* some new work. The Evidence score would wipe out most of their debts, but a spaceship is a rapidly depreciating capital asset, and if you pay docking fees instead of sitting the war out on a forest planet you're losing money two different ways.

The local job board had nothing. War, war, war. The Outreach Navy was just across the border, preparing the "one big assault" technique that had won them GWII, and every yacht and recycling scow on the Fist side was scampering off to the front to get 'rapidly depreciated'. With the cargo routes disrupted, Kol had assumed he could find someone who really needed some coffee beans moved from one place to another, but the work wasn't there. Smuggling was no longer patriotic.

Maybe there was another planet they could hide on. Someplace already terraformed, with free food swimming in the ocean. Or perhaps Kol should stop stalling and open up the personal message pulsing on his terminal. Yes, the one he'd received from the Errand Boy.

The Errand Boy was a jetk who worked for the Fist of Joy intelligence service. Kol had met him at an Outreach "military surplus" sale, where Kol had made the mistake of mentioning Yip-Goru's outstanding warrants. One shift later, police on both sides of the border had switched to looking for Yip-Goru-Toco, a dead person. After waiting a plausibly deniable amount of time, the Errand Boy had added Kol to his spam list and started asking him for favors.

Although addressed to Kol, today's message was written like a form letter—"I'm grateful for the help you're rendered in the past", etc. That was a relief; Kol did not need any attention from the Errand Boy more complicated than his countersign on a bank draft.

The Boy was looking for a marketing engineer who'd trained in the Outreach. This was war work, too, no doubt. Some kind of psy-ops pigshit. Less dangerous than storming the Ninth Wing with a pew-pew laser and an Evidence gas grenade, but probably a lot more complicated, morally.

In fact, Kol realized, the Boy had made this exact request before. Maybe something Errand Boy-ish had happened to the first marketing engineer, and now he needed a replacement. Kol found the old message, sent two hundred shifts earlier, and flipped between the two. The job was the same, but the referral fee had been doubled, and language had been added ("will pick up anywhere in Fist space, in any condition") indicating that the Errand Boy no longer cared whether his new marketing engineer joined the project voluntarily.

"Sir." Kol jump-scared. The jetk girlish was standing over him, hands clasped.

"Y-yes?" said Kol. Just thinking about the Errand Boy had made Kol afraid of the whole jetk species, even this harmless cutie.

"Dura Turwale is at home," said the girlish. And Kol smiled for the first time since Cedar Commons.

When Kol opened the apartment door he saw Turwale from behind, stirring a pot of stew over a heating element. She was a beautiful rasme thau, a bit taller and quite a bit skinnier than the Chief. The Chief got a lot of exercise but she also ate a lot of junk food.

"Hi!" Turwale called out, without looking. Kol pulled his boots off and left them by the door. "Are you doing okay, Kol? It's been a while."

"We hit a rough patch," said Kol. "I brought you lemon pickle."

"Yum!"

Kol set the lemon pickle on the eating table. There was the bonsai tree, sitting on the display arm of the couch. She'd gotten it out especially for him. It would be killed when the Outreach took the station.

"This war is insane," said Kol.

"Tell me about it," said Dura Turwale. She slurped stew from a stirring spoon.

"We were out of it," said Kol. He decided to literally tell her about it. Dura Turwale was paid to listen. "We were safe. We'd scouted out this abandoned Outreach planet. Completely useless. No reason why anyone would ever go there. And *one shift* after we landed, the Outreach Navy came and turned it into a bloody operating base. We barely made it out."

"But here you are," said Dura Turwale. "Back in civilization."

"Yeah." Kol put his arms around Turwale. She leaned back into him. He kissed the back of her neck. He was relieved that this girl was still playing Turwale. He liked her-her.

"My work went all to fuss twenty shifts ago," said Turwale. "Nobody wants to buy jewelry when there's going to be a war."

Turwale's work—that is, the character's work—was forging metal jewelry from stable transactinide elements. This was not a backstory Kol would have chosen, but it projected an appealing air of feminine competence, and it was a job that made sense anywhere Kol might meet with "Turwale": here on the frontier or deep in the Fist. Egenu men knew nothing about the jewelry business; only that women loved buying the stuff.

"Give me a box of your jewelry," said Kol. "We'll sell it on consignment. The Chief can sell EVA suits to a Cametrean priest."

Turwale nuzzled his scaly neck with her cranial fronds: "Set the table, big shot." Of course, there was no jewelry. Kol had bumped up against the limits of the fantasy.

Kol reached underneath the heating element and took two dishes off the little shelf. That stack of dishes was a stroke of genius. Of all the Fist corporations Kol had dealt with (or been owned by), Long Term Memory had the best grasp of the Outreach concept of branding. In fact, if you traced the ownership documents back, you'd probably discover an Outreach brand running the whole thing through a holding company.

Kol had met "Turwale" on twenty different space stations, and those dishes were always on the shelf beneath the heating element. The large stack implied the existence of children, or of friends who might come over. Long Term provided the outline Kol supposed you'd recognize if you'd ever lived a normal life, then they stepped back and let you fill in the details yourself.

"Table is set," said Kol.

"Food is ready!" said Turwale. She turned around and pulled the apron up over her fronds. Her breasts were smaller than the Chief's, but breasts had been very much an acquired taste for Kol.

The stew was neutral: N-beans, shen eggs hard-boiled, and rehydrated celery. It wasn't very spicy. Kol had been to cheap brothels where the girl would cook him a nice egenu dish. She'd say "That's okay, I'm not hungry," and watch him eat. Here, Kol got to eat with his girlfriend. They ate the food a real egenu/rasme thau couple would eat.

Kol served the stew and the lemon pickle with a big plastic spoon. "There's this new woman on the crew," he said. He sipped his water-laced trute. It was putting him in the mood.

"Didn't you just hire the quenny girl?" That had been a while ago, actually.

"The quenny died in an accident."

"She *died?*" Turwale might have said the same thing, but that was the prostitute, dropping the act for a moment. Did she have a quenny colleague?

"Space is dangerous," said Kol. "People die. The new one's a human. She's American. Exotic accent, you know?"

The 'Turwale' character was back and she smiled coquettishly. "Should I be jealous?"

"I'm jealous," Kol admitted. "She's caught the Chief's eye." Turwale said nothing, which was unusual, but Kol didn't notice, just kept swimming towards the whirlpool like the mehi-peri kid running his mouth in the bar. "And I warned her, I warned her that the Chief loves 'em and leaves 'em. Because this human girl is very naive, and I don't want her to repeat my mistakes."

"Uh-huh," said Turwale, flatly. Kol dug at his stew.

"And it's always the same. The Chief's relationships last fifty shifts. We're in shift twelve. They're having sex for the first time, right now. Because she structures her life like it's episodes of *Jammer Readout!!*—"

"Is the Chief a rasme thau woman?" Turwale asked, an edge in her voice.

"What?" said Kol.

"*Jammer Readout!!* is a rasme thau show," said Turwale. "It's very obscure. And now you're talking about the Chief like she's your ex. Is that why you never show me pictures? Because I'm a substitute for your dorky boss who thinks she's Tattercu from *Jammer Readout!!?*"

Some people liked lying to their girlfriends, but Kol preferred to save the lies for business contexts. "I guess you could put it that way."

"What is this, Kol?" said Turwale. "I thought we had something."

"We don't 'have something'," said Kol. "I'm paying you." A very stupid statement which made Turwale decide she had no choice but to throw her punch.

"I work with you because I want to," said Turwale. "You're

paying me to be your girlfriend; well, what the *fuck* is your girlfriend supposed to do when she learns something like this?"

"M-maybe we should reset," Kol said.

"I don't reset," said Turwale. "I'm not one of your computers, I'm an artist. If you want a whore, you know where to go. If you want a relationship, there is me, and there is your Chief. You need to choose, now."

Kol carefully put the spoon in the bowl. "It's her," he said. "I'm sorry. It will always be her."

"Then talk to her," said Dura Turwale. "Be a man. Don't ask me to be her, because I'm not. I'm me. I'm Dura Turwale." She sighed. She stood up. "You can finish your stew." She went into her bedroom, where it was dark, and she shut the door.

Kol finished the stew and lay down on the couch. Eventually the woman pretending to be his ex-girlfriend came out and washed the bowls in a gravity sink. The bonsai tree stared at Kol on its little plastic stand with its bushy face-like features. It was pretty ridiculous, if you thought about it. People were afraid of full-sized Terran trees, but everyone wanted a bonsai in the leisure room. It made them feel like they'd tamed the mighty tree.

Miss Becky Twice and the Errand Boy, Kol's two catastrophes, had taken joint custody over his mind. He'd cheerfully ignored the Boy's first message; Outreach-trained marketing professionals weren't exactly his crowd. But this time was different. Kol had heard Miss Becky Twice bragging about a marketing certificate from Los Angeles City College. Kol had heard of Los Angeles— that's where they filmed the 3-shows—so it was probably a good school.

The Chief would be pissed if Kol sold out her bed-buddy to the Errand Boy. But thirty-eight shifts from now, once someone else occupied that bed, Kol wouldn't feel bad about sending Miss Becky Twice on to her next job and pocketing that finder's fee. There was a war on, and much worse things were happening to people Kol actually cared about.

Kol drifted off to the sound of water running into the gravity sink. It was the sound of the pool where Kol had learned how to manage a wirchak water-cooled mainframe, so many kiloshifts ago. He was a scrawny boy diving into the pool with a logic probe and a multispanner. It was so nice in the pool, so cool and wet. He was so smart, so good with computers, and his parents were poor, so they'd sent him to a special school for kids who are good with computers, and when Kol came out of training he was the property of the school.

"Kol," said Dura Turwale. She shook his shoulder. It was much later. She was not wearing makeup. There was a box and a bag packed, near the apartment door.

"Huh? Yeah," said Kol. He reached for his water bottle. His skin was dry. The trute stung his throat as he gulped from the bottle; he'd forgotten about it.

"You're sitting the war out?" said Turwale. She sounded frantic.

"None of us want to paint the Fist," said Kol. "Two humans and a rre on the crew. We gotta stay neutral." A half-ring of spilled dirt on the shelf like an eclipsed moon marked where the bonsai plant had been.

"Kol, there's an emergency," said Turwale. "All the passenger ships are moving troops to the front. A friend of mine...his plan fell through. A friend of a friend. He needs someone who can go a long way in the opposite direction."

"Is this business?" said Kol. Turwale shook her head yes.

"How many passengers?"

"Five." They'd have to sleep in the cargo bay, but desperate people paid well.

"Give me his info."

The rasme thau woman handed Kol a business card. Underneath the card was something else: a sheet of plastic with a password drawn on it. It was pink and green, with much simpler lines than the rainbow-colored password Kol had given the jetk receptionist.

"What's this?" said Kol.

"This is a password for Miss Charlotte Yao," said the woman who was playing Dura Turwale. "At the same point in the relationship where you were with me. If you're going to keep doing this...I think you should stay away from rasme thau women."

"Story of my life," said Kol.

"I wish I could have met your Chief," said Dura Turwale. "I can't believe someone else remembers *Jammer Readout!!*."

Chapter 15

Second Epiphany

Dwap-Jac-Dac-Tia
Sotese Prison Red

That is the most ridiculous story I've ever heard," said Dwap-Jac-Dac-Tia. "As a soldier, or a priest."

"It makes more sense than the story your soldier bodies told us," said Bolupeth Vo. "Where the children disabled your suit through some conveniently unknown mechanism. Maybe the priest can comb the soldier's memory, and tell me where this tree research planet is."

"Tree...research planet!" said Dwap-Jac-Dac-Tia. Even as Tia thon wanted to laugh. Thon had been thinking of crawling off of the floor-mounted vocalizer and refusing to talk, but this was too good not to exploit.

"Aren't you worried, Precedent?" said Bolupeth Vo. "This genetically engineered organism that stops machines from working? We have the power to destroy this weapon before it's deployed. Isn't this what you work for?"

"If you think I'm going to lift one claw to fight your war, Bolupeth Vo, you're badly mistaken. Grafting a pacifist onto a soldier won't get you a collaborator."

"We're going to find this planet, Precedent. That's a given."

"There's no such planet and no such tree," said Dwap-Jac-Dac-Tia. "What kind of force field makes basic machines stop working? It's impossible."

"I don't believe in 'impossible'," said Bolupeth Vo. He paced around the rre on the cell floor. "Faster-than-light travel is 'impossible', but we do it all the time. It seems 'impossible' that evolution should produce the same two forms over and over, on dozens of planets, but that's what happened. Present company excluded, of course, heh heh.

"Who are you to say this 'tree' is impossible? We're not going to take your word on it. Unfortunately, genetic analysis of those mystery leaves was inconclusive, so we'll have to conquer this planet and search it. There are a number of agriculture planets near the border, therefore we need specific coordinates. If you won't give us the coordinates, we'll just have to get them out of your fellas. Or the children, heh heh."

"All right," said Dwap-Jac-Dac-Tia. "The soldier doesn't care; this is the priest speaking. Don't hurt the kids."

"Yes?" said Bolupeth Vo.

"The planet has no legal name. It has a code name which is not on any map because that name only exists in the mind of a leasing brand."

"Now we're getting somewhere," said Bolupeth Vo. He leaned down as if to pat the rre for a job well done. "Do you know the star's name or catalog number?"

"Yes," said Dwap-Jac-Dac-Tia. "The catalog number is, you should never remove a rre from thons suit."

Dwap-Jac-Dac-Tia leapt off the vocalizer and slashed one claw across Bolupeth Vo's atmosphere suit at ankle level, slitting the weave into a tangle of fibers and a puff of toxic dust. With two other claws thon pulled the hole open and propelled thonself into the occupied suit like a Terran octopus into a soda bottle. The corestin psychiatrist sputtered and fumbled for his sidearm and slapped at the rre climbing up the space between his leg and the wall of the suit. But when Dwap-Jac-Dac-Tia reached the crotch of the suit and slashed upwards into the flesh, Bolupeth Vo screamed.

Most intelligent races descended from predator stock, but rre were the only parasites. The first human visitors to their world believed they'd made contact with the rwit, an intelligent race of gentle, furry quadrupeds. They were disappointed to learn they'd been communicating with worms wrapped around the quadrupeds' brainstems.

Dwap, Jac, Dac and Tia had this in common: they'd never ridden a rwit. The former hosts of the rre now lived only in zoos. But Dwap-Jac-Dac had undergone expensive training to ensure that, at the moment of truth, thon would put civilization aside and fight like a cornered animal. And considered purely in animal terms, a rre is an endoparasite.

Dwap-Jac-Dac-Tia launched one body upward through Bolupeth Vo as far as it would go, grabbed at the source of the scream, and punctured and crushed it. Bolupeth Vo slumped against the wall, and Dwap-Jac-Dac-Tia scrambled through a maze of hemorrhaging organs and horrible tastes. A corestin is much smaller than a rwit, and anyone watching Bolupeth Vo would have seen a sizable bulge in his atmosphere suit, snaking its way up his body. But they would have been more concerned about the blood and the various stages of shit pouring out the hole torn in the suit's right leg, and accumulating in the intact boot of the left.

Bolupeth Vo collapsed to the floor. Fluids beaded harmlessly onto the stainproof surface of his atmosphere suit. Dwap-Jac-Dac-Tia wedged a small body between Bolupeth Vo's vertebrae, finally found the brainstem, and *pain* felt the psychiatrist's *pain.*

Thon dropped the brainstem like a live wire. Bolupeth Vo was dead, but until his nervous system deteriorated Dwap-Jac-Dac-Tia would read pain signals from it. The rre soldier steeled thonself, picked up the brainstem again *pain* and let instinct do its work.

The heart started pumping, sending fresh spurts of blood out the hole in the atmosphere suit to merge with the mist of imitation rwit blood that filled the air. Bolupeth Vo's corpse reached out a gloved hand to pinch closed the hole in the suit. The lungs began to work again, pulling oxygen through the respirator, and the brain came back online. Dwap-Jac-Dac-Tia sent a body further up the brainstem and tried to relax, to gain access to the mind within the brain.

The Tia body could have done this easily, but Tia was in shock, desperately trying not to be part of the colony who had done this horrible thing. Dwap-Jac-Dac-Tia felt nothing from Bolupeth Vo; only a repetitive thumping that could have been a heartbeat if thon wasn't already controlling the heartbeat. After a few minutes, the pain signals became bearable, and the thumping resolved into a thought, repeated over and over:

Sel Sel Sel I love you Sel Sel I love you I love you

Beneath that thought was a picture; not a 2- or a 3-picture but a mental image in all its holographic fuzziness, indistinguishable from Dwap-Jac-Dac-Tia's own memories. It was the memory of an egenu woman walking out of a building, maybe a spaceport, holding a bag, so happy to see Dwap-Jac-Dac-Tia that it broke his heart. And beneath the memory was the information Dwap-Jac-Dac-Tia was trying to remember: an access code, and an algorithm for responding to a challenge with a countercode.

Bolupeth Vo's corpse staggered to its feet. With one hand, it pulled the sidearm out of its holster. With the other, it punched an access code into the cell door, responded to the challenge with a countercode, and knocked to be let out.

Sel Sel I love you Sel Sel Sel Sel

Bolupeth Vo's hand fired its sidearm through the doorway where Dwap-Jac-Dac-Tia guessed the first guard would be. Thon raised the dead man's elbow and smashed it into the second guard's face with the force of someone who doesn't need that arm back. An alarm sounded, celebrating the prisoner's escape. Dwap-Jac-Dac slowly maneuvered the gun sight over the second guard's body and fired again, killing her instantly.

Dwap-Jac-Dac-Tia didn't plan to get very far. Thon had only gone after Bolupeth Vo because "killed trying to escape" sounded better on the service record than "spent the entire war in a prison cell". But thon had greatly overestimated the willingness of Fist of Joy soldiers to fire on their former comrade even as his dead body shambled towards them fumbling with an air pistol. After taking down two more horrified guards, Dwap-Jac-Dac-Tia began to entertain the possibility that thon had won. Bolupeth Vo's decaying brain *Sel* said there were only four guards stationed here, and Dwap-Jac-Dac-Tia had killed five people.

The problem now was that Sotese Prison Red only *needed* four guards, because there was no way out. The prison had no skip capability. Tactically speaking, it was a disabled spaceship stranded in interstellar space. Messages and people were skipped in and out remotely, via a large chamber with curved walls near the center of the prison. Dwap-Jac-Dac and the other prisoners had been brought in through that chamber. Every shift, four tired guards stood there and had their space-time locations swapped with those of four fresh guards, plus supplies and specialists like Bolupeth Vo.

That microsecond, once a shift, was the only moment of communication between Sotese and the outside universe. That explained the air pistols: if a singularity gun breached the hull, there was no emergency exit. The prisoners could take over the entire station, but there'd be nowhere to go next.

That said, taking over the station was the logical next step. There were several hours before the next shift change, and from Bolupeth Vo's decaying brain, Dwap-Jac-Dac-Tia had extracted the knowledge of where thons fellas were being kept. But nothing was left of Bolupeth Vo anymore. His nervous system no longer held a charge.

Dwap-Jac-Dac-Tia staggered Bolupeth Vo back to the last guard thon had killed and allowed one dead body to collapse atop another. Then the rre crawled out of the blood-spattered environment suit, and slithered into the egenu guard through his chest wound.

Dwap-Jac-Dac-Tia had learned to mostly ignore the sensations that came from being surrounded by corestin flesh, but changing to a new host species forced a new range of unhealthy chemicals onto his skin. Dwap-Jac-Dac-Tia choked back bile and burrowed for the spine, being as careful as possible with the dense viscera that held an egenu's organs in place. Thon wrapped around the spinal cord and felt for the rules that would make sense of the controls and sensations that were still sputtering up and down the electrical pathways.

Fresh blood oozed at last from the egenu's chest. He stood up, conscious of pain the way a soldier is conscious of the enemy craft in orbit. His name was Nep. He had died wondering if anyone would notice that supplies were no longer going suspiciously missing. Bolupeth Vo knew that this shift the enlisted beings were held in a recreation area, and Nep knew how to open the door.

Warrant Officer Ingridsdotter, Specialist Tellpesh and Spaceman Heiss were inside, playing cards using a cheap Red Cross deck. When they saw the shambling monster stumbling through the door, Heiss flipped the table on its side for protection, sending playing cards scattering into the air like anti-drone chaff.

"What the fuck is that?" Tellpesh screamed from behind the table. When they showed a horror movie in the mess, Tellpesh was the one watching with her hands in front of her face.

"Fellas, it's me," said Dwap-Jac-Dac-Tia, pushing down a rising sense of rage. Enlisted and noncoms got a recreation shift? Tables, chairs, playing cards? While Dwap-Jac-Dac-Tia was in solitary treated like a fucking animal?

"Bet labbri u satfat," said Nep. Shit! The dead man didn't know English, and Dwap-Jac-Dac-Tia lacked the motor control necessary to operate his voicebox. Thon could make the egenu's brain talk, but it came out in his native language.

Warrant Officer Ingridsdotter's hand briefly appeared over the overturned card table and her thrown prison slipper hit Nep in the chest. Dwap-Jac-Dac-Tia ransacked Nep's mind for words with approximately the same sounds as "Fellas, it's me."

"Stylish refusal!" thon said. "Pella sifi!" said Nep.

Nep's vision went black-and-white, then fuzzed into nothingness. Dwap-Jac-Dac-Tia felt through nerves and meat for the signal. The problem wasn't with Nep; it was with the rre who'd spent the past forty-five minutes trying to ride humanoid bodies on instinct.

"Shit! I'm losing it!" said Dwap-Jac-Dac-Tia. "Gadrawas! Sensit ahuhi ka!" said Nep. A spasm wracked his body and his spine made irreversible cracking noises.

"Oh Jesus Christ it's the LT!" Dwap-Jac-Dac-Tia heard it twice: once as a barrage of nonsense through Nep's ears, then again, in English, muffled by pounds of flesh. "Lieutenant Jac's in there!" Nep dropped to his knees and fell again, face-down, slowly remembering that he was supposed to be dead.

Stop breathing. It was Tia, the priest. Thon had been quiet, refusing to act, hiding from the facts on the ground and the horrible things their colony had done. Now the soldier was spent and the priest was ascendant. You're succumbing to nitrogen narcosis. It feels good but it's killing you.

I can't not breathe, said Dwap-Jac-Dac. It's a reflex.

Reflexes can be controlled. The voices outside were babble. I can teach you, but you have to stop keeping me out of the personality. Dwap-Jac-Dac is dying. Dwap-Jac-Dac-Tia might make it.

I'm not fighting you, Precedent.

I've killed five people today. I did it so easily. I've killed before, haven't I?

During the last war, when I was Dwap-Tuni-Dac-Sora. Those guards are on my conscience, Precedent, not yours.

We're all in this together, said Tia. I can halt the nitrogen narcosis, but you're the one who can get us out of this prison. I can communicate with your fellas, but you're the one who can command them. A slippery, subtle tug of war was happening inside the egenu corpse, and Dwap-Jac-Dac was losing. Dwap-Jac-Dac-Tia can survive, but you have to promise me: there's going to be no more killing.

No, this wasn't losing; this was dying. Dwap-Tuni-Dac-Sora had died this way. The psychological bonds connecting the colony were dissolving. A priest could keep the colony together by strength of will but Tia was holding back, insisting on the soldier's submission, even if it meant death for all four of them.

Universi sumus, said Dwap-Jac-Dac. I surrender to your judgment, Precedent. There will be no more killing.

Tia flexed, and wrapped around, and dug into Jac's flesh and Dac's and Dwap's, with claws so much more precise than the scalpel that had grafted them together. Thon twisted and wrapped and intermingled bodies in a way that a humanoid surgeon could never approximate, and Nep finally stopped breathing.

<u>Let me give you something for the transition</u>, said Tia.

The Most Sacred Memory of the Two Epiphanies of Lir was a holy relic, passed down unmodified for over a million years. It was grafted into rre who became priests of Jalir, and was sometimes given to a lay worshipper as a form of last rites. In Sotese Prison Red, it served both purposes at once.

I'm in a field, the disposal field. There are bones all around us. I'm here because when the sun came up my father discovered that old Kesaw had died. The elders dragged her body here, with the other initiate and me trotting ahead, and now we're going to eat her rre, also known as the spinefruit or the organ-that-retains.

This is my first time eating a spinefruit. I'm young and I have a lot of questions. My father pushed to initiate me as soon as possible, because he thinks taking on Kesaw's wisdom will answer some of my questions and teach me not to ask the others.

We're gathered around the corpse, in the spot where we'll let it rot. "Why do we only eat the rre?" I say.

My father pulls the knife out of his mouth with his trunk. "Look at my teeth, Lir." He swings his head as if to butt me in discipline, and bares his teeth. "Flat teeth, broad teeth. Our teeth do not tear flesh. We have to use knives to even get to the rre. We eat it because that's the only way to preserve Kesaw's wisdom. Everything else belongs to the predators."

"Is Kesaw's wisdom more important than the wisdom of the way our teeth are shaped?"

"Yes, it is, because we can't completely rebuild our damn civilization every time someone dies. There has to be continuity."

My father picks up the knife in his herbivore teeth. The other elders have theirs at the ready. Together they cut Kesaw's back open and expose the rre. It's grey and green, a lattice of worms, a net wrapped around Kesaw's spine, and it thrashes in the light, as though it were still alive.

The older rwit take part, carefully snipping off chunks of the lattice with their teeth. They do not swallow; they let the rre burrow into them. There is blood, and great pain. One of the elders collapses and quivers and does not speak. We'll be eating *his* rre soon enough.

The other initiate and I are left with the leftovers. Although I have been trained to tolerate pain, they say this will be worse than anything we can imagine. But this is what I asked for. This is adulthood.

I lower my grazing head, and at that moment, before my mouth even touches Kesaw's body, I achieve wisdom. Not from Kesaw's rre, but through what I can only think of as a divine epiphany.

I am not the rwit. These flat teeth are not my teeth, these dull eyes are not mine. I am the rre, the spinefruit that grows on a rwit. I am a parasite on a dumb animal. That's why we're doing this to Kesaw. She's not even dead. She was inside a rwit that died.

Once I look at it this way, everything makes sense. I know why wild rwit stay stupid and docile their whole lives. I understand the trite sayings that once seemed like excuses to ignore the reality of death. I see how Kesaw can "live on through us". I see how eating her rre "preserves her wisdom". We're not eating her; she's eating us.

I glance up at the groaning elders, my mouth still

open in the Kesaw-rwit's viscera, and the world now seems an unwelcoming place. My father, the others, their obsession with continuity, with preserving the old wisdom at the expense of anything new. They keep it this way. Our civilization is based on using this truth—that our natural habitat is not the plains or the mountains but the interior landscape of the rwit—without ever acknowledging it.

And now I achieve a second epiphany, the really important one: *I cannot be the first person to have made this discovery.* It's very close to the surface. Thousands of people throughout history have learned this before me. Yet, I have never heard this idea before.

I am not the first to learn that I am not the rwit. But perhaps I can be the first to talk about it, and live.

A dead man's lips moved and he wheezed out: "Fellas, this is Lieutenant Dwap-Jac-Dac-Tia. I have secured the area. For the next six hours, we are the only living people on this station. Unfortunately, this nitrogen atmosphere is poisoning me, and if we don't act quickly I will leave your august number."

"Who's Tia, aer?" said Ingridsdotter.

"Another prisoner of the Fist." Nep the dead egenu rolled over onto his back. His clothes were soaked in stringy blood. "Ingridsdotter, Heiss," he said. "Carry me to the sickbay on this deck. Don't worry about damaging the host: as you can see, he's already dead.

"In the top shelf of the supply closet you'll find an atmosphere tent. In the space in front of the shelf should be a tank of mkire. Keep me covered. If I'm still conscious, I'll help you cut me out. Otherwise, find a knife and do your best." Ingridsdotter rushed to Nep's head, leaving Heiss stuck with the blood-covered feet.

"Tellpesh," said Dwap-Jac-Dac-Tia.

"Yessaer."

"The armory is one deck up. It's stocked with riot control gear and very small arms. Do not take the small arms. I do not and will not authorize deadly force. We're going to get out of here without killing anyone else."

Heiss paused, stooped, his hands on Nep's bloating ankles. "Are you nuts, aer?"

A blood bubble spanned Nep's nostrils and popped. "Of course I'm nuts," said Dwap-Jac-Dac-Tia through wide-split gushing lips. "What kind of question is that. Would a sane person break out of a cushy officer's cell so thon could lead thons fellas back into the war?"

Half of Spaceman's Heiss's mouth curved into a smile. He was the hotdog, the risk-taker. This was the kind of eccentric attitude he expected from a rre C.O.

"Let's do this," said Heiss.

Chapter 16

Folds

Myrus
Somewhere in space

M yrus was eating lunch after the *Real Heroes* recording when a big soldier climbed through the door and told the kids they were leaving.

The first thing he said was "You all speak D?", in D. The soldier was an uhalti, believe it or not, a spiralhorn who wore 'em tight and sharp, but he wasn't a commando busting in to rescue them. He or his father had defected from the Outreach and he worked for the Fist of Joy. There was a sidearm strapped to his hip, and a knife in a holster.

Myrus and the other kids all said yes, they spoke D. The uhalti had trouble thinking how to respond to that. "Here's the deal," he said finally, "you are going on a nice trip." There was clearly more to "the deal", but the only other thing he said was what adults say to kids before a trip: "If you have to pee, do it now."

Everyone had to pee. Dad had instilled a Navy rule in Myrus that if someone offers you a chance to do something, you do it, because it could be up to two years before you get another chance. Myrus sat in a toilet stall and quietly imagined Warrant Officer Ingridsdotter yelling at him to do more pushups, then sighed and got out.

After everyone had to pee, everyone had to get pushed into an inflatable spacecraft: a transparent sphere that dangled off the space station like a lure on a fishing line. The craft was too small for artificial gravity. Too small for anything, except for three humans and Myrus to be cocooned into a material that wasn't quite brand-name sturdi. The walls of the sphere rippled like the skin of a scout balloon.

The Fist uhalti stood just outside the airlock in the gravity, grimacing into the inflatable spacecraft and watching his fellas entomb the four kids. Dad had come back once tipsy from a sales meeting and told Myrus "Nobody hates uhalti more than a Fist uhalti!" but this guy had no special hatred for Myrus; he didn't like kids in general.

Myrus craned his neck and looked out into space. There was no nearby star: the Fist of Joy had built a space station with a television studio in the middle of nowhere. Myrus guessed it was the only way to hide their stuff from the Outreach Navy.

Finally everyone was bundled up, and the airlock was shut. An inflatable airlock! That'd be good for a few nightmares, Myrus reckoned. The sphere was pulled down a metal track, away from the station, so they could skip from a safe distance. Then it happened: Myrus's stomach jumped and there were stars where the station had been.

Now they were *really* in the middle of nowhere. No planet, no station. Nothing except that metal track, and their inflatable sphere moving slowly down the metal track. They passed a small fusion generator on one side of the track and a dark emergency shelter on the other. Inside, Myrus saw some vending machines, illuminated from within.

The ship moved down to the end of the metal track and they skipped again, to the beginning of another metal track, with its own fusion generator and emergency shelter. The only difference between here and the earlier place was the position of the stars and the colors of the things in the vending machines.

This repetitive pattern happened a couple more times before everyone decided it would keep happening indefinitely and stopped looking. "Can we escape?" said Myrus. "Hide in one of the shelters?"

Wei Nzeme ignored him and started whining, like usual. "You know, I wish they'd tell us where the devil they're sending us."

It was a rhetorical question, but Myrus had an answer. "Look how the stars are moving," he said. "We're going towards the galactic core."

"Yes, but *where?*" said Wei.

"Your destination!" said a booming male voice, in English.

"Oh hell!" said Teresa Inez. Everyone looked around for a stowaway but there wasn't one.

A 3-projection appeared in the middle of the spacecraft. Plinky piano music played as the projection zoomed in on a blue and yellow planet. "The Fist of Joy Youth Festival!" said the male voice, who was the video's narrator, not a stowaway.

"Dear Lord," said Wei Nzeme, struggling in his cocoon. "They're using public domain music."

"The brightest young minds in the galaxy," said the narrator. "Their latest accomplishments! Their fresh collaborations!"

The 3-tank showed a group of kids of different species crowding around something they'd just built. Some of them had their fingers up in the human peace sign. An Outreach 3-tank would have projected a shape that showed the same 2-image no matter which direction you saw it from. But this was a crummy Fist tank, so Myrus was stuck looking at the back of everyone's head.

"Thrilling athletic competitions!" Kids were hiking through brush, and then other kids were fighting with swords. "Leisure activities typical for your age group!" Now some kids were walking on a beach. Others were running on the beach. A few were swimming just off the beach. The spacecraft was skipped to another transit station, which triggered a glitch in the recording. "Free—free-ranging political debates. The exploration of difficult issues. Tomorrow's leaders."

"That might actually be interesting," Wei Nzeme said. In the 3-tank, a corestin girl was giving a speech in a room built to look like the Interstellar Cooperation and Security Assembly. Or maybe it was the actual ICSA; the Outreach would have abandoned its half when the war started.

"The youth culture of every homeworld." Same shot of the kids fighting with swords. "All of these things!" said the narrator, closing the sale. "Their presence at the Fist of Joy Youth Festival! Our decision to send you there! And you!" The 3-projector shut off with a loud click, and nothing happened after that.

"Was that supposed to be an *advert*?" said Teresa Inez. "You know, sometimes I actually feel sorry for them."

"Honestly," said Sanjit Mathis. "Leave it to the Fist to make summer camp look dreary."

"It didn't look that bad," said Myrus.

"Myrus is right," said Wei. "The kids at this festival are our counterparts. They will decide the future of the Fist. This is our chance to start a dialogue."

"What about the fact that *we are currently at war*?" said Sanjit. This was a classic ignorable argument. Myrus retreated into his terminal and picked up the book he'd been reading the other night, when his dad and Wei's dad had been having *their* argument.

The Object of Power was a fantasy novel about a bumbling computer programmer named Castorak and his assistant, who used magic to compensate for Castorak's failings. They were searching the universe for a guy named Stoterwanny, who owned the vaguely-named Object of Power. When they found him they were going to kill him and take the Object. It was pretty similar to all the other books like that, except that woven into the adventure was a running argument between Castorak and his assistant about whether killing Stoterwanny was the right thing to do, ethically speaking. Myrus liked this part of the book a lot. He also liked that basically every woman Castorak encountered was in the mood to screw, which meant a sex scene every three chapters, like clockwork.

But something was off, and after a few minutes Myrus realized he'd grown up a lot since he'd set down *The Object of Power*. He'd been through the crash of *Jaketown*, gone into love, been drafted into the Navy and captured by the Fist of Joy, he'd told some very important lies, and he'd even appeared in the 3-tank. Now he was being sent to a summer camp full of aliens in a rickety inflatable spaceship. All this real excitement overshadowed what you could get from reading about some dopey guy and his assistant. It felt like something that had already happened, a long time ago.

Myrus stuck with the *The Object of Power,* because the real payoff of this book was the sex scenes. Finally, things started getting hot between Castorak and a desk agent for Teris, a travel brand Myrus had never heard of. (Myrus got his books cheap at used bookstores, and their product placement was always out of date.)

Myrus read through the sex scene slowly, but not in a lingering way that would draw suspicion. He didn't want to start getting embarrassing contextual ads from related brands, and he sure as heck didn't want Dad to find out he'd been doing this.

Except, no! That was pre-capture thinking. Dad was ten thousand light-years away. They didn't have brands in the Fist of Joy. They didn't even have Internet.

That meant *no one was watching Myrus read.* Nothing and no one would ever learn how his eyes had moved across the page, or how many times he'd gone back to a particular description of Castorak's rough hand moving down a mysterious tangle of curls. Myrus could do whatever he wanted with this book. He could read all the dirty parts right in front of the other kids, and they would just see him zoned out on his terminal.

Oh, my gosh. Myrus could *search* for the dirty parts, and read only those parts. And he knew just how to do it. Uhaltihaxl authors seriously overused the word "folds" when describing women's pussies. It was "glistening folds" and "tripartite folds" and "winking folds" and every kind of folds you could think of. Den had shown Myrus her 'folds' on their last planetfall, with Myrus a little disappointed after all the hype (he had not said this out loud). But now it was time to use that information. To find the next sex scene, Myrus just had to search for

folds

    it? Surely you agree that a leader who
    folds under the slightest pressure

Next.

    gasped as his engorged width separated
    her swampy *folds.* With each heartbeat

Yes, this was the stuff! Myrus skipped back to the beginning of the sex scene and read it carefully, savoring every word. But it wasn't as good as he'd hoped. He went three chapters back, but that sex scene wasn't as hot as he remembered either. Myrus's taste in pornography had changed along with the rest of him.

Today's worldly Myrus noticed something that had been invisible before: Castorak the incompetent sysadmin was only doing it with uhalti women. The guy who wrote *The Object of Power* was apparently grossed out by the idea of an uhalti having sex with a human. Admittedly human women were not appealing to everyone, but the intellectual tone of *The Object of Power* had promised Myrus a level of adult sophistication that was not being met.

Unless...maybe the human sex was located further into the book. You had to build up to the good stuff; that's why porn always started out with oral.

human

    reasonable, for a *human.* Wouldn't you
    say, Stelfet?"

    unfortunate *human* who had preceded
    them by some hours and succumbed to

    cold, and the *human's* bulk did nothing
    to make the journey through the water

find anything. As I told your friend,
the **humans** came through long ago and

"Naturally," chortled the jovial **human**
harbormaster. "But by the same token,

And that was it. Castorak the "ladies' man" went through an entire dirty novel without so much as unobtrusively sampling a human woman's delicate musk. Thinking about it, Myrus had *never* seen an uhalti-human sex scene, outside of a single *Down Under Crew* fanfic. He'd skimmed over the 'gross' scene, heart pounding, but now he saw that fic author was his only kindred spirit in the universe.

Here was the reason he and Den had never gone into love, even though that's what Dad was clearly going for with his fake-subtle suggestions. Myrus had a wire crossed. He was *abnormal*. He—

"Myrus, have you been listening to one word we've said?" said Teresa Inez.

Myrus came out of his terminal and glanced at the other kids, trapped in sturdi. "No," he said. "I'm busy."

"What could you possibly—" Myrus just closed his eyes and ears. He had no time for their whining. This was a disaster. He knew exactly what the human kids would say if they knew he'd been fooling around with his "half-sister". (How could you have half a sister? It made no sense.) And he knew exactly what *Dad* would say if Myrus miraculously snagged Warrant Officer Ingridsdotter with his woodworking skills and brought her to lunch in the cafeteria.

Myrus had spent his whole life being shoved around by human culture on one side and uhaltihaxl culture on the other. Now he was caught in the middle and being squeezed to death. So he did what he always did when he had a problem he couldn't solve or talk about. He went into his terminal, picked up a book he hadn't read, and started to plow through it.

Chapter 17

Unicorn Sector

Lieutenant Rebtet
Magna Carta
Unicorn Sector, Fist of Joy space

Green dots. Red dot. Red dots!

Texchiffu Rebtet squeezed open the global channel, but his human counterpart on *None of the Above* got there first.

"*None* here," said Prasad. "Enemy forces are in system. All teams to combat posture. Human crew, deploy your gas masks. Over."

"*Magna Carta* copy," Rebtet subvocalized. He forwarded the message down the chain of command, but Captain Hsu and the rest of the bridge crew had seen the hostile red dots in the 3-tank, and were already implementing the procedure they'd hastily trained on, clicking open storage compartments near their seats and retrieving translucent plastic full-face masks.

To hear the 3-tank tell it, the tactical situation was the classic face-off of tanks against artillery. Several big green dots (Outreach) keeping distance from a lot of small red dots (the Fist). Each lumbering Outreach spacecraft a nucleus surrounded by an electron shell of tiny drones.

The Fist forces had already begun skipping about, converging on Outreach green, relying on lightspeed lag to confuse *Magna*

Carta's sensors. Some gravity wells were scattered here and there to complicate the calculations: the uninhabited planets of the Mas'pl system, about to earn their footnotes in the history books.

Trujillo and Pickering had slipped on their masks. They now had the aspect of ghosts, or actors from old-fashioned uhaltihaxl theater. Captain Hsu's features were still human. The old man sat with his chin on his fist, looking into the tactical 3-tank. His mask dangled from one hand.

"Gas masks, captain," said Rebtet. "That means you, sir."

"I hate these bloody things," said Hsu, but he pulled his mask on.

"Groups Alfa and Charlie, move in," said Commander Prasad over comm. "Delta and Bravo, you're in the capable hands of *Magna Carta*. Over."

"*Magna Carta* copy."

"Let's hold back a bit," said Hsu through his mask. "See what we're up against." It was difficult to gauge the strength of a Fist formation because they always looked the same: a messy flotilla of repurposed civilian ships.

"Groups Bravo and Delta, hold back," said Rebtet. "There'll be plenty of action for everybody." Later on, Rebtet would identify his careless remark as the dreaded *chenexmar thame*, the 'invitation to Providence', because this was the point at which the Situation started going Normal.

Most of the ships in groups Bravo and Delta did not acknowledge Lieutenant Rebtet's hold-back order. They didn't grumble or second-guess, but neither did they acknowledge, or take any other action.

Foul-smelling mists drifted across the bridge. The Evidence weapon, silently skipped through the shields by some new enemy delivery device. Rebtet scrambled to higher ground—weaponized Evidence was heavier than air— and switched to the global channel to report the attack. His ears drowned in babble: people screaming, crying, laughing. It sounded like an attempt to jam the comms, but it was the sum total of activity across the Fifth Wing. The humans had been hit.

"Captain, we got trouble," said Rebtet.

"Take us into the anomaly," Hsu murmured.

"Sir, it's not that kind of..." But Hsu's eyes were blank inside his gas mask. He had two fingers pointed at the 3-tank, the way he did when he gave orders. Pickering stood at attention, looking at nothing. Trujillo paced and compulsively ran his hands through his hair, muttering too quietly to hear.

"Oh, Merciful Providence," Rebtet swore. Evidence had fucked them all up in less than one minute. Rebtet turned down everything but the coordination channel. "...down," Lieutenant Prasad was saying. "All craft stand down. This operation is deeply immoral. Over."

Rebtet opened the coordination channel and shouted over her. "All human crew have been compromised!" he said.

"This is my channel, Tex," said Commander Prasad firmly. "I am opening up a space for dialogue. Over."

"Dialogue? We are in the middle of a battle!"

"A battle that will not be won with weapons. Over."

"It will if we *use* the bloody things!" Lieutenant Rebtet formulated a protocol message to mute Prasad from the coordination channel, but there was no need. The enemy skipped five red nukes into the vicinity of *None of the Above*. Three of them were decoys; two were not. Together they drifted lazily through a cloud of confused drones, towards the flagship.

"*None*, get control of your cloud!"

"We're hit," said Prasad calmly. "Over." In the 3-tank the atomic nucleus that was *None of the Above* shattered. Its useless electron shell spun off in all directions. Rebtet was alone on the coordination channel.

"All human crew have been compromised," Rebtet repeated. "*None of the Above* is lost. *Magna Carta* cannot cover you. Devolve strategy to the queens and retreat to the rendezvous point. To confirm: I am sounding retreat."

Lieutenant Rebtet had no right to sound retreat. He was Prasad's backup, and she was only supposed to relay decisions made higher up. But Prasad and 'higher up' were dead, Hsu was compromised, and no one on the coordination channel could speak in complete sentences. Rebtet was the trusted voice in the chaos. In the space of ninety seconds he'd been field-promoted to fleet captain.

How many ships in the Fifth Wing had uhaltihaxl or rre in command positions? The database said eighteen; half of the thirty-three ships could possibly carry off a retreat. *Magna Carta* qualified, barely, thanks to Commander Axlithwol in engineering. Rebtet sent a protocol message muting every human crew member in the Wing. That eliminated the laughing and crying, and most of the screaming. Now just a few officers and noncoms were trying to coordinate in Narathippin and English.

Retreat acknowledgments were trickling in. Eight of the eighteen saveables had responded. "Engine room," Rebtet subvocalized out of idle curiosity, just checking whether he himself would survive this.

"*Working* on it!" Axlithwol screamed in Narathippin.

In the 3-tank a cluster of enemy red was thrown in all directions before fizzling out like firework sparks. The shockwave came in a little ways behind the sensor reading, sending Rebtet tripping two steps back from the tank like a child fumbling at hopscotch. Someone in the Fifth Wing had skipped a C-21 planet buster ten light-seconds away into a concentration of Fist craft. A queen would never dare such a tactic. That was the work of a soldier with a brain—probably Captain Pir-Nuri-Stap of *Five Demands, Not One Less.*

I HAVE TWO MORE OF THOSE, said *Five Demands* on text channel. Lieutenant Rebtet nearly smiled.

"Tex, what the hell is going on?" Captain Hsu was pulling himself up off the floor in front of his chair. Red pressure marks ran down his cheeks, parallel to his goatee, where his gas mask had been—*The masks. They sabotaged the gas masks.*

Hsu found his answer in the pandemonium of the 3-tank. "A battle?" he said. He seemed personally hurt. "We're on a peaceful mission of exploration. Who would attack us?"

"No, sir, you have been misinformed," said Rebtet. "This is war, and we are losing."

Five Demands, Not One Less went up in plasma. Her drones fell back, coalescing around their queen. Five red dots skipped across space, appearing a few kilometers from *Magna Carta*. Three were decoys; two were not.

"Engine room!" said Rebtet.

Big red dot. A few stray drones caught in the skip overlap. No red, no gravity wells. Empty space on the edge of Unicorn Sector. Rebtet slapped the side of the 3-tank in relief.

"You're welcome, *lieutenant*," said Commander Axlithwol.

Two green dots appeared in *Magna Carta*'s new light cone. Two ships with engineers or navigators who'd been able to pull off the first retreat skip. The downstream channels came to life with checkins. Three ships, four, eight, nine. Back to eight—*Notwithstanding Clause* had brought a live missile along in its skip overlap. Nine, ten.

Ten.

Ten ships out of thirty-three. The Fifth Wing was dead.

Part Three

Princess Denweld and the Magic Trees

Chapter 18

Make It Happen

Den
Jaketown

Denweld Xepperxelt had turned fifteen. Her mother had baked her a lemon cake—it was from a box, but still. She was still apprenticed to Myrus's dad, but in every other respect she was a legal adult. She could drink. She could vote. She could, theoretically, leave home. She could join the Navy.

But adulthood also came with responsibilities. She had to vote. Instead of an allowance, her mother was now charging her rent. She could be drafted into the Navy, the way Myrus had. Most important of all, adulthood meant constantly lying to everyone about everything.

Yeah, Den knew what was up. Adults lied about how much work they had done and what they were doing next. They'd lie about their own emotions. They lied during election week, and when you cast your vote you were whispering someone else's lies, adding to the chorus to drown out the opposing lies.

Most of all, adults lied to children. Human parents lied to their children about Father Christmas, and when the children discovered the lie they were brought into the conspiracy as a coming of age. Uhaltihaxl parents lied to their children about *themselves.* Lies of deflection. "Is Mr. Wectusessin my father?" Denweld had asked, point blank. Nothing else made sense. "Nice girls don't use that word," her mother had said.

Children lie, but when adults catch them lying, it's bad news. When an adult lies to a kid, the kid has to sit there and take it. That's why Mrs. Chen was so frightening. She had the same power over adults that adults have over children.

Mrs. Chen wasn't really with the War Duties Board. Nobody believed that. She was someone who could *pretend* to be with the War Duties Board and get away with it. Nobody had the courage to say, "You're lying, get out," because the reality, whatever it was, was worse.

When Mrs. Chen came down the elevator, Jiankang Nzeme shook her hand and led her into his office. Tip-Iye-Nett-Zig went in a few minutes later. The mayor and the solicitor left the office after an hour or so, but Mrs. Chen stayed inside. She'd claimed the office.

Then Mrs. Chen started calling people in for interviews. Den's father (ssh!), then the other council members. *Jaketown's* skipper and first mate, the security chief, the head of production, head carpenter, head lumberjack, ship's engineer and shop steward; then Den's mother, as the head of marketing. And then Mrs. Chen wanted to interview Den.

"Just go in and talk to her," Den's mother had said. Den had only come along because it was lunch break and now she was... damn it!

Mrs. Chen sat in the mayor's chair behind his desk. Mounted on the wall behind the human was a very old picture of Wei Nzeme, the mayor's son, holding a football and smiling with a huge gap in his teeth. It was so creepy, until Den remembered humans grow two sets of teeth.

"Hello, Miss Xepperxelt," said Mrs. Chen, as though Den were an adult. Then she undermined it by pushing a glass dish across the mayor's desk and saying, "Have some candy!"

Den reached into the glass dish and took out a piece of hard candy. She'd never been in the mayor's office before, but she had seen Mr. Nzeme sucking on these candies. She unwrapped it and scraped it out with her teeth and put the wrapper in the pocket of her overalls. It tasted like pra fruit.

"Sit down," said Mrs. Chen. She spoke very good Narathippin. There were two chairs; Den sat in the uhalti-sized one.

"How long have you been here?" said Mrs. Chen.

"On *Jaketown*?"

"On Cedar Commons." She said the English name but with a Narathippin accent: "Cheder Camunis."

"A couple days." Part of the candy was still dry and it smacked against Den's cheek as she spoke.

"You're an apprentice carpenter."

"Just for two years, to learn the business. I'm going into marketing."

"Like your mother. You're apprenticed to..." she checked some notes in her terminal. "Kemrush Wectusessin."

"Yes, ma'am."

"Do you like working with wood?"

"Not really."

"You'd rather be doing marketing work?" Den shrugged. "Was there anyone on Cedar Commons when you landed?"

"There was a human woman."

"You saw her, or you heard someone talk about her?"

"I saw her. She was wearing a jumpsuit."

"Have you ever gone into estrus? You don't have to answer."

Den thought about watching *The Down Under Crew* with Myrus, his hands and hers moving under the blanket, Mr. Wectusessin mysteriously absent from the apartment. "Not yet," she said.

"That must be frustrating," said the human.

"Yeah." What were these questions?

"Do you know about the war?"

"Sort of."

"Do you know why the Outreach is at war with the Fist of Joy?"

This was the first real question, one that Den could answer but where the answer wasn't obvious. The first war had been a big misunderstanding and the second one had been about slavery. So the third one... Den noticed that Mrs. Chen was smiling, and she said "No," to stop the smile.

Mrs. Chen lifted herself up out of the chair, her palms on the mayor's desk. "Let's imagine, Den, let's imagine you could come up with a weapon to win the war for us. Don't worry about the cost, or how it would work. What is your weapon that will defeat the Fist of Joy?"

"I don't know anything about that."

"That's exactly why I want your opinion, Den! Sometimes what's needed is not more technical knowledge, but a fresh, clear perspective. I want to know what kind of weapon a clever apprentice would design."

"Um," said Den. "What if we could just make everyone be nice to each other? Just, make it happen, you know? Then we wouldn't need to have a war at all."

"That's a very interesting idea," said Mrs. Chen. "Have you ever heard of a brand called Starbottle?"

"Carbonated..." said Den. She'd seen a 3-poster on a space station. "Carbonated milk?"

"That's Star Quality," said Mrs. Chen. "I'm talking about Star-bottle."

"I guess not," said Den.

"Okay!" said Mrs. Chen. "You can go now." The human blanked into her terminal and came back to reality when she noticed Den hadn't gotten up. "Hmm?"

"Ma'am?" said Den. "Do you know what happened to Myrusit Wectusessin? Is he okay?"

"*Myrusit* Wectusessin?" said Mrs. Chen, as though she'd never heard the name before.

"He's my brother." Nice girls didn't use that word, either. Den had to switch to English because the word didn't exist in Narathippin. But there were no nice girls in this room.

"I'm sorry, Den," said Mrs. Chen. "Your 'brother' and the other children went missing in Fist space. Hopefully you'll be reunited after the war. You can go now."

Den's mother was waiting outside the mayor's office. "I want to go home," said Den.

Mom took her home, and Den hid her head under a pillow and cried. Shortly after that, the really horrible things started happening, and Den remembered this conversation only as the trigger that had started it all.

But there and then, under the pillow, the most frightening thing for Den was the one thing the human had said that *wasn't* a lie. Mrs. Chen really did think Den had a very interesting idea for a weapon.

Churryhoof
Cedar Commons

Churryhoof stepped out of Scoop Alfa onto a foul-smelling beach at the edge of a burnt-out forest. The sun was just coming up. Birds and sand crabs fled from her, just as they had during her time at the Academy on Earth. To these animals, Churryhoof was an alien horror, and she didn't much like them either.

Her military terminal sensed a civilian terminal, or at least its crystalline shell. Churryhoof walked through the crunching corpses of cremated trees, sweeping the flashlight of her multitool back and forth, honing in on the anomaly.

Unfortunately there was no charred corpse attached to this terminal, no bones nearby, no teeth to compare against dental records. Just a tiny computer, now embedded in clay that had once been mud, still warm beneath its blanket of ash.

Churryhoof dug the terminal out from the clay with her multitool. The processor was burned out, but her terminal could read the ID engraved in the crystal. Rebecca Laverne Twice wuz here.

Churryhoof dropped the computer into a little plastic bag and slipped it into the pocket of her uniform slacks. She kicked over some ashes just to make sure she hadn't missed the teeth. It looked like Mrs. Chen was right: Twice had made it off-planet sans her terminal.

It really didn't smell so bad here in the former forest. The ocean was full of horrible dead things, and the beach was crawling with living things that scavenged the dead. But a "dead" tree wasn't really dead: it was furniture. Here at the equator, the planet's glowing ring was nearly vertical, like a beacon going up into the stars. In this moment, swiveling her flashlight, surrounded by barbecued furniture, Cedar Commons was a planet Hetselter Churryhoof could imagine waiting a while to escape.

The light glittered against something large and metallic thirty meters away. Churryhoof hauled ass through the warm clay, giving thanks for her Linearc boots. Ground troops swore by Linearc, but for the commander of a combat platform they were a career-limiting affectation, so Churryhoof had spent the past two years walking around *Brown* in pinchy dress shoes. It was good to have the boots back.

The metallic thing was a hovercar. It had crashed into a tree, which had subsequently burned down. Churryhoof didn't recognize the model, but it was an Outreach hovercar and the seats were sized for humans. Yes, the branding was intact on the door to the cargo hold: Tata.

This was the car that had brought Rebecca Twice from the steward station (later to be kinetically replaced by *Jaketown*) to her fate here. The vinyl seats had melted like ice cream, the glass windows and instrument panel had popped. Churryhoof tugged the cargo door: it was warped shut. She jogged back to Scoop Alfa and brought back the crowbar and the bag of logic tools.

The cargo hold was empty. The bottom was laminated with bubbled plastic—maybe it had been a tarp. Churryhoof took her crowbar to the front of the hovercraft, looking for something computer-like. Hovercars crashed into trees and caught on fire every day, although usually it was one or the other. There had to be some hardened storage for the insurance investigator to work with.

The hardened storage was way back in the bonnet, the same black box you'd find in a combat drone or a spacecraft. Its internal computer was dead, and to protect the owner's privacy the hardened storage was designed to accept commands only from a commercial tool for accident investigation.

A military terminal could easily impersonate any piece of commercial software, but without a manual handy it would take a while to decode the peripherals and protocols. Churryhoof unplugged the storage, brushed off the hovercar's melted vinyl seat and sat down to work-work.

Several hours later, Churryhoof decrypted the black box's final recording and copied it to her terminal. It was 2-video, grainy and glitchy, but Churryhoof could clearly see the view back through the dashboard.

A deepening evening on Cedar Commons, the forest unburnt. A middle-aged egenu male sat in the driver's seat, right where Churryhoof was sitting now. He had just sparked the hovercar's engine, and it was slowly rising off the ground. A ship was clearly visible in the background. Churryhoof recognized the ship as *Sweet-and-Sour*, and the egenu as her sysadmin, Kol.

Kol said something in Trade Standard D. Something like, "For safety purposes, I'll turn this into a dead machine." This would prove to be the only audible dialogue in the video. The time index said 10:43 AM. That was local time at the steward station, right around the time Churryhoof had sent Dwap-Jac-Dac down to draft the politicians' children.

The egenu jumped down onto the forest floor, out of range of the camera. There was a *click* as he carefully shut the door. The hovercraft's engine revved, it surged forward and immediately bent its hood around a tree trunk. The engine died and the hovercraft crashed to the ground.

Churryhoof glimpsed the egenu walking back to *Sweet-and-Sour*. She scrubbed forward to the forest fire, then went back a bit to watch *Sweet-and-Sour*'s motivators push the ship off the ground. The shockwave rattled the camera, the spacecraft lit thrusters before clearing the treeline, and that set fire to everything in range.

From an insurance perspective, it was clear there would be no payout. The crash was premeditated and the fire was arson. From an intelligence standpoint, Mrs. Chen was, regrettably, correct.

Sweet-and-Sour had been here, and they had taken Becky Twice alive.

Churryhoof went back into her terminal, working on video enhancement, trying to get a glimpse through *Sweet-and-Sour's* porthole. She was pulled back to reality by bright lights in the sky and the loud whirr of a *working* hovercar. Churryhoof picked up the crowbar, quietly slid out of the oversized vinyl seat, and hid behind a tree.

"It's *me*, Churryhoof," Mrs. Chen said over the ad-hoc military network. Churryhoof came out from behind the tree and watched the hovercar settle onto the ground. This was another human model: a more expensive car than the Tata, worn and dinged from use.

"How did it go with you?" said Churryhoof.

"There is no secret military research station on Cedar Commons," said Mrs. Chen. "*Jaketown* is a city of idiots and children."

"I could have told you that," said Churryhoof.

"You find anything good in that black box?" said Chen.

"*Sweet-and-Sour* was definitely here," said Churryhoof. "Rebecca Twice was not in the video, but I did see the ship and her sysadmin. You want to take a look?"

"No, I trust you," said Mrs. Chen. "Did you find her terminal?"

"Yeah."

"Hand it over, please." Her hand was out, expectantly.

"You just said you trusted me."

"I trust you," said Mrs. Chen, "to do as I tell you."

Churryhoof slowly took the plastic bag from her pocket and handed the tiny computer to Mrs. Chen. She looked it over and slipped it into the neck of her tunic, like a femme fatale hiding plastic money in her bra.

"Let's go," said Mrs. Chen. "I hope you won't mind sharing the scoop with me."

"Doesn't *Jaketown* want their hovercar back?" asked Churryhoof.

"I think a missing hovercar will soon be the least of their worries," said Mrs. Chen wryly.

Oh, shit. "Could you let me in on some of their bigger-ticket worries?" said Churryhoof.

"On her next orbit, queen Barhukad is going to drop three nukes on *Jaketown*. They're not going to survive that. And it's going to cause a forest fire that will make this one look like a fart, so I'd like to get off-planet myself. Smoke irritates my allergies."

Churryhoof took two deep breaths. "Why are you using my defense context to kill the civilians I set it up to protect?"

"I don't need to explain myself to you," said Chen.

Churryhoof gripped the crowbar. "I think you'd better!"

"It all comes down to time constraints, Commander. I wish there was a better way, but the Fist could arrive at any moment, and we have to find Becky Twice. I honestly thought *Jaketown* might be able to impersonate a research station that would stand up to scrutiny. But, no. Idiots and children, like I said. However, we can make it look like there *was* a research station here, which we destroyed rather than let the Fist take it."

"I don't even know why I bother to point this shit out," said Churryhoof, "but you're murdering three thousand civilians for a practical joke."

"We are at war," said Chen. "These people stranded themselves in a war zone trying to escape their obligations. They are going to die. Better they die now, quickly, for a purpose, than the Fist tortures them to death looking for something that isn't here."

"Don't you fucking try to out-tough me!" said Churryhoof. "I know this is war! I am proposing the radical step of saving our nukes for the *enemy*!"

"I'm afraid all these changes to her orders have made Barhukad paranoid," said Chen. "I don't think you'll be able to convince her to go back on this one."

"Maybe not," said Churryhoof, "but there's always revenge." And she swung her crowbar.

Quicker than thought Mrs. Chen chopped at Churryhoof's arm, slapping the weapon away and bringing Churryhoof down with a leg sweep. Churryhoof landed on her back, and Mrs. Chen leapt on top of her, but Chen didn't fight a lot of uhalti, and she'd forgotten about the horns. Churryhoof reared up and gouged the human in the stomach. Chen screamed, and Churryhoof threw her onto her back in the ash.

The two women scrambled to their feet. Churryhoof feinted high and punched Chen in her fresh wound. Her other hand grabbed Chen by the elbow and went for the throw, but she'd also underestimated her opponent. Mrs. Chen was old, and small for a human, but she couldn't be thrown. She turned Churryhoof's weight against her and flung her off into the corpse of a tree.

On the way out, Churryhoof managed to connect one heavy boot against Mrs. Chen's mouth with a sickening-satisfying crunch. Churryhoof heard the tree crack and went down along with its burnt-out trunk. The pain debt pooled in her joints, and her jolted mind flicked back to the last time a human had tried to murder her.

"If you nancy boys! ever have the idiot idea! to rumble with a sheephead, you! will! lose! A sheephead may look...weak! She may look... soft! But by the time she feels the pain I have taught you to inflict, you... will...be dead! Our own Midspaceman Churryhoof will demonstrate!"

Midspaceman Churryhoof would spend four days in hospital paying off the debt, but she had demonstrated. She had dodged and weaved and pinned Instructor Muang. She had blacked his eye, put a gash in one arm and wrenched the other behind him and knelt on his back and smashed his face into the padded floor until he bled, because that was the only way a uhaltihaxl cadet could stop a two-meter combat veteran.

If she survived this war she vowed to find Muang and pay him the highest honor a former cadet can give her instructor: a barely perceptible nod and a free drink. He wasn't just being an asshole. He wasn't just trying to humiliate her. He didn't give a damn about teaching the humans respect for their uhalti colleagues. He was showing Churryhoof what it would take to kill someone stronger than her.

When Churryhoof took to her feet once again, Mrs. Chen was

wiping her bloody face with a dirty hand and gauging the distance to the crowbar. She was not fighting, and not fighting an uhalti was the same as losing. Churryhoof launched at the human, head-butting her with the blunt side of her horn, trying to knock her down. But again, Chen wasn't knocked down. She grabbed Churryhoof in a bear hug and twisted at her right horn.

Churryhoof heard another crack, the crack of bone. Her horn was a stump, but Mrs. Chen was still playing the wrong game. She thought war was a contest of cruelties, and she was choosing cruelty over victory. Maiming an uhalti was a completely different task from killing her, and while Mrs. Chen was busy disfiguring her opponent, Churryhoof had wrapped her hands around the human's neck—enough of her neck to count—and begun to squeeze.

Now Chen thrashed. She easily gained control of the fight. She picked Churryhoof up and smashed her body into one hovercar, then the other, twirled her around like a discus, but she couldn't do the most important thing which was *make the fucking sheephead let go of her throat.* Finally Chen went for the eyes, tried to stab Churryhoof with her own broken horn, and Churryhoof bit down on her hand, tasting human blood for the second time in her life.

Chen dropped her weight onto the smaller woman and Commander Churryhoof took the hit and took the beating and focused all her attention on keeping her thumbs on the old woman's windpipe. Long seconds later Mrs. Chen gurgled and broke. Churryhoof rolled atop her and looked down at the human's eyes flashing hatred and betrayal, the blood foaming up between two missing teeth in the gash of her mouth.

"Revenge!" Churryhoof hissed. "Tell them it was revenge!" Mrs. Chen's eyes went blank, as though she were retreating into her capital terminal. She slowly lifted two fingers in an obscene gesture, and then she died.

Churryhoof's head was bleeding. A three-spiral horn that had taken fifteen years to grow was snapped off, just like that. She had broken a rib and who knew what else. The pain debt was a heavy weight in her stomach and her knees and her fingers, a dam about to burst.

With her two stiff fingers outstretched, the dead woman looked like she was showing the peace sign. Churryhoof's mental world enlarged beyond her body to encompass the sound of the ocean, the smell of the ash and...

The nukes. Barhukad. That's what this was about. Churryhoof had taken this drastic step because maybe she *could* do something about the nukes.

Churryhoof rifled through Mrs. Chen's tunic and took back Rebecca Twice's burnt-out capital terminal. If Mrs. Chen had thought it was so interesting, Churryhoof would save it. Then she ran through the dead forest, ran for the crab-infested beach and the scoop ship.

Before even getting into the scoop Churryhoof had coupled its radio to her terminal. She broadcast on the drone queen's comm frequency. "Barhukad, this is your deployment officer." She was panting from running; was she calm enough? Hetselter Churryhoof was calmer than she'd ever been in her life. But no, calm would tell her body that it was time to start paying off the pain debt. So, Hetselter Churryhoof was icy calm but in a state of life-threatening peril at the same time. That was the only way to make it through this.

"Hello, Commander," said Barhukad. "How can I help you?"

Churryhoof let slip a nervous chuckle. In the predicament she was about to describe, being *too* calm was a sign of psychopathy. "Barhukad, we got kind of a Situation Normal down here. I understand you just got some...inaccurate orders."

"I hope you're not trying to get me to cancel the strike."

The nukes hadn't dropped yet, thank Providence. "No, of course not, perish the thought. Cancel a strike, everyone knows you can't do that. But, uh, what coordinates were you given? Seventy, zero, zero? Something like that?"

"Something like that." Uh-oh. The queen was being cagey.

"The problem is, that is *exactly* the wrong side of the planet," said Churryhoof. "I need you to strike the point antipodal to the measurement you were given. On the other side."

"Commander Chen gave me a navsat measurement. The possibility of sentient error is remote."

"You underestimate our ability to commit errors. The measurement is precise, but it's not accurate. You're about to nuke a city full of civilians. I need you to strike the point on the opposite side of the planet. *Not* the city full of civilians. That would be silly."

"Oops!" said Barhukad with canned helpfulness. "It looks like you're trying to call in a strike on your own position."

"That's, that's correct," Churryhoof said. The pain debt was starting to come due. "I'm actually buggering off right now. I'll be out of range shortly." Churryhoof leaped through the Scoop Alfa airlock and kicked on the motivators. The autopilot could bring her back to *Brown*. She searched beneath the pilot's seat for a survival kit, searched the kit for the painkillers.

"Let me see what I can do," said Barhukad. That was a basic ruse. The queen was stalling, unable to determine which version of events was more believable, waiting for Churryhoof to drive a suspicious request into illegitimacy by showing unwarranted anger or eagerness. Churryhoof gritted her teeth and kept quiet. Gee forces plastered her against the metal wall of the scoop and there was a pill in her mouth which she couldn't swallow, and she kept quiet.

"Okay, I'm changing the strike coordinates," said Barhukad at last. "Strike time has been reset to T minus twenty-three minutes. Is there anything else I can help you with today?"

"No, that's it," said Churryhoof. Best not to push her luck.

"Have a nice day, Commander."

With the channel closed, Commander Churryhoof was finally, finally free to scream. Her fucking *horn* was torn off. She was losing blood, she'd just strangled a fellow officer, and she'd expended a big chunk of *Brown*'s nuclear stockpile to buy how much time for a bunch of worthless carpenters? One day? Two? How long until the Fist of Joy finished the job Churryhoof had interrupted? She put her mouth over the pill bottle and rattled as many of the bastards into her cheeks as she could.

A miniature eternity later Scoop Alfa swerved around the space elevator and backed smoothly into *Brown*'s docking bay.

Maybe the nukes had landed, maybe not. Churryhoof no longer cared if everyone died. She curled up on the floor, quaking, trying to gather strength for the trip out the scoop and up the ladder into the inhabitable portion of the ship. And then the airlock slid open, all by itself.

Looking down at Churryhoof was a featureless shape: smooth, menacing, dark as space. It was Thrux, the Horns of Providence, the angel of death. He had come for her. Hetselter Churryhoof had robbed Thrux of three thousand souls, and now he would have his due.

"Hello, Commander," said Thrux. Churryhoof tried to scream and actually managed to swallow one of the pills. The pain as it screwed down her throat was unbearable.

"I should have known you'd be behind this," said the featureless shape, which wasn't the angel of death at all. It was Tip-Iye-Nett-Zig, *Jaketown*'s rre solicitor, in thons finely-carved obsidian suit. "You just can't seem to leave *Jaketown* alone, can you?"

Churryhoof made a helpless choke and Tip-Iye-Nett-Zig leaned in for a closer look. "You're leaking," thon said, disappointed; these confrontations have a dress code, don't you know, old chap.

Churryhoof sucked on her mouthful of pills. *The enemy is coming. Your planet is burning.* She couldn't speak.

Two big humans in private security uniforms climbed down into the scoop and stood backup to Tip-Iye-Nett-Zig. "You look like you've had a difficult day, Commander," said the solicitor, "so I'll make this very simple: you are under arrest."

Chapter 19

Human Style

Rebecca Twice
Sour Candy, **at Spark Station**

Becky and the Chief were having sex on the bed. The Chief called this "human style", as if everyone else did it standing up in a dressing room. Her bed was not the four-poster monstrosity of Becky's fantasy. It was smaller than the bed Becky and Hiroko had shared back on Cedar Commons, and the only bondage gear was four metal brackets attaching it to the hull. Two people could not fit in this bed unless one was on top of the other. Thus, "human style".

Becky lay on the bed, spreading her arms for imaginary ropes, and the Chief got on top. She worked her black trousers down her hips and pulled her panties aside to show Becky her pussy. It was a little miracle of convergent evolution, an alien orchid, a few striated bands of flesh finely wrought in green brushstrokes and leaking a fluid that was hopefully *inrahi*, because Becky was about to get a mouthful of it.

Under the Chief's guidance Becky lifted a finger and ran it along the inside of the Chief's v-shaped ridge. The ridge was like a thin, broad clit, and Becky's gentle touch made the Chief blow air out her lips the way she'd never done with Becky fumbling beneath her skirt in the dressing room. Becky's fingers spent a while learning about rasme thau pussy, and then she switched to applying those techniques with her lips and tongue, and before long the Chief purred like a chainsaw as she came.

"Good?" said Becky, looking up at the Chief.

"Yes!" she said.

"Me?"

"Yes." The Chief snuck under the bedsheet and went down on Becky with her ass sticking up and her feet curling off the end of the mattress. That was human style, the Terran Outreach's gift to galactic civilization.

The best part about human style was, you could cuddle afterwards and watch the 3-tank and never acknowledge that the sex was over. The Chief stood naked on the bed between Becky's legs and fiddled with the ceiling tank, her body looming over Becky and shifting entertainingly as she worked.

"Do you have the new *Down Under Crew?*" asked Becky. "I think I missed one."

"A better idea," said the Chief. "A 3-video I watch with special people."

"Oooh," said Becky. "I hope it's a 3-video of your ass."

"My ass, in person!" said the Chief. She turned her head and looked down at Becky with a stern look which turned into a snorting giggle.

The air around Becky came alive with a rhythmic throbbing not much different from the noises outside. One at a time, *Sour Candy*'s neighbor ships were lighting their motivators and leaving to fight the war. The Chief lay down and pulled the bedsheet's grommets up along the railings that held everything in place during weightlessness. Becky hugged her from behind and rocked back and forth.

The spaceship-like noise that filled the surround-sound system was revealed to be, in fact, the in-flight noises of an onscreen spaceship. In the 3-tank a rasme thau woman lay on her back in a maintenance shaft with a screwdriver clutched in her teeth, grunting and pulling herself forward by grabbing onto strategically placed metal pipes. "What's this?" Becky whispered.

"Quietude!" the Chief shouted.

The camera cut to a bank vault, full of aluminum Toblerone bars painted to look like gold. A metal vent dropped onto the floor with a loud clank, and the rasme thau woman climbed out of the air duct. Becky and the Chief both laughed.

"The largest such duct ever created!" said the Chief.

"No kidding, why would you put that in a friggin' bank vault."

The rasme thau walked with mincing steps to the stacks of 'gold'. She took a cloth bag out of the pocket of her big baggy green trousers and started looting Toblerones. The throbbing sound erupted into alien music similar to the big-band jazz Hiroko favored. Fiery 3-letters erupted from the center of the tank, with 2-subtitles in English to match.

JAMMER READOUT!!
Starring Soema Toslie as Tattercu the Thief

"All that gold must weigh like a hundred kilos," said Becky.

"Her ability to carry it!" said the Chief indignantly. Apparently there was a limit as to how much you were allowed to make fun of *Jammer Readout!!*.

The bank vault creaked open and a beam of harsh light spread across Tattercu the Thief's shadowed face. Silhouetted against the vault door was another rasme thau wearing a cheap toupee. Those 3-ideograms popped up again, but this time there were no English subtitles because the other character was speaking English to begin with. "Woman, you cannot do this!" the other character shouted. "This is that bloody bank of the England!"

"Wait a minute," said Becky. "Is this guy supposed to be a human?"

"His hair!" said the Chief, pointing at her own cranial fronds.

Tattercu fled the bank vault and ran down the hall of a spaceship with the 'human' in hot pursuit. She leapt into an escape pod and slammed the door shut. Then she turned, saw the other door, and realized that the escape pod was actually an airlock. Uh-oh.

The 'human' peered coldly through the airlock window. Tattercu the Thief blew him a kiss as the external airlock door opened and she was sucked out into space. Becky tensed up; the Chief squeezed her hand.

In an unconvincing 3-matte effect the rasme thau woman flew unprotected into the void. But what's this? Without letting go of her bulky cloth bag, Tattercu the Thief twisted a bracelet on her arm. A skip bubble appeared around her and zapped her to safety.

"It's cooooool," said the Chief.

It was cheesy. In the chaos that followed that little cold open, Soema Toslie ended each of her lines staring at a random 3-camera with a huge hammy Emotion fixed on her face. She was a stage actress in a culture that had just been introduced to motion pictures. But it was not boring. It was firearms and chases and kissing boys while wearing glamorous clothes. It took no imagination to draw a line between Tattercu the Thief and the real-life smuggler playfully humping Becky's thigh.

This was the source of the Chief's calm: an unrealistic 3-show made by a species new to space. People who had never fought an interstellar war, who saw the faraway Outreach as bumbling toffs who couldn't hurt anyone if they tried. For years the Chief had held on to that insane optimism and belief in cliffhanger resolutions, while the universe around her had gotten harsher and bloodier. Now she was kissing girls and watching TV while a navy advanced on her little smuggling ship.

The Chief climbed off of Becky's now-slick leg. "The second episode?" she said.

"Actually can we talk about something?" said Becky.

The ship intercom beeped. "Gnaharnity *chief job*," said Kol's voice. "Harnagnar gra *very* grana!" The Chief bounced off the bed and sorted through Becky's clothes, looking for her own.

"What is it?" said Becky.

"A job, Miss Becky Twice," said the Chief. She struggled to pull her black jeans over her big ass. "Our timely escape from the war zone!" Becky winced as the Chief's fly sliced upwards, millimeters from her sensitive wet pussy flesh.

Becky picked clothes off the floor until she got enough to cover everything. She couldn't find her bra. She tried to assemble the wirchak clothes the way she remembered them fitting in the dressing room.

Special people, she was thinking. The Chief showed *Jammer Readout!!* to special people. She'd had a version with English subtitles all queued up. She'd followed every twist and turn of the plotline.

How many special people had lain in that bed before Becky, watching Tattercu the Thief kiss a boy who by the end of the episode would die to save her? How many humans? How many more would there be, later on, once Becky was no longer special?

Kol
Sour Candy, at Spark Station

Kol sat in the kitchen, the dome of Yip-Goru's suit just visible above the plane of the dining table. They were waiting for the Chief and Miss Becky Twice to come down the ladder so they could all vote on whether to do this job, or stay on Spark Station and die in the war.

"You saw the contract?" said Kol.

"Yes," said Yip-Goru.

"What do you think?"

"We'll see." Yip-Goru played it cool, but thon was a reliable vote for anything that wasn't dangerous.

"Where's Mr. Arun Sliver?" said Kol.

"I'm calling the pubs."

"We need him here for the vote."

"I'm calling all the pubs."

Democracy was all very well and good, in Kol's opinion, but it was no way to run a smuggling business. Surprisingly, a fictional character disagreed! Chief Mene from *Nightside* got a glassy look in his dreamboat eyes whenever the topic of democracy came up, and naturally the Chief was a big fan. So dutiful Kol had run some simulations and read some papers, and figured out how to make it work, most of the time.

Those papers were an eye-opener. Kol had never realized that the core of democracy—the voting—was a sideshow. The power lay in being the person who brought things up for vote in the first place. Translated into those terms, running a democracy wasn't much different from being an executive officer. At this Kol was not competent at all, but a bunch of criminals would probably never do better.

Right now, Kol had a problem the size and shape of Miss Becky Twice. Everyone knew two things about Americans: they loved voting and they hated slavery. The human would vote this job down, and the Chief would vote with her new bedmate. Which meant that Kol, in violation of the first rule of democratic procedure, was bringing up a vote he wasn't sure he could pass.

Now the Chief climbed down the ladder, surreptitiously looking up Miss Becky Twice's flowing skirt as it fluttered and swayed above the Chief's head. The human sat in the dead engineer's chair. The Chief stood with her knuckles on the table.

Kol clapped his hands. "Miss Becky Twice," he said, "I'm sure you know about voting. Let me explain how it works on *Sour Candy*. I describe the job. You ask questions. You read the contract if you want. We take a vote, and then *we abide by the result of the vote*. The last part is important! It's our own little twist on the way the Outreach does things."

"What if there's a tie?" said Miss Becky Twice.

You couldn't sneak anything past an American. The need to avoid a tie was the main reason Miss Becky Twice was a member of the crew instead of a small pile of ash on Cedar Commons. It was funny how these things worked out: she was about to turn a sure thing into a 2-2 split.

"If there's a tie, Mr. Arun Sliver will cast his vote once he's here," said Kol. "And conscious." There was no comfort in that. Mr. Arun Sliver was unpredictable when given power.

"I found him," said Yip-Goru. "I'm having someone drive him over in a cargo loader."

"We have here a pretty standard contract," Kol told them, "to transport some passengers to the corestin homeworld."

"Our carefully crafted neutrality," said the Chief.

"There are no neutral ships in a war," said Kol, the only crew member old enough to have learned this lesson. "This is our chance to get away from the action without having to paint the Fist on *Sour Candy*'s hull."

"The passengers?"

"Five in all," said Kol. "Distinguished physicians and computer experts."

Miss Becky Twice perked up, right on cue. "Doctors and computer experts?" she said. "Are we talking about enslaved people?"

"Yes, we are," said Kol. "The company that runs Spark Station needs to evacuate its slaves for insurance reasons. We are the only available ship, so we can name our price."

"Absolutely not," said Miss Becky Twice. And so it began.

"Wonderful," said Yip-Goru. "Now the American is going to lecture us on the evils of slavery."

"I'm a *Black* American," said Miss Becky Twice. "My ancestors were born and died in slavery, and they are going to rise from their graves if I work on a slave ship, and I don't understand how we can sit around a table and talk about it like it's even an option!"

"This is not a 'slave ship'," said Kol. "We are carrying passengers who happen to be slaves." He was so calm it was uncanny. "We are the Fist of Joy, not the fucking Appalachian Empire, and I would appreciate if you didn't apply your hypocritical standards to a situation you don't understand."

"Oh, I don't understand?" said the human. "Why don't you learn the first God-damn thing about slavery before you start using cultural relativity as an excuse?"

Kol didn't say anything. He just turned his left hand over and held it across the table. Miss Becky Twice looked in silence and confusion until the pattern of discolored scales around his wrist made sense. They showed where Kol's bracelet had been.

The human made a little choking noise. "How can you do this?" she said quietly.

"How can I evacuate a bunch of old people from a war zone?" said Kol. "Because it's the right thing to do. I vote yes."

"I vote yes," said Yip-Goru. Below them the sound of *Sour Candy*'s airlock opening and someone—either Mr. Arun Sliver or his reanimated corpse—staggering into the cargo bay.

"No," said Miss Becky Twice, making her stand. Kol looked at the Chief.

"Deference to crew morality," said the Chief, and in case that wasn't clear enough, she added, "No."

That was what she did best. The grand moral gesture; the adoption, in every serious moment, of whatever ethical system seemed most noble. She'd done the same thing for Kol. They'd dug up the jug of Evidence, and she'd offered to pour it out onto the ground and bankrupt them. And Kol had said *No, go ahead and sell it,* because Kol was an adult.

"All right," said Kol, "it's up to the other human." Slowly, awkwardly, Kol endured the clanking echoes of Mr. Arun Sliver's climb upladder. Finally his head rose into view. His eyes were bloodshot, halfway between drunk and hung over.

"Hello, fellas," he said. He pulled himself up another rung. His 2-glasses were folded up and fastened to his shirt pocket.

"We are voting on a job," said Kol. "Evacuating the station's slaves to the corestin homeworld."

Mr. Arun Sliver clung to the ladder with the strength that humans, with atypical modesty, called "superhuman". He panted and looked up at the three unhappy faces. "Sounds all right, mate," he said, and he felt for the next rung.

"Go to the medical chamber," said Kol. "Cycle your blood. We need you awake." The human nodded and climbed up, out of sight.

"The motion passes," said Kol. "*Sharki jurna, tarki jur.*"

"What does that mean?" said Miss Becky Twice, trying to find a way out of the vote. "What's with the secret talk? I thought we agreed to use English."

"That's the lovely motto of the Fist of Joy," said Kol. "It reminds us that even our disagreements tie us together. If you want to ruin it by translating it into English, it means 'Many fingers, one Fist.'"

"That's our motto!" said the human. "That's the same as 'We're all in this together!' You stole our motto!"

Kol pushed his chair back along its microgravity-safe runners and pulled himself up and across the table. "That was the motto of our *interstellar civilization*," he snarled, "back when your ancestors were slaves and their masters were fucking pigs up the ass because they were too stupid to find the vagina!"

"Kol!" said the Chief, in D. "Your attitude."

"Oh, I bet you wish you hadn't freed me," Kol told her, "since apparently, slaves have to do whatever you tell them!"

"Stop it, Kol!" Kol sat back down and glared around, so angry he wanted to cry. At least Mr. Arun Sliver wasn't seeing him like this.

"The vote," said the Chief in English. "Its conclusion. The job, the division of labor."

"Yip-Goru," said Kol, "what's our ETA?"

"For a crew that doesn't constantly attract insane drama, thirty-two point two shifts. I can't predict how long it will take *us*."

"Plot a course and get ready to cast off," said Kol. "Tell the passengers to bring their own food. Chief, sign the contract." Now, in English: "Miss Becky Twice."

"What."

"Since you are so concerned with our passengers' welfare," said Kol. "You are responsible for making sure they're comfortable."

"I'm...in charge of the slaves," the human said.

"Meet them in the cargo hold," said Kol, "and get them whatever they need. I'm sure they would love to hear an American explain their situation to them!"

Thirty-two shifts to the corestin homeworld. That would bring the Chief most of the rest of the way through her *Jammer Readout!!*-length relationship with Miss Becky Twice. Then the human would be gone, and Kol's only problems would be the ones he'd made for himself.

Chapter 20

Compliance

Dwap-Jac-Dac-Tia
Sotese Prison Red

Instead of designing their own transport box for rre POWs, the Fist of Joy attended Outreach prison trade shows and placed big orders for civilian models. Dwap-Jac-Dac-Tia discovered this when after surgically removing their lieutenant from the dead egenu, Warrant Officer Ingridsdotter and Spaceman Heiss had given thon a cursory rinse-off and stuffed thon into a transport box nearly identical to the one Dwap-Tuni-Dac-Sora had endured during SERE training twenty years earlier. It even had the same branding on the outside: Hestin Compliance Systems.

The box was one-way glass reinforced with metamaterial strands. With Dwap-Jac-Dac-Tia inside and the mkire tanks attached on top, the whole thing weighed about twenty kilos. The glass blocked all light, and dampened sound and sensation, so that when Ingridsdotter accidentally slammed the box into a wall while carrying it through the prison, Dwap-Jac-Dac-Tia barely felt it.

"Sorry, aer," said Ingridsdotter, anyway.

"Three person-days of human food," said Heiss over the comm. Dwap-Jac-Dac-Tia had sent him to gather supplies. "Eight person-days of neutral. Won't last long." There was no Internet in the prison, of course, but Specialist Tellpesh had deactivated the jammers that blocked imprisoned Outreach spacemen from forming an ad-hoc milnet.

"Don't forget a can opener," Ingridsdotter added. "Bastards don't use standard can sizes."

Dwap-Jac-Dac-Tia felt a soft crunch and a nearly imperceptible jolt. Ingridsdotter had set the prisoner transport box down onto what thons previous hosts remembered as a thick layer of sand filling the bowl-like floor of the prison's skip chamber. "Here you go, aer," she said, and left through the sliding door.

In eighty minutes a fresh shift of guards would skip in from the Kesk Crossroads Station, switching places with Dwap-Jac-Dac-Tia's impromptu strike force. The layer of sand kept humanoids from losing the soles of their shoes during the skip. Dwap-Jac-Dac-Tia sat in to wait. It wasn't difficult. Tia had also spent many hours in Hestin transport boxes, as a prisoner of conscience.

Thumps and *shuffs* of shifting sand whispered in from all around Dwap-Jac-Dac-Tia as thons fellas brought in survival gear from throughout the prison. Most important were the weapons necessary to hold the skip chamber at Kesk. Guns and grenades would allow the strike team to dispense light, electricity, and gas; the three "public services" of riot control.

Five minutes to skip. The fellas entered, picked up weapons, and stood back to back, forming a circle around their LT.

"Once I take the controls, aer," Tellpesh asked, very confident that she would, "where do I skip us to?"

"See what's in range," said Dwap-Jac-Dac-Tia. "A planet is better, rural is better than urban. Bolupeth Vo remembered Arzil being nearby. There's a big Jalian monastery on Arzil."

"Is the monastery on any particular *continent*, aer?" said Ingridsdotter.

"I don't know. It's an idea, not an order. Pick a destination that hasn't been used in a long time."

"One millishift to go," said Heiss. "Start the flashbangs two seconds before the skip."

"You timed them, spaceman?" said Ingridsdotter.

"Timed one in the locker., ma'am."

"What if they're late with the switch?" said Tellpesh.

"Can't be late in this business, buddy," said Heiss. "Skip bubble will chop your dick off."

"Let's just pretend I said the joke," said Tellpesh.

"Sounds good," said Ingridsdotter.

Dwap-Jac-Dac-Tia's body nudged against the lid of the prisoner transport box. The prison's computer had turned off the gravity in preparation for a skip. "Remember," thon said. "I do not authorize use of deadly force."

"Flashbang on," said the other three in unison. They skipped.

There is no non-lethal way for a naked rre to fight a humanoid. Dwap-Jac-Dac-Tia had planned to wait it out in the box of ignorance and hope that thons fellas could dispense the essential public services quickly. But the three strobing flashbangs illuminated Kesk Crossroads' skip chamber so brightly that the one-way glass became two-way.

So Dwap-Jac-Dac-Tia saw the wirchak woman at the skip console go down, flopping and screaming as Tellpesh moved towards her, leveling her compliance pistol with the same fear-shaky hand she'd used to carry her assault rifle on Cedar Commons. Thon saw Ingridsdotter and Heiss, generic humanoids in full-face masks, drop gas grenades and move to cover the two exits.

Tellpesh's fingers bashed the skip console, isolating it from the rest of the station's computer network. It took forty-five precious seconds for the Fist of Joy to realize that the escaped prisoners were not trying to force their way further into Kesk Crossroads. Then Dwap-Jac-Dac-Tia was squished against the bottom of the prisoner transport box, hurled to the top, to the side. The Fist couldn't shut down the skip console, so they were altering the gravity of the entire station, trying to throw off the calculations. The station lurched, Tellpesh's face ricocheted off the skip console and she twisted her gas mask back in place and kept turning knobs and tapping panels.

Then someone in another skip chamber teleported a tear gas canister and a concussion grenade directly above Dwap-Jac-Dac-

Tia's prisoner box. This did nothing much: the room was already full of gas, and the concussion blast didn't even move the box. "Nothing gets through a Hestin!" as they say in the adverts.

The Fist's third tactic was more successful. The door Heiss was guarding slammed open and a masked Fist soldier with weapon already drawn shot him with a kinetic charge at close range. Heiss went down. Another masked soldier was right behind the first and took aim at Tellpesh.

But Tellpesh was holding a weapon of her own, and Dwap-Jac-Dac-Tia saw to thons horror that it wasn't the compliance pistol. Thon saw Tellpesh drop the two hostiles with high-voltage pyrotechnic charges that sent them reeling back into the hallway, their bodies shattered.

"You son of a bitch!" Dwap-Jac-Dac-Tia screamed over the comm. "Ingridsdotter! Open this thing! Let me out!" But no one heard. Outside Sotese Prison Red, the jammers that prevented an ad-hoc network from forming had full power. Thon could see everything, but no one could hear.

"We skip in ten!" Tellpesh called out. She tossed a grenade underhand through the open doorway. Ingridsdotter picked up Heiss in a fireman's carry and climbed back onto the disturbed sand of the skip platform. The gun Tellpesh had killed with was missing from its holster.

"Heiss needs a doctor!" said Ingridsdotter.

For Dwap-Jac-Dac-Tia, the skip meant everything went dark. "The LT, get the LT out," said Tellpesh.

"Shift the gear off the platform!" Ingridsdotter yelled. "That's a fucking order, Specialist!"

The gravity here was low. There was scratching, motion, the sound of the mkire canister unscrewing, an inrush of numbing nitrogen. Dwap-Jac-Dac-Tia launched thonself through the gas intake valve and into a light too bright to see with. But rre can smell blood, and there was a lot of it.

Heiss lay out on a flat bed of sand. Not the little dish of sand used to level out a skip platform. A desert, a continent of sand. Dwap-Jac-Dac-Tia's eyepatches shuttered in the sunlight. Thon saw a chunk of

Kesk Crossroads station: metal and wire sheared off by the station computer's best guess at a safe skip radius. A whitewashed road cracked by grass and native brush. An empty sky, an empty horizon. Sand and cold. A sun that visibly moved in the sky.

"He's fucked up, aer," said Tellpesh. "Can Tia do something?"

"Stop worrying about Heiss and *shift some gear*!" Ingridsdotter screamed.

Dwap-Jac-Dac-Tia gently laid a body on the intact half of Heiss's torso. A whiff of skipped-over tear gas puckered thons skin. "How is it, spaceman?"

"Not gonna lie, aer," said Heiss. "It really fucking hurts."

"Do we have cocaine or morphine?" Dwap-Jac-Dac-Tia called out.

"From a prison hospital?" said Tellpesh. "Are you kidding me, aer?"

"We have tranq pistols," said Ingridsdotter. She set down a tool chest and unholstered hers. "Not that you'd know. They've got to have something good."

"Mr. Heiss, we have no medic," said Dwap-Jac-Dac-Tia. There was the abandoned skip platform, a burglarized vending machine, a road that had once led somewhere. A forgotten part of a small quiet world. "We have tools, but no skills. All my experience is in serving as a surgical instrument. It's my advice that you make your peace."

"Oh, God!" Heiss sobbed. "I never fucked an uhalti girl!"

Tellpesh set down a jug of sterilized water, reached down and squeezed Heiss's hand. "I would have fucked you," she said.

"Thanks, buddy," Heiss croaked. Ingridsdotter carefully pressed a small tranquilizer dart between two of Dwap-Jac-Dac-Tia's claws.

Thon took up the dart. "I can administer Christian last rites," thon told Heiss. "I'm not qualified, but at least Tia knows the words."

"Last rites is some Catholic shit, man." Heiss coughed. "I'm a Lutheran. Gimme some Jalir stuff."

"I really think Catholicism is closer to what you're used to."

"I don't wanna go to Catholic heaven, man! All those...saints and popes and peoples' moms."

"There is no Jalir afterlife. I can give you the Two Epiphanies, but they won't mean anything to a human."

"Come on, aer, who's dying here, you or me?" said Heiss. Around them the boxes and bags and jugs were piling up. Tellpesh tossed the cargo off the skip platform with incredible force. It had always been the uhalti soldier's first rule: *keep moving*. Keep the adrenaline flowing, keep the pain debt at bay until it's safe to be hurt.

Dwap-Jac-Dac-Tia carefully pinched Heiss's arm, held the little dart between two claws and pushed it into what Tia said was a vein. Heiss relaxed immediately. When his C.O. sliced open the back of his neck, he sucked in breath through his teeth but said nothing. Dwap-Jac-Dac-Tia carefully burrowed in, found the spinal cord and began to give memory to the dying man, through the universal and now depressingly familiar language of the vertebrate brainstem.

> I'm in a field, the disposal field. There are bones all around us. I'm here because when the sun came up my father discovered that old Kesaw had died. The elders dragged her body here, with the other initiate and I trotting ahead, and now we're going to eat her rre...

"I'm not the rwit," said Heiss sleepily. He laughed, and his mouth stuck open, his next words reverberating down his spine as unvoiced thoughts. "No worries, aer, it makes sense. I'm not the rwit. Thank you."

Bolupeth Vo's last thought was a static image; Nep's was a regret. An eavesdropping parasite saw whatever came to mind in that final moment. But Spaceman Heiss had prepared something ahead of time. He'd poured a thought into a two-dimensional pan and baked it into a tombstone. Perhaps a prayer was the best way to think of it. A secular form of the last rites, a recitation spread among enlisted beings and saved for one's dying breath. Spread among *human* enlisted, because the inanity of this prayer was of a particularly human kind.

We civilized ourselves and then set out to civilize the stars. We extended our hand and we gave it a name: the Terran Outreach. We taught a peaceful race to defend itself, and showed a warrior race the arts of peace.

For me, Thom Heiss, the story ends here, and only God can say whether I discharged my duties. But the story of humanity will never end. We will never stop exploring, striving, fighting to uphold our common values of decency and democracy.

Whatever comes next, I will be ready. May God have mercy on my soul and take pity on our enemies.

"He's gone," Dwap-Jac-Dac-Tia told thons fellas. The numbing of a nitrogen atmosphere tinted with tear gas rushed in to replace Heiss's waning consciousness.

Did you experience that? Dwap-Jac-Dac asked Tia in native-voice. What was that shit? That is how he repays me for the Two Epiphanies?

I experienced it, said Tia gently, like a priest does.

Is that what they think of us? We taught ourselves the arts of peace, fuck you very much! What do you do, Precedent? When you look into someone's soul, someone who respected you, and you see this hoo-ah pigshit?

Please remember, Lieutenant, said Tia, smoothing at the cracks in the colony, that you yourself were not at your best when you died.

Something evaporated from Dwap-Jac-Dac-Tia and thon saw thonself spread out beneath a dead human in a poisonous atmosphere. Together Ingridsdotter and Tellpesh carried the last supply box off the ruined skip platform.

"Would you really have fucked Heiss?" Ingridsdotter asked the uhalti woman.

"He was dying, ma'am!" Dwap-Jac-Dac-Tia's two living fellas dropped the box in the sand, and Specialist Tellpesh fell to her knees alongside it and pulled her gas mask up over her horns. A bruise in the shape of the mask covered the right side of her face, where she'd banged it against the skip terminal. She snorted fresh air and blood bubbled from her nose like sea foam.

"Oh fucking coin-flipping Providence," she said, feeling it run down over her lips, watching it drizzle into the sand of Arzil, feeling her body start to pay off the pain debt. And only now did Specialist Tellpesh, who had never lifted her hand in anger until just now, when she had killed two people unnecessarily and in violation of a direct order, feel safe enough to scream.

The officer's rule for applying discipline was similar to how an uhalti body pays off pain debt: you do it as soon as the situation is safe. It's the only fair way. Your fellas can't be wondering if you're going to come down on them for a fuckup two days old.

But what's 'safe', in wartime? Once you escape the POW camp? Once you've hidden yourselves in a desert behind enemy lines? Once you've dug a hole in the sand and buried your dead spaceman?

Maybe the best you can do is to discipline as soon as it's quiet. Once Heiss was buried and Tia had said some words over the grave, once Tellpesh had stopped moaning on the ground, Dwap-Jac-Dac-Tia decided to get this over with.

"Specialist Tellpesh," thon said, in a synthesized voice that left no doubt what was on the docket. Stuck inside the prisoner transport box, Dwap-Jac-Dac-Tia saw Tellpesh through a low-fi view of the desert, captured by the terminal behind Ingridsdotter's right eye.

"Yessaer." Dwap-Jac-Dac-Tia saw Tellpesh from the side, standing up, facing the prisoner transport box, standing to attention.

"I believe I told you to leave the pyro pistols in the arms locker."

"Aer, I needed the pyro to generate an EMP. To wipe the skip computer, aer."

"And I'd let that slide," said Dwap-Jac-Dac-Tia, "except that you also used the pyro to kill two people."

"Two enemy, aer. They got Heiss."

"Do my orders cease to apply when we take casualties?" said Dwap-Jac-Dac-Tia. "Once the shit hits the fan, you can do whatever you want?"

"With respect, aer, I question the...provenance of your orders."

"You don't say that 'with respect', Specialist. You say that to someone who needs to be removed from command. Is that where we are?"

Before Kesk Crossroads, Tellpesh would have backed off, but she'd crossed a line and her only choice was to run for the finish. "You were tortured, aer," she said. "They surgically modified you to change your worldview. I don't know what the regulations say about this, but we don't have the luxury of pretending you're the same person as you were. Aer."

What does she think she can do? asked Tia. I'm her superior.

No, she's right, said Dwap-Jac-Dac. My commission expired the second your nervous system intersected with mine. If my fellas are going to argue the legalities, I've lost them.

Then don't let them argue! said Tia. Let me handle this.

"Specialist," said Dwap-Jac-Dac-Tia, "Before we were captured, when we were scooping onto Cedar Commons, what rules of engagement did I set?"

"Weapons off," Tellpesh quoted reluctantly. "Weapons stay off."

"Did I have a Jalian priest grafted on to me when I gave that order?" said Dwap-Jac-Dac-Tia.

"No, aer."

"Okay," said Dwap-Jac-Dac-Tia. "Would you *prefer* that Ingridsdotter take command of this unit, or would—?"

"Aer!" said Tellpesh. "Giant reptile on your six!"

"Not a good time, Specialist."

"The reptile disagrees, aer." Ingridsdotter's glance was down as she drew her Fist of Joy tranquilizer pistol, but then she swung her head towards Tellpesh, and yes, there it was: a four-legged reptile-type predator, loping towards the two humanoids from behind a dune, a large shining flap of skin flaring from its neck.

"Tranqing it!" said Ingridsdotter. She dropped to one knee. The video feed fuzzed in and out, tinted red and white in time to her heartbeat. The predator wheeled, stung by Ingridsdotter's dart. It pawed up sand, flailing at the unseen enemy, then resumed its cagey advance.

"Ingridsdotter, what is the scale on that fella?" said Dwap-Jac-Dac-Tia.

"I would estimate approximately the size of a fucking dinosaur, aer!"

"I'm not familiar with Terran wildlife. Is it the size of a scoop ship?"

"Smaller."

Predators that size quickly learned to stay away from humanoids. Why was this one attacking? Encounters always ended the same way. Stung by darts, the creature collapsed on its side and lay its head on the sand, its broad grey tongue spilling out of its mouth. At least it wasn't dead.

"Reptile down, aer," Tellpesh reported.

"How many darts did that take?"

"Five or six," said Tellpesh. That made the creature's mass around ten humanoids, larger than a rwit. "I think Ingridsdotter missed once."

"In my judgment," said Ingridsdotter, "Tellpesh was aiming a little high."

"Nice shooting, you two," said Dwap-Jac-Dac-Tia, shutting it down. "Where were we? Ms. Ingridsdotter, would you like to take command of this unit?"

"Uh, more than willing to let you have this one, aer," said Ingridsdotter.

"Then pick me up and bring me over to the animal. Tellpesh, trail ten meters and cover us. If it moves, take it back down."

"'Towards' seems like the wrong direction with this fella, aer," said Ingridsdotter. She stooped and picked up the prisoner transport box. "It's not sentient, and there's no guarantee we can eat it."

"We're not going to eat it," said Dwap-Jac-Dac-Tia. "I'm going to ride it."

"Kinda tacking away from 'reassuring C.O.', aer," Ingridsdotter said privately.

"Do you want to carry me through this desert?" said Dwap-Jac-Dac-Tia. "We've found a vehicle; let's use it."

Through Tellpesh's eyes, ten meters back, Dwap-Jac-Dac-Tia watched Ingridsdotter slowly carry thon towards the downed predator. Thon saw its chest slowly moving with its breaths, but there was no sound; only subvocalizations transmitted over the military network.

"Tellpesh," said Dwap-Jac-Dac-Tia. This place wasn't safe, would never be safe, but it was quiet again.

"Yes," said Tellpesh, and added, "aer." Her breathing was heavy.

"We are a combat unit," said Dwap-Jac-Dac-Tia. "I appreciate that this is a different sort of combat than we trained for. You are a computer programmer and Ingridsdotter is a pilot. I myself haven't slept outdoors since the last war. That is not our primary problem. Our problem is, you do not understand the task of *any* combat unit. We are not here to rack up a bigger kill streak than the other fella."

"What is the task of a combat unit, aer," Tellpesh said without enthusiasm.

"The task of a combat unit is to degrade the enemy society's ability to make war," said Dwap-Jac-Dac-Tia. "That is what we will do. It requires precision and unit cohesion. It does not mean shooting peoples' faces off, one at a time. Do you understand, Specialist?"

Tellpesh considered her options. "Yessaer."

"On close approach to the giant-ass lizard, aer," said Ingridsdotter.

"Set me down near the mouth, crack the box and back away." Entry via the mouth was how they did it to rwit in the olden days, and Tia had no ideas for a less invasive approach. Ingridsdotter opened the transport box, getting bubbling mkire all over her hands, and quickly backed out of swiping range, wiping her hands on her trousers.

Finally Dwap-Jac-Dac-Tia could hear again. The desert sand hummed in resonance with a distant wind. The predator's breaths were rattling snores. Its teeth were sharp and bloody. Rwit were herbivores, so going in through their mouths was no problem. This was a problem.

"I'm going in through the neck," said Dwap-Jac-Dac-Tia.

"Fine, aer—just, hurry please," said Ingridsdotter.

The predator twitched when Dwap-Jac-Dac-Tia made the cut, but it stayed tranquil. Dwap-Jac-Dac-Tia pushed in and was immersed once again in a sort of mkire that was real blood and muscle. The blood oozed out and the muscle split apart, but there would be no organ damage. This animal had plenty of room to accommodate a four-member rre.

In fact, there was a parasite in here already, a nasty desert worm in the predator's gut. Dwap-Jac-Dac-Tia gently threaded a body down through the esophagus into the digestive tract, and punctured the worm's scolex, killing it.

She was a spine with a mind at one end, and she struggled through a knee-deep storm of sleepiness. Her eyes twitched into a blinding light, then shut again. Now her hunger returned, and the memory of a smell that promised to hold the hunger off.

She was old and successful. She had no name, but there was a preference, something that made her different from others. Sunlight didn't bother her. Anything that died in the daytime was hers. She could scavenge while her rival slept in his cave. She lived by sunlight, and if a name was necessary, Sunlight would do.

Sunlight straightened her slack mouth and sucked precious saliva from her sand-covered lips. She coughed and ropes of blood dribbled from the wound in her neck, but she felt no pain. The Outreach military officer wrapped around her spinal cord saw to that.

Dwap-Jac-Dac-Tia-Sunlight stretched her clawed toes and padded along the sand back to the vandalized skip shelter. She saw twice: once in color, through Spaceman Ingridsdotter's terminal; again in black and white, from the opposite perspective, with shadows and edges exaggerated. Everything alive within a kilometer was a smell in her nostrils. Metamaterial combat suits could grab vacuum. This was a steed worthy of a rre soldier.

"Fire the netting guns," said Dwap-Jac-Dac-Tia-Sunlight. "I can use the nets as saddlebags. This body can carry a lot of cargo." The strange smell strengthened as she moved back towards her fellas. Were they the smell?

"Shit, there's another one!" said Ingridsdotter. "On six!"

"Tranqing it," said Tellpesh, despair in her voice. Sunlight tensed and prepared to flee, but Dwap-Jac-Dac-Tia-Sunlight held her ground and looked through Ingridsdotter's eyes.

It was the rival. He had smelled the same strange smell. He was larger than her. He took her kills. He had smashed her eggs and drank her children. He would kill Sunlight if he could, and eat her, too. Now he was after—

"He wants Heiss," said Dwap-Jac-Dac-Tia-Sunlight. "They're scavengers. They're both after the body." That was the smell! Delicious, exotic molecules of human flesh, whipping through Dwap-Jac-Dac-Tia-Sunlight's nostrils with each fresh inhalation.

Dwap-Jac-Dac-Tia-Sunlight rushed her rival, frilling and roaring, throwing up clouds of sand as she ran between Tellpesh and Ingridsdotter. The uhalti and the human cursed and flung themselves to the sand. Her rival hissed in unbelief, snarled and snapped his jaws, trying to warn off a suicide attack that would leave them both dead.

"Dig up Heiss!" said Dwap-Jac-Dac-Tia-Sunlight. "We fucked up!" The thought of *him* eating her fella made her ill. A dart whistled in and stung her rival's side. His legs buckled.

"Aer, we have to leave him!" said Ingridsdotter. "We cannot tranq one of these bastards every five minutes!"

"Then we kill this one," said Dwap-Jac-Dac-Tia-Sunlight.

She sank her teeth into her rival's neck and pulled away a chunk of flesh. The gurgling wound poured out wholesome mind-clearing blood that drowned out the toxic sweet smell of the alien corpse behind her. Dwap-Jac-Dac-Tia-Sunlight chewed and swallowed and stood over her dead rival and bit again. The sore bleeding muscles of her throat constricted, pulling the meat into her stomach, sliding it past the body of the embedded parasite that had given her what she had wanted most.

You are not the rwit, Tia was saying, over and over, as the dying meat rubbed across thon on its way down the animal's gullet. *You are not the rwit!*

The squad slept outside that night, huddled in a burrow Sunlight dug. They all slept, except for Dwap-Jac-Dac-Tia, who lay awake inside Sunlight, cramped in a way thon had never been inside a combat suit, surrounded by the disturbing symphony of the predator's internal mechanisms.

Nights on Arzil were only about three hours long. In the morning Sunlight walked along the whitewashed road with Ingridsdotter and Tellpesh on her back, and the day after that—ten hours later—they found a monastery, forty-one klicks down the abandoned road from the skip point. But it wasn't the Jalian monastery Dwap-Jac-Dac-Tia had heard was on Arzil. That was probably on the other side of the planet. This was a Cametrean monastery.

"That is a military base," Tellpesh had said, scooting forward along Sunlight's broad neck and closing her swollen eye. Her terminal zoomed and enhanced the image it saw through the other eye.

"Was a military base," Ingridsdotter had said. "It's abandoned since the first war."

Five hundred meters out, the road became a checkpoint, passing through the only intentional gap in a razor-wire fence that was now more gap than fence. Next to a concrete shack stood a primitive air-defense launcher standing high on a decorative pedestal. Isolated, disconnected from its supply chain, unusual. A piece of branding, like a regimental mascot.

"It is not abandoned," Dwap-Jac-Dac-Tia-Sunlight had said. "I smell humanoids. Take off my cargo nets; I'll check it out."

The cargo nets were noticeably lighter than they had been the day before. The frozen food was gone and the packaged food was dwindling. The water they'd gathered on plastic sheets overnight had been barely enough to rehydrate breakfast.

Sunlight did not like this place. The smell of humanoid was a temptation to be shunned, and there were other strong smells from deep underground which were not food at all. But Dwap-Jac-Dac-Tia-Sunlight loped around a dune and came at the checkpoint from one side, like an animal who didn't know any better.

Ingridsdotter was correct about the timeframe, at least. The rocket launcher was a show piece. Ground-based systems like this had been ineffective for fifty years. Sandstorms had pitted the obsolete weapon's metal, and at some point someone had been sent out with a can of polish to undo what nature had done. And then sent out again a few years later to polish the launcher again. Over the generations, this cycle of *hless*, useless work, pitting and polishing, had given the metal a complex texture like the grain of Terran wood.

The concrete shack was unstaffed, but it was being maintained. Its windows were intact and modern; shatterproof glass of the sort used to make, let's say, prisoner transport boxes for rre. Attached to one wall, where someone in a passing vehicle could reach out and grab, was a clear plastic box filled with faded paper brochures. Past the checkpoint, a klick further down the road, the shadows of buildings shimmered in the heat.

A tattered plastic shape lay folded across the guidance piece of the air-defense system, limp in the brief desert afternoon. Even without color vision, Dwap-Jac-Dac and Tia both recognized it through Sunlight's eyes as a Cametrean caution flag.

"This is not a military base," Dwap-Jac-Dac-Tia-Sunlight told the fellas. "It's a Cametrean Zone of Reality."

"Cametreans in the desert?" said Tellpesh. But that explained the pamphlets at the checkpoint, the polished machinery. The air-defense launcher was the perfect metaphor for Cametreanism: an antique, vaguely rocket-shaped piece of technology that pointed at the sky and didn't work.

"Bloody Cammies," said Ingridsdotter. Just like that, over open comm. Dwap-Jac-Dac would have reminded her that there was no place for bigotry in this Navy. But Dwap-Jac-Dac was now only the dominant voice in the choir that was Dwap-Jac-Dac-Tia-Sunlight, and there were other opinions to consider.

Dwap-Jac-Dac had read the holy scriptures of Cametre. There was nothing holy about them, of course. They were standard adventure literature from the powered-flight era of Quennet. But it was good literature, and easy to find—people in shame robes set up tables at every space station from Terra to Fit Keade, and spammed copies into anyone who looked their way.

Dwap-Jac-Dac respected *In Cametre's Clutches* the same way thon respected *Undeclared* and *The Down Under Crew*. But Tia had experienced the nightmare of achieving interfaith dialogue with real, believing Cametreans. And Sunlight just wanted to eat these fellas based on their smell. Overall, Dwap-Jac-Dac-Tia-Sunlight's position on Cametreanism was not far from Ingridsdotter's.

"What do we do, aer?" said Tellpesh. "We can't keep going like this, and we can't attack a monastery. Even a Cammie monastery."

"Used to be a military base," said Ingridsdotter. "I'm just saying, honest mistake, wink wink."

"We'll talk to them," said Dwap-Jac-Dac-Tia-Sunlight. She sniffed around in case anyone was watching, and fled back towards the sand dune the humanoids were using for shelter. "They're supposed to be neutral. They might even help us."

"Might kill us, aer," said Ingridsdotter. "Cammies are mad. They'll convince you your lungs don't exist and you'll suffocate."

"I am a priest of Jalir," said Dwap-Jac-Dac-Tia-Sunlight. "Nobody is going to out-logic-chop me. Ingridsdotter, how's your Trade Standard D?"

"It's...it's all right, aer. I took a refresher before I went to Cedar Commons."

"Very good." Dwap-Jac-Dac-Tia-Sunlight lowered her hind legs and sat on the sand. "Climb on my back."

"I am as gung-ho as the next pigfucker, aer," said Ingridsdotter, "but respectfully I suggest stealth should be our watchword here. Not, uh, riding through the front door on a giant carnivorous beast wearing a prison guard uniform."

"Have you read the sacred writings of Cametre, spaceman?"

"I am pleased to be innocent of such matters, aer."

"Tia the scholar would tell you that two competing viewpoints run through Cametrean thought. One comes from *In Cametre's Clutches*, in which an angelic being with a sword visits an office worker and presents a quest. The other comes from *Don't Go Out There*, in which a scientist realizes someone is sneaking around tampering with her experiments.

"The Cametreans are going to see us through the lens of one story or the other. And, Ms. Ingridsdotter, we really need it to be *In Cametre's Clutches*, and not *Don't Go Out There*."

"You're the boss, aer."

"And I thank you for realizing that," said Dwap-Jac-Dac-Tia-Sunlight. "Tellpesh?"

"Yessaer."

"Go through those nets and clean out the junk." That was classic military *hless*, something to keep the fellas occupied. "Bury it. Work on the comm if you have some free time. If you don't hear from us in an hour, arm up and come in after us."

Dwap-Jac-Dac-Tia-Sunlight loped back past the shredded security fence. Ingridsdotter bounced around on Sunlight's back and braced herself against the hard bony protrusions on Sunlight's hide. "Eyes up, Ms. Ingridsdotter," said Dwap-Jac-Dac-Tia-Sunlight. "Zoom in." Through the human's terminal Dwap-Jac-Dac-Tia could make out something green near the black buildings, and a moving shape: a humanoid working in a garden.

"Wave at them," said Dwap-Jac-Dac-Tia-Sunlight. "Show you're not hostile."

"I'm super-hostile, aer."

"Wear the mask, spaceman. Or I'll turn us around and do this with Tellpesh."

"Well, we don't want that." Ingridsdotter waved and called out "Hallo hallo!" in D. The humanoid in the garden looked up and fled. "Oh, brilliant," said Ingridsdotter. Dwap-Jac-Dac-Tia-Sunlight just kept trotting into enemy territory, friendly as you please.

The garden was large and stood out against the desert. Its dark soil had been brought from somewhere else. The humanoid returned, and more figures joined it at the place where the soil ran into sand. This was the monastery's operational border, the furthest point they were willing to claim as true reality.

They were corestin, ears floppy with sweat, and they were definitely fans. They all wore crude hand-stitched clothes that, if you weren't too picky, resembled the archaic quenny fashions described in Aquadale Selmar's *Cametre* novels. Patterns had been adapted to the corestin frame by lengthening the legs and letting out the chest. They all wore the emblem of Cametre: a glittering cloth patch in the shape of a lens flare. Tia had been told once what it meant and then forgotten, but Dwap-Jac-Dac recognized it as the hole-in-space from *Don't Go Out There*.

Businesspeople and cops and angels and horrors from beyond reality, all chewing some kind of drugged leaf and spitting darkened saliva into the sand. The fans' eyes were on the shuffling predator. Some of them held their tools as though they had once heard you could use them as weapons.

One stood in front, fearless, wearing a tight shiny stillsuit painted to look like the uniform of the fictional Quennet Exploratory Patrol. An orange-skinned reptile-type surrounded by cat-eared mammals. The monastery's abbot was a real live quenny.

"Good morning, ma'am," the quenny said to Ingridsdotter, in D. His face was weathered and wrinkled by the desert air, so unlike anything on Quennet. Inside the stillsuit he was probably as smooth as an embryo sac.

Ingridsdotter dismounted and sent up a cloud of sand with her prison-guard boots. "Hiroko Ingridsdotter, at your service." A bit over the top, but only the quenny was looking at her. All the corestin fans were still looking at her mount, the dangerous animal standing calmly before them.

"Tell him I'm a Jalian priest," said Dwap-Jac-Dac-Tia-Sunlight, "and that we have a message for them."

"My friend here is a Jalian priest, you see." Ingridsdotter slapped Sunlight's bumpy hide. "We bring a message."

"Your friend is a surk," said the quenny. "You've been in the desert too long."

"Hoot," said Sunlight. Then "Hoot," a little lower. "Hoot, hoot, hoot." She was singing the Sure Recognition, a sequence of tones described in *Behind Cametre's Windowblinds* and used by Cametreans to recognize fellow travelers during shared hallucinations.

The corestin were shocked and stepped back. The quenny walked towards the two intruders, cocked his head and considered the rre-sized wound in Sunlight's neck. He looked at Ingridsdotter and gave a sardonic smile. "A surk who can sing. So what?"

"We've come a long way to deliver a message," said Ingridsdotter.

The quenny issued some perfunctory orders in Mirret, presumably in the form of a quote from the *Cametre* stories. Four of the corestin fans ran off to secure the perimeter.

"I'm listening," said the abbot.

"Quennet is under siege," said Ingridsdotter. "The Outreach and the Fist are both blockading the planet. Did you know about this?"

"Our focus is on lowering the fourth wall in the here and now," said the quenny. "What happens outside Arzil's atmosphere is not our concern." But he was rattled. His gills rippled, and the dark flesh between was visible as he struggled to draw moisture from the dry air.

The abbot certainly had family on Quennet. He'd had a life there, before whatever trouble had exiled him here, the way Tia had been hounded out of the Outreach for taking Jalir's liberation theology too seriously.

Quennet was still the abbot's home, and it hurt him to see what the galaxy's two great powers were doing to her. Tia understood this pain, and Dwap-Jac-Dac was willing to push on the part that hurt. To avoid thinking about his home, the abbot was letting a pious story do the talking for him. Like the customer support rep who takes on the voice of the brand as you describe your problem.

"We know that the fans of Cametre have a special bond with Quennet," said Ingridsdotter. "We are here...we were sent here to ask your help in protecting your home."

"Sent here," said the quenny, not missing the implication. "Human, tell your 'friend' that Quennet is neutral, and so are we."

"My friend says that Quennet is neutral the way a prize is neutral," said Ingridsdotter. "Quennet will be the spoils of this war, if she survives."

"Your friend doesn't talk like a Jalian," said the quenny. "Talks like a gangster."

"Not your typical god-botherer, I admit," said Ingridsdotter. "My friend wants to make sure you know that disabled spacecraft are falling into Quennet's gravity well. Spacecraft full of technology that should not exist."

"Does not exist," murmured one of the corestin.

"Things that do not exist are dropping from the sky and exploding in quenny cities," said Ingridsdotter. "The people of Quennet are starting to demand that someone go out there and see what's going on. Do you see where this leads? Do you want to help us stop it?"

"So that your...employer can claim its prize?" said the quenny.

"Make a deal with us," said Ingridsdotter. "We are not making demands. You can get something out of this for yourself. But you will not find a better offer."

The quenny dismissed all but the oldest corestin, whose costume marked him as Star Proctor Qued Ethiret, primary hero of the *Cametre* series. The two fans conversed in Mirret, shouting and stomping on the dirty sand, lowering their voices now and again to rattle off story citations like quick prayers. Finally the quenny looked up and barked at Sunlight: "What do you propose?"

"That's up to you, sir," said Ingridsdotter. "Is there something we can do for you, here on Arzil, that will end the war sooner? If so, we're at your service. Perhaps you're having trouble with the local authorities?"

The religious dispute had gotten only as far as was necessary to voice that question, and it now resumed, twice as angry as before. "You know what they're saying, aer?" Ingridsdotter asked.

"They're quoting precedent at each other," said Dwap-Jac-Dac-Tia-Sunlight.

"Who's winning?"

"*In Cametre's Clutches* is winning," thon said, "which means we are winning."

Finally the quenny stepped toward Sunlight and tapped the wound in the predator's neck as if to heal it with a touch. "Bring in the others," he told Sunlight.

"The others, sir?" said Ingridsdotter.

The quenny scowled at the human as though she were a hindrance. "Whoever you brought with you," he said. "Out there, in the desert, providing covering fire. I don't imagine your *employer* would have sent two people here by themselves."

"You'd be surprised, sir," said Ingridsdotter, without prompting from her LT.

"Bring them all here," said the abbot, "into the zone of reality, where we can speak free of tricks and threats."

"There's one other," said Ingridsdotter, again without prompting.

"I don't trust numbers," said the quenny. "I only trust what's real. Bring them here. I will see how many, and what you might be capable of. That is my offer."

"Tellpesh," said Dwap-Jac-Dac-Tia over the ad-hoc milnet.

"Tellpesh here."

"We are headed back to your position. Sort the weapons out of the cargo. Wrap them in plastic and bury them. We may need them later."

"Oh, now Cammies don't believe in weapons?" said Tellpesh.

"They believe that weapons exist," said Dwap-Jac-Dac-Tia-Sunlight. "I just don't think they want any in their monastery."

Chapter 21

Neutral

Myrus
Twelstee?

Myrus and the others were asleep during the final skip. It showed itself as a horrible feeling in the pit of your stomach that interrupted your very vivid dream about (let's say) a sexy human; but when you woke up you discovered the feeling was just your rumen rediscovering gravity after two days away.

The inflatable spacecraft was descending down one track of a space elevator, towards a yellow planet with blue oceans. According to the travel staff who'd "escorted" them through their pit stops, the planet was called Twelstee. But "Twelstee" was obviously the Trade Standard D acronym for "Fist of Joy Youth Festival" (*twar ellin stayankrop eern*), so the planet itself was probably called something else.

"D'you suppose the spacecraft hull will hold?" said Sanjit Mathis, kind of academically as they inched down Twelstee's air column in a big party balloon.

Shut up shut up, Myrus thought.

Despite all this foreshadowing they didn't die. The space elevator came to rest on the edge of a beach, and Myrus and the others were unloaded from their sturdi netting. Holding on to railings, they staggered into a steel-reinforced grass hut where an old hopore sat reading a book. She wore a doctor's apron and a jewel-covered slave bracelet that jangled when she stood up.

The hopore peered closely at the kids on their wobbly legs and clucked to herself softly. She hopped back a bit and took everyone in.

"Exists one...with talking ability...Trade Standard D?" she said, in English.

"Yes!" said everybody. They'd been asked this nineteen times.

"Oh, that makes this easier." said the hopore, switching to D. "I am a doctor. Human boy! Stick out your tongue!" Wei Nzeme stuck out his tongue, and while he was distracted with that, the hopore stabbed a suction gun into his arm and took a blood sample.

"Ouch!" said Wei. "Now, see here!"

"Keep yourself calm!" said the hopore doctor. She checked a red light on the suction gun. "I'm only ensuring you don't introduce any diseases to the Fist of Joy Youth Festival."

"Now, see here," Wei repeated. "We're not carrying any ruddy diseases!"

"That's what they all say," said the slave doctor. She chuckled and handed Wei a food bar. The suction gun glowed for a bit and then she stabbed Myrus, who bit his lip and said nothing. There was no pain debt, just the sharp of the jab.

After stabbing everyone the hopore stroked her beak and said: "All of you are clean, so go out and have fun!" That was the only adult supervision at the Fist of Joy Youth Festival. As long as you didn't have any diseases (STDs?), they didn't seem to care. The slave doctor sat back down and picked up her book. Myrus and the other council kids left the tent and walked onto the sand.

The humans gasped in amazement. A planetside beach was an awful place to dock a city-ship, so they'd only been to small recreational beaches on space stations. This blew them all away. The beach was insanely long, klicks and klicks, and the ocean was terrifying. Myrus couldn't even see the other side of the water.

About ten meters into the ocean was a pile of Fist of Joy teenagers building a tower out of plastic sticks. Kids were climbing up the tower and pushing each other off into the water. It looked like there were two teams: one trying to build the tower higher and one trying to tear it down.

The council kids loved tearing things down, especially things other people cared about. They started talking excitedly and looked around for a changing room, or swimsuits to change into. Myrus swiveled and walked in the other direction without even saying goodbye. He decided to find a restaurant or a bookstore and hopefully avoid his fellow prisoners until the war was over.

Some blocky Fist buildings huddled together behind the beach and past the space elevator. The ground here was mostly sand, held together by the stringy roots of scrub bushes, clinging to the ground in defiance of hundreds of kids who had kicked them and tripped over them.

"Could be worse," Myrus said experimentally. Dad said this a lot, and Myrus had always been like, *How do you know? How do you know it could be worse?* Because Myrus had only ever had one thing happen to him. He was born and raised on *Jaketown*, and had never been allowed to seriously consider leaving.

Now that his life had been ruined, Myrus saw lots of ways it could be worse. He'd narrowly avoided being drafted into the Navy, suffocating in a scoop ship as it ran out of oxygen, being locked up in a tiny cell until the end of the war, and suffocating in a defective inflatable spacecraft as *it* ran out of oxygen. All those things were 'worse'.

Myrus was a prisoner in a cell the size of a planet, but within that cell he was free. The adults who'd captured him cared just enough to make sure he survived to become someone else's problem, and now he'd been shipped to a place where kids did as they pleased. Maybe Myrus could exploit the difference between this situation and an imaginary worse situation, the way a skip capacitor exploits a gravity differential.

Maybe that was why Dad always said that stupid, obvious phrase. He was telling Myrus to look at what he had available, options that he wouldn't have if the situation were worse. It was a lot of work, finding the hidden wisdom behind Dad's clichés.

By following the teenagers who weren't heading to the beach, Myrus honed in on the Youth Festival's cafeteria. It was a long flat building and its double doors sent out the delicious smells of foods from strange places that would make Myrus incredibly sick if he ate them. A whirlpool of chattering kids of all races slowly drained through the doors. Myrus joined the mob and rode it.

Alien kids shoved Myrus, did double-takes, gawked and in broken English demanded explanations for his existence, then ignored him when he refused to take the bait. Myrus had one instant to grab a white porcelain bowl with ledges arranged around the inside, and then he was spat out into the cafeteria.

At this point the mob dispersed. On *Jaketown*, uhalti and humans and rre had separate cafeterias. But, no surprise, the Fist of Joy had much looser rules about food safety. So the wirchak kid and the mehi-peri kid would grab their bowls, break off their conversation, and split to adjacent stations to get their food.

Myrus hadn't seen another uhaltihaxl since the soldier who'd put them in the inflatable spaceship, so he figured the uhaltihaxl food station would have the shortest line. Myrus made his way to an abandoned station in the middle of the cafeteria, dodging bigger kids whose bowls were piled with sizzling meats, only to discover this was where they kept the neutral food. White glop and yellow beads and green leaves. Everything labeled with that safety logo, like on bottles of neutral Coke.

There was no uhaltihaxl food station. This was it, and Myrus had already been eating this stuff for days. At least he wasn't alone. A human adult with long dirty hair and a beard was poking at a pile of jewel-studded grey squares resembling the food bar in Myrus's pocket.

"Hello?" said Myrus, in English, afraid he was blowing a spy's cover.

"Ah, young person, hello," said the human. "In English thoda my words form unhappily. Might we take pleasure in Trade Standard D?"

"Uh, sure," said Myrus, in D. "What do you recommend?"

"Huh?" said the human. It was like he had to stall for time every time someone spoke to him.

"What food? What food is good?"

The human gazed into his bowl. "That's a subjective question," he said. He seemed to have been transported to a faraway land where subjective questions ran free. "We'd have to simulate your pleasure model, and—no, no, no, what am I thinking? You already have a pleasure model! It just needs calibration. Ah, what I mean is, try everything, and see what you like! You see?"

The human took Myrus's bowl, smushed it atop the food in his own bowl, and started grabbing at tongs and spoons, filling the bowl with a little of everything from the neutral station.

"You're supposed to keep things separate on these protrusions," said the human, "but it all ends up in the same place, doesn't it?" He handed back Myrus's bowl. There was a ring of syrupy stuff around the bottom where the bowl had touched the human's food.

"Starbottle is the name," said the human. "Thaddeus Ganapathi Starbottle, Ph.D., Ph.D., at your service. The youth call me Professor Starbottle."

"Which youth is that?" said Myrus.

"You're supposed to tell me your name, in return," said Professor Starbottle. He moved one hand in circles, like, *Hurry it up!*

"My name is Myrusit," said Myrus, leaving out the family name.

"Myrusit, Myrusit," said Professor Starbottle, in the rhythm of someone who forgets names five minutes after learning them. "Okay. Which youth, you ask? My answer is, the ones here at the Youth Festival. I'm a research instructor. Follow me, Myrusit. It's rude to get between hungry people and their food."

Professor Starbottle hurried over towards a sign saying "Eat In Here", and Myrus followed him because this guy was the first person he had met since being captured who was neither angry nor amazed at the fact of him.

"I move my laboratory here during the festivals," said Professor Starbottle. He was walking barefoot through a food service facility! "The youth act as inexpensive research assistants, and hopefully they learn something they can apply to their own studies. I like working with youth. They are the future of the Fist, after all. But of course, you would know; you're a youth yourself."

Beneath "Eat In Here" was another double door. On the other side were the benches Myrus had been expecting, full of kids eating and chatting. Professor Starbottle kind of stumbled upon a free seat and Myrus scampered to sit across from him. The human held a spoon in one hand and a piece of stiff flatbread in the other and started painting food onto the bread in swirly patterns.

"Um," said Myrus. "I'm getting the feeling you're not from the Outreach."

"Oh, no, I was born here," said Professor Starbottle. "The Fist, I mean, not this planet. No one is born on this planet, although quite a few are conceived here. I take it you're...differently situated? In terms of citizenship?"

"I'm actually a prisoner of war," said Myrus. "You know there's a war going on, right?"

"Oh, my, yes. And don't think I think any less of you, Myrusit. I respect the military ethos, but I have no political opinions. Unless you count a general belief in the desirability of peace, which is radical enough these days, I suppose. I'm neutral, like our food."

"I'm not a soldier," said Myrus. "I was just caught in the middle, you know?"

"Oh," said Professor Starbottle. "Well, then, Myrusit, what *is* your chosen path in life?"

"I'm a woodworker," said Myrus, very reluctantly.

And indeed, Professor Starbottle said "A woodworker!" as though the word had zapped him in the butt. "Are you religious, Myrusit?"

What was it about telling humans you were a woodworker? Did Myrus have "Bother me about your stupid religion!" written on his back in a color only humans could see?

"No, I'm not," said Myrus. "And if this is about Jesus, I'm not interested."

"What? Oh, I see, also a woodworker! Very amusing. No, I was contemplating the Hasithenk concept of Merciful Providence."

Myrus lowered his voice. "The thing about that is, it's not really merciful. Providence is kind of a..." Yeah, Myrus didn't know *any* of the swear words in Trade Standard D. "Kind of cruel!"

"Oh, yes: my good fortune is your misfortune. Providence aligns cause and effect without regard to our feelings."

"You said it." Myrus cast glances at Professor Starbottle's flatbread painting and tried scooping the corresponding foods into his mouth all at once. It definitely tasted better than eating them separately.

"But I was thinking, Myrusit: just as I need someone to teach me woodworking, here you come, from halfway across the galaxy. And we run into each other based on nothing but our shared appreciation of healthy vegetarian food. A cynical person might say that Providence arranged this entire unpleasant war to bring you to me at just the right time. 'A poison to Fet, a delicacy to Fritl,' as they say."

"That's all-me thinking," said Myrus, who had been to enough church meetings to pick up the lingo. "If Merciful Providence was even a thing, which she's not, she would use a war to do eight billion things at once. You're not that important. Why do you need to learn woodworking, anyway?"

"For my research project," said Professor Starbottle. "Any kinesthetic skill will do, but the youth here are designers, speakers, athletes, and so on. You see, it's not that they don't use their bodies in their work..."

"They don't put things together," Myrus suggested.

"Exactly! I was going to try to find a sculptor, but woodworking...that's so much better! It's a very *human* art, wouldn't you say?"

"No," said Myrus, his mouth full.

"I see your point. But if you could teach me to make something simple, like a chair..."

"A chair's not simple."

He laughed. "Oh, well, you see, I don't know anything, do I? What would you recommend?"

Myrus thought about what he could teach an old guy who couldn't even remember to wear shoes. "A stool," he said. Even that was dubious.

"Then a stool it will be, Myrusit!" said Professor Starbottle.

"But we need tools," said Myrus. "And wood. Like, from trees. Terran trees, which you don't have."

"Don't worry about that," said Professor Starbottle. "I'm sure we'll find the appropriate tools in the Festival's equipment library. We're not much for exotic materials, but my personal assistant will be happy to send us all the wood we can use."

That was weird. Personal assistants were for executives and celebrities. Maybe Myrus didn't have the word right. "Won't that be expensive?" he said.

"I don't like bringing this up, Myrusit, but the Fist of Joy now controls a certain volume of Outreach space. Only temporary, I'm sure, but there is such a thing as the spoils of war."

Myrus imagined the Fist military tearing up Cedar Commons for the wood, Dad and Den dead in the crossfire. This was the sort of ironic fate Merciful Providence arranged for people who denied her power. "Why do you need to learn woodworking?" he asked, hoping to talk the human out of it.

"I've developed a way to record one person's brain activity and play it back in another person's body. I'm ready to create a recording of myself as I learn a skill. Hopefully it's transferable, you see." Professor Starbottle scraped a little bit of brown gel from the side of his bowl and sighed with a contentment that Myrus didn't feel at all.

"Not on the level of brain chemistry!" he said, as if Myrus was a rival neuroscientist trying to discredit his research. He licked his spoon. "It used to be brain chemistry, but now I can record the subjective experience! Which means you must do a good job teaching me woodworking, or the whole thing's useless, you see?"

"Could you record me already being good at woodworking?" said Myrus.

"Great question! That will not work! It would feel like a pleasant dream, and the skill wouldn't stick. Anyway, my process only works on human brains." At this point the human noticed Myrus's empty bowl. It had been empty for a while, because Myrus *ate* instead of talking all the time. "Are you full, Myrusit?" asked Professor Starbottle.

This was an interesting question. Myrus's new diet had made him realize just how little he needed to eat to stay alive. But was not wanting to eat the same as being "full"? "Full" was a human thing: the stomach was "full" of food. How did that translate to uhalti? Was it when the rumen was full? Must be; otherwise you'd have to eat to fill the rumen and then *keep eating*, a little bit at a time, as it drained—

"We can go back, you know," said Professor Starbottle. "There are no food shortages in the Fist."

"I'm full," said Myrus quickly.

Professor Starbottle wiped his mouth with a cloth he kept in his jacket. "Then shall we get started?" he said.

Professor Starbottle pushed open a flap in the wall of the cafeteria building and dropped his bowl into what looked like a swimming pool. A big cloud of steam blasted Myrus in the face when he pushed the flap up to do the same.

"The thing is, woodworking isn't that interesting," Myrus said. "It's all muscle memory, like washing dishes. You should come up with a drug for learning calculus."

"Calculus is far too abstract," said Professor Starbottle. "You cannot inject knowledge into peoples' brains. You *can* give them a new sensory experience. If it's the experience of learning something that engages their body, the skill might transfer. Woodworking is our test case, my young friend."

Myrus had never been anyone's young friend before. Outside the cafeteria the sun had set. The beach was dark and the sky was bright. The galactic center basically had control of the sky and you couldn't see many normal stars. The little scrub bushes illuminated the paths with bio-light.

"Hey, Professor, is this like Evidence?" said Myrus. "'Cause they sound pretty similar. Like, you do some Evidence, you're King Arthur; you play back this memory formation thing, you become a woodworker."

Professor Starbottle gave Myrus a suspicious look. "How do you know about Evidence?" he said. "It's a very dangerous drug! I suppose your human friends..." He threw up his hands in disgust, as if he'd heard a news article about teenagers doing oral.

"There was this hitchhiker laborer who got high on Evidence," said Myrus. He laughed at how ridiculous it was. "She thought she was a pegasus! You know, from mythology. She jumped off a balcony." Myrus saw the look of horror on Professor Starbottle's face and stuttered. "She—she's okay! She just broke her legs." Except maybe Dad had lied about the broken legs, the way he lied about everything else.

Professor Starbottle just worried his beard. He tracked sandy footprints up a ramp and into a large building which advertised itself as Twelsteekarako, the Fist of Joy Youth Festival Equipment Library. Myrus followed him in and stopped dead in the entrance with his mouth open.

High-end furniture brands had physical showrooms. Myrus had been walked through 3-maps of these stores as part of his apprenticeship, and they had seemed like a big waste of space. In fact, a lot of the *product* Myrus worked on seemed like a waste of space, but you got more real estate on a planet, since you didn't have to defend every cubic meter against vacuum.

So now here was the Youth Festival's Equipment Library, the size of a SuruBo or bigger, but instead of disconnected planetside living rooms it was full of shelves, aisles of shelves that stretched on into the back, shelves with *stuff* on them. There were a few kids carrying cardboard boxes up and down the aisles, looking for something in particular. A mehi-peri adult slowly pulled a smoothcart towards the front of the building, reshelving things the kids hadn't put away properly.

The shelves glowed with different colors of quiet light, and bright panels in the floor and ceiling fuzzed in and out. The Fist of Joy had a big problem lighting anything the normal way, and it meant a lot of extra shadows. Down a ramp was a big basement area with more aisles, more shelves, more stuff. A large sign hovering over the basement area said SAFE in D. This was when Myrus noticed that every aisle on this, the ground floor, had a large hovering sign reading DANGEROUS.

A big pile of different-sized cardboard boxes sat between Myrus and the smoothcarts. Behind the boxes Myrus could see the tangled nest of Professor Starbottle's long hair.

"Hey," said Myrus, coming out from behind the boxes. "Sorry about..."

Professor Starbottle had unlatched a small smoothcart from its power socket and now he switched it on. The cart was big enough to carry some two-by-fours and not much else.

"Myrusit," Professor Starbottle said. He was facing away from Myrus and he wasn't pushing the smoothcart. "You deserve to know this, I suppose."

"Okay," said Myrus.

"I developed a computational biochemical for my work on experience formation. That chemical is the basis for the substances grouped together under the street name of Evidence. You understand what I'm saying?"

"I get it," said Myrus.

"I am responsible," said Starbottle, even though Myrus had said he got it. He punched the smoothcart. "I started an epidemic and there's nothing I can do about it. I can't stop people from making drugs or using them. I can't change the social conditions that make people feel they need to escape reality. All I can do is continue my work and try to make something good come out of this."

"Is it really that good?" said Myrus. "If you could turn random people into woodworkers, wouldn't it put us out of business?"

There were grips all over the cart, for people with differently arranged hands, and Professor Starbottle, who was very tall, slammed his hands around two of the grips that were highest up.

"This is a test case, Myrusit. As you say, woodworking is the interest of an enlightened few. A calculus drug would be a viable commercial application. Here's what I'm after: what if we could teach *empathy*? What if you could literally experience what it's like to be someone else? Learn to understand your enemy? You wouldn't even call it a drug. It would be a medicine. It would solve so many problems. Maybe as many problems as I've created.

"But the next step is to capture something simple and physical, like woodworking." Professor Starbottle had a faraway look in his eyes, but he was just looking down the ramp, into the basement, trying to figure out where they stored the wood. SAFE or DANGEROUS?

"Are there any other POWs here at the Festival?" he asked Myrus. "Perhaps a human?"

"No, just me," Myrus lied.

"That's a shame," said Professor Starbottle. "We will eventually need to test it."

Chapter 22

Smoke

Captain Styrqot
Small but Sharp
Approaching Seeder Commons

They nuked it!" said Styrqot. His pipe dropped from his beak. "The Outreach nuked their own damn planet."

"Pathetic," said Vec. She walked up the bridge and stared through the front window into space, looking up at the burning planet. "Trying to destroy your magic plants, eh?" she said. "Trying to hide your secrets from Vec."

Unlike the average, sane egenu, Vec carried no water bottle. She went naked, her body glistening with natural mucus. Her mercenaries, dressed in the heavy shame robes Cametreans wore in space, stood at the rear of the bridge, murmuring to each other.

"The fire and the radiation are localized," said Byrno, a navigator on loan from the professional military. "Our big problem is the smoke."

"What's wrong, Byrno?" said Vec. "All your high-tech fart-cleaners and environment suits, and you're afraid of a little smoke?"

Byrno opened his beak for a comeback but Styrqot cut the navigator off. Discipline had to be maintained. "Young lady," he said, "I don't want to make you look bad in front of your fellas, but you clearly have no experience with magic plants."

"And you do?"

"I know how you get the magic out of one." Styrqot picked up his pipe. He held it by its silicone bowl and tilted it so Vec could see the superheated ceramic coal, the sizzling leaves. "You burn it. The magic's in the smoke.

"That's why they nuked their own planet: it keeps us at a distance. If we try to land, the smoke seizes up our motivators, and...well, we land, but we don't survive the landing, if you catch my meaning.

"Byrno, take a high orbit. I don't trust a smoke cloud to know where the atmosphere stops."

"Aye, sir."

"Magic smoke or no," Vec told Styrqot, "your assignment is to deliver the Bronze Age Bastards to the surface. Not into a high orbit. A zero orbit."

In his raucous youth, Styrqot had loved to picture himself as the sort of roguish captain who'd swagger onto the bridge of his ship with a naked woman at his side. Even after his marriage and the birth of his son, he had secretly fantasized about being that guy, like Chief Mene on *Nightside*. Then a few shifts ago the naked woman had been assigned to his ship, and it had turned out not to be fun at all.

"Let's think it through," said Styrqot. "Byrno, I see a ring around this planet. What's the composition?"

"Mostly ice," said Byrno. "It was an unlucky comet. We're in orbit, now, by the way."

"Thank you," said Styrqot. He took a pull from his pipe, letting the magic smoke seep into the membranes of his mouth and throat. He peeked at Vec. The egenu woman scowled at him. She fingered the insignia of her leadership: a trophy necklace made of teeth. Styrqot had looked at it long enough to see that not all of them were uhaltihaxl and human teeth.

"Turn some of that ice into rain, if you don't mind," said Styrqot. "Let's try to put out this fire for our passengers. That should clear the smoke."

"Aye, sir. Charging weapons." Then Byrno chuckled. "Oh, that got someone's attention! Drones in the rings." A tactical view appeared in the 3-tank: half the planet, half the ring system, one moving dot in the rings, more to follow.

"Drones," Vec whispered. She walked towards the window, ignoring the 3-tank, eyeing the planet, like an idiot. How big were drones in her mind? How small was space?

Styrqot would have been perfectly happy never to have learned about a team of mercenaries who used low-tech means to break into high-tech facilities. It made sense that the shadow economy would support a few people like that. It was one of those things Styrqot didn't need to know, like which parts of which animals went into meat-sticks.

But now he knew. And having the Bronze Age Bastards as passengers on his ship, mocking his dependence on advanced technology like reheatable food containers, predicting his violent comeuppance when some vague apocalypse destroyed all advanced technology and rendered his "crutches" useless...it was not how Styrqot wanted to contribute to the war effort.

A kinetic charge slapped the ship, sending everyone lurching to one side and grabbing for handholds. For a peaceful trader like Styrqot, being shot at was terrifying, but the handholds were there and the shields stayed up. The drones were no real threat. *Small but Sharp*'s combat laser pointed into Seeder Commons's ring system, creating an imperceptible flash where it hit. *There's your drone, Vec. That's how big they are.*

"The tactics are nothing special," said Byrno. "I'm definitely feeling a queen. Where are ya, queenie?" A few more dots had appeared in the 3-tank, and Byrno worked on picking them off with the laser.

Styrqot asked the most important question. "Does queenie have nukes?"

"She usually leads with them," said Byrno. "Probably used them all igniting the planet. Oh, that's interesting..."

"What?" The appearance of something interesting never failed to put a chill down Styrqot's spine.

"There is a *space elevator* on the far side," said Byrno. And there it was, sticking out of the increasingly complete 3-map of Seeder Commons in the center of the bridge.

"How does that work?" said Vec. "I mean, how does it work when it's surrounded by magic trees. I don't need to know how a space elevator works."

"It probably doesn't work, anymore," said Byrno. "Should we take a look, sir?"

"Go for it," said Styrqot. "Might be queenie's nest."

Vec walked to the rear of the bridge and conferred with her mercenaries. Styrqot steadied himself and continued facing the window, ignoring the Bronze Age Bastards. He wished for his body armor. It might not do much good against a powered weapon, but it was guaranteed to turn a knife in the back.

"And now we're...receiving a hail," said Byrno. "From the planet's surface."

"Again, how?" said Vec. "They're covered in smoke. They shouldn't have working wheels."

"I don't think the magic trees are real," said Styrqot. "The intelligence came from a little boy. Kids make things up. My son created this elaborate—"

"The call, sir," said Byrno. "What do I do with the call?"

"I'll take it in the tank," said Styrqot. "Keep killing drones." A fuzzy 2-image of a human head appeared in the tank, superimposed over the map of the increasingly mysterious planet. The human said nothing.

"Hello?" said Styrqot.

"Hello," said the human in stilted Trade Standard D, "ah, and whom am I addressing?"

"You are addressing the Fist of Joy," said Styrqot. "In the person of its humble but well-armed representative, Niuquo Styrqot Tukl."

"Mr. Jiankang Nzeme," said the human. "Mayor of Chaiktan settlement. Uh, first order of business: as the elected head of government on this planet, I offer our surrender under the terms of the Treaty of Ois."

"It's customary to break off your attack before trying to surrender," said Styrqot.

"You're under attack?" said the human.

"Yes, sir, we are."

"From whom, may I ask?"

"From the military drones guarding this planet! If you're trying to divert my attention, I should let you know that there is more than one person on my ship. We are more than adequate to the task of stopping your little machines."

"Those drones are not ours," said the human. He licked his lips. "Forgive me, sir, but the past few days have been...bizarre and unsettling. I am going to have a talk with someone, and hopefully we can resolve the drone situation. In the meantime, please don't do anything rash. Legally speaking, this planet's civilian authority has surrendered, and there are children in this settlement."

"Children?" said Styrqot. "You know, I have a son myself. He loves running. In fact, he tried out for one of the Youth Festival teams, and—"

Static and interference broke up the 2-picture, but not so badly that Styrqot didn't recognize the telltale shoulder movements of someone pumping a dimmer switch to create fake interference. "You're breaking up," said the human. "Chaiktan out."

"That man talks like a brand," said Byrno.

Styrqot toked his pipe again, hoping for enlightenment. "Nothing about this makes sense. Why would you light a planet on fire and *stay on the planet?* Not even to evacuate the children?"

"Stop thinking like a soldier," said Vec. She'd dismissed the Bronze Age Bastards and they were climbing below decks. "Think like a criminal, if you can."

"This may surprise you, Vec," said Styrqot, "but *Small but Sharp* has occasionally carried 'unlicensed' cargo."

"Then you ought to recognize a front operation when you see one," said Vec. "Some idiot gets a mysterious stream of money to support his business that makes no economic sense. Like, ah, what do Terrans *do* with their trees? What are they for?"

"Fruit," said Styrqot. "Trees grow fruit." Moving Terran fruit across the border was good business. In fact, if the war ended at the right time, Styrqot could potentially bring back a load from this trip...

"Let's say it's fruit," said Vec. "But a few shifts ago, Mr. Jiankang Nzeme discovered he's not in the fruit business at all. His real job was to run interference for a military research lab. Now the military's buggered off, nuked his planet, he's staring down the Fist, and he's in the mood to think back on everything he ignored back when the money was flowing."

"Like mysterious drones in orbit that he can't control," said Styrqot.

"Ships skipping in unannounced," Vec added. "People seen around town who didn't belong. If you can get over your fear of smoke and set us down on solid ground, I think we can 'persuade' the frontmen to remember what the back office was doing."

"Drones have gone cold, sir," said Byrno. "Retreated into the rings. Still no sign of queenie."

Military grand strategy was not Styrqot's strong point, but he had ran a shipping business for twenty kiloshifts. He could think a step ahead, and he was used to being the middleman between two parties whose only shared interest was in screwing him.

"Go back to smash-and-skip on the ring fragments, Byrno," said Styrqot. "Let's make sure it's safe to land. Vec, when you and your fellas put your feet on the ground, I will be with you."

"Sounds like fun," said Vec.

"I'm going to change into my body armor. If Mr. Human calls back, let him sweat for a bit."

Vec snorted. "Body armor!"

"You know what, Vec?" said Styrqot. "I don't like your attitude."

The egenu touched her necklace. "Don't think you're safe, old man," she said, "just because hopore don't have any teeth."

Churryhoof
Cedar Commons

Every time Dr. Sempestwinku came in to Churryhoof's room with his white lab coat and his thin fake smile, Churryhoof wished she'd drafted him instead of going for the dentist. A human doctor would have looked at a patient in Churryhoof's condition and dispensed steroids and opioids until *Jaketown*'s stores ran dry. Sempestwinku held the belief, unsubstantiated by medical science, that the body would only heal properly if pain debt was paid off naturally.

Churryhoof had sweated through two days as a living control group in Sempestwinku's sadistic experiment. She was a prisoner on Cedar Commons awaiting trial on trumped-up charges, so a human doctor might have been worse. Might have "accidentally" put something nasty in her IV.

"We are coming along nicely," Sempestwinku told her. "As you'll be walking soon, I'd like to suggest trimming your horns to a consistent mass." He meant hacking off her left horn to match her right.

"They trimmed my horns at the Academy," said Churryhoof, "and Thrux will take them when I die, and no one is touching them in between."

"You cannot walk like this," said Sempestwinku, who dropped the nice-doctor act at the slightest provocation. His own horns were a six-month growth, barely curved. He'd probably been meaning to make an appointment with the cornicurist when *Jaketown* crashed. "One side of your head weighs a kilo more than the other. You'll have vertigo, balance problems."

"Cast me a prosthetic," said Churryhoof.

Sempestwinku scoffed. "We don't have the tools."

"You have wood, don't you? The miracle organic material! Your economy is based on making shapes out of wood!" Churryhoof dropped her head back onto the pillow. "Make something useful for once."

The doctor went into his terminal for a few seconds, probably to write 'still cranky and uncooperative' on Churryhoof's chart. Then he leaned over the bed and spoke quietly. "There are two beings here to see you," he said.

"Are they the 'beings' I warned you about?" said Churryhoof. In stolen moments of consciousness, and then in hours of paralyzed boredom, she'd planned out how a city of carpenters could carry out resistance once the Fist invasion fleet put them under occupation. No one had asked her advice.

"Speaking as your doctor," said Sempestwinku, "it would be bad for your health if they found out you're a Navy officer."

"What do they know?" said Churryhoof.

"Nothing about you. You're just a prisoner. A prisoner who will not say anything. The civil authorities have this under control."

Sempestwinku put his hands in his coat pockets and walked out through the door. "She can speak," he said in Trade Standard D to someone outside. "Don't speak for too long."

An nude egenu woman slinked into the hospital room/prison cell, followed by a hopore man with an awkward gait. Before the door hissed shut, Churryhoof caught a glimpse of another nude egenu standing guard outside.

"Hi there," said the hopore, in Trade Standard D. He stuck a fuming pipe in his beak and sucked on it. He moved stiffly because he was wearing body armor under his ribbon suit. Churryhoof folded her arms and shut her eyes.

"What are you?" said the egenu, in much worse D.

"My name is Rebecca Laverne Twice," said Churryhoof, in uncooperative Narathippin. "I work for Trellis On-Site Security."

Oddly enough, the hopore understood her. He conferred with the egenu for a while in Trade Standard A, the Fist's military language. Not-so-oddly, Commander Churryhoof understood Trade Standard A, but the hopore was just translating what she had said.

"I believe Rebecca is a human name," the hopore told the prisoner at last, in serviceable Narrathippin.

"What are you, the racial name police?"

The hopore man held a terminal in one hand and with the other trained a little cubical scanner on Churryhoof's face. Churryhoof twitched at a burst of infrared and the military-grade capital terminal implanted behind her left eye did absolutely nothing. But the burnt-out crystal she'd hidden under her pillow buzzed imperceptibly and filled up the hopore's terminal with a detailed employment history for Rebecca Twice.

"Ms. Rebecca Twice," said the hopore, reading the name off his terminal. "my name is Styrqot. This is Vec." He gave a self-satisfied shudder, as if to illustrate that most decent people had exactly the sort of name you'd expect. "Your planet is under a new government, and as part of the handover we are investigating how prisoners are treated. You seem to be the only prisoner, so...what happened to you? You don't look so good."

"Resisting arrest," said 'Rebecca Twice'. "That's what they call it when they want to smack you around. 'Resisting arrest.' What do you call it?"

"We don't do that," said Styrqot. The smoke from his pipe filled the hospital room and numbed the throbbing pain in Churryhoof's head. It sure made a better narcotic than whatever was in this IV drip. The whole experience would make for an amusing malpractice suit after the war.

"How do you do?" Vec asked Churryhoof in D. An oddly formal thing to hear from someone wearing a trophy necklace made from teeth.

"*What*," Styrqot corrected her. "*What* did you do? Why were you arrested?"

"They say I set off some nukes," said Churryhoof casually.

That got their attention. The hopore and the egenu conferred in A, and this time the conversation was worth overhearing. "For the brand Trellis, she works," Styrqot muttered. "To the military, the research project, the brand operates, the benefit accrues."

"To the former authorities, of the back ???," said Vec, "she certainly knows, she conceals. Her tongue, in her, trust, they lack, my knife will engage."

This made Styrqot uncomfortable for some reason. He leaned over Churryhoof's bed, trying not to stare at her horn stump. "Did Trellis tell you to set off the nukes?" he asked.

"Ha ha ha," said Churryhoof. "You're cute. We call that one 'leading the witness'." Styrqot must have thought Churryhoof actually believed he was cute, because he looked pleased and then disappointed.

"What do you know about...trees?" asked Vec, eager to seize on a wrong answer.

"Never heard of 'em," said Churryhoof. Vec made a disgusted let's-go gesture.

"Do you need anything from us, Ms. Rebecca Twice?" the hopore asked Churryhoof. "Are you still being mistreated?"

"No, no," said Churryhoof, storing up his pipe smoke in her lungs for later. "I'm fine! Best medical care in the galaxy!"

"If you cooperate with us," said Styrqot, very cleverly baiting a trap, "we have a lot of leeway under treaty to shut down prosecutions ordered by the previous regime."

"Do you know," said Churryhoof, jamming her own bait into the same trap. "The one thing I hate more than cooperating with the police is cooperating with the mother-fucking Fist of Joy."

"For her benefit, the attempt, I made," Styrqot muttered in A. They left in a huff and 'Rebecca Twice' stretched painfully and fell asleep, aware as she'd recently been that she might not wake up. But she did wake up, in the middle of the night, in darkness with her window lit by the planet's ring above and a few streetlights below.

"Hey, ma'am," a teenage girl was saying in Narathippin. "Wake up, ma'am." The girl was jiggling Churryhoof's hospital bed in a way that replayed every moment of her fight with Mrs. Chen. Churryhoof slowly turned her head. The girl was a straighthorn uhalti. From the shadows she held out a bar of Just Me kelexn. "The doctor told me to give you this," said the girl. "For your blood sugar."

"No, I don't think so," said Churryhoof.

"That's what I was going to say if someone stopped me," said the girl, a cunning smirk in her voice.

"Good thing nobody stopped you."

"Take it," said the girl.

Churryhoof had eaten nothing but bland Terran fish for two days. She hadn't had kelexn for over a year. It was junk food for middle-aged women.

"Thank you," she said. She took the kelexn and pulled the tab. The inside of her elbow screamed. She gritted her teeth and tore the top off the wrapper.

"What's your name?" she asked. She bit into the food bar. The kelexn was greasy and sweet. It had sat in someone's purse for a while.

"Den," said the girl.

"Den what? Denweld? Denmax?"

"Denweld Xepperxelt, ma'am. My mother is *Jaketown*'s head of marketing."

"Why are you giving me your mother's kelexn, Denweld?"

"To get on your good side."

Denweld Xepperxelt was the most honest person on Cedar Commons. "And why is that somewhere you want to be?"

"I'm trying to find out what happened to my read-only."

Churryhoof had had vivid dreams before, but they always fell apart eventually. "Happened to your what?" she said through her second mouthful of kelexn, trying to get through it before waking up.

"Myrusit Wectusessin. My read-only."

"Oh, your brother." Denweld didn't know the Narathippin word, so she'd used the English, *burathar*. "What's a nice girl like you doing with a brother?"

"Not a nice girl, ma'am."

"I'll tell you what I told Councilman Wectusessin," Churryhoof said. The last bit of kelexn was smeared on her finger; she sucked it. "Myrusit is probably in a foster home in Fist space. You'll get him back after the war." *Or maybe he suffocated after being skipped into nowhere.*

"I have to go and rescue him," said Denweld.

"Why do you care so much about your 'brother'?" said Churryhoof. Denweld stammered and looked away and Churryhoof had her answer. "I see. Does your mother know about this?"

"It was her idea!" said Denweld. "Her and Mr. Wectusessin. To sort of...concentrate our genes."

Churryhoof felt pride, an emotion she'd thought the Navy had hammered out of her. Out here in the boonies, a few people were keeping the old traditions alive. The humans hadn't human-ized all the uhaltihaxl; not yet.

This was her opening. Churryhoof could use Denweld to split Mr. Wectusessin off from the rest of the council. She made her voice stern. "You'll never make it off-planet," she said. "You're under military occupation. We need to bunker down and form terror cells."

"Can't we just kill them?" said Denweld. "We could take their ship."

Churryhoof's groan introduced her to a whole new form of pain. "There's *only one ship?*"

"Only one landed. Might be more in orbit."

"How large is the occupying force?"

"It's pretty big, but I think most of it's cargo space."

"How many *people?* How many soldiers on the ground?"

"I don't know. Ten? They don't look like soldiers."

Ten enemy in one cargo ship. Fucking PSYOP. Mrs. Chen had nearly killed five hundred people to make ten scratch their heads. And Churryhoof was no great strategist herself. Thinking she could tie down a Fist of Joy task force by lying in a hospital bed and claiming to have started a fire. This op was a joke.

"What's wrong?" said Denweld.

"I...thought they'd send more," said Churryhoof.

"But that's good!" said Denweld. "We outnumber them. They don't even have good weapons. Just knives and stuff. We just... we've got nothing."

"You have weapons," said Churryhoof. "There are always weapons! You even have drones." She'd seen them through the window, buzzing in and out of the forest. She made a little flying-drone motion with her hand across her stomach, and barely felt the pain.

"Those are harvesters," said Denweld. "They're for cutting down trees."

"They're flying robots with laser cutters!" Churryhoof said. "You have electric knives for shaping wood. You use high-powered lasers to monogram cricket bats. Do I have to spell it out for you?"

"We don't *do* that," said Den. "That's why we have the Navy. I can't tell my mom to form a terror cell. You're trained for this. We need you."

They said a Navy uniform gained you respect from civilians, and that was true, but it was an anemic ten-percent-discount kind of background respect. Or else a respect based on fear: respect from cowards eager to turn the tables the moment you weakened. Everyone agreed that the Outreach needed a strong military, but up to now nobody had needed Hetselter Churryhoof in particular.

"Given your...family situation, I expect you have some clout with Councilman Wectusessin."

"He's my father," said Denweld, a child taking pleasure in a dirty word.

"Your *father*'s the reason I can't leave this room. Talk to him. Tell him if he wants the occupation force to leave, the city should put me in a safe house and give me control of the harvester drones."

"He'll say no," said Denweld.

"He'll say yes once it gets bad enough," said Churryhoof. "Just, stop being helpless, Den. Stop saying there's no weapons to be had. You're not out of weapons until Thrux takes your horns."

Denweld shook her head yes. "And find out how many people they actually have," said Churryhoof. "How many ships. I can kill ten people, but if there's another ten in orbit, we're all going to die afterwards."

"You talk so much about death," said Denweld. There was so much fear in her.

"You brought it up," said Churryhoof. *And you have no idea how close you came, Denweld Xepperxelt.*

Chapter 23

The Side

Rebecca Twice
Sour Candy

Becky met the enslaved doctors and sysadmins at *Sour Candy*'s entrance hatch and helped them up into the cargo deck. They were cargo and she was a slave driver. The cargo had cargo: big bags and suitcases brought on a smoothcart by a delivery guy who resembled a younger, healthier Crazy Rooroo.

The slaves were five ancient, slow-moving men and women with heavily decorated ownership bracelets. There was a mehi-peri, a corestin, a wirchak, a reptile-type species Becky didn't recognize, and someone whose species and gender was unknown because they were wearing a black Cametrean shame robe with a one-way veil. They grumbled at each other in D and ignored Becky the same way they ignored the delivery guy.

Becky loaded the suitcases onto the cargo lift. The delivery guy had also brought five cheap sleeping bags with weightlessness tethers, and left without waiting for a tip. By the time Becky and the sleeping bags had made it up the lift, *Sour Candy*'s latest passengers had taken over the cargo bay. Two of them were playing a game that involved slapping magnetic tiles onto the hull, and the Cametrean was snooping around, audibly disapproving of anything that looked modern.

Becky tethered the sleeping bags to the wall of the cargo hold and the wirchak woman kicked at the not-quite-cotton stuffing. "Gahaven *is* hoonar," she said.

"Do any of you speak English?" said Becky.

The mehi-peri hobbled over to the accident scene. "She says the bed is shit."

"You angry mouth!" said the reptile-man of unknown species. "She says the bed is irrational!"

"In English is that class of metaphor unused!" said the mehi-peri.

"Okay, folks," said Becky, feeling the situation slip out of her control. "My name is Becky and I am your cruise director. These are the beds I was given. In about eight shifts we'll hit Twist Station and we'll see what they have there. In the meantime, if there's anything that will make you more comfortable, I can make a quick trip to the Obahan before we leave."

Becky and Arun had just come back from Obahan, the Fist version of a chain convenience store. She was terrified of returning on her own with her tourist-level D, but more afraid of these folks finding out she knew what their bracelets meant. She'd hoped one of the English speakers would translate her offer, but the mehi-peri just squinted at her and said "Miss Becky?"

Oh, God, 'Miss Becky'. *Gone With The Wind* over here. "Yeah?"

"Aber greens. Get some aber greens."

"Aber greens, okay," said Becky. "Are you gonna cook them or...?"

"I suggest them for you," said the mehi-peri. You have a calcium deficiency."

"Vitamin B-12," said the reptile man, abandoning the magnet game for something much more fun. "Stopping you eating meat suddenly?"

"Genetic factors may be to blame," said the mehi-peri. He groped at Becky's face with his trunk, pulled her eyelid open and peered into it.

"Hey!" said Becky.

"High blood pressure," said the mehi-peri.

"Don't touch me!"

"I only give information about your health," said the mehi-peri. "Check your blood pressure. And make juice into the aber greens. Humans have trouble digesting cellulose."

"What the hell do you know about humans?" said Becky.

"I know it all!" said the mehi-peri. "I am the most gifted doctor! On a human I performed a second autopsy. Cyanide poisoning! The authorities missed it! Hah! The mighty human, brought low by mere cyanide!"

"Tithnal the Autopsy King!" said the reptile man. He put his arm around the mehi-peri's shoulder. "He once performing an autopsy and two hundred fifty-five times telling the story." Tithnal made a noise like a fart and struggled out from beneath the reptile's oppressive grip.

"For some tough love the time coming, Miss Becky!" said the reptile man. "Your health suffering because you living in space and eating treats every meal! Aber greens, raw! Your digestion cleansing!"

Over the comm, Yip-Goru's synthetic voice said "Hargoo nar *spaceship* goo hern-hara hesrurri hotga." There was a click and then a second click as thon immediately switched the comm back on. "Confidential to Becky: we're undocking. Gravity will return at point two gee to conserve energy."

"Okay, look, fellas," said Becky. "I don't know how we're going to do this, but when we get to Twist Station I'm going to free you. I'll cut off your bracelets and...sneak you into an old folks' home or something. I don't know. I welcome your feedback. I'm sure you've thought about this more than I have. But I am one hundred percent on your side. So...stop hassling me, you cranky bastards."

The lizard-man looked at Becky in a new but equally unflattering light. "Being you...American?" he said.

"Jesus," said Becky.

"Ho ho!" said Tithnal. He deepened his voice. "'Four score

and seven years ago!'"

Becky looked around for help that wasn't there. The Cametrean was sitting quietly in the lotus position, waiting for the gravity to go off. The wirchak and the corestin were pressing magnetic tiles against each other's face in a way that verged on flirty. Only the two doctors spoke English, and they were using English to mock her for doing the right thing.

Becky reached for the ladder. "I'll let you know when we heat up dinner," she said. "You can eat in the kitchen if you want." This had the same knee-slapping effect as telling the patrons of a restaurant that they were allowed to eat in the kitchen.

"Eat some calcium, young girl," Tithnal heckled as Becky fled abovedeck. "You'll feel better!"

Arun Sliver stood at the kitchen sink, putting a damp teabag into his mug for a second go-round. A pouch of Tetley's with the tamper seal ripped off sat nestled in a plastic Obahan bag next to Becky's luxury item: an undersized jar of off-brand peanut butter, whipped full of palm kernel oil to keep it from separating all these light-years from Earth.

Off in the bridge Becky could hear Yip-Goru going back and forth with station control. There was a huge jolt as the station released the docking clamps, but Arun's bendy legs absorbed it and he screwed the cap onto his teacup. Becky said "Hey, Arun," and then he turned around. It was the first time Becky had seen him smile.

"Glad to have some real doctors on board," he said. Two circular bandages covered the vampire wounds in his neck where the medical chamber had cycled the alcohol out of his blood.

"Listen," said Becky, "can I talk to you, human to human?"

"Oh," said Arun, diagnosing her wet cheeks. "I suppose you think I let the side down during the vote on the slaves." As if there were only one side. He snapped the teacup into the hot-water cavity.

"Yeah, I do, actually!" said Becky.

"You must understand. The Fist of Joy is twenty-six species. That's twenty-six ways for people to fall ill and twenty-six ways for computers to crash. They had to train generalists. They can't keep two dozen doctors on every space station in case someone gets an air bladder infection."

"I know why they do it," said Becky. "I just don't care."

The angle of gravity took a sharp turn downwards from the perpendicular as *Sour Candy* pulled out of Spark Station. The peanut butter and the tea bags slid down the counter, and Becky stumbled and fell, but by the time her knee glanced the deck there was no gravity at all, and she ricocheted off what had been the floor.

Arun grabbed a handhold and reached out to stop Becky's caroming. "Becks," he said in a chummy way, and when Becky grimaced he overcompensated and went over to "Rebecca" before returning to his starting point.

"Becky, we won the war. There are no more slaves. Just these old geezers who can't make it in private practice. Let's be nice to them for a few years and they'll die out naturally."

"I can't do this, Arun," said Becky. "Just, the looks on their faces, and they *made fun of me* for giving a damn!"

"This is not America," Arun said with zero sympathy. "You must adjust. You live here now."

"I don't! I can't."

"You had a job with a security brand, and you left in a way that made the brand look bad. You're done, love. Consider how I might know this." The singularity pistol peeked out of Arun's hip holster. He'd worn it openly out on the station. It wasn't illegal here.

"Since we've chosen a life of crime, we can visit the Outreach now and again." Arun slurped his tea and winced; the water was too hot. "But you can't go back. You must adjust."

Becky had been eight years old when GWII ended. She remembered a special church service, candles, "Down by the Riverside". Afterwards had come a warm feeling that Becky had drawn on as far as her college years, that there *was* now only one side. That the Fist and the Outreach were now morally the same, and there was no longer any reason to go to war.

But the sides *weren't* the same; the Outreach was better. There were still problems, but humans and uhaltihaxl had spent hundreds of years reckoning with the horror of being owned and the sin of owning. Now Becky was trapped in this evil realm where modern corporations put people on balance sheets and wrote off their depreciation.

The Fist of Joy hadn't learned the lesson of the second war. Their long reckoning hadn't even started. Now another war was coming, and Becky's new home was going to lose this one, too.

The first sleep shift after leaving Spark Station, Becky's relationship with the Chief advanced to the moving-in-together stage. At the Chief's invitation, Becky brought her Obahan bag into her girlfriend's quarters and didn't come out.

They made out through the new episode of *The Down Under Crew* and then the Chief put the lie to stereotypes of inferior Fist electronics by slipping on a vibrating wetglove that approximated the experience of being gang-banged by an Olympic women's netball team. She held Becky down on the bed in the lowered gravity and with gentle circular motions worked the glove into every relevant nook and cranny while firmly kissing Becky's belly button.

When Becky limply offered to reciprocate, the Chief just started kissing her, big hungry kisses from her oddly-shaped mouth, combined with a cuddle-hug that filled Becky with dread precisely because it was so well designed to make her feel protected and loved.

Becky couldn't get Kol's cruel timetable out of her mind: fifty shifts, the pages falling to the floor like a cartoon calendar. So far everything was proceeding on schedule. But nothing said Becky had to wait it out and become a sad-sack like Kol. She could flip the script.

Every minute Becky spent in enemy space showed her that the Fist of Joy just didn't understand marketing. The Obahan stocked everything twenty-six spacefaring species might need, but it wasn't presented attractively or in any coherent way. Becky had sat outside counting while Arun queued for a meat smoothie next door, and found that twenty percent of Obahan customers left without buying anything.

There was a lot of money here, just waiting for a smart consultant to pick it up. It would be honest work, enough to support a family. Becky and the Chief could live on a planet like a normal couple, with the kidnapping-hostage thing blurring over time into a naughty meet-cute. "You know, your mom used to be a *pirate!*"

Becky recalled her first-kiss courage. "I want to ask you something," she said.

The Chief misunderstood stupendously. She smiled and looked Becky in the eyes and said with rehearsed diction: "I love you, Becky." And that was the moment Becky knew it was over. She'd just *said* it. No struggle, no questioning. The Chief found the syntax tricky but the emotion was simple and easy. She'd memorized 'I love you' in every language. She'd said it to Kol, and to however many between Kol and Becky.

Becky could understand a fling, or a lie, or trying out 'I love you' to see how it sounded, but this was terrifying sincerity. The Chief *did* love Becky, more than anything. She would do anything Becky wanted. Until they made it to the corestin homeworld, or whatever destination came after that, and some other hot-assed humanoid caught the Chief's eye.

The Chief hadn't wanted the wetglove because she already knew what it was like to cum that way. She only loved new things, and Becky's newness was slipping away. You couldn't flip that script. Asking the Chief to settle down was like throwing her in jail. She'd go quietly, probably, but before long she'd be mapping out escape routes.

Well, Becky knew when a relationship was over. She usually knew it before the other girl did. She forced a smile and looked the Chief in the eye and said, "Good night."

"To sleep well," said the Chief. She was asleep in six seconds, her every limb still wrapped around Becky's body. Becky struggled free and the Chief just muttered in her sexy native language.

Sleeping on the floor was better, emotionally and practically. Becky had to get up in a couple hours for Yip-Goru's weird secret meeting. She lay on her side and sipped water from a bag and looked out the porthole at the stars, thinking about the life she'd given up, about the enslaved senior citizens down in the cargo hold, wishing the universe would just be not-fucked-up enough that she could fix any of this.

She didn't remember falling asleep but now she saw a gas giant hanging in the porthole. A green and orange crescent of sherbet swirled together in nature's majestic display of tackiness. *Sour Candy* had skipped and it was time to get up. Becky's stomach moved uncomfortably through the reduced gravity as she twisted and kicked her feet up to put her slippers back on. Going barefoot on *Sour Candy* was like having a death wish plus a dirty-feet wish.

The secret meeting was being held down-ladder on the bridge, where Yip-Goru apparently lived. In a compromise for the sake of the humans, the rre had turned on the running lights and it was possible to walk around the consoles without banging your knees.

Arun Sliver sat in what Becky had thought of as the Chief's chair, leaning forward and murmuring with Yip-Goru. Becky ahemed and Arun sat up and said "You're late."

"Let's cut to the chase," said Yip-Goru. "There are three of us. Three to two. We outnumber them."

"That's what I told you," said Becky. "On Cedar Commons. Like, a week ago. Thanks for joining up with Team Outreach, now that it's too late."

"There is no Team Outreach," said Yip-Goru. "The Outreach is a joke. We are three rational individuals with a mutual interest in not being shot by some trigger-happy humanoid because we're on the wrong side of a border."

"You should have thought of that before you voted to take us fifty thousand light-years into Fist space!"

"Becky makes a good point," said Arun.

"I have a plan," said Yip-Goru. "Secret plan for a secret

meeting. Before I reveal my plan, I need to make sure you two will vote for it when I bring it up."

"You, made a secret plan," Arun said in disbelief.

The lights inside Yip-Goru's suit refracted at Becky. "Arun thinks I'm a coward."

"I don't think you're a coward."

"A coward doesn't join a smuggling operation, does thon?"

"I know you're no coward, mate. Tell me your plan."

"I don't want to die, is all. Yip-Goru-Toco died. I was there for it. Yip-Goru is not going to die! So a kiloshift ago, I bought a safe house, in case I was in Fist space when the war happened." Yip-Goru's cheap vocalizer made everything thon said sound like a ransom note.

"Wait wait wait," said Becky. "A kiloshift ago? How did you know?"

"I predicted the war," said Yip-Goru. Becky glanced at Arun: seriously?

"Yip-Goru predicted this ages ago," he said. "Credit where due."

"How do you predict a war?" Wars started for good reasons that everyone could see coming, like the second war. Or they started from random accidents, like the first war, and probably this one.

"Buckle up, buttercup," said Yip-Goru, a classic crackpot, eager to share. "Every five Terran years, we have our general elections, right? And you vote, I'm guessing, weak sauce Dem-Soc."

Becky's family had been proudly Dem-Soc since before there was an Outreach Parliament. "That's none of your business," she said.

"And in the run-up, the entire Outreach starts screaming for blood. It's time to get tough on the Fist. Take the gloves off. The party in power is coddling the enemy, but the opposition's willing to make the tough decisions. Right?"

"It's not that bad," said Becky.

"Maybe not in *Los Angeles*," said Yip-Goru.

"What's that supposed to mean?"

"*Meanwhile,*" Arun said, interrupting to make peace, "the Fist renegotiates its overall military posture every three kiloshifts. That's approximately three Terran years. That's when everyone over here has *their* chance to demand *their* government get tough on the nasty humans and their uhalti pets and their rre attack dogs."

"Woof, woof," said Yip-Goru.

"Most of the time this is just a bit of harmless fun," said Arun, "but every fifteen years or so, the cycles line up, and we actually have to go to war."

"That explains the last two wars," said Yip-Goru. "And this one, and the next one, and so on forever."

Becky felt the sinking feeling of not being able to spot the obvious flaw in the conspiracy theory. "Did you *tell* anybody about this?"

"I tell everybody!" said Yip-Goru. "Nobody listens."

"'Cause if this was true, we could work with the Fist," said Becky. "Just stagger the elections."

"If we were smart enough to do that, we'd be smart enough to not have the wars," said Arun.

"And because we're not smart enough, I bought the safe house. Hollowed-out asteroid, deep in Fist space, fully supplied. We just have to make it there. And the corestin homeworld is on the way, which is why I voted for a job Becky thinks is 'evil'."

Arun folded his arms. "How'd you afford a posh place like that?"

"I don't have full ownership," said Yip-Goru. "It's a time-share."

"Time-share on a safe house. Sad to say you got ripped off, mate."

"No, no," said Yip-Goru. "I went through a very reputable broker."

"You can't go time-share on a bloody safe house!"

"Yeah, no way to send quality signals in that kind of market," said Becky.

"This fella," said Yip-Goru, "she does asteroids for big names. I happen to know she does the safe houses for Crazy Rooroo's operation."

"Have you actually been there?" said Arun.

"Did I leave the ship for fifty shifts and then come back?" said Yip-Goru. "No, I haven't been there."

"Let's suppose it exists," said Arun. "What if we get there and one of the other owners is using it? You know, as might happen during a war?"

"We share it?" Becky suggested hopefully.

"No, no, we kick them out!" said Yip-Goru.

"So at any given time your asteroid is occupied by whoever's the hardest bastard. That is the opposite of a safe house. That is a dangerous house."

"The asteroid is our best option," said Yip-Goru.

"That says more about our shit options than any salutary thinking on your part."

"I told you my secret plan!" whined the ransom-note voice. "You have to vote for it!"

Arun got off the chair and squatted next to the rre. "Tell *you* a secret, mate," he said.

"What?"

"You're a crap negotiator." Arun dramatically turned and left the bridge, but Becky had left ahead of him and collared him in the kitchen.

"How quickly can you teach me Trade Standard D?" Becky asked.

Arun wasn't thrilled. "You *hogana* from the Chief," he said, in D.

"I need to *hogana* faster," said Becky. "I have to get out of here. I can't go live inside an asteroid for who knows how long."

"It's the same as living in a spacecraft," said Arun.

"I need to leave the *crew*," said Becky.

"Leave the crew?" Arun briefly seemed to believe this was impossible, as though *Sour Candy* were a cursed ghost ship. "Oh, I see. The asteroid's twenty shifts out. By the time we get there..." He glanced upladder, towards the Chief's quarters. "Look," he added, "I tease Yip-Goru, but you can see thon's smart. There'll be five people in that asteroid, max. I can kill five if I have surprise. And it's just 'til the war's over."

"What if you didn't have to kill anybody?" said Becky.

Crazy Rooroo had flatly rejected this lifestyle change, but Arun, whose livelihood was more closely tied to manslaughter, seemed open. "Are you wistfully saying it would be nice, or is there a way to make it happen?"

"I have my own secret plan," said Becky. "It involves you and me leaving together."

"Why me?" said Arun.

"I'll need a bodyguard," said Becky. "Until the war's over, like you said. You just have to look tough, and show me how the Fist works. Maybe some light shoving."

"I'm listening," said Arun, and Becky had him.

Chapter 24

Pain Debt

Captain Styrqot
Seeder Commons

Sometimes the worst thing the enemy can do to you is surrender. Styrqot was thinking of issuing a small book of such maxims, called *The Paradoxes of War.* He was aware that this was a daydream he used as a way of escaping his problems, and that the one really good paradox he had encountered was the one that had created the problem he wanted to escape. This was a paradox, but not a Paradox of War.

The slippery tactic of surrender had transformed the population of Chaiktan from a hated enemy to the backslapping Chamber-of-Commerce types Styrqot dealt with in peacetime. Styrqot did not want to have Ois Treaty obligations to these people. He wanted to negotiate a load of fruit from them and get out.

The Bronze Age Bastards were here to infiltrate the putative facility and capture the secrets of the energy-suppressing plants. As an occupying force, they weren't worth a slab of frozen piss. Byrno had sent a message back into Fist space asking for assistance, but Seeder Commons was shaping up to be the least important planet in the war. There were no magic trees. That uhalti kid had made it all up. No one was coming to help them.

Styrqot sat in the mayor's office, looking out onto the town square. The sky was hazy, but the fire on the other side of the planet was long since out. "Let's wreck their elevator and leave," he told Vec. "Let them occupy themselves."

Vec was eating a raw fish she'd caught in a lake. "We need to know what happened to the magic trees," she said, in a singsong voice.

"I don't think there are any magic trees," said Styrqot.

"You don't *think*? I would love to see your so-called civilization collapse because you overlooked the weapon that destroyed it. But my fellas don't get paid until we *know* what happened here. If there are no magic trees, we need to find out how the rumor got started."

Styrqot rummaged through the mayor's desk once again, looking for nothing. "It's misinformation," he said. "I mean, we're calling them 'magic trees' because the whole thing sounds ridiculous. Chaiktan is a front for something that never existed."

"Ms. Rebecca Twice knows," said Vec. "The carpenters caught her. She set off the nukes. She will explain why, to my knife."

"You can't torture an uhaltihaxl," said Styrqot. "It's physically impossible!"

"Of course you can," said Vec. She sucked the fish blood off her fingers. "You torture someone else, and you make the uhalti watch."

Styrqot's stomach sank to new lows. "She'll just tell you what you want to hear."

"Yes," said Vec. "I want to hear what I want to hear."

So they did it, that night, in a building the Bronze Age Bastards had found and secured for the purpose. The branding on the front door said "1-2-3 Quick Loan and Wire Transfer". Inside were three cubicles made of shatterproof glass, a place for loan sharks to run their evil trade, safe from their customers on the other side of the glass. It seemed the Bastards would use high technology so long as it could be explained in simple terms, like "glass that won't break even when someone's life depends on breaking it".

Styrqot could have sat the whole thing out, and he should have. He should have gone back to *Small but Sharp* where Byrno was sleeping and gunned the motivators until it was safe to skip far away. But he felt that if Ms. Rebecca Twice had to watch what was happening, he was honor-bound to watch as well.

Vec had claimed the middle cubicle. When Styrqot entered she was duct-taping a struggling Councilman Kemrush Wectusessin to a rolling office chair. The Bastards herded the other members of Chaiktan's city council into one of the adjacent cubicles. Another of them presented Styrqot with Ms. Rebecca Twice.

Styrqot marched the uhalti woman with the human name ahead of him into the last unoccupied cubicle. The uhalti leaned forward and rested the side of her face against the shatterproof glass that separated their cubicle from Vec's. She seemed about to pass out, and they hadn't even started.

"I'm a Navy veteran," Mr. Kemrush Wectusessin said, looking straight ahead at nothing. "I took SERE training. You'll never get me to talk."

"I don't want you to talk," said Vec. To prove her point she squeezed some glue from a tube onto her plastic glove and smeared her fingers over the man's lips. "I want *them* to talk." She swept her hand around to cover the other two cubicles.

Mr. Kemrush Wectusessin tried to spit out the glue, but he couldn't spit anymore. Vec teased her gluey fingers near his nostrils. Then she removed her sticky glove and dropped it on the floor.

Vec activated the electronic speaker a loan shark would use to communicate with his victims. "Let's avoid a painful misunderstanding!" she said to the assembled prisoners. "There's only one thing I need to know: what is the purpose of the secret research installation?" Then she took out the knife she'd used to fillet the fish in the mayor's office. "Has anyone seen one of these before?" she asked.

"I didn't want to do this," Styrqot told Ms. Rebecca Twice. "I said we should leave." She just stared blankly at Mr. Kemrush Wectusessin. What could Styrqot do? He couldn't force her to acknowledge him. He could force her to watch, but she was already watching.

Mr. Kemrush Wectusessin snorted, breathing as deeply as he could with his chest bound up in the duct tape. Vec held his head in place and carefully drew a square on his cheek with her knife. She stopped halfway through and looked again at Ms. Rebecca Twice, who didn't acknowledge.

So Vec completed the square, as perfect as if she'd used a straightedge. She pried out a little bar of skin and muscle and blood, like a pastry from a pan; pulled it out expertly balanced on her blade, and she flipped it onto the white plastic counter where the money changed hands.

Any normal person would by now be screaming through the strange new hole in their mouth, but the uhaltihaxl only quivered and grunted. There was no pain, only terror. Through the cross-section of his head Styrqot could see the man's teeth, strange white shapes slowly being painted in with blood.

Vec hit the button again, and this time she was looking at the humans and the rre who made up Chaiktan's city council. "Any ideas?" she said. "Does anyone have anything? Maybe a bunch of experts coming in, acting like they own the place?"

Two of the humans were weeping. The rre was silent, an abstract shape disconnected from reality. The human with the beard pounded on the unbreakable glass, yelling something about the Outreach Navy, but two panes separated Styrqot from the information, and despite her invitation Vec didn't seem to be listening.

She picked up a pair of pliers she'd taken from a tool shop along with the glue. With the other hand she pinched Mr. Kemrush Wectusessin's nostrils shut. He struggled and took a wheezing breath through the hole in his face, and that was enough for Vec to get the pliers in.

Styrqot saw that his own hand was pressed against the glass. He saw Ms. Rebecca Twice lick her dry lips, finally reacting. Vec rocked the pliers back and forth, and with a twist and a pull, she yanked out one of the bloodstained teeth.

Styrqot knew that would happen. But it was the way she *looked* at the tooth, appraising it. Styrqot bolted from his cubicle and hammered on Vec's. One of the Bastards squeezed through the door he'd left through and held Ms. Rebecca Twice firmly by the shoulders. Vec slid her door open and walked outside to meet Styrqot. "Yes?" she said, in A. She brandished the bloody tooth at him, childishly. Styrqot refused to flinch.

"Not one word, Vec," he said. "She did not say one fucking word. What did you think you would accomplish with this stunt? This is *illegal.* How am I supposed to explain to my son what I did in the war?"

Vec shut the door behind her, leaving a red smudge on the glass. Styrqot was afraid she would start licking the blood off her hands. "Why tell him anything?" she said. "Children don't need to know what goes on in the real world." She squeezed open a leather envelope full of sand, and dropped the tooth inside.

Now three Bastards were escorting the uhaltihaxl doctor and a human dentist into the middle cubicle. Styrqot had insisted on this. Torture was one thing; murder quite another.

"Oh, by the way," Vec added. "I got the information we need. From the humans." She gave a nasty little smile. "Ms. Rebecca Twice does not work for Trellis. She's Navy. Her real name is Commander Curryhu."

"Oh, let me tell you something interesting," said Styrqot. "You always have so much wisdom, Vec, so much advice to give. Let me tell you a fact based on my dealings with Outreach craftsmen. If we leave right now, we *might* make it off this planet alive."

"What are you talking about?" Inside the middle cubicle, Mr. Kemrush Wectusessin had finally started screaming.

"Those humans who gave you your precious information?" said Styrqot. "After what you just did, they want us dead. I doubt you noticed, because so very many people want you dead already."

"Those people are locked up," said Vec. "What they want doesn't matter."

"Shut up, shut up," said Styrqot. "Just stop talking. You live in the past. Those people have communication devices embedded in their skulls! Everyone in Chaiktan knows what you did. There's 3-video. They'll use it in our war-crimes trial."

"Trial?" said Vec, in the quiet tones of a concerned friend. "You're acting like we're going to lose this war."

"There is *evidence!*"

"There is evidence of a lot of things!" said Vec. "In the end, we are the ones who will decide which evidence matters!"

Styrqot flipped on his own communication device. "Styrqot to Byrno!" It would take a moment to wake up the pilot.

"Tell him to run an intelligence report on this Curryhu," said Vec, uninterested in the topic of her own supreme stupidity and arrogance.

"Stop talking," said Styrqot. "Stop *doing*. I am trying to clean up your mess."

"Byrno here."

"Warm the elevator hookup and start pulling potential. We are leaving now."

"Uh, just a reminder sir? We can't leave without completing the mission." Byrno's voice oozed the condescension of the full-time military man. Styrqot suppressed his rage. It's not personal, it's business. Everyone's out to get the best deal for themselves.

"The mission is complete, I assure you," he said. "See if you find anything in the intelligence database about a Navy officer, Commander Curryhu."

"How is that spelled, sir?"

"I don't know. Sound it. Styrqot out."

"I'm going to talk to your prisoners," Styrqot told Vec. He was so calm, in charge of everything. He slipped the comm back into his pocket. "I'm going to make them a deal. We will take *their* prisoner, the hated Curryhu, and we will leave their planet and never come back. They will take this deal. Do you know why? Because they're not idiots."

"There are other undercover agents besides Curryhu," said Vec. "I can feel it."

"Curryhu is the one I can get," said Styrqot. "If you want more, you're free to stay here and follow your feelings. Make some more *videos*. I don't think you'll last one shift."

Styrqot walked a few steps and unlocked the clear glass cubicle where the Bastards held the humans and the rre. Why were there locks on these doors? What sick mind locks its employees in their place of work? Only a brand would do something so pointlessly cruel.

Styrqot slid the door open and stood blocking the doorway. He was a man of business, like them, not like the brutes who had pushed them in here, who had done...this. He was appalled by Vec's behavior. It made him physically ill. It would not happen again. He was a family man himself. He only regretted that it had taken such drastic measures to get them to come clean about Commander Curryhu.

He took a breath and parted his beak slightly to show a smile full of sorrow and sympathy. The Chaiktan city council were not free of the thugs, yet; but they could be, very soon. It would be the simplest thing in the world. All they had to do was give him something to take back to his superiors. Anything would do, really.

Churryhoof
1-2-3 Quick Loan, Cedar Commons

Churryhoof stood helpless with her ribs taped up and her face pressed against a pane of glass. Insanity was sinking in to Councilman Wectusessin's eyes, and once the torture stopped, the pain would flow into the channels the insanity was cutting.

She could stop the cut. She could tell a lie about the supposed research station. But the Fist wanted one specific lie. They were fishing for the other half of a puzzle-locket which the late Mrs. Chen had tossed into their intelligence stream.

If she could talk to the city council, they could all agree on a lie. They were right over there! Even if it didn't match what Vec and Styrqot were expecting, a unified lie would stop the torture. It would be so believable, because the city council all hated Churryhoof, and would never agree with her on anything, so the plan was hopeless. She didn't even have their contact information. The only person on this planet who she could call was

Incoming call from Denweld Xepperxelt.

"Churryhoof here," she subvocalized, and just afterwards she saw Jiankang Nzeme's screaming mouth move in a way that also said "Churryhoof". He was selling her out.

"Ma'am?" came the voice through her terminal. "I...?" She made some sounds that weren't even sobs. Churryhoof pictured her curled up on the floor of her flat, a little girl who has just discovered there is more than one kind of pain debt. "I...I need to know how to kill somebody."

You strangle them, came into Churryhoof's mind, but she didn't let it out over the comm. "I told you, Den," she subvocalized, keeping all kindness out of her voice. "You kill somebody by giving me control of the harvester drones."

"They don't trust you!" said Den. "You brought the bad guys here! They're...right now!"

"Don't go through the council. Talk to the people who actually operate the drones. Tell them to subordinate the drones to my terminal. I will handle this, Den. This is my job."

"I have to do this myself, I don't want to but I have to because it hurts so bad."

Churryhoof kept her expression blank. These were the dead eyes that met Councilman Wectusessin's as he was tortured. This was the slack face she would have when her consciousness was distributed across seven flying robots. An egenu grabbed her by the shoulder and didn't move her, so she didn't move.

"Do you know something, Den?" she subvocalized. "Six percent of uhalti recruits can't bring themselves to kill in a real combat situation. That's people who choose to enlist and go through training. Everything we can do to get them to pull the trigger when the time comes. Six percent would rather die and let their buddies die. They don't tell you this, but you hear it from someone and then you always wonder if you're in that six percent. You understand, Den? You're not a killer. Not being a killer is *normal*. Don't throw that away because you want to kill right now."

"How do I know you're not six percent?" said Den. "Have you ever killed anyone?"

"Yes." Churryhoof's thumbs pushed against a vanished throat.

"Who?"

"I killed a human," she said. The truth sounded so good.

Outside, Vec and Styrqot were arguing in Trade Standard A. they were saying 'Churryhoof'. They were saying it a lot. Churryhoof kept her jaw loose, her eyes blank, her shoulder limp under the hand of the egenu guard.

"Okay," said Den at last. "My mom and me will talk to the lumberjacks."

"Quickly, Den," said Churryhoof. "They're going to hurt me next." And Churryhoof stood there, waiting in line for torture, watching Dr. Sempestwinku and a human in a surgical mask fight over who should treat Councilman Wectusessin's disfigured face. Watching Mr. Nzeme use his only remaining power over the woman who'd taken his son: handing her over to the coward Styrqot and the sadist Vec. And then the torture began: the egenu with the hand on her shoulder started making small talk.

"The chief say you not the private security after all," she said in lousy D. Churryhoof said nothing. "They say you the Navy."

"What if I am?" said Churryhoof, looking straight ahead. "What are you going to do? Pull my teeth out through my cheek?"

"Hey, I not make the rules," said the egenu.

Captain Styrqot
Seeder Commons

Dawn was coming, and the streetlights of the ruined city-ship were getting the message. Styrqot jumped like a startled animal every time a light shut off, and Vec mocked him for it.

Styrqot tried to think tactically. Reduce the whole thing to dots on a 2-map. He and Vec surrounded—flanked was the word—one of the Bronze Age Bastards, who pushed a cheap Outreach smoothchair down the early-morning avenue. Commander Curryhu, who after strenuous negotiations everyone had agreed to treat as the prize of this operation, sat in the smoothchair. Curryhu was catatonic, not having responded to Styrqot's hand-waving or Vec's slaps. Styrqot wondered how she had lost her horn. It looked painful. He imagined his beak being snapped off. He thought of the tooth.

Tactics, tactics. Behind Styrqot was another Bastard handling the hostages—the three human members of the city council, their hands bound with plastic zip-ties. Behind him, a third Bastard carrying the rre hostage. Tip-Iye-Nett-Zig had been extracted from thons suit and sedated by immersion in a plastic container full of alcohol. A volume of Terran bourbon! That alone would have paid for this trip.

Two Bastards were stationed on the other side of the planet, investigating the nonexistent research station and the now obviously non-magical trees. One Bastard was with Byrno at *Small but Sharp*, guarding the space elevator. The space elevator, visible from here but a brisk walk if you couldn't fly. The three Bastards not yet accounted for in this inventory fanned out around the procession, glancing around like tourists in a bad neighborhood. And Styrqot the only one with a gun.

What were the obstacles? Snipers, on the higher levels of the city-ship, possibly on the space elevator itself. At *Small but Sharp*, the main obstacle would be convincing Vec not to kill the hostages. *That's later. Survive this now.*

Styrqot's communicator crackled. "Byrno to Styrqot."

Styrqot took it out of his chest pocket and flipped it open, keeping his attention on the best place to point his singularity pistol. "Styrqot."

"There is nobody named Curryhu in the Outreach Navy," said Byrno. "I did find a Commander Churryhoof who was near this planet recently."

"Interesting but irrelevant. Can we discuss this once we get to the ship?"

"We discuss it now," said Byrno. "Here's the thing: your Churryhoof is an expert pilot. She was Master of Drone on *What is to be Done?*."

Styrqot glanced at the uhalti in the smoothchair. She had been nonresponsive since the tooth extraction. A hopore doctor would have said *pu gare beheitukea*, 'her mind went somewhere else.' But where, exactly, had it gone? A bored secretary in an Outreach branch office wouldn't look much different playing a game in her *terminal!*

Whatever Byrno said next was drowned out by a *whir-thump-splat!*. Some kind of viscous liquid plopped into Styrqot's trouser leg and he looked over to see a tree standing between him and Vec, right where the Bastard pushing the smoothchair had been standing.

The tree was very tall, it had been stripped of leaves, and *fuck* it just *crushed* that guy, and at the top of the tree was a hovering robot, safety-green, manipulating the tree like a puppet with some kind of articulated harness and up there were three more robots each with—

"Kill the uhalti!" Styrqot screamed. He leveled his pistol at Curryhu/Churryhoof and the butt end of the tree slammed into his side, throwing him across the avenue into the wall of a shop. His body armor saved his life twice: once from the initial impact, and again a millishift later when he was able to stand up and take the drone's second attack in the chest instead of getting his head caved in. The wooden staff crushed him against the wall and pulled back for a third strike.

Styrqot ran. Something inside him had torn and was leaking. A whirlwind of hardwood clubs surrounded the drone pilot in her smoothchair. The Bastards had their knives out and were darting back and forth, hunting for an opening. Styrqot's gun and communicator were in there. So were Vec and the chair-pusher, two puddles of green vomit that had once been people.

Someone really ought to kill the hostages. Styrqot darted into an alleyway, where the drone couldn't follow. It hurt to breathe. He heard the grinding whine of the machine trying to gain enough altitude to track him.

There was an office here, on the ground floor. The window was covered with a heavy anti-theft chain wire. The door was flimsy plywood. Styrqot bashed the door with his increasingly useless body and fell through into the office. They couldn't get you indoors, not without missiles.

There were desks here, and a vinyl banner that was upside-down if you were lying on the floor, but Styrqot could recognize the famous English proverb: "Engage With Your Favorite Brands!"

Footsteps. Styrqot scuttled away from the door and tried not to cough and coughed anyway. A young uhaltihaxl girl stood in the shattered doorway. She held an human-sized industrial nail gun in both hands: one hand wrapped around the grip, the other propping up the barrel by the air compressor. Tears streamed down her face. She was too young to be a soldier, too old to be Churryhoof's daughter. She moved in and pointed the gun at Styrqot.

Styrqot tried to put his hands up and couldn't. "I have a son," he said, in Trade Standard D. "About your age." Inside his chest his disconnected organs were migrating, helpless against gravity. "Please."

The uhalti girl stooped over Styrqot's body and looked in his eyes. One of her tears spattered on his chin. She didn't speak D. They only taught kids Narathippin and English. Styrqot tried to think of the words that would reach her. He tried to take one more breath.

The uhalti girl butted the nail gun against Styrqot's forehead. "I'm sorry about your son," she whispered, in perfect D. Then she pressed her finger onto the trigger, and as far as Styrqot knew, she never took it off again.

Chapter 25

Canon

Dwap-Jac-Dac-Tia-Sunlight
Arzil, outside the Cametrean monastery

I n their field of imported dirt the fans of Cametre grew a bushy plant with flat leaves: the corestin version of quenny syncweed. Each row of the plant was shorter than the one behind it, planted later, to be harvested later. The curious fans that surrounded Dwap-Jac-Dac-Tia-Sunshine idly pulled leaves off the mature plants and chewed them to maintain their shared hallucination in which the universe made sense.

There was some loose relationship between the Cametreans' costumes and the jobs they did at the monastery. The fan dressed as a cop had appointed herself customs inspector and was going through Dwap-Jac-Dac-Tia-Sunlight's cargo nets, separating the contents into two piles: things that existed in Cametre continuity and things that did not.

The sun abruptly set, and a corestin dressed in a manual-labor overall came through with a handheld hose, watering down the plants and anyone unfortunate enough to be standing nearby. Warrant Officer Ingridsdotter sat on the ground a few meters away, reading a crinkly comic-book pamphlet she'd taken from the checkpoint. Tellpesh was having some fun taunting the customs officer.

"Heat-sealed food in metal tin exists as per *Darker than Anticipated*," said the customs officer. "Heat-sealed food in metal bag exists as per same. Electric lantern exists," and it was a good thing it did, because she set it down on the ground and switched it on to continue the inspection. "This..." she held a sonic sanitizer up to the lantern light. "Unknown. Does not exist." She tossed the sanitizer into the second pile.

"Hey, hey, you," said Tellpesh. "Do uhaltihaxl exist?"

The fan glared at her. "Everyone exists."

"Tellpesh, stop it," said Dwap-Jac-Dac-Tia-Sunlight. Ten sets of syncweed-dazed corestin eyes followed the predator as she walked around piles of stolen prison equipment to the seated uhalti. "Get back to the comm."

Tellpesh was responsible for a Fist military communicator taken from the pocket of a dead prison guard. She'd disabled it with a tiny multitool taken from a different dead guard, and since their arrival on Arzil she'd been working on getting it to pick up Fist military transmissions without activating its tracking beacon.

"Yessaer," said Tellpesh. She took the comm and the multitool from the pocket of her ill-fitting and increasingly implausible guard uniform, and went to work, talking to herself and cursing. After about ten minutes the comm popped onto their Outreach ad hoc military network, and Tellpesh said "Try it now, aer."

Dwap-Jac-Dac-Tia-Sunlight coupled the comm to thons terminal and said "Testing." The comm was silent.

"Shit," said Tellpesh. "Sorry about that, aer." Three more minutes of work. "Try it again, aer."

"Testing!" said the comm. The customs inspector's ears twitched and she whipped her skull around like it was on a rubber band. "Hey!" In three long steps the fan in the cop outfit stood over Tellpesh and snatched the communicator out of her hand.

"Where's the wire? You can't send voices to a machine if there's no connecting wire!" She waved the comm in Tellpesh's face. "Where's the wire, huh?"

Tellpesh's D was very poor and she wasn't following any of this. "Whoa, whoa, calm the fuck down, fella," she said in

Narathippin. She slapped the custom inspector's hand away from her face. "What the fuck."

"Ahem," said Dwap-Jac-Dac-Tia-Sunlight through the communicator. "If you'll recall, ma'am, in *The Kind Permission*, two characters were able to telepathically communicate across the entire galaxy, without the use of a wire. Why can't I communicate telepathically with a machine that's right here?"

The customs inspector pulled herself up to her full height and looked into the communicator as though she had finally found a worthy opponent. "I think you'll find," she said sarcastically, "that in *Doing Without Cametre*, the events of *The Kind Permission* were revealed to have been a *dream sequence*? Yeah? I thought so."

The quenny abbot had never been far away and now he intervened. He gently pried the comm out of the customs inspector's hand. "No, boss, this thing needs to stop talking, boss," said the customs inspector, as though the abbot were holding a live grenade. "No talking without a wire!"

"Mechspeech is possible," said the abbot. He held the communicator close to his stillsuit. "Radisik the Community-Minded Robot had mechspeech. What's impossible is that with no wire, mechspeech should convey the thoughts of this surk here. But everyone knows that animals can't talk, so the point is moot." The abbot gave Sunlight an ironic glance. "Walk with me, Precedent," he said. "Something tells me we will be retconning this entire incident as a dream sequence."

They walked along the edge of the field towards the monastery buildings. Sunlight once again resigned herself to copying the slow pace of a humanoid. Now there was a gap in the syncweed, an empty row that had just been harvested, and beyond it, new seedlings tasting the short desert night.

A teenage fan dressed as a scientist, perhaps the astronomer from *Don't Go Out There*, rushed up and handed the abbot a tattered plastic scroll. The abbot muttered "Thank you" in Mirret and didn't open the scroll. "It's a poor kind of hospitality we can offer you, Precedent," he said instead. "You won't be able to enter any of the buildings."

"Why not?" This was Tia's third visit to a Zone of Reality, and nothing had been off-limits before.

"You will not fit through the doors," said the abbot. "I'll have the fans set up a tent for you."

"That's very kind."

Now the abbot expressed interest in the plastic scroll. "I had this brought from the litstash hardvault," he said, "to show you what we risk by helping you." Holding one end of the scroll awkwardly in the same hand that held the stolen Fist communicator, the abbot tugged one end of the scroll to reveal a reproduction of a painting.

Dwap-Jac-Dac-Tia-Sunlight could see the shapes but not the colors. The painting showed a rocket-propelled spacecraft poised in launch position. Tiny quenny figures were frozen in motion, scampering up and down gantries that surrounded but could not contain the enormous machine.

For civilians, that sleek phallic shape was a skeuomorphism. On every planet it signified space travel, even in the modern era of motivators and skip engines. But soldiers still knew that shape, from in-atmosphere drones and missiles. And Cametreans of every species knew it, because this scroll was a sacred text. When it was published, Quennet had just entered the era of powered flight, and that shape had been state-of-the-art.

"Is this an original Aquadale Selmar novel?" said Dwap-Jac-Dac-Tia-Sunlight. Even Tia was impressed. (Sunlight was not.)

"This is a periodical," said the abbot. "Ours is the honor of safeguarding a complete edition of Selmar. The arid air here preserves the pigments. We have his *Cametre* stories in their original periodicals, his novels, and a few miscellaneous quickreads. Ours is one of only seven complete editions in the universe." He snapped the scroll closed. "Condition near-mint to good. Some pieces have significant creasing."

"The original manuscripts are on Quennet, I take it," said Dwap-Jac-Dac-Tia-Sunlight. "They are not safe either."

"I don't need you to remind me," said the abbot. "During the Upheavals, many manuscripts were destroyed. Mint copies were removed from their wrappers. The loss was incalculable.

"You don't appreciate how tenuous my position is, Precedent. My Zone operates on land leased from a belligerent military. My fellas see me talking to an animal through wireless mechspeech. I reach out to you because I'm a desperate man. A man who believes there are things more important than whether a lit or a man or a monastery survives a war."

On what had once been the parade ground, a more-or-less permanent hut was set up. Through the open door Dwap-Jac-Dac-Tia-Sunlight saw some fans dressed as Selmar-era quenny soldiers, pushing little tokens around a map. The way real soldiers did, back when wars were fought in two dimensions. Dwap-Jac-Dac reckoned they were simulating the battle from *Through Cametre's Prism* that finally killed Qued Ethiret and all the other big-name characters. Trying to uncover some new bit of canon that up to this point lay implicit in the text.

The soldier-fans peeked curiously through the hut's door at their abbot and the carnivorous beast. When they saw the look on the abbot's face they quietly shut the door and hid from everything outside.

"Let me speak plainly, Precedent," said the abbot. "I want you to take revenge on Cametre's behalf."

"You know, sir," said Dwap-Jac-Dac-Tia-Sunlight. "As a follower of Lir I try to recast thoughts of revenge in terms of other emotions. I find it helps my blood pressure."

"Keep your syrupy Jalian double-talk to yourself. I am an old man trapped in a universe that refuses to operate according to rational principles. I want revenge for an infamous robbery!"

"A robbery here?"

"On the human homeworld," said the quenny. "Twelve kiloshifts ago, in a place called Botswana. The Cametrean monastery of Botswana has one of the other six editions. We assumed the sacred lits would be safe on Terra."

"Someone stole the scrolls?"

"You'd think so, wouldn't you?" said the abbot. "No, someone broke in and they *didn't* take the lits. They took the cattle the human fans used to produce adrypoxine."

"I don't have any chemistry," said Dwap-Jac-Dac-Tia-Sunlight, "but I assume adrypoxine is the human equivalent of syncweed."

"They use something different now. Some kind of fungus. But twelve kiloshifts ago it was genemod kine milk. I didn't hear about this at the time, you understand. It wasn't a religious issue. Cattle theft is a common crime on Terra.

"But then...recently..." the abbot stopped talking for a while and looked up at the sky. He could not tell this story to anyone else. He whispered into the comm. "There was an...incident here in the Zone, involving fourteen jetk soldiers and a human named Starlight-in-a-glass. After the incident I traveled to the city and made a farcall to Quennet, to ask what I should do. I was told to file a formal complaint with the Fist of Joy. I was not to mention the incident itself. I was to complain about some stolen cattle, on Terra, twelve kiloshifts earlier.

"You know, we get the newsfax here. I have to go through it and put it in sync for the fans. A while ago, the newsfax started talking about this new human drug. Evidence. How it was derived from adrypoxine. At that point the incident with Mr. Starlight-in-a-glass made sense.

"They made our sacrament into a toy," said the quenny. His neck trembled inside the stillsuit. "And then they turned the toy into a weapon. I don't expect to be taken seriously by those who lack truesight, but I would prefer not to be exploited. Every team like yours, sent to a place like this, every one of them is going to hear this story. We want revenge. We want the Evidence destroyed."

"Where are they making the drug?" said Dwap-Jac-Dac-Tia-Sunlight. "Is it on this planet?" *Is it, perhaps, right here, on this military base?*

"It is not," said the abbot. "They make the drug in a place I shouldn't even be thinking about." This meant offworld. Dwap-Jac-Dac-Tia-Sunlight began the perilous project of talking this guy down.

"We can't leave Arzil," she said. "We don't have the capability. That's why we came to you instead of the Jalians. There are not as many of us as you seem to think."

"The Jalians won't help you," the abbot snapped. "Bloody hypocrites. No offense intended. We will get you off this planet. I've been out there before, you know. Obviously! I'm not from Arzil. Do you know why I was sent here? Sent through an unplace so I could live in a desert? It's quite a funny story!" He was angry now, angrier than the customs inspector had been at the communicator. Angry at an imaginary box he chose to live in.

Dwap-Jac-Dac-Tia-Sunlight chose her words with care. "Sending a quenny to the desert; one might view it as a punishment."

"I'm not saying it was not a punishment," said the abbot. "But I was sent to root out a headcanon. You know what that is?"

"In Jalir we would call it heresy," said Dwap-Jac-Dac-Tia-Sunlight. "And we would not make a big deal out of it."

"Would that we could all be so lax," said the abbot. "The fans in this Zone were abusing their access to the original periodicals. They had gotten the idea that everything on this litscroll," (he held it up) "from the beginning of the Aquadale Selmar story to the end, was canon. Including classified ads, editorial notes, and interstitial stories by other authors. All of it. They spun elaborate theories, new categories of reality. They thought they could lower the fourth wall by destroying the other three. It was insanity.

"To clean up that sort of mess, Precedent, they don't send the most imaginative fan. I don't get wild ideas and I don't mind turning a theological dispute into a fist fight. Those are my virtues. You may not appreciate them. But you will appreciate this one, Precedent: I am sharp enough to see when the author of my fate has handed me a plot device. You've seen Qued Ethiret? The old man I spoke with earlier."

"That's actually his name?" Apparently the corestin in the Star Proctor Ethiret outfit took his role-play more seriously than the average Cametrean.

"Qued Ethiret is our chief heretic. He used to run this monastery. I was sent here to deal with him. He is still...not fully reformed. Have you read the lits? Do you know what Qued Ethiret does, in canon?"

"He's the leader. He's the proctor of the ship that discovers the hole in space."

"Qued Ethiret is the troublemaker. He gets into trouble. And then he comes up with fucked-up, impractical plans to get out of trouble. And—this is where I struggle with my own faith—the plans *work*. Qued Ethiret's stupid plans save the day and he's a big hero. Not the ordinary people who work, day in and day out, to keep reality running. They're never the hero. It's always the con-man Ethiret with his bluffing and his shit-eating grin.

"But we use the tools we have. I have a Qued Ethiret on my hands; let us make use of him. You tell Ethiret your problem and he'll come up with a plan. I have faith the plan will work. Qued Ethiret can get you and your fellas into space, into the unplace where no one should ever go. Then you can do a favor for Cametre that will benefit the Terran Outreach. You will be the instrument of our revenge, and Ethiret will be a big fucking hero for coming up with the idea, and I will somehow manage not to care."

"When shall we start?" said Dwap-Jac-Dac-Tia-Sunlight.

"I assume your fellas are hungry?" said the abbot.

"In the Navy we have a saying," said Dwap-Jac-Dac-Tia-Sunlight. "Never turn down a plate or a bed. Or a shower, or a flush toilet, or...the saying goes on for a while."

"I have heard the first two volumes of this saying," said the abbot. "We don't have any of the items further down the list, but we can offer you food and beds." He stopped at a greenhouse with fogged-up windows. Tia had never before seen a structure like this in a Cametrean monastery.

"What's in here?" asked Dwap-Jac-Dac-Tia-Sunlight.

"This is where we grow *my* syncweed," said the abbot. He unlatched the door and clouds of water vapor poured out: a little bit of Quennet in the desert. The abbot knelt in the mud of his home planet, stuck his hand down his throat and vomited into a pool of filthy water. The smell arrived a little later, like thunder after lightning, and to Sunlight the quenny man's vomit had the exotic smell of strange proteins.

The abbot stood, wiped his mouth and brushed ineffectively at the mud that now filled the grooved knee joints of his stillsuit. "All right, the weed is out of me," he told Dwap-Jac-Dac-Tia-Sunlight. "It will take a decishift for Ethiret and me to go completely out of sync." He pointed north, to the monastery's nearest edge. "Please wait for us outside reality."

The fans had set up a small red catering tent just outside the broken-down fence at the property line. Dwap-Jac-Dac-Tia-Sunlight stepped towards the fence. She was being followed; she turned her head and saw a young corestin woman dressed as an elected member of the Grand Council of Quennet. The woman was struggling across the sand holding a large ceramic pot in both hands, and when she saw the surk's turn head towards her she startled and nearly dropped the heavy thing. It was the sort of pot that contained food, but Sunlight detected no smell except the sweat beneath the woman's satin tunic.

Ingridsdotter and Tellpesh sat beneath the catering tent on simple Fist folding chairs, dozing with their heads on a fancy dining table with embedded cupholders. They woke when the elected representative sat the pot on the table with a throat-clearing clank. The lid came off: now Sunlight smelled the soup inside, bland and meatless. Four short ladles swiveled around in the pot. The elected representative said "neutral" in English. She'd learned it phonetically. She repeated it: "New-trull." Then she left, carefully picking a path around Dwap-Jac-Dac-Tia-Sunlight, walking back into the Zone.

"Did you learn anything, aer?" said Ingridsdotter.

"Just relax for a while and eat," said Dwap-Jac-Dac-Tia-Sunlight. It was a nice order to be able to give.

"I'm bloody starving," said Tellpesh. She pulled out one ladle and slurped at the soup. In the midday heat, the plastic of the tent's ceiling sagged near its melting point.

"You fellas have any idea how I'm supposed to drink from a ladle?" said Dwap-Jac-Dac-Tia-Sunlight.

"We'll give you the pot, aer," said Ingridsdotter.

Tellpesh rattled her ladle around in the pot, trying to get more than her share of vegetables. "Aer, I got the enemy terminal picking up planetary broadcasts," she said.

"Nice work."

"I heard them talking about us. They're saying a rre quartet and two humans in the desert. They don't seem to know about me."

"They think you're the second human," said Ingridsdotter.

"Except I'm not a human."

"The enemy commonly assume uhaltihaxl to be a human ethnic group," said Dwap-Jac-Dac-Tia-Sunlight.

"They're gonna find out different when they fight a ship full of us."

"Where do we get a ship full of uhalti?" said Ingridsdotter.

"We better find one quick," said Tellpesh. "There was a big engagement in Unicorn Sector. They've deployed their Evidence weapon." She sneered playfully at Ingridsdotter. "Team Human's been knocked out of the game."

"That's just propaganda," said Ingridsdotter.

When half the soup was gone, Ingridsdotter set the pot on the sand near the reptile head of Dwap-Jac-Dac-Tia-Sunlight. The surk pushed her snout into the pot and slurped at the lumpy green liquid. It was tasteless; she forced herself to swallow. Before she'd taken two bites, the elected representative of the Council of Quennet was standing inside the tent, setting a fresh pot of soup on the table.

The quenny abbot and an elderly corestin, Qued Ethiret, stepped gingerly outside the Zone of Reality and took seats at opposite ends of the table. Ethiret's hand-sewn rendition of the Quennet Exploratory Patrol's EVA suit was less than impressive. It was a fabric copy of a nonsensical piece of futurism described in vague detail by an antique fiction writer. It would never have taken vacuum. Qued Ethiret didn't care. He wore his cosplay with a dignity that none of the younger fans had mastered. The Quennet Exploratory Patrol was a made-up military, but it had one real spaceman and he honored the uniform.

The quenny drank a ladleful of soup, burped and for a moment seemed about to vomit again. "Esteemed Outreach soldiers," he said, "allow me to introduce Ethiret, the scourge of our little Zone."

"Gentlebeings," said the corestin.

"Ethiret is an intellectual," said the quenny, "which is to say he is an heretic. When I arrived to take control of this Zone, he had introduced a 3-tank to the common area. A commercial 3-tank! Showing..." (He was trying to think of the most insulting term.) "...movies."

Ethiret leaned forward like a card-player who cannot conceal his excellent hand. "The Ancestral Device described in *Within Cametre's Absence*," he began.

The abbot screamed at Ethiret in Mirret. His stillsuit crinkled as its fists clenched. "You see what I have to deal with," he told the soldiers, switching quickly back to Trade Standard D. "You've never seen shit strained so fine."

"Sir, the incident?" said Dwap-Jac-Dac-Tia-Sunlight.

The quenny's outburst had given him access to an inner strength. He leaned forward in his seat. "Two kiloshifts ago," he said, "the military invaded our Zone. They naturally chose Ethiret the intellectual as their collaborator and guide."

"Fourteen jetk soldiers with pulse rifles," said Ethiret. "I did as they told me: I showed them the hardvault. They copied our lits and they used the information to create a drug that kills human Cametreans."

"They should have come from the city," said the quenny. He frowned at his guests. "If the government wants to come here, it's supposed to come from the city, on the road, in a wheeled vehicle, as a sign of respect. These jetk just dropped their...VTAL vehicle... right here where we're sitting! So everyone could gawk at it over the fence!"

"'VTAL vehicle.'" Ingridsdotter laughed at the term, archaic even by the standards of D's technical vocabulary.

"What's that, a spaceship?" said Tellpesh.

"Yes, small human," said the abbot. "A 'spaceship'."

"You see the horns?" said Tellpesh. "Uhalti all the way, motherfucker."

"They didn't even come in from the city," said the abbot to himself.

Ethiret pounded the table. "They are killing our human siblings, and you speak of protocol!"

"Sir, why were they all jetk?" Ingridsdotter interrupted politely.

"Why is anyone jetk?" said the abbot. "Why does Cametre, or God or Providence if you prefer, create one soul jetk and the next one quenny?"

"I don't think those were soldiers," said Ingridsdotter. "They were mercenaries or con artists. You'll never see a Fist military unit all the same race. It gives people treasonous ideas."

"Ship full of uhalti," Tellpesh muttered.

"Did you actually see the Fist painted on the ship?" asked Dwap-Jac-Dac-Tia-Sunlight.

"The Fist was engraved in the metal!" said Ethiret. "This was a military vehicle and its intentions were altogether violent."

"The soldiers were jetk," said the abbot, "but there was a human civilian. They gave him an English code name. What was it? Starlight-in-a-glass."

"Star bottle," said Ethiret in heavily accented English.

"Yeah, Mr. Star Bottle." The quenny gave an angry smile. "Mr. Star Bottle was a real V.I.P. Ethiret escorted him into the hardvault. He was the one who actually read the litscrolls."

"The human could read Mirret?" said Dwap-Jac-Dac-Tia-Sunlight.

"He took notes," said Ethiret, as if that answered the question.

"He took tintshots," said the abbot. "Photography of the sacred lits is expressly forbidden!"

"Nevertheless we followed the soldiers' instructions," said Ethiret, "because we did not want to die or lose the lease on our Zone. We allowed the human to tint our lits. The abbot put a screen around the...'vehicle'...so we wouldn't have to look at it. Apparently our faith is so weak it cannot survive the sight of a spacecraft."

"Fuck you," said the abbot.

"I'm the scapegoat, as you can see," said Ethiret. "They were here for ten shifts. A kiloshift later comes the war."

"While you were in prison," said the abbot, "there were a number of border engagements. The largest at Mas'pl."

"We heard," said Tellpesh.

"We learned the Fist of Joy uses the blasphemous drug Evidence to make chemical weapons. Weapons that prey on a soldier's ideology or religion." He choked up. "I didn't even know there were Cametreans in your Navy...Christians, too. Why would you join a military? These are peaceful religions!"

"Not every believer is a monk, sir," said Dwap-Jac-Dac-Tia-Sunlight.

"Find the fourteen jetk and Mr. Star Bottle," said the abbot, "and kill them. Kill everyone involved in the project. Kill the Terran cattle they use to synthesize this weapon. Destroy the notes and the tintshots used to invent it. Destroy it all!"

"We would very much like to destroy this weapon for you, sir," said Dwap-Jac-Dac-Tia-Sunlight, "but I am not promising to kill anyone."

"You're a rre soldier in the body of a surk!" the quenny screamed. "And you have a problem with killing?"

"Ethiret, when the ship left," said Ingridsdotter, "where did it go?"

"Up." The corestin pointed away from his planet, his face free from sarcasm. Ingridsdotter and Tellpesh exchanged glances.

"I'm afraid this gives us very little to go on," Dwap-Jac-Dac-Tia-Sunlight told the fans.

"We cannot give you more!" said the quenny. "Once you leave here, you are beyond our power. We have no guarantee you will do what we want."

"There was a place called Nimar," said Ethiret. "The jetk kept mentioning Nimar. 'Let's just take all this shit back to Nimar.' That sort of thing."

"Never heard of it," said Ingridsdotter.

"Probably a code name," said Dwap-Jac-Dac-Tia-Sunlight.

"If you can find out where Nimar is," said Ethiret, "I have a plan to get you..." he pointed away from the planet again. "Up."

"Of course you have a plan," said the quenny, supremely annoyed even though this was the outcome he'd been hoping for.

"Master, I am about to say something," Ethiret told the abbot, "which you will please not mention to the other fans." There was a gleam in his eye like the actual Qued Ethiret might have had in the early stages of his latest insane scheme.

"What is it?" said the quenny, promising nothing.

"In the city," said the corestin fan, "we have a 'VTAL vehicle' of our own. It is kept in long-term storage and registered to a shell corporation. When I took over the monastery, I was told I should use the 'vehicle' in the event of catastrophe, to return the sacred lits to Quennet."

"I did not ask for a vehicle!" said the abbot.

"The vehicle predates your arrival by kiloshifts," said the corestin. "It is a logistical matter that has nothing to do with you."

"Why was I not told about this vehicle?"

"It has nothing to do with you," Ethiret repeated.

"How large a craft are we talking about?" said Ingridsdotter.

"Large enough to fit the lits, presumably," said Ethiret. "I've never seen it and I don't think about it. I'm not comfortable with it myself. I recall the manufacturer is Oena."

"That's a Fist company," said Ingridsdotter. "They went out of business about five years ago. They made sexy fast birds that exploded."

"This...could work," said Tellpesh. "We go into the city, get the 'vehicle' out of storage. We wear your trendy shame robes and no one will notice us."

"The shame robes would be *inside the vehicle*," said Ethiret. "They are for travel through places that do not exist. You people seem to think we wear them all the time."

"Because people see stereotypes," said Ingridsdotter. "Cametreans always in their shame robes. Uhalti are lovey-dovey hippies. Humans are loud and obnoxious." (Tellpesh snorted cynically.) "A stereotype is a disguise. Someone sees the stereotype and they stop looking. If we had those robes we could walk around any city in the galaxy, in broad daylight, and everyone would just see a bunch of Cammie crackpots."

"We could sew new garments that resemble shame robes," said the abbot, "and I would like nothing better than to rid ourselves of this vehicle which I was *never told about*! But we can't exactly put a robe on a surk."

"I can't be seen in this," said Dwap-Jac-Dac-Tia-Sunlight. "We install spies and commandos in megafauna. I'm the first place they'll look."

"I know what they can do, master," said Ethiret, openly smiling now.

"Well, tell us."

"One sees so many more possibilities once one leaves sync, wouldn't you say? Unfortunately, by definition, the possibilities one sees tend to be...morally reprehensible. The way it is reprehensible, let us say, for an *unbeliever* to wear an *imitation shame robe* as a disguise!"

"Point your hate at its target, Ethiret," said the quenny. "The fourteen jetk and Mr. Star Bottle."

"Aer?" Ethiret scanned the surk from side to side. He wasn't sure whether to address the head, some unseen point inside the animal's body, or the forbidden box on the table that spoke with the voice of the rre. "How many are you? How many bodies?"

"Four rre and a surk," said Dwap-Jac-Dac-Tia-Sunlight.

"Then the planetary authorities will be hunting a four-bodied rre," said Ethiret. "Such a colony requires a very large host. Very easy to spot. If instead you were four singletons, you would need four hosts, but each host could be much smaller." He looked down the table at the other spacemen. "The size of a human."

"Oh God," said Ingridsdotter.

"Brother Ethiret, you have outdone yourself." The abbot set down his ladle. "I should have let you keep the 3-tank."

"They tried rre hybrids during the last war," said Tellpesh. "It didn't work."

"It worked fine during the war," said Dwap-Jac-Dac-Tia-

Sunlight. Her precedent Dwap-Tuni-Dac-Sora had served with some of the 'hybrids'—an inaccurate term that had become tragically more accurate over time. "It didn't work so well once the war was over."

"Perhaps you didn't notice," said Ethiret, "but you are once again 'during a war'."

"Splitting up a rre colony is risky on its own," said Dwap-Jac-Dac-Tia-Sunlight. "There must be targets on this planet we could hit."

"Of course there are," said Ethiret, "but there's no reason why the Keepers for Cametre should help you 'hit' them."

Dwap-Tuni-Dac-Sora would never have agreed to this, but Dwap-Tuni-Dac-Sora was an unimaginative grunt. Dwap-Jac-Dac was an imaginative officer—too imaginative, some had said—but thon had no experience riding anything but an exobody. Whereas Dwap-Jac-Dac-Tia now had a disturbing amount of practice at integrating with the vertebrate nervous system, and even Dwap-Jac-Dac-Tia-Sunlight was starting to feel comfortable with herself; less like a parasitic infestation and more like a partnership, albeit one that hadn't been bringing in very much meat lately.

"There are only two of us," said Ingridsdotter. She shuddered. "Two hosts."

"You're a healthy specimen," said Ethiret. "Plenty of room in your chest cavity. You could support a colony of two."

"Tia could stay here," said Tellpesh.

"No, I volunteer myself as a host," said Ethiret.

The abbot looked like he wanted to pitch face-first into the soup. "I knew this would happen," he muttered.

"Master, consider the advantages," said Ethiret. "If I go with them, I ensure they complete our mission instead of rejoining their fleet. More importantly, I *leave*. You and I are no longer disgracing Cametre in each other's eyes."

"It would let me get rid of you without the bother of a trial," said the quenny.

"I will not order anyone to go through with this—" said Dwap-Jac-Dac-Tia-Sunlight.

"I'm in, aer," said Ingridsdotter.

"Let me finish."

"Sorry, aer."

"It's not the done thing, to say the least. It will probably kill us and it certainly won't help our careers. I myself am not looking forward to being dissected by a monk who's never seen a rre. But if we can pull it off, it would be a way to get us back into the fight. What do we say?"

Tellpesh groaned. "Why do I let people talk me into this shit?" she said.

"Because you're a badass lady," said Ingridsdotter.

"Dead-ass lady."

Ethiret
The monastery clinic, the hardvault, and *Brown v. Board of Education of Topeka*

Qued Ethiret hadn't known how many memories he'd accumulated until Jac bit into his brainstem and the past started oozing out. Numb from a canonical anesthetic that immobilized you without putting you to sleep, Ethiret felt his lucid thoughts take on the character of a dream: his life seen through another's eyes.

To Jac it was clear that Ethiret had two distinct sets of memories. There were the exploits of Star Proctor Qued Ethiret—a roguish but ultimately good-hearted fella—all completely correct and canonical. And tagging along on the edge of those memories was a pathetic side-story about a corestin kid who'd joined an alien religion trying to stop a war, who'd spent the next fifty kiloshifts in a haze of syncweed, watching helplessly as his religion failed to stop the war and went on to not stop the next two.

The most painful spots were the times when Ethiret had gone out of sync and the two sets of memories had collided. Most recently the incident with the human in the hardvault, which...*I mean, Jac, the whole thing's a wash. I've wasted my bloody life and*

What happened in the hardvault? said Jac.

I don't want to think about it. Ethiret's pulse was elevated; his nervous system lost homeostasis and opaque electric messages ran down his spine.

You're thinking about it now. Why does thinking about it do this to your body?

Can't you look and leave me out of it? said Ethiret.

We're the same mind. We look together.

Okay, damn, damn it all, I'm standing in the hardvault, watching the human rummage through the sacred lits of Cametre. Are you happy?

We've been locked in here together by the leader of the jetk soldiers. Mr. Star Bottle refers to the jetk as his errand boy, but it's clear that the "errand boy" is the dominant one in their relationship.

This is the sixth shift since the VTAL vehicle landed, and my fourth shift spent in the vault with Star Bottle. It's very unusual to see someone study the lits without using syncweed. The very idea has the abbot in a fury. Whenever I leave the vault, he's waiting right outside. He interrogates me. He thinks the human is reading the lits out of sync deliberately, to find continuity errors. This terrifies him—as if we didn't already know about the errors. He hates that the jetk trust me over him, because I'm a Fist citizen and Quennet is neutral.

What I haven't told the abbot is that after watching Mr. Star Bottle, I've decided that the human *is* in sync, after a fashion. On the table, next to the box of scrolls I fetched for him, Star Bottle has set a medical inhaler. Periodically he sucks on the inhaler, like an initiate putting a fresh leaf into his mouth, and goes back to reading. There is also a box of needles, and several times a shift he sticks a needle into a valve implanted in his neck and draws a small vial of blood. Whatever he's inhaling is not syncweed, but the rhythm is unmistakable.

Each time we leave the vault, Star Bottle's errand boy picks up the box of blood and carries it under his arm to the VTAL vehicle. We sleep for a bit, Star

Bottle and I, and we go back into the vault. He reads; sometimes he asks questions. He keeps a pad of paper next to the scroll and on it he maintains plot diagrams that look like chemical formulae. The "errand boy" doesn't care about the diagrams; he only takes the blood.

In this memory we're watching, just as the thing is preparing to happen, Star Bottle is reading *Doing Without Cametre*. Sretho the oblivious security guard is about to be killed by the outcritter. Star Bottle's finger stops on the scroll just before the attack. I hold my breath.

"What is *aunau tequeket sue*?" Star Bottle asks.

I manage to breathe. "Guard duty," I say. "I'm doing it now. I could be doing something useful, like working the garden. Instead I'm standing here watching you, because my abbot doesn't trust you with our lits. Jalians call it *hless*."

Star Bottle cocks his neck in a way that says he's tired, but he's just matching the needle to the valve. He pushes it in without looking and the meaning of *aunau tequeket sue* gushes out red into a vial. He reads a few more sentences and the outcritter strikes. Sretho the security guard dies horribly, and I groan, as I always do. But Star Bottle does nothing. He circles a box on his diagram of the plot of the story and his finger keeps moving.

This is the moment, in the middle of my fourth shift of guard duty, when I know that I have to stop this. Star Bottle doesn't *care* about Sretho. She's not even a fictional character to him; just a box on a diagram. That's how he sees everyone. The human is *eating* Cametre, a little at a time, removing our truth from the lits and distilling it into his blood and drawing a diagram to show how it works. I don't know what's going on, I don't know why the Fist of

Joy takes such a sudden interest in the Cametrean secrets, but the plan must be worth the stopping.

Yet what can I do? Qued Ethiret would birth a scheme effortlessly, but I am not Qued Ethiret at the moment. I've gone out of sync to perform my *aunau tequeket sue* and I have reverted to that corestin boy run away from home. No plan will come from this mind that can deal with the brute facts of a defenseless monastery and fourteen jetk soldiers.

Except for this: the hardvault stores relics on sturdy earthquake-proof shelves. I am standing next to a collectible plaster bust, a million shifts old and barely chipped. Star Bottle's back is turned. I could take this priceless bust and smash it against the human's head. Beat his brain to paste. Spill his blood all at once rather than letting it trickle into vials destined for some secret centrifuge.

There would be no hiding my crime from the jetk outside. The errand boy would have me killed. Probably kill the abbot as well—there's some comfort—maybe raze the Zone with laser fire. It would have no effect on the universe as a whole, but I have been given a glimpse into a secret pipeline of misery, and killing Star Bottle would disrupt it for a while.

I can't do it! Such an act would never be canon. Even out of sync, I know that Qued Ethiret would never commit murder, strike down a man while his back was turned. I've spent fifty kiloshifts as Qued Ethiret, and this was why I chose to be him: he will lie, bluff, bribe, humiliate himself—anything to avoid taking a life.

So I humiliate myself. I put my plan on the shelf of collectibles and I step away, to remove the temptation. I answer Mr. Star Bottle's trivial questions about words and etymologies. I help him until he leaves Arzil. The day he leaves, I creep outside the Zone after hours and dig a hole in the sand. I kneel down and I cry into the hole until my eyes are swollen, and then I sweep my hand across the desert and bury my tears.

A few shifts ago I learned what Star Bottle did, what I could have prevented if I'd killed him. I thought to curse myself, but I pointed my anger at its target. I cursed Qued Ethiret, who made me too good to do evil but not good enough to stop it.

As a man of peace, I am a failure. I want to be a killer.

I want to be you.

Okay, well, said Jac. Now perhaps I can show you a memory?

I am riding my Navy exobody, half-sitting above the couch in the ready room of *Brown v. Board of Education of Topeka*. We were ordered to requisition the factory city-ship *Jaketown*, which has evaded her legal responsibilities by wrecking on a planet near the border. I am discussing our options with my C.O., an uhalti woman named Churryhoof. She proposes harsh retribution. I have a better idea.

"We could declare *Jaketown* a munitions factory, ma'am," I say.

"Clarify?" says Churryhoof. She does not seem to believe this is legally permissible.

"Your authority under martial law is very broad," I assure her. I have complete mastery of the regulations, as befits a junior officer. "In particular, I'm thinking of your ability to commandeer production facilities for defense purposes. You can give *Jaketown* production orders and we can head back to the fight."

Commander Churryhoof looks at me—looks at the head of my exobody—and I see I have misjudged her. The commander is not looking for the most effective solution. She wants vengeance. To an uhaltihaxl, pain is a commodity to be borrowed and repaid. The books must balance. Evil must be returned for evil.

So we do it her way. I am captured, my fellas taken prisoner, Spaceman Heiss is killed, and four children are separated from their parents. Why? Why not use my simpler solution? Because it sounded silly. It would have been humiliating. I was willing to be Qued Ethiret, and my commander was not.

Each of us has a gap shaped like the other, Jac said to Ethiret. Together we can actually be Qued Ethiret. I need your fluency in Trade Standard B, the skill in twisting words that comes from a priest who thinks like a con-man. I need your body—not to steer, like a puppet, but as a place to live. I can help you be the man you wish you'd been, and together we can stop this war.

Was I not clear? Ethiret-Jac told himself. This body is useless. Take it.

Chapter 26

Destiny

Churryhoof
Little Dagger
in orbit around Cedar Commons

ll indicators are red," said the woman who had been *Jaketown*'s chief sysadmin before the crash. Her name was Natal and Churryhoof disliked her. She was competent enough, but sloppy. She would never have cut it in the Navy.

"Red is good, yeah?" said Singh, *Jaketown*'s former skipper.

"On a Fist system, red is good," Churryhoof told them.

Dr. Sempestwinku tapped Churryhoof on the knee. "You were telling me about the fire," he said.

Hetselter Churryhoof was nominally in charge of *Little Dagger*, the cargo vessel brought to Cedar Commons by the late Mr. Styrqot. A plastic-coated wire connected her capital terminal to the ship's systems control point, giving her control of everything wired through it. In particular, her terminal was the only thing suppressing the security checks that had disabled the ship after the timely death of its navigator, Mr. Byrno.

Despite single-handedly freeing the people of Cedar Commons, Churryhoof was still their prisoner. She couldn't be trusted to run the evacuation. So Dr. Sempestwinku had been assigned to distract her with mindless conversation, to keep her from making sudden use of the tools she could feel through her terminal.

"We vent the whole access tube," said Churryhoof, "but it doesn't help, because by this time the PRX line is busted. PRX is what we use to print torpedoes. You do not want it in your fire because it acts as both a fuel and an oxidizer. So now the fire is happily burning in vacuum, like a thruster. Except this thruster is located a hundred meters *inside* the hull of *What is to be Done?*."

It seemed a thousand years ago; it had been two. Hetselter Churryhoof had been a hero. She'd saved the ship, gotten her own command. Now she was a key in a lock, a minor part of a plan to evacuate an uninhabited planet. She sat in a fancy wooden chair with her hands cuffed to the arms, guarded by a sadistic quack who'd slid a plastic-coated wire in beneath her eyeball.

"Skip on my mark," said Mr. Singh. And then, shockingly: "Mark." Where did they get that? War movies? Why give two orders when one would do?

Ms. Natal put one finger on a slider and then took it off and blew air through her lips. "Capacitor has discharged. No skip." The big window at the front of the bridge proved itself useful for once: it was blindingly obvious that the commandeered hopore vessel hadn't moved. Cedar Commons still hung above them, quiet and hazy.

Why would Churryhoof even want to take over *Little Dagger*? What would she do with a starship? Where could she go? She'd failed her mission, lost her fellas and murdered a colleague. Killing a thousand enemy wouldn't cancel that out.

"Reinitialize the calculation process," Churryhoof muttered. That was the order she would give if she was in charge of anything.

"Hey, hey, now," said Dr. Sempestwinku. *Get your hand off my knee, you fucking birthday aunt.* "The fire?"

Ms. Natal moved from the navigation console to the systems control point, nearly brushing the wire that leashed Churryhoof's optic nerve to *Little Dagger*'s internals. "It's not a process," she said. "It's a dedicated analog computer. It needs to be reset mechanically." She hunted around the back of the panel, looking for the switch.

"I do wish you hadn't killed Mr. Byrno," said Singh. Now that it was once again acknowledged that Churryhoof was a sentient being you could speak to.

"Yeah, fabulous, do you know what?" said Churryhoof. "I wish I wasn't handcuffed to a chair."

"How did you put the fire out?" Dr. Sempestwinku was losing control of his 'patient'. "You're here now, so you managed it somehow."

Churryhoof let her head drop onto her chest. This made her once again aware of the block of wood bonded to the stump of her horn, pulling her off-kilter. "I got..." she said. "I fetched up one of those little-buddy drones from maintenance. The ones that hand you the tools."

Mrs. Chen was dead. Tip-Iye-Nett-Zig the asshole solicitor was dead. Dwap-Jac-Dac: too stupid to live without adult supervision, ergo probably dead. Tellpesh, Heiss, the children, that reservist. Dead; her fault.

"Help me visualize it, Hetse," said the doctor. "Is it like a medical Atlkit, or is it more like the old Solid Mechanics construction models?"

"I don't know the brands, sorry," said Churryhoof. Then a high-pitched alarm went off and she and Sempestwinku both winced.

"Hrgh—Providence, what now?" Dr. Sempestwinku shouted, his hands over his ears. Churryhoof couldn't move her hands. The muscles of her left eye twitched around the plastic-coated wire.

"What's wrong, doc?" said Mr. Singh. He heard nothing. The alarm was out of the range of human hearing.

Churryhoof saw what was wrong, saw it through the ship's sensors. "Bogey in system!" she called out. Something with huge displacement had skipped in, seven light-seconds away. Its Doppler shift, practically a blue shift, indicated that it was hauling ass towards Cedar Commons and *Little Dagger.*

"Commander, please!" said Dr. Sempestwinku. Churryhoof killed the alarm with a stray thought.

"Natal, get it in the tank!" Mr. Singh was saying. Yeah, that 'mark' shit went right out the airlock when you needed something done quick. Churryhoof was quicker than the tank. Her terminal merged the barrage of Fist-format media types into something her brain could make sense of, and she saw the ship.

It was a titanium mountain, half illuminated by the star EGS-RC121 and fully outlined by *Little Dagger*'s sensors. Churryhoof recognized the hull shape and the deployment bays of a Heavy Combat Platform. The mountain was now well into visual range. English lettering was spotlit on the dark underside of the hull, but the words weren't in English. They said NTO HCP 011 MAGNA CARTA.

"Thank God," Churryhoof heard Mr. Singh say. "It's one of ours."

"Yes," said Churryhoof, "but we are in one of theirs."

"Hailing frequencies!" said Singh. Churryhoof already had them open. "This is Commander Hetselter Churryhoof of Naval Intelligence, Echo Division." She spoke aloud, in English. She had control of the ship; she would use it. *Little Dagger*'s combat laser was autonomously powering up; she expanded her suppression of the security systems to cover offense as well.

"Hopore vessel *Little Dagger* has been commandeered. Repeat, hopore vessel is a friendly. More to the point, I am on hopore vessel. Please acknowledge through non-kinetic means."

Kinetic means were the only ones forthcoming. *Magna Carta* unfolded her armament arrays and the sensor readings multiplied as the drone swarms deployed. Five swarms, then ten, twelve, too many to count. Big swarms, more drones than an HCP's full complement, deployed through orifices that didn't normally exist. What had they done to *Magna Carta*? She'd been a good ship. Now she was some idiot admiral's idea of a superweapon. An entire battle wing crammed into a single point of failure.

Churryhoof glanced at Dr. Sempestwinku and the humans. They were staring at the solid green clouds in the 3-tank, mouths agape. Sempestwinku was praying, pressing his thumbs against each pair of fingers in turn.

They didn't know this was unusual. This was what an HCP deployment looked like to civilians. It was all a space show to them. They thought the problem was that they, personally, were going to die. But Commander Churryhoof now saw that her death was just a pimple on a much larger problem. You didn't change the order of battle like this. Not in the middle of a war. Not unless you were losing the war.

"This is *Outreach Navy* Commander Churryhoof to *Magna Carta*. I am aboard hopore vessel. Please respond."

Magna Carta's deployment collapsed. The swarms spun away and out of formation. There were too many drones. The best company in the Navy couldn't coordinate that much firepower. One swarm skimmed the top of Cedar Commons's atmosphere and disappeared from sensors. The rest established orbits at various heights, under the control of their queens, and waited to hear from the parent craft.

Magna Carta veered uncomfortably close to *Little Dagger*, fired her motivators and climbed into a parking orbit. The HCP's hull lights went dark. Both ships were dead in space.

The three civilians let out their breath at once. "What in the hell?" said Mr. Singh quietly. Churryhoof's breathing stayed quiet and careful. She wasn't about to die. If Providence was going to kill her with friendly fire from an HCP, it would use *What is to be Done?*, the ship she'd served on and had just been talking about. There was no irony in dying to *Magna Carta*. Not enough, at any rate, to satiate the bloodlust of Merciful Providence.

A young uhalti male winked into the 3-tank and incidentally into Churryhoof's optic nerve. He stood on the bridge of *Magna Carta*, hands behind his back. Some shiny humanoids rushed in and out of the picture behind him: rre in combat suits.

"Commander?" said the uhalti male. "Are you all right?"

"Um," said Churryhoof. Her lips felt numb. Perhaps there was some deeper underlying irony here that she was too dense to comprehend.

"Captain Texchiffu Rebtet of *Magna Carta*. We received a distress call from a queen in this system, so we thought we'd come over and shake the bugs out of our tactical context."

Churryhoof felt an itching sensation running down her spine. If this guy was a captain, the Outreach was well and truly fucked. Churryhoof hadn't exactly been slow to rise through the ranks, and now someone five years younger was commanding a flagship.

"We do appreciate that, sir," said Churryhoof, "but I was able to neutralize the enemy on my own."

"Commander..." Rebtet wasn't sure how to put this. "Would you mind addressing me through the tank?"

"Sir, sorry, sir. My terminal is suppressing hopore vessel's security systems. I'm connected optically to the systems control point. Can't turn my head, sir."

"I'm not a stickler for regulations," said Captain Rebtet, "but under the circumstances I would at least like to get a salute out of you."

"Sir, really wish I could, but unfortunately I am also handcuffed to this cushy Strigl Modern Design armchair, sir."

"And is that a...block of wood stuck to your head?" Captain Rebet touched his own horn, a nice tight spiral and then some.

"Prosthesis, sir. Broke a horn in a fight, sir."

"I had no idea Echo Division's work was so interesting," said Captain Rebtet.

"You just made it a little more interesting than we'd like, sir."

"Lucky for you it's a Situation Normal over here," said Captain Rebtet. "We can't splash a fethen turd without targeting it manually. Our tactical context crashes whenever it enters a live-fire situation. Do you or your fellas have any experience..." Churryhoof was finding it hard to concentrate because the itching sensation was spreading through her entire body and—

Antiestruals!

That was the problem! Churryhoof's clicker of antiestrual pills was over on *Brown*, the vessel no one would allow her to board. Dr. Sempestwinku hadn't prescribed any, because antiestruals aren't medicine, because heat isn't a disease. It's a natural part of life, albeit one that makes it really difficult to be active-duty military. And when you took away the drugs an uhalti had been taking for fifteen years, you were pretty much guaranteeing he or she would go into heat for the first suitable match.

And let's be honest, Texchiffu Rebtet was a real stud. He'd made captain halfway through his second spiral, no desk-job gut to push out his uniform tunic. His features were solid and masculine but retained something gentle, a reminder of the boy he'd so recently been. Yeah, Hetselter Churryhoof wanted to pin Captain Rebtet to the floor of *Magna Carta*'s bridge and mount him and not stop riding his thick-headed cock until she had to go to sickbay to deliver the baby.

Churryhoof took a deep breath and thrashed, once, in her handcuffs. This was idiotic. She was a decorated military officer, not some teenage spring-breaker ready to flip a coin for her future at the first rush of keproserathone. Captain Rebtet wouldn't respond to that. She had to be adult about this.

"Maybe I can help, sir," said Churryhoof with confidence. "I was Master of Drone on *What is to be Done?*. Captain Kidare thought I was pretty good at wrangling them."

"Who am I to second-guess the great Kidare?" Captain Rebtet nodded to one of the outtank rre, and through her terminal Churryhoof saw *Magna Carta* slow down to match delta-v with *Little Dagger*. "Oh, Commander?" he added, his dark eyes flashing in the 3-view.

"Yessir?"

"No funny stuff, please? We are a normal unit and our tolerance for black-ops pigshit is very low."

"Wouldn't dream of it, sir."

"*Magna Carta* out."

"Ms. Natal," said Churryhoof, "please spark the thrusters and dock us with *Magna Carta*." She said it with confidence, as though Natal had ever taken one damn suggestion of hers.

Natal looked at Singh, who nodded. 'Mayor' Nzeme would have fast-talked the Navy, tried to get them to take the evil Churryhoof into custody. Singh and Natal just wanted to evacuate Cedar Commons before the enemy showed up for revenge.

"Doctor," Churryhoof said. They had antiestruals down on

Jaketown. She just had to tell Sempestwinku about her problem. Just ask him for some time-release keproserathone. It wasn't too late. You felt like crap for a couple days and the problem went away.

"Yes?" Dr. Sempestwinku looked into Churryhoof's eyes with the expression that had never quite managed to be concern or compassion. What had she been thinking? This guy didn't even believe in painkillers.

"Would you open the handcuffs, please?" Churryhoof jangled her wrists. "I'm sorry I didn't finish the fire story. Maybe another time."

"It's all right, commander." And they were back to "commander".

Churryhoof rubbed one sore wrist with the other. A strange churning dominated her stomach: the gravitational negotiations of a small ship docking with a much, much larger ship. It had been a close call, but she felt okay. She was a grown woman. She didn't need keproserathone pills to keep her sane. Unless...

The uhaltihaxl mating hormone had lost some of its effectiveness as its host civilization developed niceties like mattresses and birth control. In response, biology had evolved iricisnene, the rationalization hormone. Iricisnene did to your higher brain functions what keproserathone did to your crotch: focused you, concentrated you, all towards one pleasant purpose.

An uhalti who overcame his or her initial keproserathone rush and then made a cool, considered decision to make a baby with the person who'd caused it, sometimes wondered if this very calmness wasn't the iricisnene talking. It was an interesting hypothetical, but after considering it for a moment, Churryhoof decided the question was moot.

Two uhaltihaxl marines in combat armor stormed *Little Dagger*'s bridge, brandishing charged weapons and barking orders to do what everyone had done automatically: stay still and put their hands on their heads. Dwap-Jac-Dac had pulled the same trick on *Jaketown*, and the results here were identical: civilians cowering in fear, or at least submission.

The marines were a man and a woman. The man corralled Dr. Sempestwinku and the two humans near the decorative window. The woman powered down her rifle and sauntered over to the edge of the bridge to Churryhoof's little chair. She kept her visor down. Her nameplate said AXQUATETTERPET.

"Ma'am." Space Marine Axquatetterpet shifted her rifle into her left hand and saluted.

"As you were, marine." Churryhoof could smell her own must. That meant Axquatetterpet and every other uhalti within a parsec could also smell it. She envisioned roiling cartoon clouds visible in the marine's HUD. She'd have to mask it; selectively, of course. Pharma brands had probably researched this; she could look up some papers on *Magna Carta*.

"Ma'am, I have here..." Axquatetterpet patted a Micro 4501 logic tool attached with a carbine clip to her belt. "A Micro 4501 logic tool. This can take over the job of suppressing *Little Dagger*'s security protocols."

"Proceed," said Churryhoof.

"Yes ma'am." Axquatetterpet used her laser bayonet to bore a hole in the plastic casing of the systems control point. She pushed the Micro 4501 logic tool into place and Churryhoof allowed it a connection to her terminal.

"We're green, ma'am. Or red, I guess." Churryhoof relaxed her mind. No alarms went off and the reactor didn't explode.

"I'm free," said Churryhoof.

"Bridge is secure!" said the uhalti man, simultaneously shouting it and blasting it out as a high-priority status message that hit Churryhoof's terminal like the drunk buddy you had to walk back to quarters. A rre noncom quietly clanked through the airlock and looked around.

"Can you stand up, ma'am?" said Axquatetterpet.

"Negative; I'm still optical."

"Hey Toos," the woman marine called to the man, "send the bones over." The man gave Dr. Sempestwinku a shove and let him walk the rest of the way under his own power, brushing the dust of indignity off the sleeves of his white coat.

"We're done, bones," Axquatetterpet told him. "Take the wire out."

"Are you certain?"

"Take it out!"

"Hold still," said Sempestwinku. He quickly, painfully jerked the wire out from beneath Churryhoof's eyeball.

"Fuck!" said Churryhoof.

"Ma'am," said the marine.

"Don't rub it, you'll make it worse," said Sempestwinku. Churryhoof continued to rub it.

"You a real doctor, bones?" said the male marine.

"Of course I'm a real doctor."

"He's a sadist," said Churryhoof, finally free to speak the truth.

"We got work for you." Axquatetterpet took up her rifle again. "Ma'am, the old man wants a word." She escorted Dr. Sempestwinku back towards the front of the bridge. Churryhoof gripped the armrests and levered herself up. She wobbled across the bridge towards the open passenger airlock, ignoring the stares from the humans, rubbing her eye.

Captain Rebtet was standing just inside the *Magna Carta* side of the airlock. *Little Dagger*'s grainy 3-tank couldn't convey how well he masked the look of being in over his head. The look Churryhoof had probably shown when she'd first stepped onto the bridge of *Brown v. Board of Education of Topeka*. He wasn't some unattainable wonder kid; just a good officer who'd gotten a battlefield promotion.

Churryhoof saluted. "Permission to come aboard, sir."

"Commander," said Rebtet. A rre lieutenant stood next to him. "Let me introduce my Master of Drone, Ja-Iyo-Cat."

"Ma'am."

"Lieutenant. Sir, real quick, if you would remind your fellas that my crew are Outreach civilians?" *My crew.* Was there a helpless idiot anywhere for whom Churryhoof wouldn't take responsibility?

Rebtet nodded. "Stand down, fellas," he said through his

terminal. Inside *Little Dagger*, the marines' weapons noisily powered off and helmet visors slid up.

"Lieutenant," said Rebtet, "Commander Churryhoof is now your special assistant. She is going to fix the problems with our tactical context, and then we're going to go kick some ass. Sound good to everyone?"

Everyone agreed that this was a swell idea. Ja-Iyo-Cat even made the metamaterial head of thons combat suit nod back and forth. Churryhoof was not going to make the mistake of bitching about being made assistant to a first lieutenant.

"I so authorize," said Captain Rebtet in response to something Churryhoof didn't have clearance to hear. Lights went on in her terminal—searing, blinding lights that overwhelmed her optic nerve. She'd been granted access to *Magna Carta*'s systems.

"Access received, sir," said Churryhoof. At a glance, it all looked familiar. She could access all the systems she remembered from serving *What is to be Done?*. But there was a layer of gauze between her and the controls. She wasn't Master of Drone here, and she couldn't do anything without Ja-Iyo-Cat's okay.

"Let's go," said Rebtet impatiently.

Churryhoof followed Rebtet and Ja-Iyo-Cat through an airlock, a nonfunctional decontamination chamber, an unstaffed security checkpoint, and a second airlock. Beyond, inside the familiar hallways of an HCP, Churryhoof was assaulted by a bitter smell like the rotten milk of Terran kine. It was the smell of Evidence.

There was no way out of this hallway. Doors to adjoining rooms were powered down, and whenever they came to a crossroads, two of the paths would be physically blocked off with emergency bulkheads. There was only one path from the docking airlock through the ship, and it led directly to the main lifts.

"Where is everyone, sir?" An HCP normally crewed over a thousand.

"Where are the humans, you mean?"

"Is that what I mean, sir?"

"You want to take this one, Lieutenant?"

"The war has hit a little snag, ma'am," said Ja-Iyo-Cat. "The enemy is using an illegal weapon that makes humans stop fighting."

Of course. "Weaponized Evidence," said Churryhoof.

"*Magna Carta* was hit at Mas'pl," said Rebtet.

"I served on *The Case of the Armie Truly Stated*," said Ja-Iyo-Cat. "We got it in the Rira system."

"Were people not wearing their gas masks?"

"Unfortunately the enemy have some way of skipping it directly into the gas mask. Parallel universes are involved."

"Fucking Providence, sir." While Chen had been screwing around with fake secret research labs, the Fist of Joy had been systematically dismantling the Outreach Navy.

"We've had less than a week to retool around a posture that eliminates eighty percent of our personnel as potential security risks."

"But they're not dead, right? Just...risky."

"There's nothing wrong, medically, with a human who's been hit," said Captain Rebtet. "But they're not spacemen anymore. Something has changed inside them and they won't fight."

It was now clear how Rebtet had gotten his promotion. "Captain Hsu...?"

"Sits in a therapeutic 3-sim, peacefully exploring the bloody galaxy." They'd arrived at the lifts. Five of the six doors stood open and waiting. Captain Rebtet walked into one of the lifts. Churryhoof made to follow, but Ja-Iyo-Cat went into the lift adjacent. Rebtet turned around and looked Churryhoof in the eye for the first time since she'd boarded his ship. "Hsu was a good man," he said. "We're going to get the people who did this to him. Bridge." The doors closed.

"Ma'am, follow me to the awareness stations," said Ja-Iyo-Cat. Thon had moved into an adjacent lift and Churryhoof was still staring at where Rebtet had met her gaze. Unprofessional.

The lift whirred and moved belowdecks. Dust and something that looked like paint chips had collected in the corners of the lift. *Magna Carta*'s janitor drones weren't working any better than her combat drones.

"Lieutenant," said Churryhoof. "I would like a straight answer as to how this vessel can function even at the sub-standard quality on display here. I look at the roster and I see a lousy sixty crew."

"Seven officers, counting you, ma'am," said Ja-Iyo-Cat, "ten noncoms, forty-four enlisted support staff and grunts."

"And you have one fella stationed in awareness. So who's managing the hundred fifty queens I just saw you puke out?"

"The idea was, we'd have the brand do it," said Ja-Iyo-Cat.

"Deck four," said *Magna Carta*'s computer. The lift slowed and stopped. "Awareness. Drone control."

The lift doors opened on to chaos. The awareness 3-stations had been moved to the far end of the room, stacked on top of each other like ballast. Discolorations on the walls showed where the stations had been before they were moved to make room for...

In the center of the room, where the Master of Drone should have been supervising, stood a cylinder of metal and plastic three meters tall. After processing what the lieutenant had just said, Churryhoof recognized it as a brand tower. Thick sec-data and power cables ran from the skirt at the bottom of the tower, through bayonet holes in the hull and into *Magna Carta*'s guts. A rre noncom in an amorphous utility exobody crawled down the brand like a slug.

"Who..." Churryhoof was dumbstruck. "Which brand is this?"

«Gearu Media is the industry leader in the design, execution and marketing of transmedia IPs for children and families. Owner of some of the galaxy's most beloved properties, it has brought up generations of children to respect the universal values of tolerance, friendship, and good citizenship. Although its techniques are always innovative, the messages Gearu conveys are timeless.»

"Holy butt-fucking Providence!" Churryhoof gripped her head; the pain was behind her already sore eye. "Does it always do that?"

"You get used to it, ma'am," said the rre in the utility exobody.

"Toh-Gak is our expert," said Ja-Iyo-Cat. "In civilian life thon is a PR engineer on Boeing-Quickdark."

"Why didn't thon bring Boeing-Quickdark with thon?" said Churryhoof. "If we're going to use brands in combat, which I'm fully aware is illegal, why bring a fucking media company?"

"We've lost fifteen percent of our fleet, ma'am," said Ja-Iyo-Cat. "We need Boeing-Quickdark coordinating the shipyards."

"Gearu was deemed non-essential to the war effort," said the noncom.

"I don't know what to tell you two," said Churryhoof. "Your context collapses because you've put twenty thousand military spacecraft under the control of a computer that makes toys for children."

"A common misconception, ma'am," said Toh-Gak. "Gearu and Boeing-Quickdark are actually quite similar. They both manage a complex interstellar logistics chain. This is an NP-equivalent task which can be mapped onto any other NP-equivalent task, such as building a tactical context."

Churryhoof had never ordered someone to map an NP-equivalent task onto another NP-equivalent task, but you didn't need to be an expert to point out the obvious. "So why doesn't our context work?"

"It works in simulation, ma'am. There's a mapping problem in the interface between brand and swarm." Toh-Gak latched on to one of the sec-data cables and oozed down its length, checking for flaws. "This is where we hope you can give some insight."

Churryhoof had nothing to give. She was an old-fashioned pilot in an era when piloting tasks were being devolved to the queens. The logical next step would indeed be to devolve the whole shebang onto a brand, but this next step was insane, which is why the queens had been developed in the first place.

But what if you went the other way, and treated Gearu Media as a super-charged queen? Churryhoof had seen queens consumed with paranoia, unable to trust their orders or the outputs of their own algorithms. Those problems didn't show up in simulation because queens could spot simulated data.

You fixed a queen by talking to it, helping it through its neurosis to a point where it could trust its environment enough to take action. But Churryhoof was terrible at talking to brands. That was why she'd joined the Navy: it was a good career that didn't involve working for a brand. Military service was the only way off of a boondocks colony like Fallback, unless you had no pride and were willing to end up like...

"Oh, hey," said Churryhoof. "You know who else makes useless shit?"

"Uh..." said Toh-Gak.

"I'm not confident I can guess which producer of shit you have in mind, ma'am," said Ja-Iyo-Cat.

"The people of *Jaketown* make wooden furniture," said Churryhoof. "They have to sell it, right? They must have someone who negotiates with consumer brands. Someone who can talk some sense into Gearu Media."

"Like a solicitor, ma'am?" said Ja-Iyo-Cat.

"Their solicitor's dead," said Churryhoof. "I am thinking more like a chief of marketing."

Den
Cedar Commons

Den had locked herself in the bathroom and was rifling through the first aid kit, looking for a weapon. She could hear Mom rushing around the flat, muttering to herself, adding things to her fake Louis Vuitton purse and removing them again.

"*Providence*, Den," said Mom. She rattled the door. "What are you *doing* in there?"

"I'm getting ready!" said Den. "I want to go with you."

"What? No! What?"

"I know Commander Churryhoof," said Den. She snapped the first aid kit shut and tied it back under the sink.

"You don't 'know' her," said Mom. "You...we talked to her about the drones."

"Before that," said Den. "I visited her in hospital. She likes me." This was a stretch. Den activated the bathroom door and looked out and made her eyes big at Mom. "I don't want you to go up there and not come back," she said. "They won't do anything to you if your daughter is with you." Mom stared at Den and weighed the options on some parental scale while squeezing one foot into a high-heeled shoe. "I'm an adult," said Den, throwing that on the pile.

"Make yourself presentable," said Mom.

"I'm presentable," said Den.

"You look like a hitchhiker. Put on a jacket at least."

While Mom took her turn in the bathroom, Den opened the dishwasher and pulled out the knife they used on-planet to gut fish. She hid it in her jacket pocket. If the Navy tried anything on Mom, the thing-trier would get this knife right in the stomach, and damn the consequences.

After killing Mr. Styrqot, Den had used her T-shirt to wipe her fingerprints off the gun, and hidden it in the alley behind the bank. But there was no murder mystery. Nobody cared who'd killed Mr. Styrqot. He was a bad guy, and more important people had died at the same time.

When the space elevator started lifting, Mom got all twitchy, fiddling with her purse as though she knew she'd forgotten something. "What do we get out of this?" Den asked her. "For helping them."

"What do we get?" said Mom. "We get to stay alive! The bloody council. Marketing always has to clean up the mess."

"You should make them evacuate the planet," said Den. "It's too dangerous here."

"Honey, you see this ship?" Mom pointed upwards and Den caught her first tiny glimpse of *Magna Carta*. "You don't 'make' this ship do anything. This ship sets the rules. You do what you have to do to survive, and get out as soon as you can."

The ride took about fifteen minutes, with the car moving up the elevator a lot faster than normal. Mom took out her compact and brushed powder onto her face. She was wearing big hoop earrings. Mom's motto was "dress to impress" and apparently hoop earrings were the most impressive kind. Soon enough the car docked with *Magna Carta* and when the doors hissed open there was Dr. Sempestwinku, and, oh shit! there was Dwap-Jac-Dac, the rre soldier who'd kidnapped Myrus.

"Please hand me your weapon, ma'am," said the rre. No, it wasn't Dwap-Jac-Dac, it was someone else in an identical exobody. Thons synthesized voice was different and thons name plate said JA-IYO-CAT.

"This is a purse!" said Mom, clutching it to her side.

"Not you, ma'am," said Ja-Iyo-Cat. Thons head turned towards Den with a snake hiss. "Your apprentice."

"Denweld?" said Mom in disbelief. Den sheepishly removed the knife from her jacket and handed it to the rre, who pinched it by the blade. "You brought a *knife?* What were you *thinking?* Providence, that's my Resusis silver!"

"You'll get it back when you disembark," said the rre. Thon pressed the knife into the shoulder of thons exobody and it slowly sunk into the metamaterial.

Dr. Sempestwinku coughed. "Ms. Xepperxelt." He held out his hand.

"Doctor," said Mom with strained politeness, keeping her arms at her side.

"Please come with us," said the doctor. "There is a sick brand aboard this ship."

All of Mom's anger was instantly transferred to the doctor. "You have a *brand?*" she said, in exactly the same tone she'd objected to the knife. "Do you mind explaining what in horn-plucking hell a brand is doing on a military ship?"

"Not my brand, not my ship," said Dr. Sempestwinku. "We need you to find out why it's sick."

"It's sick because it's tied into a bloody *death machine*! Now let me repeat my question: *why is it here?*"

"Professionals like ourselves must deal with the situation as we find it. If I see a man dying from a drug overdose, I don't lecture him; I save his life." Mom put her hands over Den's ears and cursed at the doctor in Narrathippin.

"I can hear you, Mom," said Den.

"Well, don't look those words up, honey."

The inside of the ship was cramped and smelled bad. Its streets were tunnels, like hallways between rooms. No passageway on *Jaketown* was this narrow, not even the alley where Den had dropped the nailgun. This was a ship that never landed, never unfolded into sunlight and air. There were no buildings, only doors that were shut and powered off. The walls were white, like a doctor's office, but they hadn't been cleaned. It felt like a slum.

Mom was muttering to herself again, searching through her anger like her purse to see what was available. This was very nearly the angriest Den had ever seen her. Angrier than when Mom had learned that Sefa de Gier's birthday party had featured the hazardous combination of Spin the Bottle and human boys. But not as angry as when Den had told her what Vec the egenu had done to Myrus's father. Vec was now dead, so you saw what happened when Mom got really angry.

The four of them got in a lift and the lift moved down, or at least along the gravity vector. Den listened to the thrumming of the lift and tried to figure out how fast they were going. Mom's teeth were clenched, her body stiff. Then the lift opened on a large messy room and there was the brand, all right.

The messy brand room was full of an *amazing* smell, eye-watering, like a bakery that only made flowers. Den wondered if this was some defense mechanism of the sick brand, but it was an uhaltihaxl kind of smell. A sick brand would smell human, like the smell in the corridors, which was like human food left to rot.

Mom let out her breath in a whoosh, either at the smell or the sight of the brand itself. Commander Churryhoof and a rre soldier were crawling up the floor with hand tools, checking wires. Commander Churryhoof looked up at them and stood up, and Den realized that the uhalti woman was the source of the flower-bakery smell. The two rre didn't seem to notice it.

But Mom sure noticed. She frowned and rummaged around in her purse and whispered to Commander Churryhoof and surreptitiously handed her something that Den couldn't make out. Commander Churryhoof spoke quietly to Mom for a while and then waved at the brand, using the sort of giving-up gesture the schoolmistress used to give to Mom when Den was being particularly impossible. Mom walked forward. Everyone watched her.

"Hello, qui," she said.

"Qui" was the polite way in English to address a brand in and of itself. Den and Myrus were brought up to be gentlebeings and they used "sir" and "ma'am" and "aer" all the time. But "qui" was a part of English that wasn't used very often, and hearing Mom say it brought up the shock that probably should have come when Den first saw the brand.

Nothing happened, so Mom just kept talking. She wasn't intimidated at all. "How are you, qui?" She walked around the tower, gently dragging her hand through water condensed on the metal. Den noticed that the seating panel ringing the tower was made of mahogany. Someone like Myrus or Den had carved that from a tree. Still nothing from the brand. "Tell me about yourself, qui," said Mom, almost flirtatiously.

«Gearu Media is the industry leader in the design, execution and marketing of transmedia IPs for children and families. Owner of some of the galaxy's most beloved properties, it has brought up generations of children to respect the universal values of tolerance, patriotism, friendship, and good citizenship. Although its techniques are always innovative, the messages Gearu conveys are timeless.»

Den went into her terminal and turned her privacy settings as high as they would go. Mom just smiled gently. "What are your core values?" she asked Gearu.

«Seven core values inform Gearu's growth: innovation, pride, respect, competitive spirit, a sense of fun, diversity and integrity.»

Gearu was actually a brand that Myrus liked. Den remembered a logo that popped up while a 3-game was loading, and a dopey voice saying "Gear-ooo". That singsong was nothing like the in-your-head voice of the brand itself. Now Mom turned away from the brand and looked at the Navy soldiers. "Do I even want to know what you told this poor brand to do?"

"We don't have time to coddle a bloody computer," said the rre in the blobby suit.

"This is not a 'computer'." Standing in her high heels Mom was fierce and tall enough to stare down a human. A wormy rre was no problem. "A computer does whatever you tell it to. A brand is a *person*."

"A brand is! a! computer!" snapped the rre in the squishy suit.

"Don't spook the talent, spaceman," said Commander Churryhoof. Her eyes were tired. "We brought her here for a reason."

«Would you like to hear a story?»

"Ma'am sorry ma'am!" said the rre. Den looked around. No one else had experienced the brand.

"You've compromised its core values," said Mom. "You've drafted a civilian without putting it through boot camp. I'm amazed this thing isn't flatlining!"

"Lady, I happen to be a PR engineer," said the wormy rre. The rre in the biped combat suit just stood at the door with arms crossed, watching.

«I really need to tell you a story.»

The brand's flat telepathic tone hadn't changed but its words were more insistent. Den looked around again and subvocalized: "All right."

«For many years the queendoms of Pampaxet and Urdicet had been happy neighbors. Their rivalry—for no great nation can truly believe another its equal—was the stuff of sport and drinking competitions. Words of challenge flowed across the border, but so did trade, and love letters.

«A silent change came scant days ago. In a moment, as if the world were a jewel that had turned to show another facet, every peaceful mind turned to thoughts of war. Soft-handed merchants in cafes smiled to imagine their competitors bloody and dead on a battlefield. A game became popular in the play-pits: the smallest child in a group was declared a citizen of the 'enemy' nation and beaten by her former friends, then abandoned so that the pain would take effect.

«Of course the culprit was the sorcerer Enxech, that would-be conqueror who never seemed far from the troubles of both countries. From her underground fortress of Nimar, Enxech magicked subtle paths and breathed a numbing fog up into the valley. Enxech whispered to Pampaxet, she hinted at Urdicet, and each nation obediently sharpened steel for the other.

«Far from this trouble, a young princess of Pampaxet was serving her apprenticeship, learning the art of government by ruling an island chain of no importance. When word came to her from a Pampax traveller that her country was at war, no hatred for Urdicet entered her. She was too distant for Enxech's spell to take effect. She saw through the Enxech's plan to make two great nations destroy each other so the wizard could pluck baubles from the wreckage.

«This princess used the remnants of her trade routes to gather her intelligence. From the best a small island could offer, she mustered an army to march on Nimar. She was the only one capable of stopping Enxech. She was the only hope of both nations. What was her name?»

"I don't know this story," Den subvocalized, though the parallels were clear. 'Pampaxet' and the rest were normal fantasy names; but 'Nimar' was really weird, more like a human or corestin name.

«Her army prepares to ride with her, to reclaim her birthright. Her commanders merely await the word. What is her name?»

"Wait wait wait," said Commander Churryhoof, staring into her terminal. "Coordination just spiked. It's gone now. Play it back. What happened?"

"Commander Churryhoof, ma'am!" said Den. "I need to talk to you! In private. It's urgent."

Churryhoof seemed skeptical. "Urgent *and* important," said Den. She cast eyes at Mom so that Churryhoof would think it had something to do with her. The two women were about the same age, so similar techniques should work on both of them.

Commander Churryhoof waved Den forward down the long room, through an uhalti-width crevice in piles of metal furniture and out a door Den hadn't seen. Out the door was another dirty white hallway. Churryhoof sealed the door and said "What is it?"

"This isn't private," said Den. "The brand can hear."

"What do you suggest? Shall we go EVA?"

She was probably being sarcastic. Mom had to deal with this situation on business trips. "Is there a restroom?" said Den.

There was a restroom, a big unisex thing twenty meters down the hallway. It was cavernous: scummy white tile, showers and stalls, exposed plumbing, alternating uhalti- and human-sized urinals. Den saw herself in a mirror that ran across a row of sinks.

"They're not allowed to watch you in here," said Den. "Unless they make soap or something. Then it's research. But sometimes they listen from outside." She checked her terminal for the sinks in front of her and couldn't find them. They were locked-down military sinks. She put her hands on the metal counter. "Can you turn on the water?"

Commander Churryhoof got it. She glanced at the sinks and they all started gushing. Den leaned in close, into the older woman's overwhelming perfume, and whispered: "The brand is talking to me."

"It talks to me. This is different?"

"I'm in its demographic. Older young adult. It trusts me."

"What does it say when it talks?"

"It's telling me this stupid fantasy story about an evil sorcerer. It's clearly a metaphor for the war. It wants me to engage."

"I wouldn't engage if I were you."

"I'm not asking for your advice," said Den. "I'm trying to help you. Gearu won't do what you want, right? That's what my mom is saying. But you already knew that. What Mom won't tell you is how to change its mind."

"How in...how do you change a brand's mind?" To Commander Churryhoof this seemed on the level of convincing rain not to fall, but Den knew better.

"You tell it a story," she said. "You align whatever you want it to do with its values. Brands are really messed up. We give them all these moral rules they have to follow, but then they also have to sell more furniture than they did last year.

"That's why the adverts have all these fake stories. The baby in the crib and the family sitting around the table. That's how Mom sold it. When actually the table and the crib were made by Ms. Sun who's got to apprentice five kids because her *husband*" (Den jumped briefly into English) "left her for a stripper and she needs the money."

Den backed off a little and squeezed her legs together. Being inside Churryhoof's scent was making her a little horny. What was going on? Was Den a lesbian? Myrus had never had this effect on her, nor the dreaded 'human boys' at the party; but neither had Churryhoof, the first time they'd met.

Around the fingers of one hand Churryhoof was unconsciously twirling the thing Mom had given her: a blister pack of little white pills, like antiestrual pills. Some of them were missing—Mom had been taking them—and that's when naive Den realized what the yeasty flowery smell was.

"So Gearu will manage the swarm," Commander Churryhoof said, "if it can pretend it's just a story?"

"It needs a way of filtering the data," said Den. "It'll do whatever you want if I can sell it as an adventure for young adults where I learn a lesson at the end." Then she sprang the trap. "But you need someone in-demographic to keep the filter going. So you'd better let me come with you."

"This is a real war," said Commander Churryhoof. "Not a metaphor with evil sorcerers. We are going into enemy space."

"Yeah, that's where Myrus is," said Den. "I told you, I'm going to rescue him."

"You're..." She was thinking how to say this without hurting Den. "You're not a soldier."

"I killed Mr. Styrqot. The hopore."

Den was sure this was the winning play, but Commander Churryhoof just nodded slightly and said, "Yes, you did."

"I thought I'd feel bad about it," said Den, "but I had to do it. And once I did...I don't feel bad at all. He deserved it."

"Den, you're in shock and you're not thinking clearly."

"You said six percent of uhalti soldiers won't kill. What about the people on the other end? What if six percent of us can kill without feeling bad? Those are the ones you need, right? We'd be the best soldiers of all. I'm an adult. I can join the Navy if I want to."

Commander Churryhoof finally seemed aware of the blister pack in her hand. She glanced at it and tucked it into a pocket in her uniform tunic. Her body language said she was embarrassed about this, but her face showed only determination.

"You have a theory," she told Den. "That's not much, except the rest of us don't have shit. Providence knows it's not a problem with the wiring. So I will give you authority to *test* this theory, and if it works out, I will *talk* to your mother about inducting you. But you need to know, and she's gonna know, that this is a suicide run. I can't share the details, but we are not expected to come back."

"No, we'll make it back," said Den. "It's destiny."

Commander Churryhoof sighed. "All right, Den," she said. "You've had more warnings than most people get. Let's test your theory." Den let herself smile a little. She knew she would remember this as the moment when Commander Churryhoof finally started treating her like an adult.

The instant they left the restroom, a stack of messages crash-landed in Den's terminal like papercraft launched across a schoolroom. «What is her name?» «What is her name?» «Where did she go?» «What is her name?»

"Den," said Den, out loud. "My name is Denweld Xepperxelt."

«Princess Denweld, my liege. It has been too long. I await your command.»

This was a private message, but Commander Churryhoof must have experienced something in her terminal, because she stopped in her tracks and looked at Den.

"Well, that got its attention," she said, and she was kind of scared when she said it. But Den was smiling a smile as big as all space.

Chapter 27

Save the Day

Kol
Sour Candy, **at Twist Station, Gontonbaine System**

s there any way," Kol asked the Chief, "do you know any way at all we could take on some more cargo? It doesn't have to be fancy. I'll move deuterium at this point, just to offset the cost of maintenance. But I've been all over this station and I have found nothing."

Cargo or no, it felt good to be doing business in a language designed specifically for doing business. Miss Becky Twice was making an honest effort to learn D, but things still went more smoothly when she was not at a meeting.

"How about that mehi-peri who does the forged artwork?" said the Chief. "Isn't she somewhere near here?"

"Those weren't forgeries," said Kol. "They were her original compositions, and I couldn't give them away."

"We trusted her!" said the Chief.

Kol opened a frozen fruitpack he'd bought from a vending machine. "What about the planet-sized turd we're orbiting?" said Kol. "What's its name?"

"They just call it Gontonbaine VI," said the Chief. She reached into the pack and stole a fruit slice. "It doesn't have much of an underworld."

"What are the legitimate exports?"

The Chief tried to think of some. "They export venomous animals," she said eventually, "but only by accident."

"Can we get more passengers? Someone who missed the Red Fist ship?"

"We're having trouble with our current passengers," said the Chief. "Sysadmin Gazak handed me a very angry note saying there's nothing to do on board."

"He handed you a note? That's pretty passive-aggressive. And has Gazak tried *leaving* the ship?"

"Maybe he likes Twist Station even less," said the Chief.

The seal on the access hallway cracked with an ear-splitting pop and Yip-Goru came out of an access corridor that had been exposed to vacuum for maintenance. Thons exobody was covered in the waste oil that Twist Station dragged behind it like a comet. "Good news, everyone," thon said. "I got us a full set of capacitors from a destroyed Outreach LCP. We're ready to leave."

Kol stood up. "Undock on the Chief's order."

"No, we got a problem," said Yip-Goru. "I should have led with the bad news. While the mechanics were installing the capacitors, they saw our...compartment. Where we keep the things. The *things*."

Kol sat back down. "Unfortunately, I haven't turned up any new 'things' to put in there," he said.

"That's your problem. The secret's out. We need to reconfigure the ship."

"We can reconfigure when we acquire some 'things'," said the Chief.

"My recommendation as the pilot is that we reconfigure now."

"Nice try. That's not the pilot's call. Shall we take a vote on it?"

"Hey, anybody seen Arun recently?" said Yip-Goru, pulling for the dreaded tie.

"He's on his pub crawl."

"Don't blame me when we get busted. I'll turn state's evidence on all of you."

"Speaking of which," said Kol, "call the pubs. Get him back. We're leaving."

"There's only one pub," said Yip-Goru. "I'll call while I pay the mechanics." Yip-Goru clanked down the access hallway to the bridge.

"How about Miss Becky Twice?" said Kol. "She's not chained up in your quarters or anything?"

"The humans left together," the Chief said without much interest.

"Uh, fellas," said Yip-Goru over the deckwide comm. "This is probably nothing, but there's a lot of money missing from the company account."

"Shit!" said Kol.

"And the pub has been closed since the war started."

Kol stood up and deliberately walked to the food storage cupboard above the sink. Strapped to the inside of the door was a 300-count box of Tetley's tea bags. Kol slipped a finger under the cardboard flap. opened the box, and reached inside. "The tea is gone," said Kol.

"We trusted him!" said the Chief. Betrayal never got old for her.

"Bloody humans!" said Kol. "They're in it together. He knows the account code, and he was teaching her D."

"She must learn D," said the Chief, in D. "It's the language of business!"

By an act of will Kol forced the panic-causing chemicals in his bloodstream not to interact with the anger-causing chemicals. "Yip-Goru, how much did they take?" he called down the access corridor.

The comm crackled. "Six hundred forty thousand in microcash."

This was the exact number Kol was hoping for. He sat down with exaggerated calm. "That's two shares of the Crazy Rooroo job," he told the Chief. "They only took what we owed them. We're even." There was no need for drama, for elaborate proclamations of revenge, or—perish the thought—actual revenge.

"She left," the Chief said to herself. Kol was a little shocked as well. He'd seen a number of bedmates go through *Sour Candy* and Miss Becky Twice was the only one who'd voluntarily left while still the center of the Chief's attention. Again two bands of chemicals warred in Kol's brain: pride that someone had finally listened to his warning, and anger at this demonstration of his own weakness.

Kol took out his 3-terminal and opened the letter he'd composed to the Errand Boy. It was just missing one sentence—a date and a place. Kol added that bit of crucial information and sent the letter. This wasn't revenge; it was business. Miss Becky Twice was no longer a crew member, and her safety was not his concern.

The Chief was trying to disguise her crying as a coughing fit, but the quantity of mucus dribbling from her nose—not sexy egenu mucus but the gross mammal stuff—meant Kol wasn't fooled. Kol reached across the table and put his hand on the Chief's trembling arm.

"Hey," he said, not exploiting this, just being there for her. "Let's get out of the war. Drop off the...doctors at the corestin homeworld and then act surprised when Yip-Goru brings up thons asteroid."

The Chief looked up. "What about Mr. Arun Sliver?" she blubbered, having discovered something else to be sad about.

"He is a grown-up," said Kol. "He can make grown-up decisions." Unlike Kol, apparently.

Rebecca Twice
Twist Station

"What happened to our tickets?" said Becky.

"Those are decoy tickets," Arun said, "for a flight we won't be taking." A mehi-peri family attached itself like a bolus to the end of the queue: two parents, genders indistinguishable to human eyes; a sullen teenager and two screaming younger kids. Just like that, the two humans went from being the conspicuous end of the queue to part of the unremarkable middle, invisibly shuffling towards the Red Fist refugee ship.

"Isn't that the most obvious plan ever?" said Becky.

"It would be more obvious to buy the tickets and take the flight." Arun flipped the hoodie of his ribbon suit over his head. You could still see he was human, but not identify him as any particular human.

"I'm asking these questions which may seem elementary to you," said Becky, "because you're acting like they're gonna come after us."

"These are the professional services I provide," said Arun. "But, no, we're probably not worth it. Unless you gave them a reason to come after us, for instance by stealing something on your way out."

The line lurched forward and the little vial of chemicals jostled on its chain around Becky's neck and her heart just about stopped. Too late to go back now.

"This is queer as all hell," Arun said, when they finally peered through the hatch. The Red Fist transport was a captured Outreach military ship, *I Am an African*. It had English wall signs saying POWER OFF ALL WEAPONS and SECURITY CHECK AHEAD. Instead of buttons and switches, everything ran on terminal connections. Stepping on board from a thousand-year-old Fist space station reintroduced Becky to everything she'd left behind.

"Fucking creepy is what it is," said Becky.

"It's effective propaganda," said Arun. "They captured so many Outreach vessels they could donate one to charity."

"SECURITY CHECK" was a cheerful human woman wearing an Outreach Navy uniform with the unit patches ripped off and the Red Fist logo embroidered in their place. A buzz cut and septum stud gave her an adorable soldier-boi look. "Greeting!" she said. The language was Trade Standard D but her accent was Chinese colonial. "You being *kiygahar*?"

"Uh, hi, what's—" said Becky in English. Arun lightly stepped on her foot.

"We being married," he said in D, ruining Becky's chances with the cute girl. "Safety being better than sadness. Maybe neutral hot drinking, *gahan?*"

The cute girl checked them in on a Fist clipboard. "Hot drinking, hot clothing, *garhey hoo* forward. Others having *gluy*ing the rooms, you staying in the *benhan*. Moving, please!" She beamed as she waved them on, so happy to be helping out these unfortunates.

"Coming with me, my love," said Arun, and guided Becky down the queue with a hand on her arm. Even in D, Becky could hear him ramping up the poshness of his accent, like a pufferfish inflating itself for protection.

"Who blew smoke up Miss Perky's ass?" Becky whispered.

"Not smoke," said Arun. "Evidence."

I Am An African's rec room was now a smelly common area. Most of the refugees were mehi-peri, but there were quite a few corestin and some feathered reptile-types. They all had crying children. Becky momentarily thought she saw two other humans, but they were jetk in Mormon-missionary shirts and ties, frightened expressions on their exaggeratedly masculine features.

"Home sweet home," said Arun.

"I worry that we're taking resources from legitimate refugees," said Becky. This was the sad tableau Becky saw in the 3-tank as part of a charity pitch, not something she'd ever imagined participating in.

"There are no refugees this side of the border," said Arun. "These good people saw their chance to escape Gontonbaine VI, the bloated appendix of the galaxy." He used his British radar to locate another queue, and steered them into it. "Coffee," he said, pointing at two large metal tanks down at the end of the queue. "Tea."

"Is it real coffee?" said Becky.

"You won't be drinking real coffee for a while," said Arun.

The queue shuffled forward. "Hey, I was thinking about Yip-Goru," said Becky. "How thon said there'd be a war every fifteen years."

"Don't be so loud when you speak English," Arun muttered. The jetk Mormons got in line behind them, dashing Becky's last hopes that the liquid at the end of the queue would be anything like coffee.

"Thinking I Yip-Goru anticipating a war happening, I having—"

"Hearing you the first time," said Arun. He tore a flattened microgravity-safe cup off of a big roll, popped it into the third dimension like you would a top hat, and filled it with 'tea'. Becky took lukewarm 'coffee'. She was pretty sure both tanks contained the same liquid. They sat down near the least crowded stretch of wall, leaning back on their bags, and let the screaming babies drown out the sound of their English.

"The math doesn't work," said Becky. "GWII was fifteen years ago, but GWI was twenty-four years before that. I don't see how Yip-Goru predicted anything."

"Don't look at the wars," said Arun. "Look at the elections. There's a war that didn't happen, a war single-handedly prevented by the greatest hero in modern history:"—he actually put his hand over his heart—"M. M. Jilani."

"Jilani?!" Becky coughed and spat. "The prime minister—with the—?"

"The very same. You all right?" Arun waited a bit. "The fall of the Jilani government resulted in new elections. That reset the Outreach election cycle, and our parents enjoyed nine more years of peace, until the cycles synced again. But no one will ever appreciate M. M. Jilani for his service, and it makes the pattern too hard to see."

Becky hugged her room-temperature coffee. "I don't think I want to live in this universe anymore," she said.

"Oh, don't take that view, love," said Arun. "It's actually quite comforting. Sometimes you can save the day by being incredibly crap at your job."

I Am an African shuddered and Becky felt the side-gravity of thrusters pushing them away from Twist Station and the job they'd left. A job at which Becky had, indeed, been incredibly crap. Arun, on the other hand, was a pro. The Chief had not run onto the fugitive transport, flailing her arms, looking for her former crew. She probably didn't even realize they were gone yet.

"I'm just hoping I'm not gonna be crap at this job," said Becky.

"You'll be fine," said Arun.

"I was a bad security guard," said Becky, "and I was a bad smuggler. And I probably should have told you this earlier, but I've never had a real marketing job before."

Arun wasn't fazed at all. "How hard can it be to get people to buy shit?" he said. "Some things are illegal and people *still* want to buy them. You'll do fine."

Part Four

The Brand Engagement

Chapter 28

P-A-R-E-N-T-S

Myrus
Interstellar Cooperation and Security Assembly (replica)
Fist of Joy Youth Festival

A few days into his imprisonment at the youth festival, Myrus learned, by way of some cruel teasing, that the Outreach was losing the war. Like, losing really badly. All at once he felt his love for the absent Warrant Officer Ingridsdotter flaring up again. He'd had it under control! He'd been thinking about other things. But one shock to the system, and the dam broke and all the itchy feelings came rushing back.

About a year ago Dad had suddenly started drinking a lot of licorice-nel tea. He'd winked at Myrus and said it helped a guy stay calm when "your chemicals can't find her chemicals" (Dad's phrasing). A week later he'd gone back to ruxlt and never mentioned it again. But there was no licorice or nel in the cafeteria, of course not, because this was the Fist of Joy, where everything was left over from something else.

Myrus found some tea-like stuff in a cupboard beneath the chafing dishes, and brought a steeping cup of it outside, but sipping the tea gave him double vision and did not help his hormonal problem at all. At the entrance to the replica of the Interstellar

Cooperation and Security Assembly, he'd poured the awful tea into the sand and crumpled up the paper cup.

"The occupying power has an obligation to allow neutral-party inspections of the occupied territory," Wei Nzeme was saying in English.

The replica ICSA had only five seats on the Outreach side of the semicircular table, versus twenty on the Fist of Joy side. Myrus was pretty sure the real ICSA had it even on both sides, but nobody wanted to RP some middle-tier Outreach colony, so the good guys were limited to Terra (Wei Nzeme for the human homeworld, of course), Akset Swy (the uhalti homeworld, represented by Teresa Inez, because Myrus sure wasn't doing it), Bex (the rre homeworld, some hopore girl), Temporary Junction (a jetk who wasn't showing any particular gender), and Centaurus (Sanjit Mathis).

"The party controlling the pending holdings must permit a neutral party to examine the pending holdings," said the translator, in Trade Standard D.

Over on the Fist side of the table they had all twenty homeworlds, but no effort was made to match up the species with the planet, so the hopore homeworld was represented by a mehi-peri, and vice versa, and so on. The debate was run through two translators who sat in the center of the space enclosed by the table. This was a big waste of time because all the kids on *Jaketown* learned Trade Standard D in school. But the real ICSA did things through translators, so that's how they did it here. Sitting between the translators was the parliamentarian, the only adult sitting up front.

"That provision applies to specific, named facilities, not entire sectors of space!" said the rasme thau boy representing the aausq homeworld.

A few other adults sat in the observer's gallery, watching and taking notes. Myrus scooted in a couple rows behind them and sat in a now-familiar Fist metal folding chair.

"The restriction of that obligation to specific locations identified by name," said the other translator, in English. "Its inapplicability in general."

Up in the front row Myrus spotted a very young boy whose species he didn't recognize. The boy was wearing a Cametrean shame robe, role-playing the neutral observer from Quennet. It was a job you could give to a little kid to get them out of the way. Myrus wondered if a species could quietly join the Fist of Joy without anyone noticing. With everyone thinking someone else had invited these weird-looking people.

"Your failure to provide a list of 'locations' is an Ois Treaty violation," Wei Nzeme said in English, "designed to cover up other, more serious violations, ah, some of which we have brought to this assembly's attention, only to be met with procedural minutiae and irrelevant counter-accusations." His voice was amplified so everyone could hear, and there was some murmuring over on the Fist side but things didn't get really rowdy over there until the translator had finished saying the same thing in a combination of D and B.

Myrus sat back and watched the fireworks. It was nice to watch Wei Nzeme go after the other team for once, instead of tearing down Myrus all the time with his obnoxious sarcasm. The Fist side didn't like what Wei was saying at all, but they had no way to respond except with the irrelevant counter-accusations he'd just accused them of using.

Wei and his debate team had a big problem. The Outreach was losing the war, and the only thing you could do in the ICSA was argue about how you should be allowed to lose. The Fist of Joy controlled about six thousand Outreach star systems, which seemed survivable, but when you looked at it on a 3-map you saw they weren't all in one place. The Fist had moved the entire border inwards about a hundred light-years.

Now all the border stations were behind enemy lines. There was nowhere to focus a counterattack. And nobody knew what was happening in those six thousand systems, because the Fist of Joy wasn't letting the Red Top, Red Cross, etc. into the occupied territory.

Dad is in there, Myrus thought. *Our parents are in that space and all you care about is making sure the enemy knows how angry you are.* As much as he hated the other council kids, they were the only people at the Festival on his side of the war. He'd come here hoping they had a plan to save their parents, but they were still doing what they did best: complaining.

Dad was safe for a while. The Fist of Joy couldn't possibly keep the lid on all these systems. It would take ten billion soldiers. That was why they couldn't let the Red Top in; it would make it obvious that thousands of technically "occupied" planets were presents that hadn't been opened.

Hopefully that was it. The alternative was Wei's next insinuation: that the Fist was carpet-bombing the colonies with Evidence to enslave the humans, then killing everyone else (how?). Just to score points in a debate, Wei was claiming the Fist of Joy was casually murdering billions of people.

Myrus was also annoyed at Teresa Inez, who was doing a really poor job of representing Akset Swy. She was actively trying to sell out the rest of the Outreach, even other uhalti colonies, to protect the homeworld. Myrus had never been to Akset Swy, but he was pretty sure this said more about Teresa as a person than about the political situation on the homeworld.

Within minutes of Teresa's big sell-out maneuver, the mock ICSA session turned into a massive argument over the precise meaning of the Trade Standard D word "tehenrehureha", which translated to "chen thewel" in Narrathippin but to the much stronger "intolerable" in English. This was the exact problem D was supposed to fix, so the parliamentarian, the only person who could resolve things with the awesome power of adulthood, refused to give a ruling. Everyone yelled at the translators, the chair banged his gavel a lot, and the session ended with nothing being decided. It was, Myrus had to admit, an accurate model of the real ICSA.

Wei and Teresa and Sanjit frequently made lifelong friends during a four-hour stopover at a space station, so once the meeting ended Myrus was expecting everyone to drop their differences and hang out together and shun Myrus. But the kids on the Fist side stood up and milled around a little and swirled towards the exit like water down a drain, without even looking at their make-believe opposition. Maybe they thought Wei went too far accusing their parents of mass murder.

The adults had been the first to leave. The Outreach representatives now had the run of the ICSA, but they were staying near the desks they'd been sitting at, leaning on the chairs, talking in low voices like they were discussing where to have lunch. Myrus gathered his energy and walked up the ramp to make a plan to escape this POW camp.

Wei Nzeme seemed really friendly with the hopore girl who represented Bex. They were actually holding hands, until they saw that Myrus had noticed. Myrus imagined the hilarious sight of Wei kissing his hopore girlfriend right on the beak. Of course, Myrus was in no position to judge anyone: he'd gone into love for a human. However, Wei was crossing the mammal/reptile line, so if you were to create a ranking of perverts, Wei would be near the top, with the gendered rre and the people who could only get off engaging with brands, with Myrus closer to the middle.

"Well, look who it is," said Teresa. "The prodigal son returns."

"I don't even know what that means," said Myrus. Was this his idea of a clever comeback? Come on!

"Myrus, you should join us," said Wei.

"I did, I'm here, I'm right here."

"You know what I mean. Join the model ICSA."

Teresa didn't like this but Sanjit did. "It would look better if we had an uhaltihaxl representing Akset Swy," he said.

"Why?" said Myrus. "They don't match the species on the other side."

"And that's sloppy," said Sanjit. "We should hold ourselves to a higher standard."

Myrus switched to subvocal over the private capital-terminal network. "This isn't a game, fellas," he said. "There is a real war happening. Those thousands of systems you're whining about? The Fist of Joy took them over in real life. Including the system where..." He grabbed at Wei's wrist to start a bone-conductive data transfer and Wei slapped his hand away, so Myrus just said "where our P-A-R-E-N-T-S are."

Wei folded his arms. The human kids looked at each other. This was not a normal interaction. They no longer thought they were better than Myrus. They were suspicious of him. Myrus had some new power he didn't know about.

The hopore and the jetk weren't on the private network, of course. They'd never met Myrus or, apparently, been told that he existed. He was a whirlwind out of nowhere. Wei whispered in the hopore girl's ear. She left and tugged the jetk kid along with her. They walked down the rows of folding chairs towards the exit.

"All right, *Myrus*," said Teresa, as though Myrus's name was something to be used against him. "We weren't going to bring this up, but since you're so concerned about politics, maybe you should explain why you're spending all your time hanging out with a bloody war criminal."

"I don't know what you're talking about."

"Your Mr. Starbottle is the man who created Evidence," said Wei. "Everyone knows this, so I'm sure you know it as well. He is the *reason* the Fist is able to run right over our defenses and take those six thousand fifty-nine systems and do God-knows-what in there."

"Yeah, okay, well, he didn't design it as a weapon. He wanted to help people. He's totally clueless. He doesn't even have a proper lab. He's teaching kids at this festival in the middle of nowhere. They're, like, exploiting him."

"Myrus, you are an idiot," said Sanjit. "Mr. Starbottle is a bloody war hero. He can have any job he wants. He wants to work with kids? They let him work with kids. They give him whatever he asks for and hope he comes up with the next big thing. And you...are...helping him!"

Sanjit's pointing finger was getting pretty close to Myrus, and Myrus wanted to hit him, so he took a step back and lowered his eyes to calm down. "He's a human," Myrus said. "He's not going to do something that will kill a bunch of humans."

"You need to wake up, my friend," said Wei. "There is no racial loyalty in the Fist. They don't want it, they can't afford it. That's why they don't match the species to the homeworld."

These people were like Myrus's personal chorus of doom. For years they had teased him because he was short and uhalti and his dad was a woodworker instead of something posher. Now they were badmouthing Professor Starbottle and implying that Myrus himself was a war criminal.

"You know what?" said Myrus. "Fuck you. Fuck all of you. I do not want to talk to any of you, ever again." He kicked over a folding chair and left. He heard Wei Nzeme mutter "Bloody hell!" but no one came after him, which was fine. He would rescue all their parents, all by himself.

In the next building over, down the elevator, Professor Starbottle was sitting on the stool they'd just made, working on his terminal. One leg of the stool was a bit shorter than the other two, but the thing was holding the old fella's weight. It was not a bad accomplishment, considering the wood came from scraps donated to the Festival for a tax write-off.

"Hello, Myrusit," said Professor Starbottle.

"I was gone for a while," said Myrus. The professor hadn't even noticed.

"You've returned, so no harm done."

"Professor Starbottle, I have discovered an emergency," said Myrus.

The human finally looked up out of his terminal. "Emergencies don't wait, do they? What is it?"

"My dad is in a lot of danger. I need to get off this planet. I need to get back into Outreach space. Like, as soon as possible."

"That's not a problem," said Professor Starbottle. "I'll contact my personal assistant and we'll charter a ship."

"The jetk guy? I really don't think he can help."

"My personal assistant is very competent, and, Myrusit, you shouldn't make assumptions about a jetk's gender."

"I saw you talk to him in the 3-tank," said Myrus. "He said he would bring us some more wood. Which is nice, but he's *not* nice enough to return an Outreach prisoner of war."

"Oh, this damn war." Professor Starbottle threw up his hands like an interstellar war was a big hassle when making travel plans.

He stood up off the stool and started pacing, as he did when he didn't understand the next step in Myrus's instructions.

"Can you get him to send a ship?" said Myrus. "He doesn't have to show up. Just drop something down the elevator."

Professor Starbottle looked at Myrus as though he'd caught him cheating. "What sort of trouble is your father in?"

"He's shipwrecked," said Myrus. "In the occupied space."

"On the planet with the...unusual flora?" said Professor Starbottle. Myrus had been too embarrassed to tell him the 'magic trees' story but somehow he'd found out anyway.

"Not there," Myrus lied. "Nobody else knows where he is. If they find him they're going to think he's a spy and kill him."

"But he's not a spy, correct? He's a woodworker, he taught you your trade."

"Yeah," said Myrus. If Dad was a spy, it was the galaxy's deepest undercover job.

"Okay, Myrusit," said the professor. "Actually, my personal assistant has been asking me to leave the Festival early. He is trying to pull me back in to work on an old project. A...military project that's run into some very serious problems. I've been telling him no, but if I say I've changed my mind, he might send a ship for me. We can take the ship into Outreach space and find your father. It will be—"

"Make sure the ship has uhalti food for two people."

"That will sound suspicious," said Professor Starbottle. "I think we should start stockpiling food from the cafeteria."

Myrus's stomach started to knot up. Partly from the idea of living on cafeteria food for another who knows how long, but mostly because he had just realized what probably went on with Professor Starbottle's "military project".

Chapter 29

Illegal Order

Princess Denweld
Above Cheder Camunis

O ut of the mountain pass Princess Denweld came, atop a broad-backed panh whose steaming breath lifted the stench of raw meat into the royal litter. All warm-blooded creatures were unwelcome here, and only starveling boreworms lived this deep in the permafrost.

At a signal the panh halted and gasped, sucking thin air into its lungs. Denweld looked down the mountain, past the treeline, into the blue-green Pampaxet Valley and the walled city of Cheder Camunis. This city produced nothing of value, but it controlled trade through the pass, and Denweld had to conquer it to protect her supply lines.

Denweld had led her army through the pass, but now as she contemplated the situation, the front-line soldiers were filing past her. Sure-footed crossbow snipers patrolled crags at the top of the mountain, protecting the ground troops from aerial attack.

A saddled dohredaw ran back up the pass from Cheder Camunis, its feet fitted with cleated snowshoes, its tiny forearms bound uselessly into plate-mail gloves. Riding the dohredaw was Gearu, Denweld's chamberlain and scout. She was short and plump, her horns filed down to nothing. "My liege!" she said, looking up to Denweld on her panh. "They have a rock-hive!"

Denweld took her spyglass from its case and focused on the city. Her uncushioned seat swiveled wildly beneath her, keeping her steady despite the panh's shuffling movements on the packed snow. Through the glass she saw the walls of Cheder Camunis, the tall clock tower of the armory, and surrounding it all she saw a blur of living rocks: the fragments of a disturbed hive. Anyone attempting to storm the city would be battered and crushed by whirling stones.

"Let us simply bypass the city," said Gearu. "By breaking a hive Cheder Camunis have isolated themselves. They cannot get out any more than we can get in."

Den sighed. This was the problem: Gearu's core values were in conflict with the mission. It couldn't stop looking for the lateral-thinking nonviolent solution. Princess Denweld lowered the spyglass and looked sternly at...him?

Gearu wasn't a woman with filed-down horns. He was a geld, his horns stunted and ingrown, smaller than Myrus's. This made historical sense—no man but a geld could serve a queen's court—but Den had never seen this detail used in a sim. It was too gross for kids and too unsexy for adults. Why not just be a girl?

"The city controls access to the pass," said Princess Denweld. "If we don't take it, Enxech will. Then her influence will spread even further. Is that what you want?"

"No, of course not, it's just..."

"An agitated rock-hive is unstable. Send a few bolts into the swarm and the rocks will panic. They will turn on the people they should be protecting, and pound the defensive walls to rubble."

"Yes, my liege." Gearu rode back up the pass, calling out orders to the clifftop snipers. Denweld heard the *twang* of a crossbow. Displaced air sang around her, brief gaps appeared in the city's moving shield of rock, and the view through Denweld's spyglass was soon obscured by the dust thrown up as rocks smashed against the city walls.

"My liege, this is most unusual!" Gearu's dohredaw had

silently trotted back to Denweld's side. "The people of Cheder Camunis are sending a message of surrender!"

"*What?*" said Den.

In the distance the bells on the clock tower rang out, their lower harmonics muffled by the roar of the collapsing city walls. "The chimes!" said Gearu. "They sound the ancient Chord of Peace! They're suing for peace!"

Fucking... Gearu thought Den was worried about realism! Consumed by logistical questions of how 'Cheder Camunis' had sent Gearu a message of surrender in a fantasy world with no instantaneous long-range communication.

"Halt the attack!" said Den. "Wait until I come back." She disengaged her terminal, took a deep breath and opened her eyes. She was standing in the drone control room, alone with Gearu. The brand was sweating. Water ran down its tower and dribbled over the heavily shielded cabling that connected it to the ship and the drone swarms.

«Don't leave me.»

Den walked down the hallway to the large unisex restroom. The Navy was not supposed to be like this. Den didn't even get a uniform. She wore a tomboy dress from *Jaketown*'s hand-me-down shop so she'd look younger and the brand would identify more strongly with her.

«Please come back.»

An enlisted rre stood just inside the restroom, on the tile, where Gearu could not look. The three senior officers of *Magna Carta*—Captain Rebtet, Commander Churryhoof, and Lieutenant Ja-Iyo-Cat—stood in a perfect triangle around a portable 3-tank showing the damage Gearu and Den were doing to Cedar Commons.

Gearu had called off the attack as ordered, but the swarm had already nudged hundreds of ring fragments out of their orbits, and the green dots were winking out, burning up in-atmosphere or becoming radiating circles of shock spreading over the surface. The map displayed *Jaketown*'s space elevator specially, a thousand times its actual size.

"Specialist Xepperxelt?" said Captain Rebtet with the hostile curiosity that would like to know what you think you're doing, you punk kid.

"Sir, Gearu is receiving a surrender message from the planet," said Den. "There's not supposed to be anyone down there."

Oddly enough, Jiankang Nzeme, the mayor, was also here, sitting in a toilet stall with his pants up. "I'm sending the surrender message, Den," he said. "*Jaketown* is evacuated. There's nobody down there; just a relay."

"It's a little creepy," said Den.

"I don't give a damn if you think it's creepy," said Captain Rebtet. "Over and over I have been assured that Gearu is ready to serve as a weapon rather than a storyteller. Again and again, the brand has curled up the second it thinks it's put someone in real danger. The bar is now set very high. You lot are going to have to show me that your setup works in every scenario we can throw at it."

"It would have been better if she didn't know the signal was false," said Lieutenant Ja-Iyo-Cat. "Gearu is very good at picking up on humanoid body language."

"That's not reasonable," said Commander Churryhoof. "This has the appearance of an illegal order. We should be glad that Specialist Xepperxelt pushed back."

"It would be easier to get Gearu to destroy the hopore ship," Den suggested. "It's a military target." Captain Rebtet wound up to yell again, but Commander Churryhoof had once been a teenage girl, and she knew that this would not work on Den.

"Your mother is on *Little Dagger*," Commander Churryhoof told her. "We need that vessel to evacuate the people of *Jaketown* back to Outreach space."

"This is Outreach space," said Den.

"No, Den," said Commander Churryhoof. "Not anymore."

Den looked at the 3-globe. Cedar Commons was uninhabitable. The atmosphere was choked with smoke, dust and ice.

"All right," said Den. "But...you're sure there's no one down there."

"Hold on to that doubt, Specialist," said Captain Rebtet, "and take it into the drone control room, and stop throwing snowballs. Get Gearu to break the seal on a nuke. Convince me that I can take this configuration into battle without getting us all killed."

Clearly, Gearu was not the only part of the 'configuration' that Captain Rebtet considered unreliable. Den said, "Yes, sir," and turned and passed the guard, and made the walk back down the hallway to the drone control room.

This wasn't the military; this was the mob. Commander Churryhoof said she'd killed a human. What would Den end up doing before this was over? Maybe Myrus wasn't worth all of this. But she and Myrus had been designed for each other. If Myrus wasn't worth it, Den had no way to tell if anything was worth anything. And with no way to tell, Den might as well do what she'd sworn to do.

"My liege," said Gearu, still mounted on his dohredaw with its ridiculous gloved forearms, still looking up at Den, as if no time had passed. The crossbows still snapped around them, the city's walls still cracked. "What is our response to the notice of surrender?"

Princess Denweld arranged herself like someone about to make a difficult decision. "Gearu, do you believe that the trials we face in life are arranged by Providence?"

"Of course," said Gearu, so happy to have a question with an easy answer. Den did not believe this, but a brand that told stories to uhaltihaxl children would have to believe it.

"And why do the scriptures say Providence gives us these trials?"

"They say there is no reason," said Gearu. "Providence cares nothing for us and we will never understand her motives. Our lives are ripples atop her perfect indifference."

"Providence, in her indifference, has ordained this war," said Denweld. "Today the people in this city must die. Tomorrow, we may have to accept our own deaths with the same equanimity."

"But surely—"

"Fire the cannon," said the princess sharply. "One shot to the center of the city. I give the order; the responsibility is mine."

Gearu whimpered and gave a signal to the artillery officers. The ugly metal barrel of the cannon was lowered down the cliff on thick metal chains. Its report was too loud to be heard; its recoil cracked the mountain. Princess Denweld's snipers leaped to higher ground as a minor avalanche rolled into the valley. A snowdrift dribbled down the back of Princess Denweld's neck and she saw the projectile soar into the city.

Its explosion lit up the dust cloud that now enveloped Cheder Camunis. The clock tower briefly sailed into view, a pile of masonry that didn't yet know it was rubble. A moment passed and Denweld heard the explosion and the final, discordant ring of the bells with their Chord of Peace or whatever.

Cheder Camunis had been destroyed. Nimar, the evil one's fortress, would soon see the same fate. The sorcerer Enxech would be hearing from Princess Denweld and her army. Gearu looked up with begging eyes at Denweld on her snorting mount.

"You did the right thing," said Den, and that was all he needed to hear.

Chapter 30

Essential-Skilled Civilian

Rebecca Twice
I Am An African

B ecky woke in the night to the sounds of a struggle. These weren't unusual sounds in a transport full of refugees who'd abandoned their old lives to camp on the rec deck of a military cruiser. If anything, this was quieter than the usual domestic disputes; no yelling, just grunts. Becky only really woke up once it became clear that she herself was the object of the struggle.

A jetk individual, new to the ship, believed that Becky should stand up and face him. Arun opined that it was Becky's right to sleep on the floor with the other refugees. Unfortunately the jetk had a bunch of cronies, also jetk, who pinned Arun's arms behind his back and stuffed something in his mouth. Their leader yanked Becky off the floor and stood her up. They then stepped back and held up their hands, as if they'd used up their quota of violence for the day.

Becky glanced at the wirchak couple camped on the floor next to her, and saw the fully aware and active ignorance practiced by people in big cities. Then the wirchak were blocked by a stand-up curtain like you'd see at a job fair. The jetk's cronies worked around Becky, extending the curtain, pushing PVC pipes into joints, boxing her and the jetk leader into a little square cocoon.

There was no reason why the Fist should be yanking people off a refugee ship, unless someone had squealed on Becky in particular. Trellis On-Site Security was certainly displeased with Becky, but sending out a hitman seemed a little excessive, and why a bunch of jetk? This was probably Kol or Yip-Goru's fault.

"What do you want?" said Becky. The jetk held up a finger for silence, and then looked up at where the finger was pointing. One of their minions was covering the job booth with a tarp, glowing brightly on the side facing Becky and blackout dark on the side facing out.

Now that there was decent lighting Becky could get a good look at her attacker. The jetk presented male and was sharply dressed. A fuzzy felt coat pulled tight with gold thread around his androgynous frame, shiny red knee-high boots that ended in big round clown shoes. Antique gold-rimmed glasses rode high on his nose. Not smart 2-glasses like Arun's, just panes of glass that bent the light a little on its way to the eyeball.

This was the costume of the jetk privateers who'd terrorized the expanding Fist of Joy around the time of Europe's renaissance. It was not technically a military uniform—Becky was pretty sure that was illegal—but it was close enough to act as a portable slap in the face. Like a guy with a big blond moustache wearing a grey outfit that wasn't quite a Confederate battle uniform.

"Miss Rebecca Twice," the jetk said in perfect BBC English, "you are moderately difficult to find." He had no visible weapons... except for Arun's singularity pistol, which he held awkwardly, like the playbill of a musical he didn't want to watch.

"Actually, my name is Jane," said Becky. "Jane Doe."

"No, it's Becky," said the male-presenting jetk. "At some point in your hopefully long and prosperous life, you may need to lie to me and have me believe you. Please do not give away your tells trying to maintain a fragile fiction."

Becky started fumbling around for her will to live. Hitmen, even fancy ones like Arun, didn't talk to their victims like this. They just garroted you while you sat on the toilet. She might get out of this.

"What was your plan?" the jetk asked. "Why did you flee further into Fist space? I am not asking out of curiosity. I need your help, and whatever enticements my civilization might have to offer, I can get them for you."

"I was going to start a marketing consultancy," said Becky.

"Why in the Fist?"

"That's where the demand is. You people are terrible at marketing."

"This is excellent," said the jetk. "We want the same thing! I need to hire a marketing professional. You were recommended."

"By who?"

"Maybe 'recommended' is not the right word."

The whole ship shuddered. Becky looked down and realized she wasn't touching the ship anymore. At some point she'd stepped back onto a sheet of stainless steel, and the jetk's henchmen had picked up that sheet and were carrying the whole setup like a litter. The tarp above her rustled like a flag as she was lifted up. The jetk gently shifted his weight around on the plate like he'd done this a thousand times.

"I've spent some time in the Outreach, Rebecca," said the jetk, "and I've noticed that people who work for brands start to use the brand as a crutch. The brand is right so often that the sentient can't correct it when it's wrong.

"The nature of the work I'm offering requires a dynamic, independent thinker who can get along without a brand whispering in her ear. You have one centishift to prove you are that person. Otherwise I'll kill you." He said the last part quickly, like it was a legally required disclaimer.

"How do I 'prove it'?"

The jetk made the smallest possible motion necessary to convey that he didn't care how. "Sell me something," he said.

The only thing Becky had queued up was the pitch she'd been perfecting to pick up Fist clients. She could deliver the spiel in D, but she stuck to English for easy improvisation. "Okay. What is your opinion of branding? Probably not positive."

"Brand-ing? The creation of a brand? Why must English always be gerund-ing nouns?"

He didn't even know the word. "When I say 'America', what do you think of?"

"The Corn Palace," said the jetk.

Of course. "What else?"

"The Statue of Liberty. Mr. Abraham Lincoln."

"Personal freedom?"

"Sure."

"But America was built on slavery."

"I'm in no position to condemn that."

"America invented the hydrogen bomb."

"You and thirty other cultures."

"See, you're arguing with me. Not because the things I'm saying are false, but because they don't fit America's branding. You're doing the cognitive work to maintain the image we project."

"America's not a brand."

"The word 'brand' comes from 'branding'. This is the thing you don't get. The Fist has terrible branding because you won't acknowledge the concept. America has great branding because we invented it.

"You have this logo—" Becky got a little bold and poked the insignia on the jetk's felt coat—"which is a great logo, very Black Panthers, but the logo means 'war'. Nobody looks at this and thinks about your great artists, or pretty girls, or how they've always wanted to visit the Fist on vacation. This is something you paint on a spaceship when you want to kill some humans."

"I don't see why I should care what you think of our 'logo'."

"But you *do* care. You're inside the ship, but you paint the logo on the outside. This symbol is how you present your core values to the universe. And the message we're getting is: the only time the jetk will actually stand with the egenu and the mehi-peri is to fight a war."

"All right, you're hired," said the jetk. "I disagree with everything you said, but you've got balls and you're not stupid."

"I guess I start immediately?"

"You'll be in transit for a few shifts. Get you a decent bed, at least."

"Can we stand down the wobbly-ass platform?" said Becky.

"When we get back to my ship." The jetk sighed. "It'd look off-brand if my fellas set us down in the middle of an access hallway." He pulled off his antique glasses. "I'm very tired," it said. "It feels like I have to run the whole war myself." It rubbed its eyes and looked at Becky and for the first time Becky wanted to just throw herself through the curtain and *run*.

The glasses were the prop the jetk used to perform masculinity. Without them, it was a blank doll in a pirate outfit, a horrific shape in the false sun of the glowing tarp. Its face was a surface that absorbed Becky's attention and gave nothing back.

"Oh, sorry, sorry, I'm so sorry," said Becky, disgusted by her reaction, palm over her face, apologizing to the thing that had kidnapped her.

"No, no, it's all right." The jetk put its glasses back on and wrinkled his nose. "It happens." He must have so much practice ignoring that.

"What exactly is the job?" said Becky, trying to scope out how dearly she'd bought her survival.

"I'm not an important person," said the jetk. "I'm just an errand boy. But I run errands for some *very* important people who asked me to locate a marketing expert trained in the Outreach. Someone who can troubleshoot a failing ad campaign, that sort of thing.

"You're what the Ois Treaty calls an ESCOT. Essential-Skilled Civilian in Occupied Territory. We can require you to work, and we can move you around, but we have to pay you, and we'd be absolutely mad to hurt you." Becky was absolutely not an Essential-Skilled Civilian, but convincing the jetk of this would just get her moved further down the list of PWGFODW (People Who Get Fucked Over During Wartime).

"You won't need to worry about the war," said the jetk. "We'll protect you; we'll even give you a nice recommendation once it's all over. Depending on performance, of course."

"What about, uh, my husband?"

The jetk looked momentarily puzzled. "Oh, Mr. Arun Sliver? His Ois status is...complex. But my job is to make you happy, so we're bringing him along."

The quality of the artificial gravity changed slightly and the litter dropped to the ground with a clang. Becky fell on her butt and grasped at the curtain just as it was yanked back by the jetk's minions. *I Am An African* had been off-white plastic; this spaceship gleamed stainless steel. It had once been sleek and impressive, but these idiots kept dropping heavy things on the floor, and now everything was dinged up.

Arun stood over Becky, safe but ashamed, looking down at her like the Monopoly man with his pockets turned out. "What the hell good are you?" Becky asked him.

"We're still breathing, yaar!" said Arun.

The jetk reached for his glasses again and thought better of it. "I like the Outreach," he said. "I really do. A wonderful culture. You know exactly what you stand for. Unfortunately your 'core values' require you to do things you're bad at, just to get money. Intelligent people like you, Rebecca, guarding forests. You were meant for better things."

"I was doing okay," said Becky. "I was doing just fine!" The fact that she was still alive was proof that her business plan was sound.

"Things will go even better for you," said the jetk, "with me acting as your personal assistant."

Chapter 31

Space Adventure

Ethiret-Jac, Ingridsdotter-Dwap-Dac and Tellpesh-Tia Arzil, en route to Tired Gulch

Ethiret-Jac and Ingridsdotter-Dwap-Dac jostled in the open rear payload of a wheeled vehicle normally used for grocery runs. I swear this bastard's aiming for the potholes, said Ingridsdotter-Dwap-Dac, amplifying her native-voice over the ad-hoc milnet. The driver was a Cametrean fan whose qualifications for driving a wheeled vehicle were limited to owning a historically appropriate costume. Dwap is bumping Ingridsdotter's lung.

Give it a rest, ma'am, said Tellpesh-Tia. Sitting in the abbot's two-seater behind the pickup, she saw the conversation through a haze of static and quiet bursts of military data from orbit. The stolen Fist terminal sealed to her ulna by a plaster cast was sending data through to her capital terminal through her skeleton. I don't think there's a guardian force, she added. Every ship up there is either coming or going.

The abbot had insisted on driving Tellpesh-Tia to Tired Gulch in his personal vehicle, a quiet battery-powered thing used mainly for running errands around the Zone of Reality. Ostensibly this was the logical choice—an uhaltihaxl would take up less room in the minuscule cockpit than a human. But as soon as he started the engine, the abbot revealed his true agenda. This was his last chance to argue with a real Jalian priest, and he was going to make Tellpesh-Tia suffer through every minute of it.

"And if you think you're doing anything differently," the abbot was saying, "you're fooling yourself! We all interpret reality through the lens of a few well-chosen stories. Cametreans have the advantage that our stories are self-consistent parts of a single continuity. You must admit that this is elegant and rational."

"I will admit nothing," said Tellpesh-Tia. "Dwap-Jac-Dac-Tia-Sunlight thought your stories were childish amusements. Then we took Tia, the part of her who liked your stories the least, and symbiosed thon with Specialist Tellpesh, who thinks they are pigshit. Now you have me."

The quenny kept one hand on the steering controls and draped the other out the open window as the barren landscape slowly bumped past. The wind (despite appearances, they were going fast enough to create a wind) whistled oddly through the creases of his stillsuit.

"Yes, your lieutenant was far too polite," he said. "There was too much of the ecumenist in thon. But people like you and me, Tellpesh-Tia, we want the truth. We will not settle for coexistence or syncretism. We must have the whole truth! We must fight for it!"

"You don't fight," said Tellpesh-Tia. "You don't argue. You just restate your position, over and over."

The abbot cackled and abruptly turned the wheeled vehicle ninety degrees, nearly drifting it into a concrete post. "I'm not ashamed to admit that I'll miss you, Precedent," he said. "After breaking Ethiret I've come to crave the thrill of argument. But have no fear; I'm confident we'll meet again, and soon enough you'll see things my way."

Tellpesh-Tia had rarely had cause to fear anything more. "The only way I will be coming back to this planet is to lead a boycott," she said.

"Your desires and plans are quaint but irrelevant. The author of our shared narrative cannot afford to waste any characters.

There must be a resolution! Think about it, Precedent. Why should we appear in each others' stories and then part at a spaceport, never to see each other again?"

Tellpesh-Tia disconnected from both terminals and brought her full consciousnesses back to the cramped two-seater. "I don't know why we should," she snapped, "but it happens all the damn time. Tellpesh has served with hundreds of spacemen. Some of them are dead now. I never saw them again. Tia has met three high priests of Cametre, just like you. I'm never going to see them again. Unless you think they'll all line up as I lie on my deathbed, so you can have your narrative closure."

"But have you really met four high priests?" said the abbot. "Or have you met a single stock character four times? People are not as complicated as you seem to think, Precedent."

"People are simple because you make them simple," said Tellpesh-Tia. "You work so hard to put everything in sync with your stories, and then you marvel at how simple and predictable everything is. Your fake compliments and your shifting terms and your selective ignorance. I am done with you! This story has reached its end! I don't care if I have to walk the rest of the way."

"We will all be walking the rest of the way," said the abbot. He stomped his foot and the vehicle lurched to a stop. With a wave of his hand the abbot calmed the engine. "This is the parking lot."

Tellpesh-Tia forced the exit hatch open and escaped her prison. Ingridsdotter-Dwap-Dac flipped the hood of her imitation shame robe over her head and leapt out of the pickup, holding a large canvas bag full of supplies. Ethiret-Jac, dressed in a genuine shame robe, slowly scooted his ass down the cargo ramp.

They stood in a small lot for wheeled vehicles, next to newer, but dirtier, vehicles from other desert communities. At the edge of the parking lot was a corrugated-metal fence protected by a force shield. Through gaps in the fence they could see the spaceport: a few small offices and a few large hangars. Rising into the sky like a vertical scan error was the final target of this conspiracy between the Outreach Navy and the Keepers for Cametre: the city's space elevator.

Everyone all right? said Ingridsdotter-Dwap-Dac. The monk who'd driven the large vehicle pulled her hat over her head and crossed her arms in a sleeping pose. She was no longer necessary to the plan, but if she drove back to the monastery, it would be clear to anyone watching that some of the people now arriving at the spaceport did not intend to return.

I do not feel well at all. said Ethiret-Jac.

Ethiret is not the youngest of us, said Ingridsdotter-Dwap-Dac. I'll carry your bag.

"Follow me," said the abbot, the only one of them who'd been here before. They walked near the fence on a sidewalk cracked nearly to gravel.

"The local gentry keep their private craft in those hangars," said Ethiret-Jac. "My understanding is *Distributed Heartbreak* is in one of them."

"Can you just take it?" said the abbot. "Just break in and fly it out, without involving me?"

"It'll have no potential, sir," said Ingridsdotter-Dwap-Dac. "We gotta push it up the elevator."

At the gate, for the first time, they could see clear to the base of the elevator. Shit. said Ingridsdotter-Dwap-Dac. Enemy's using the lift.

An egenu cargo vessel was mounted on the elevator. It was an engine and a small crew module bolted onto a shipping container the size of a supermarket. A net of skip positioners, winking in the ultraviolet, laid out Cartesian coordinates around the cubical container. On both sides of the passenger mountup, a shape had been stenciled on the hull in purple paint: the eponymous Fist of Joy.

A hopore and an aausq stood to either side of a hose connecting the engine module to a grounded hovertanker. The aausq was wearing Bermuda shorts but they both had rifles slung over their backs.

Can you identify the vessel? said Ethiret-Jac.

Single-crew egenu cargo ship, said Ingridsdotter-Dwap-Dac. The manufacturer is Tokras. They're fueling up. They'll be up the

<u>lift by the time we get our ship out of storage. We just need to tone down the theatrics in there.</u>

The corestin guard at the gate smiled at them. "Hello, Father," she said. "Such a shame about Quennet."

"What happened to Quennet?" the abbot shrieked.

"Just, the war, you know," said the guard. She waved them through.

Tellpesh-Tia and Ingridsdotter-Dwap-Dac mounted a ramp towards the office of the spaceport administrator and shed their robes, leaving poor Ethiret-Jac to drag his canvas bags up the ramp behind them.

"The manager for this shift," said the abbot, hurrying to keep up. "His name is—"

"Don't tell me his bloody name," said Ingridsdotter-Dwap-Dac.

The office was a little building on stilts, smaller than the egenu craft it was currently handling. The abbot rapped on the door with the flats of his fingers and pushed it open. Inside were a small metal desk and a corestin man, name withheld, who divided his time between manipulating bureaucracy through his desktop terminal and eating a large dumpling out of a wrapper optimistically labeled HOT FOOD.

"Mmm," said the corestin, not looking up.

"Dawn greetings, Olalish," the abbot called out cautiously. "Have there been any farcalls from Quennet for me?"

"Mmm, just one moment, Father." Olalish chuckled. "Honestly, if you ever stop talking fancy the way you do, I—" He'd looked up. Standing before him were a human and an uhaltihaxl, probably the first he'd ever seen. "Holy fucking shit." Dumpling crumbs fell from Olalish's mouth.

"I would appreciate some service, my good fellow, if you don't mind," said Ingridsdotter-Dwap-Dac, adding as much contempt as you could possibly add to Trade Standard D without using any B.

"Who the shit are you?"

"We found them in the desert," said the abbot. "They were in a bad way. I'm neutral, all right? We're neutral, they were injured, we took care of them."

Tellpesh-Tia leaned forward slightly, resting her fake cast against Olalish's desk. I'm in his terminal, she said.

"I know you're neutral, Father," said the corestin, holding up one hand. "I'm asking these...people. Who are you? What are you doing on Arzil?"

"Who am I?" said Ingridsdotter-Dwap-Dac. "I am the Right Honorable Dame Nadia Chelwether, M.P., Second Baroness of New Scunthorpe. Don't bother trying to remember all of that, as you will soon be seeing it as the first party in a lawsuit unless I get clearance to leave your planet in the next thirty minutes."

"Uh, well, that takes care of you. Who is..." Olalish waved at Tellpesh-Tia with one hand while surreptitiously tapping at his terminal with the other. "...what about her?"

He thinks he's sounding an alarm, said Tellpesh-Tia.

"Miss Watkerrywun," said Ingridsdotter-Dwap-Dac. "My native guide to your godforsaken planet."

"Native guide?" said the Olalish, as if trying to understand an obscure multilingual pun.

"Don't get ideas above your station," said Ingridsdotter-Dwap-Dac. "When it comes to foreigners, one native guide is as good as another. I *came* to Arzil for the big-game hunting. Get a genuine surk head for the smoking room. Unfortunately, after spending three weeks in-country without seeing hide nor hair of a surk, Miss Watkerrywun here broke her wrist. The more useful of her two wrists, I might add. We were forced to take hospitality from these mad monks who spend their days in the most disgraceful manner, ingesting controlled, or at least controllable substances."

Big problem here, fellas, said Tellpesh-Tia. The database says *Distributed Heartbreak* is gone.

Ingridsdotter-Dwap-Dac didn't miss a beat. "And now you're going to tell me my ship has been stolen or burglarized, because God forbid I should trust a corestin with anything valuable!"

Fix the data-thing! said Ethiret-Jac.

The ship is gone! Changing the database won't bring it back!

"Your...ship?" said Olalish, perpetually two or three clauses behind in this conversation.

"Yes! My. Ship!" said Ingridsdotter-Dwap-Dac. "*Distributed Heartbreak*, an Oena model 540-1 registered to my personal holding company, Jabeho Enterprises."

I know what it's called! said Tellpesh-Tia. I have the record. This bird went up the elevator ten shifts ago.

"Well, ma'am, your ship..." said Olalish.

"You don't have it, do you?" said Ingridsdotter-Dwap-Dac. "You stripped it for parts as soon as my back was turned!"

"No, I believe that's against our policy, but you see, all the pleasure craft have been impressed, for the war."

"War?" said Ingridsdotter-Dwap-Dac. "What war? I leave on holiday and a bloody war breaks out?"

"Yes, a most lamentable state of war exists between our governments. Now perhaps you'll understand my surprise at seeing you. I hope you will extend this same spirit of understanding to the security personnel who will, ah, a mere formality, should be here any...any moment, actually."

Well, gents, we're fucked, said Ingridsdotter-Dwap-Dac. I'll stall while you dream up another scheme. "There's no war! It's impossible! There's some foolish misunderstanding."

We'll steal the egenu ship, said Ethiret-Jac.

Thanks for being quick, said Ingridsdotter-Dwap-Dac. "I'm the Shadow Minister for Culture and Sport! They can't declare war and not tell me!" Is Ethiret any good at fighting?

He doesn't need to be good at fighting, said Ethiret-Jac. He just needs to be bad at dying.

Ingridsdotter-Dwap-Dac and Ethiret-Jac slipped out the office door and ran down the ramp. They pulled up the hoods of their shame robes, and when the hopore and the aausq looked up, they saw a harmless crackpot coming toward them, his eager subordinate following close behind. "Take this, take this!" said Ethiret-Jac, holding out a hand with nothing in it.

"Shove off, Cammies," said the aausq. The hopore applied a wrench to the fuel hose and started unbolting it.

"What the...?" said the spaceport manager. He leapt to his feet and saw dull grey metal shining underneath the uhaltihaxl's cast as she unholstered her not-broken wrist from her sling and pointed it at him.

"You make any noise, you die," said Tellpesh-Tia. The metal was just her Fist terminal, but when you've been trained to deal with hijackers pointing guns at you, you tend to see guns where there are none.

"You're the escapees!" the corestin gurgled. "The humans and the rre. Where's the rre? I'll do whatever you say, just don't put the rre on me! Father! Help me!"

"They made me do this!" said the abbot. "Help! I'm a hostage! I'm also a hostage!"

"All right, you're a hostage," said Tellpesh-Tia.

"You are in danger!" Ethiret-Jac called to the aausq. "Every time you form a skip bubble, you fracture the fabric of space-time. The influence of Cametre our Protector leaks out of this universe, and horrible things from beyond ooze in through the cracks. I can't stand the thought of you facing these awful creatures. Please, read this! It will explain everything! Stay on Arzil! We will shelter you!"

"Get off the tarmac!" said the aausq.

The distraction was working, so Ingridsdotter-Dwap-Dac copied it. "Take this, take this," she told the hopore.

"We are currently military!" said the hopore. "Go tell your master urk." Ingridsdotter-Dwap-Dac slipped the wrench out of his hand and brought it down on his head. The hopore's skull divided around the wrench and he fell back against the fuel tanker, dead.

The aausq yelped in surprise and reached to sling her rifle. Ethiret-Jac tackled her, she tripped over the fuel hose and the bodies went down in a tangle of limbs.

Help! said Ethiret-Jac. It seems she's much stronger than I!

Get on your back, said Ingridsdotter-Dwap-Dac to the squirming dogpile. I can't get a good shot.

I think I am on my back! said Ethiret-Jac.

Deployment orders are going out, said Tellpesh-Tia. We need to leave! "You two, stay in here," she told the spaceport manager and the abbot. "Guard each other. Or there'll be trouble."

Ingridsdotter-Dwap-Dac fired the hopore's rifle. The aausq's head went 'splut' and she stopped trying to choke Ethiret-Jac. A thick spray of blood and bone sprayed across the corestin's features. He shut his eyes and mouth as tight as he could and screamed in native-voice <u>Sweet Cametre, she's dead!</u>

<u>What's the matter, brother Ethiret?</u> said Ingridsdotter-Dwap-Dac, a cynical sneer on her borrowed human face. <u>I thought you liked eating brains.</u>

Something had to be done about this. Dwap and Dac should not have been put into the same body. They had turned Ingridsdotter from a competent noncom into a serious discipline problem.

<u>Dead?</u> said Tellpesh-Tia. <u>Who is dead? We agreed there would be no more killing!</u> She ran out the door, vaulted over the railing, and dropped three meters onto the tarmac.

"Wait for me!" said the abbot. "I'm a hostage! Help me!"

<u>Ninety percent chance there's an egenu pilot locked in the cockpit,</u> said Ingridsdotter-Dwap-Dac. <u>I need Tellpesh to break the lock, and I need everyone else providing covering fire.</u>

<u>Don't kill the pilot!</u> said Tellpesh-Tia. She was running towards the egenu ship on a sprained ankle. There was no second-guessing the implant decision, Ethiret-Jac realized. If Tellpesh hadn't taken Tia, *she* would have become the discipline problem.

<u>Get over here and I won't have to.</u> Ingridsdotter-Dwap-Dac rolled the aausq off of Ethiret-Jac and tossed him the dead woman's rifle.

<u>Ethiret's body doesn't know how to use this,</u> said Ethiret-Jac.

<u>It's at half charge,</u> said Ingridsdotter-Dwap-Dac. <u>You've got ninety chances to figure it out.</u>

The trembling abbot and the station manager peered out through the office doorway, then quietly crouched on the floor and pushed the door closed. The corestin guard who'd waved them through the gate was now running towards them from the guardpost, her weapon drawn. Ethiret-Jac pointed the rifle at her and yelled "Drop it! We have hostages!", hoping he wouldn't have to pull the trigger.

Tellpesh-Tia and Ingridsdotter-Dwap-Dac leapt onto the passenger mountup and entered the cargo ship. They stood in a common area the size of Dwap-Jac-Dac's cell on Sotese Prison Red. Two secure airlock hatches led out of the common area: a small one to the cockpit and a large one connecting the crew module to the cargo container.

Break the lock, said Ingridsdotter-Dwap-Dac.

I broke it on the way, said Tellpesh-Tia.

Really?

This is a crappy little cargo ship, said Tellpesh-Tia.

So why did you snap your ankle running over here?

Because you kill people if I'm not here to stop you!

Ingridsdotter-Dwap-Dac rolled her eyes and spun open the cockpit hatch. A gush of water poured out of the opening, sweeping Tellpesh-Tia back through the common room and pinning her against the door to the cargo hold. Ingridsdotter-Dwap-Dac spread her legs into a split that held her steady against the hull. Like a duck looking for food she dunked the upper half of her body into the onrushing torrent, and extracted a struggling, naked egenu from the cockpit. Ingridsdotter-Dwap-Dac slammed the stunned man against the hull and threw him out into a puddle of water in the common room.

The common room overflowed. Water poured out the external airlock and splattered steaming onto the hardened concrete outside, pooling around the bodies of the aausq and the hopore. Inside, the egenu pilot blew red bloody bubbles in the water.

Toss him out. Ingridsdotter-Dwap-Dac climbed into the cockpit and started flipping switches.

He's bleeding!

We killed his buddies. We can't keep him prisoner. Throw him out is the only way he lives. Tellpesh-Tia winced and dragged the unconscious egenu towards the exit airlock. Ethiret-Jac pulled himself up the passenger mountup, waving the rifle in a threatening manner which he'd copied from a brief description of Qued Ethiret doing the same thing in *Seeking Out Cametre*. He collapsed into the airlock.

A little help? Tellpesh-Tia asked him. Ethiret just wheezed and coughed. Jac struggled to stabilize the old man's pulse and sweated out stored-up oxygen into his blood.

The Tokras Bat cockpit was designed to be operated with a full load of water. Now that it was drained, some of the controls were on the ceiling and difficult to reach. But the functions of the controls were fairly straightforward, copied from older Outreach designs; and there was a 3-tank hanging from the ceiling, showing Arzil, its space elevators, and the Fist convoy in orbit. Ingridsdotter-Dwap-Dac quickly traced the power tree and engaged the elevator hookups. We are leaving.

Police hovercraft is moving to intercept, said Tellpesh-Tia.

I see it, said Ingridsdotter-Dwap-Dac. Come a little closer, asshole. Ingridsdotter-Dwap-Dac lit up one of the side motivators. The cargo vessel lurched slightly, impaled on the space elevator. The police craft flipped over, went into a tailspin and crashed onto the tarmac.

With one huge effort Tellpesh-Tia shoved the unconscious pilot out of the airlock. His body fell to the tarmac, knocking off the corestin security guard who'd been climbing the ladder.

Off we go. Ingridsdotter-Dwap-Dac drafted the lower motivators to the elevator's power cable, and the egenu craft lifted off.

We're losing air! said Tellpesh-Tia.

What the f—okay, airlock is shut, said Ingridsdotter-Dwap-Dac.

Excuse me, but I'm in the airlock, said Ethiret-Jac, quivering under the g-forces, green aausq blood swirling out from his shame robe into the water that pooled between the two hatches.

We've got ten thousand kilos of cargo, said Ingridsdotter-Dwap-Dac. I'm going to drop it.

That's where the food is, said Ethiret-Jac. We need that. None of our bags made it.

The ship lurched to a stop and gravity reverted to Arzil normal. Shit, they shut off the lift, said Tellpesh-Tia.

It still works, said Ingridsdotter-Dwap-Dac; we just can't ride for free anymore.

She gunned the lower motivators and the egenu craft moved upwards again. There was a horrible squealing sound: the sound of space-elevator filament being run through a pulley system a hundred times faster than designed, coming out the other end stressed and melted smooth.

Hey, I don't want to tell you how to do your job, Tellpesh-Tia told the pilot, but there's now a ship coming *down* the elevator. I don't think there's room for two.

We don't have to make it to the top, said Ingridsdotter-Dwap-Dac. We just have to make it past the Feronato radius. And Arzil is a very small planet, so the Feronato radius is just about...here.

The motivators went silent. The cargo ship crested, held motionless thirty kilometers above Arzil, and then it dropped.

"Help!" said Ethiret-Jac. He tripped on a wall and pitched headlong through the writhing ball of water that filled the center of the airlock. "Help, I'm falling! Everything's falling!"

Okay, let's hie from this motherfucker ASAP, said Ingridsdotter-Dwap-Dac.

Is there a flashbang? said Tellpesh-Tia.

I don't see one, said Ingridsdotter-Dwap-Dac, but we are about to destroy a space elevator; that should keep them busy. She skipped them.

They were in open space. Celestial features whirled in the 3-tank as the navigation computer tried to get a bearing. Ingridsdotter-Dwap-Dac took three deep calming breaths and then decided that getting a bearing wasn't so important after all.

"We are still falling!" said Ethiret-Jac. "Is this...space?"

Uh, fellas, said Tellpesh-Tia, this vessel is booby-trapped. There's some kind of smoke grenade on the wall of the common area.

There was one in the airlock with Ethiret-Jac, too: a small metal cylinder spinning slowly, hissing and oozing mist. It had been on the wall, one piece of the complex machinery that worked the airlock, but it had been knocked loose by the ascent or the skip or the drop. A blinking light on one end refracted through clouds of weightless water. Ethiret-Jac watched the grenade, hypnotized by the mist spreading like egalitarian incense in all directions.

<u>Shit, Ingridsdotter's unconscious,</u> said Tellpesh-Tia. <u>Dwap-Dac? Do you hear me? Jac, Ingridsdotter took it bad. It's some kind of gas. It smells like bad milk.</u>

<u>Don't smell it!</u> said Ethiret-Jac, now unable to smell anything else. Jac shut down Ethiret's breathing, but it wouldn't do any good at this point. <u>What kind of milk? Panh milk or kine milk or what?</u>

<u>I don't know. Milk is milk.</u>

<u>Don't you remember the briefing?</u> said Ethiret-Jac. <u>That's the smell of Evidence!</u> He pounded his fists uselessly on the metal hatch, trying to get in and save his fellas. Satellites of his own vomit splattered across his forehead. "Help me!" Ethiret's body vocalized. "I'm trapped! Let me out!"

<u>The manual controls are inside the airlock,</u> said Tellpesh-Tia.

"Oh, I see, yes." Ethiret-Jac worked a lever one way, then the other. The hatch cracked. He pushed against it and only succeeded in throwing himself back towards the tiny metal door, the only thing protecting him from the infinite void that had swallowed Qued Ethiret in *The Empty Box*.

Ethiret-Jac climbed back up to the internal hatch—every direction now seemed to be up—and braced himself by grabbing a handle that got hotter and hotter the longer he held onto it. He pushed the hatch open and climbed out onto what had been the ceiling. Ingridsdotter-Dwap-Dac's body drifted below him, looking like the corpse from *Behind Cametre's Windowblinds,* set adrift on the water. The metal booby-trap was still floating but no longer hissing out gas.

Tellpesh-Tia's legs slowly kicked out of the cargo area. "Cargo area is safe," she said. She banged one slender horn on another one of those handles that seemed to be everywhere. "Ow! Help me move her!"

"I can't move myself," said Ethiret-Jac. "Ethiret has never been above sea level." His head passed through a large globule of water, which came away tinged with vomit and aausq blood.

"Ethiret," said Warrant Officer Ingridsdotter, as if asleep with her eyes open.

Dwap? Dac? said Jac. No response. "Are they dead?" said Ethiret.

"Let's get the rwit back before we worry about the rre inside," said Tellpesh-Tia.

The rre are gone, said Jac. I saw it with the hybrids in the last war. The host body goes into shock and the rre merges with it. Sometimes they all die.

"You tell that to a doctor, when we get to a doctor. Don't tell me, because there's nothing I can do." Tellpesh-Tia grabbed Ingridsdotter-Dwap-Dac under one arm and pulled her into the cargo hold. "I'm trying to save what I can. Help me!"

Ethiret-Jac held on to the ceiling and reached towards the floor. His homemade boot grazed the top of the metal table molded to the floor of the common area. He'd made no progress and he was nowhere near the cargo hold. I will try to move Ethiret's body into the hold, said Jac. That's all I can promise you.

He began the slow process of pulling off his sodden shame robe. The robe was just a tradition, a way of apologizing to Cametre for leaving the safety of home. Ethiret wasn't sorry. He had work to do out here, and for that he needed the clothes he wore beneath the robe: Qued Ethiret's proctor's uniform.

"There must be an antidote," Tellpesh-Tia said. "There are humans who fight for the Fist. Holy shit! This is high-end stuff. There's a few million credits worth of equipment in here."

Ethiret-Jac pushed his head through the connector into the cargo container. It smelled like the night side of Arzil. He saw their cargo for the first time: large beige pallets threaded on cables, floor to ceiling, like the seagrass forest in *The Second Copy*. White plastic crates stacked on the pallets with one-time tear strips around the lids.

A purple Fist of Joy was spray-painted on each crate in an attempt to deter theft, or at least resale. The sacred lits of Aquadale Selmar were kept in crates like these. Ethiret had thought they were a special quenny reliquary, but they were standard crates for interstellar transport.

Tellpesh-Tia was swimming through the seagrass forest, with Tia translating the labels through Tellpesh's eyes. "Blank logic boards. Precision controls. Fist explosive printers. Radiation counters, recognizers, frequency scanners, medical chamber!"

"Can we set it up?" said Ethiret-Jac.

"We can give it power," said Tellpesh-Tia. "We don't have the sixty thousand kinds of glop it needs to fix somebody."

The unconscious human bumped into one of the cartons and slowly ricocheted back towards Ethiret-Jac. "Ingridsdotter responded to my name," Ethiret-Jac said. "She might remember me. Ingridsdotter-Dwap-Dac! Warrant Officer! This is Ethiret-Jac! We served together! We were the same person. Are you in there?"

Ingridsdotter's eyes closed and flashed open again. "Ethiret! Shit! What happened?" The human tried to come to attention and flailed in space, finally grabbing hold of a crate that outmassed her. "Ethiret! Proctor, sir!"

"You're all right," said Tellpesh-Tia. "You got hit with a chemical weapon, but you're all right." She peeled back Ingridsdotter's furiously blinking eyelid. "Can you raise your arm? Just raise your arm for me, please."

"Chemical weapons?" said Ingridsdotter. She obediently lifted her arm to her head. "Who would do that? We're on a peaceful mission of exploration."

Tellpesh-Tia and Ethiret-Jac exchanged a glance. <u>Dwap, Dac, are you in there?</u> said Jac.

<u>I don't hear anything,</u> said Tellpesh-Tia.

"Do you remember me?" Ethiret-Jac asked Ingridsdotter.

"Star Proctor, sir. I'm sorry, I had some sort of dream we were quennies. This is right strange. Reality is bent. I recognize you now."

<u>Well, shit,</u> said Tellpesh-Tia. <u>She got the Cametrean flavor of Evidence.</u>

"This is a more important question," said Ethiret. "Do you know who *you* are?"

"Hiroko Ingridsdotter, sir. I'm your XO."

"Not quite," said Ethiret.

"We were in a starship, not a warehouse," said Ingridsdotter. "We were at the Hishbi system on..."

"...a mission of peaceful exploration?" said Ethiret.

"Did we have the same dream?" said Ingridsdotter.

"Let's find out," said Ethiret. "What do you remember about Hishbi VI?"

"Everyone thought it was a dead world," said Ingridsdotter. "The hishbinny had wiped themselves out thousands of years ago."

"But we got a distress message," said Ethiret-Jac. "You theorized a ship had been caught in Cametre's web and crashed."

"But you, Proctor sir, you determined that the message was coming from below the planet's surface."

"The hishbinny were still there," said Ethiret-Jac. "Living below the radioactive surface, drinking contaminated water."

"God, it was horrible!" Ingridsdotter let a tear slip. "They'd been at war for generations."

"Let me guess," said Tellpesh-Tia. "None of them remembered what they were fighting for."

"You saw it too," said Ingridsdotter. "We were all there!"

"They were stripping the planet's minerals," said Ethiret-Jac, "sapping geothermal energy from the mantle, eating the planet from within, the way a teque vitter eats a squelt."

"Worms in an apple," said Ingridsdotter. "If we were there, where is this?"

"There's a very simple explanation!" said Tellpesh-Tia. "None of that actually happened! We were attacked with a hallucinogen. There is no Hishbi system and no hishbinny. It is an adventure story for the emotionally stunted."

"Hallucination or no, it bloody well happened," said Ingridsdotter.

"Well, yes," said Ethiret-Jac, "there is a sense in which it happened—"

"Okay, wait, wait, yeah," said Ingridsdotter. "What if this drug was designed to get me to trust you? I mean, it is a bit over-the-top, yeah? Star Proctor Ethiret, greatest man in the service, privilege serving with you, sir. And now here you are, dressed in the outfit and everything, an outfit I notice I am not wearing myself."

Ethiret-Jac smoothed down the wet tunic of his uniform, his wrinkled hands catching on the crooked buttons. "The story is called *Doing Without Cametre*," he said. "I read it when I was a little boy. Then the war happened; the first war. I knew I couldn't have anything to do with it. I joined the Keepers for Cametre because they were the only ones who realized how important this story was. I took a new name—Qued Ethiret, the name of the man in the story who stopped the pointless hishbinny war."

"So you're not really Ethiret," said Ingridsdotter.

"I am not *Star Proctor* Ethiret," said Ethiret-Jac. "I am Lieutenant Ethiret-Jac, of the Navy of the Terran Outreach. I am far from the greatest man in the service. I dream, I lie, I bluff, I steal. The monk half of me couldn't run a monastery worth shit. The soldier half drove thons commanders insane with too-clever plans.

"The enemy captured me. They took me out of uniform, and I had to find another one. I chose this uniform because I value Qued Ethiret's ingenuity, his sense of duty, his absolute commitment to his fellas and to the cause of peace.

"The story of Star Proctor Qued Ethiret has been turned into a weapon. We stole this vessel to try to destroy that weapon. You are not bound to this mission. I understand if you want to head back to the fleet. You can drop me off somewhere and I'll get to Nimar on my own. You can take Tellpesh-Tia with you.

"But let me warn you, the brass back at the fleet? To them, you're damaged goods. You've been infected with subversive ideas. They'll never trust you with another mission."

What the coin-flip are you doing, Lieutenant? said Tellpesh-Tia.

I am rallying my fellas. It's a little trick called leadership.

You don't have fellas anymore. You have a conscientious objector and a casualty. I don't even understand why the Cametrean Evidence affected Ingridsdotter.

It's not Cametrean Evidence; it's space adventure Evidence. You don't join the Navy unless you have a weak spot for that shit. I don't suppose you've actually read *Doing Without Cametre?*

<u>We need to get to a doctor. We needed a doctor *before* this happened.</u>

<u>We are past the doctor stage,</u> said Ethiret-Jac. <u>We are merging with host and there's nothing we can do about it. But we can still carry out the mission. I have two talented spacemen who have ceased to be discipline problems and become committed to the principles of nonviolent resistance.</u>

<u>You still don't know where Nimar is,</u> said Tellpesh-Tia.

"Ingridsdotter, those desk jockeys will tell you you're not a soldier anymore!" Ethiret-Jac said aloud. "They'll call you a casualty! But I think you can still serve. I believe that intelligence and cunning can triumph over brute force and violence, and I'd be proud to call you my fella again. If you're willing, let's go together. Let's avenge the real, completely fictional Qued Ethiret, take back his story, and stop this war."

"As long as you're serious about intelligence and cunning," said Ingridsdotter. "I don't want to hurt anyone."

"You hurt people for a living!" said Tellpesh-Tia. "You killed two, less than an hour ago! I had to stop you from killing the pilot!"

"I don't think so," said Ingridsdotter. "That doesn't sound like me."

"Am I the only sane person on this vessel?" said Tellpesh-Tia.

"That does seem to be your particular skill, Specialist," said Ethiret. "Let's not waste it. Ingridsdotter?"

"Yeah. Uh, yessir."

"Specialist Tellpesh-Tia here is going to connect her capital terminal to yours. Then she's going to go into the cockpit, and you're going to help her get the navigation computer working. You'll set a course for the nearest space station."

"And then what, sir?"

"We're going to have a little race," said Ethiret. "I'll try to find the coordinates of the planet we're attacking. Meanwhile, Tellpesh-Tia will try to locate a doctor who's willing to extract four rre from three humanoids and keep quiet about it. And we'll see who finds what they're looking for first."

Chapter 32

Inside the Trap

Myrus
Above the Fist of Joy Youth Festival

Myrus and Professor Starbottle inched up the space elevator towards the ship the personal assistant had sent for them. Myrus pressed his hands against the glass of the egg-shaped elevator car, looking down at the planet they'd finally escaped.

Their quest and its hardships were only beginning. Myrus wore a rucksack full of stolen cafeteria food, which would have to last them to Cedar Commons. The rucksack was a craft project made from recycled bicycle tires, and despite the three layers of tinfoil he'd lined it with, Myrus knew the food was gonna taste like tires.

"Oh," said Professor Starbottle suddenly. In one word he sounded disappointed and angry, two emotions he tried to hide from Myrus, but Myrus knew very well what they sounded like. Myrus followed his gaze upwards and saw nothing but a star glimmering at the top of the elevator. "Damn it!" said Professor Starbottle. "I ask my personal assistant for a single-crew ship and he sends me *Wedge of Endt*!"

"What's that?"

"Only the headquarters of this whole operation! The personal assistant has gallantly arrived to personally 'escort' me to Nimar. Bloody hell! I do apologize for my language, Myrusit. Fuck! Sorry."

"What do we do?" said Myrus.

"We have to go through with this," said Professor Starbottle. "Or he'll get suspicious. This gets us off the planet, at least."

"What is Nimar?" said Myrus.

"Nimar is the safest place in the universe," said Professor Starbottle. "Bloody *Wedge of Endt.*"

Bloody *Wedge of Endt* went from a star to a blob and then to a spaceship made entirely of stainless steel. Finally a docking interface opened up around the elevator and swallowed the shuttle. The egg latched onto something, its walls dissolved and foreign-smelling air rushed in.

Myrus stood on the floor of a cargo bay with big stacks of wood pinned precariously to one of the walls. Standing on the same wall was a jetk showing woman and dressed in an old-fashioned outfit with a cloak and red boots. Her hair was pulled into a tight ponytail which dangled towards the wall, perpendicular to the floor.

Myrus's mind focused on the ponytail and reoriented itself. *He* was the one standing on the wall. The shuttle had come into the cargo bay at a ninety-degree angle to the gravity vector used on the rest of the ship. To adjust to the gravity aboard *Wedge of Endt,* you had to walk up a curved ramp. By the time you got to the bottom, the grav would be pulling you towards what everyone had agreed to call the floor.

"Who are you?" said Professor Starbottle to the sideways jetk.

"My name is Tvez," said the jetk. "It's my honor to serve as your pilot to Nimar."

"I told the personal assistant to send a *small* vessel, which I would pilot myself."

"I'm sorry," said Tvez, "but we have other passengers to pick up. You are essential to the war effort, Professor, but you are not the whole thing."

"Madam, I must insist," said Professor Starbottle.

"Discuss the matter with the personal assistant," said Tvez, and Myrus once again got that tingly suspicion that 'personal assistant' was not the right translation. "You're not piloting anything until the war's over. We do not want one of the galaxy's greatest scientists dying in a skip accident." Tvez walked down the gravity ramp and grabbed two of Professor Starbottle's bags. "Do you need anything else from the planet?"

Professor Starbottle froze up. He couldn't think of anything that wouldn't admit the truth: he'd never intended to go to Nimar in the first place. Tvez snorted like a suddenly wet animal, walked back up the ramp, and took Professor Starbottle's bags through a big set of metal doors at the far end of the cargo bay.

"Is there any way we can take over the ship?" said Myrus.

"I hope you don't see me as a warlike individual," said the professor. He sighed and started towards the doors and his vanished bags.

Myrus scanned the cargo for something he could use as a weapon. Planks and boards of pure and processed wood, factory-new and bound in shipwrap with red and green warning streamers dangled towards what was now definitely the floor. A few evergreen saplings leaned against the stacks, sweating oxygen into plastic bags. There were even a couple pieces of finished furniture: a little coffee table and a bookshelf sturdy enough to hold printed books.

"Where'd they get all this?" said Myrus.

"Where do you *think*, Myrusit?" said Professor Starbottle. Myrus thought they'd stolen it. He followed the professor through the cargo bay doors. The adjacent room was covered in dirty grey carpet but there were also five folding tables covered with large plates of food. Yeah, real, actual food! There was hot eklerust, reseprushinth, bread and hatuia and a little pyramid of individual boxes of cereal and some human stuff. Fresh fruit: pra and limes and ederwe. Milk and tea bags and a shiny machine for making ruxlt or coffee.

Myrus's rumen growled but he clenched his jaw and resolved not to eat the food. It looked so nice after weeks of neutral crap that it had to be a trap. This happened in Gearu stories all the time. You'd come through the forest to find a picnic laid out on a table, eat the too-good-to-be-true food, and fall into a deep sleep or turn into an animal. This was a sure sign that you were the first or second brother, one of the dumbasses, and not the clever third brother who was destined to sweep up all the loot.

Professor Starbottle walked right up to the bread table, smeared some brown goop on a piece of raw bread with a plastic knife and chowed down. Maybe he figured he was already inside the trap; he might as well eat the food.

Myrus picked an ederwe out of the fruit bowl. Ederwe had rinds; they had to be safe, right? Myrus picked it open with his fingers and ate the flesh in three bites. It felt so good to eat something designed just for him, something that only an uhalti could eat. His rumen wanted to barf it up so he'd have to eat more.

He turned to see if he could get some room-temperature water out of the ruxlt machine to stop the barf feeling and his foot nudged something under the table. There were cardboard boxes down there, boxes of neutral Coke branded in English and stacked three high.

Professor Starbottle came around and tried to pat Myrus on the shoulder with his mouth full of bread. "Myr..." He swallowed hard. Apparently the brown goop didn't taste as good as he imagined or remembered. "Myrusit, I'm very sorry that this has happened the way it has. Not least because of what you're going to think of me. But, uh..." He looked like he was about to cry and Myrus would not be able to handle that. He thought hard for the stupid clichés Dad would bring out when Myrus was sad.

"Work it off," said Myrus. "We work it off. We'll go into the cargo bay and I'll teach you about wood."

"I don't know if that will help," said Professor Starbottle.

"Nothing else will help," said Myrus. "The past already happened, and Providence controls the future. The only thing you can do is do some work or learn something."

"My work got you into this mess," said Professor Starbottle.

"How are we gonna get out?" said Myrus. "By doing nothing?

No. You have to move forward. Do you have any Workbench left?"

"I left it on the planet," said Professor Starbottle. "All these drugs are illegal in the Outreach. I didn't want us to get into trouble. But obviously I've failed at that." He suddenly liked his bread again, and shoved the rest into his mouth.

"Dude, we're not in trouble," said Myrus. "These people love you. They gave us a buffet. We just have to figure out stage two."

"They have Workbench on board," said Professor Starbottle. He opened a pudding cup and licked another brown goop smear off the lid. "*Wedge of Endt* has a lab. I've spent more time on this ship than I care to remember."

"Well, bring a dose down here, and I'll teach you about wood."

The gravity went off for so little time that you had to be a ship rat to even notice it. The little boxes of cereal wobbled in their pyramid and settled down. They'd skipped. The Youth Festival was far away, and Myrus was off to Nimar.

"We should do the recording in the lab," said Professor Starbottle.

"I'm not moving all that wood," said Myrus. "We're doing it in the cargo bay."

So Professor Starbottle had the crew move a minimal Evidence recording setup into the cargo bay. The crew were all jetk, dressed alike in these old-fashioned outfits. Recording went more or less the same way as at the Festival. The professor pushed a dose of Workbench into his inhaler and snorted it, like the drug balloons you could get at a space station. Now the timer was ticking and Myrus was supposed to help Professor Starbottle record a new variety of Evidence.

But instead of shaping or cutting the wood, Myrus talked about wood in general. He identified the woods in the cargo bay: mostly teak and redwood. The saplings were oak, like (Myrus didn't say) the trees on Cedar Commons. Hard wood vs. soft wood, modded vs. organic, which species smelled good vs. bland or awful. Redwood normally smelled terrible, but this species had been modded to have no smell.

"Is it still alive?" was Professor Starbottle's first question. It was the sort of stupid question you'd ask if you'd never seen wood before, but Myrus didn't know the answer, so maybe it wasn't stupid.

"I don't think so," said Myrus. "Not after it's dried. But I don't know."

Myrus talked about trees, which clearly were alive, how they were harvested and shaped into something you could build with. Every ten minutes Professor Starbottle drew some blood from his neck and labeled the vial, then huffed another dose of Workbench and got right back in. At the Festival he'd put the vials of blood in a centrifuge to extract the crystallized Evidence, the chemical record of his conversation with Myrus. Here, he just headed out into the breakfast room and handed each vial to one of the jetk crew.

The bookshelf was a mahogany antique with a lot of cracks and chips. The coffee table was a recent copy in walnut of a twentieth- or nineteenth-century design. Mahogany had been a high-end wood, until the natural resource companies got greedy and planted whole planets of it. Fifty years ago, those trees grew up, and mahogany became incredibly cheap.

But furniture breaks, and mahogany was now an antique wood. It was super valuable again, just for a moment, until the next generation of mahogany forests grew up. It was a cycle that would play out forever. Dad said that fir and hard pine were next on the list.

That got Myrus started on talking about Dad, and once he started he couldn't let up. He said how Dad had taught him the things he was now teaching Professor Starbottle, how good Dad was at figuring out ways to tweak the low-end furniture designs so they could be branded as better stuff. How he'd run for the council against this super racist lady who ran the 1-2-3 payday loan shop, and he'd *clobbered* her, and she'd been so mad she'd almost used the S-word in her concession speech.

At this point Myrus was on a roll, and he made a big mistake: he told Professor Starbottle about Den. He'd never told a human about this: how Dad, normally super strict about uhalti girls, would mysteriously let Myrus and Den watch the 3-tank together all the time. They could even have sleepovers, mainly at Den's place, and at one of the sleepovers Den had whispered the obvious: "They're setting us up. They want us to go into love."

Professor Starbottle didn't stammer or lecture, he just listened. He was a human, but he was also a scientist: nothing was weird to him. But Myrus kept talking, explaining himself to someone who didn't need an explanation.

"If you look it up," he babbled, "a lot of the old queens and sages were concentrated. Seven or eight generations sometimes. That's where the great heroes came from. But the humans made us stop doing it, I guess because they thought it was gross. And now we don't have any heroes anymore, just regular people. That's why we're so poor and everyone makes fun of us.

"And...Dad and Ms. Xepperxelt went through so much trouble to make this happen, and I screwed it up. I went into love for... well, the wrong person."

"Myrusit," said Professor Starbottle.

"I let everybody down." There was the real problem. Not that Warrant Officer Ingridsdotter was human; Dad could probably get used to that. "There was this whole plan, and I just had to do one little piece, and—"

"Myrusit, please listen!" Myrus looked up and there it was. All the anger and frustration that Professor Starbottle normally kept to himself was pointed at Myrus, and for one moment it was like seeing Dad lit up in the sweeping beam of a spatial beacon.

"I don't know anything about uhaltihaxl genetics," said the human. He paused, as though searching his terminal for an online class on the topic. "But I do know some uhaltihaxl history, and the last thing we need is more heroes like that. Those queens did nothing but kill people, and the sages did nothing but..." He sighed. "...invent faster ways to do the killing.

"This war is full of heroes. What we *need* is people like your father." He jabbed the needle into the catheter on his neck to capture this insight for posterity. "Draft dodgers. People who make furniture."

An hour later they took a break to get some more food from the buffet. It was the same stuff as breakfast, but now the bottles of Coke were on top of the tables so you were allowed to take them. Myrus drank three Cokes, and really regretted it when the ship started rotating.

Myrus had this feeling whenever *Jaketown* docked with a space station, and tried to avoid eating beforehand. Little nauseating torques at odds with the gravity vector, while *Wedge of Endt* matched orbit and rotation with something else. You couldn't hide it with fancy equipment, like you could with skipping.

"I need to go," said Professor Starbottle. He set his dinner plate on a side table.

"What are we docking with?" Myrus made the whirling-finger gesture. The other ship was either larger or more important than *Wedge of Endt*, since *Endt* was making the adjustments. They'd been skipping frequently, but Nimar was still a couple days away.

"It's...don't worry about it. I need to meet them. It's better if you don't come." Which just guaranteed that Myrus would come.

In the docking bay Tvez the pilot stood at attention, her huge red boots freshly shined. Professor Starbottle motioned for Myrus to fall back, and stood next to Tvez in his battered-up ribbon suit with his hands folded. He looked unhappy in a thoughtful way, like a kid who'd just learned that school now starts an hour earlier than it used to, wondering if that means it also ends earlier.

One by one, six more jetk in the red-boot uniform climbed through the docking hatch and lined up along the side of the gravity adjustment ramp, three on each side, facing each other. Myrus strained on tiptoe to look down the hatch and saw two dark-skinned humans coming out behind them: a man with a mustache and beard, and a lady with her hair in braids. The six jetk stood stiffly like an honor guard, but the humans didn't look honored, just tired and scared.

Then one more person climbed up out of the hatch and walked between the six jetk: Professor Starbottle's personal assistant. Myrus recognized him by his fake 2-glasses. He was smiling, a tired smile like when Dad had been working on a handmade project for a long time and was just now stepping back to see how everything looks together.

"Professor!" said the personal assistant, gesturing to the human woman with both hands. "I'd like to introduce your new troubleshooter: recently of Los Angeles City College, Miss Rebecca Twice."

Rebecca Twice
Wedge of Endt

"Do you have a capital terminal?" Errand Boy had asked Becky and Arun, back when it was just them and a few jetk toughs in a shuttle headed for who-knows-where.

"Got it taken out," said Arun. "Eight kiloshifts ago."

"The problem is," said Errand Boy, "as long as your terminal remains in your head, your activities are being written to the disposition context, and the Outreach can track you."

"That's why we had ours *removed*," said Arun, "so that we could enjoy lives of crime."

"You had them taken out?"

"Yes, sir, very much taken out."

"Both of you?"

"Both of us," said Becky.

"Ah."

After spending so much time extracting this valuable information from them, Errand Boy had not spread the word to anyone else. The first thing Becky and Arun had to do after moving from the shuttle onto *Wedge of Endt* was visit the ship's doctor, a rasme thau man named Cwess who peered into Becky's mouth and asked her the exact same question.

"In which eye do you have your terminal, Becky?" he said. (Well, not exactly the same question.)

"I don't have a terminal."

Dr. Cwess took this as a professional insult, as if Becky had lied about flossing. "Hold still, please," he said. He held up his own terminal, a large two-handed affair, and shone a bright flash of light into Becky's left eye.

Cwess had a diploma from Harvard Medical School hung prominently on the wall, which meant he probably only doctored humans. Becky squinted at the diploma with her remaining eye, trying to make out whether it said "M.D." or "torture specialist".

"Other eye," said Dr. Cwess, and flashed Becky again. She was now completely blind. "Ah, there it is."

"It's still in there?" said Becky, a little worried.

"I see where it was removed. Looks like a chamber job. You couldn't pay me enough to get in one of those machines. All right. Arun?"

"Don't shine that bloody light in my face."

"This is very serious, Arun. We cannot continue to Nimar while you have a capital terminal in your head."

"I've had it out for eight kiloshifts."

"I'm just making sure." Flash.

"Oh, God!" Arun reeled. "Are you happy?"

"Good lad. That looks like a professional job."

"Yeh, the surgeon sold the terminal to help buy out his contract."

Dark spots slowly began to form in between Becky's blinks. "One more thing we need to check," said Cwess. "Have either of you taken Evidence before, recreationally or otherwise?"

"No," said Arun. "Too expensive."

"I did it once," said Becky. "I didn't like it." What did he mean, 'before'?

"You didn't *like* it?" The doctor took this personally, as if someone had insulted his French toast. "Jesus Christ." Becky didn't mention that Jesus Christ was the reason she hadn't liked it. She imagined Dr. Cwess showing up at a Harvard reunion after the war, chortling over cocktails with Outreach hedge fund managers. They deserved each other.

Once again, all relevant information vis-à-vis Becky and Arun's capital terminals stopped dead with the person who'd heard it. When they were on the final descent to Nimar, while

Becky and Arun were actually strapping themselves into their environment suits, Tad Starbottle turned to Becky and said over the radio: "Oh, Rebecca, I'm afraid you need to have your capital terminal removed."

"Being way ahead of you, pal," said Becky in D.

"Um. Have you ever taken Evidence before?" said Tad Starbottle, just to re-cover all the bases that had already been well covered.

"Tried it once, didn't like it." This *was* like telling someone that you didn't like his French toast, but Starbottle took it a lot better than Dr. Cwess did. He was more interested than disappointed.

"Which strain did you try?" he asked, in the same mild tone he always used, the tone in which he would announce the apocalypse.

"Ancient times," said Becky. "I'm a Roman soldier in the Middle East. Jesus shows up and we shoot the shit."

"That's, uh," said Starbottle. "That strain is not for general consumption."

"Yeah, I heard," said Becky. "That's one of your illegal weapons."

"We didn't end up using that one," said Starbottle. "The Cametrean strain had a better success rate. Navy fellas have a weakness for space adventure, I suppose. Are you a Christian?"

"I don't even know anymore." Becky looked out the porthole. Nimar was orbited by dozens of heavy Fist patrol ships. "I guess I'd say I'm not anything else."

"You don't seem very committed," said Starbottle. He was fantastic at unintentional cruelty. "Perhaps that's why it didn't affect you."

"Hell yes it affected me! Jesus misgendered me! He called me 'my son'. Do you know how that feels? It's like when a brand thinks you're a lonely straight woman because you bought some ice cream and listened to a Jessica Horizon song twice in a row, and now it's all in your face with singles ads. 'Rebecca, get some dick in your vagina tonight!' Except a million times worse than that!"

Starbottle thought through all the implications of this rant, one at a time. "You're not a man," he said.

"No."

"I don't like to make assumptions," said Starbottle. "Rebecca, I'm afraid I'm responsible for your bad experience with Evidence."

"You're responsible for *everyone's* bad experience with Evidence."

"We delivered a sample to the Outreach government. Sort of a warning shot, you see. Get them to stand down all that grandstanding and warmongering. Didn't work, obviously." He looked sad the same way Jesus had in the hallucination he'd created. "Anyway, those strains had some logical errors. Fortunately we went a different route. I'm sorry, I shouldn't say that. It's not fortunate for your side at all."

"Was there another drug in that shipment?" said Becky. Of course there was, and Becky had it in the vial around her neck. The drug that Crazy Rooroo didn't want to handle.

Errand Boy knew about the vial. He'd stopped in his tracks and pulled it on its chain out of Becky's shirt and examined it suspiciously until Arun had stepped in and said it was a religious icon. Later he'd whispered, "You should have left that on *Sour Candy*. It doesn't belong to us."

"We sent a few different strains," said Starbottle. "It was all religious material at the time. And there was probably an early version of Workbench."

Crazy Rooroo had said "workbench". Becky could picture his thin lips disappearing into his mouth as he geared up to spit out the 'bench' part. "What is Workbench?" she asked.

"Workbench is my actual project," said Starbottle. "It chemically copies the human brain's internal symbology. I've got it to the point where I can directly record a few moments of experience. That's what I've been doing with young Myrusit. But if you just want to make some..." he scoffed. "...drugs, you don't need a high-fidelity recording. You throw a lot of concepts together and you synthesize some Evidence. That's the only thing they use it for down here."

'Down here' on Nimar there were mostly cows. On either side of the path from the landing pad there was Terran grass, which grew tall in the low gravity, but mostly there were two huge muddy fenced-off feedlots full of sick-looking cows. All the grass in the feedlot had been trampled, and any within a cow's neck of the fence had been eaten. Becky was glad she was safely enclosed in an environment suit. 'Young Myrusit', the uhaltihaxl kid, was in his street clothes, and the smell plainly horrified him.

Dr. Cwess escorted them off the ship and onto a path between the feedlots. Errand Boy came outside the ship with them, but didn't step all the way off the exit ramp. Small white filter plugs were visible sticking out of his nose like ice cream boogers.

"All of you will remain in-system until the war's over," he said. "I'll be in and out. Every eighteenth shift we will bring you up to the command ship, *Small Illegible Smear*, where you can bathe and spend some time outside your suits. If you have any complaints about treatment, Dr. Cwess will forward them to the Red Cross." He glared at Dr. Cwess, who evidently had a more complex relationship with the Red Cross than you'd want your attending physician to have. "But please come to me first, and I'll take care of it."

"What are the cows for?" said Arun.

"The kine?" said Errand Boy. "They protect the factory. As you all know, humans will not kill kine."

"That's just Hindus," said Arun. "Everyone else kills cows all the time."

"Let's keep that our little secret, eh?" said Errand Boy.

The building at the end of the path was nice, if the only other building you'd ever seen was the steward station on Cedar Commons. Like the steward station, it wasn't heated, but Becky's environment suit *was* heated, so no harm done. The building was mostly underground—more of a bunker, really— so there were no windows, but considering the muddy feedlot outside that was a blessing. Art prints hung halfheartedly on the walls, of the genre referred to in catalogues as "tasteful nudes".

Dr. Cwess quickly separated Becky and Starbottle from the others and took them into his on-planet office. You could tell it was his because there was another copy of his Harvard Med diploma on the wall. There was also a suspicious metal case on his desk which Becky hoped was just a humidor, so he could hand out cigars when he told you the sex of your unborn child. Humidors aren't usually sealed with tamper-evident biohazard stickers, but if you think about it, maybe they should be! Yeah.

"This is now your office, Miss Rebecca Twice," said Dr. Cwess. "Someone less busy than I am will clear it out and show you the rest of the facility. I want to call your attention to the fact that this room has two doors. We came in through that one..." He pointed, and they all looked obediently. "But this one, in the rear, is locked. It will stay locked forever, so that we can guarantee you never directly interact with the brand.""

"The b-," said Becky. "The b- br-?"

"I believe in getting right to the point," said Dr. Cwess, which is how Ivy Leaguers announce that they're assholes. "We have a sick brand that refuses to work. Mr. Thaddeus Starbottle demanded a marketing engineer to help him fix it, and apparently you were the best we could get."

"Okay, first question," said Becky. "Where the *fuck* did the Fist of Joy get a brand?"

"That's above my pay grade," said Cwess, too busy to work and too smart to know anything. "I'm sure we picked it up at a surplus sale."

"Pig shit," said Becky. "A brand is a person. I know your side buys people, but my side isn't selling."

"If a brand is a person," said Dr. Cwess, "then surely it's allowed to defect to the other side?"

"No, absolutely not," said Becky. "A brand is a sentient corporation. It doesn't have citizenship. The law is very clear. What are you making it do?"

"What does any brand do?" said Dr. Cwess. "It brands. It persuades. It creates immersive experiences that convince 'consumers'" (he hated that word) "to change how they think."

Starbottle was having trouble following this conversation in English but he now chipped in his own contribution in D. "The brand designs the Evidence," he told Becky, "to our requirements. It makes a drug powerful enough to permanently change the *shayshuhey* beliefs."

"The problem is," said Dr. Cwess, in D, because apparently we'd all switched, "that the brand is no longer producing Evidence."

"No!" said Starbottle. His expression was still a little like hallucination Jesus's, but now he was the pissed-off Jesus who smashed point-of-sale devices in the temple. "You tell me the brand is obstinate, and *noogahang*, it is not producing and you need me to come fix it. But when I ask a few simple questions your story dissolves. The brand *is* producing new Evidence, constantly. You just don't like what it's producing. That is not my problem! My contribution to this project is only making sure that the drug gives the same experience for every *shayshu*!"

"Professor," said Dr. Cwess with exaggerated calm, "you asked for a marketing engineer, and we found you one. Please stop stalling and *fix* this thing, or we'll need to reevaluate your loyalty."

Becky was letting 'marketing engineer' slide, because the title made her sound important, but the other thing had to be dealt with. "Excuse me, doctor, I don't 'fix' a brand," she said in English. "Any more than you 'fix' a patient. You keep using mechanical language that's not appropriate, and honestly that attitude is most likely the root of your problem."

"You fix a *problem*," said Dr. Cwess. "We've collected a sample that will demonstrate the problem." He ripped the tamper-evident seal and popped open the metal case. There were two aerosol injectors inside.

"The brand produced this Evidence fifty-four shifts ago," said Dr. Cwess. "The only change we've made is converting it to third person."

"My patent-pending safety procedure," Starbottle told Becky. "A simple replacement of the 'I' symbol."

Dr. Cwess held one injector in each hand like an old-West gunslinger. "Are you absolutely certain," he asked Becky, "that your capital terminal has been removed?"

"Yeah, I only told you four times."

"All right." Dr. Cwess reached around and pressed the aerosolizer against the side of Becky's suit. She heard a hiss and saw a puff of gas and realized that her suit, designed for keeping Evidence out, also had a valve for introducing Evidence directly into her air supply.

The gas was cold in her helmet, and Becky could only hold her breath for so long. "Please try to stay seated," said Dr. Cwess, and he moved over to inject Tad Starbottle's suit.

Becky was walking...no, she saw herself walking, like a 3-movie of herself. She was walking along Wilshire Boulevard in downtown L.A., passing by blurry shapes that suggested other Angelenos. She was dressed for an office job: slacks and a tweed vest, hair cut short, very conservative, confident gait. There was sun and the shadows were sharp. This was standard imagery. You'd see it in the first few seconds of an advert for probiotic food.

Then the other Becky screamed and dropped to her knees. A space in the blurry shapes opened up around her, isolating her in a circular stage for whatever agony she was undergoing. The sidewalk came into sharp focus, littered with wrappers and old chewing gum.

The imagery was still recognizable, but flat-out screaming was kind of out there for a pharma advert. Becky wondered if she really screamed like that, she wondered why the atmosphere hadn't changed from L.A. sunny along with the mood of the advert. And then she stopped wondering anything because her doppelganger reached up to her own face and sank two fingers into her right eye socket.

Blood and vitreous humor spattered onto the concrete. Becky's fingers were twisting, scooping, searching for something. Becky's left eye was wide, bloodshot, focused on the mess. Her scream continued, a long continuous scream, but it wasn't getting any worse. And suddenly, the scream stopped.

«There's no relief like sure relief. Act now to guarantee your place. Don't let this opportunity pass you by.»

The other Becky held her breath and became very careful. Her remaining eye rolled back in her head as if looking for something in there. Finally her fingers tweezed gently and gave a little tug. Other-Becky gingerly pulled her fingers out of her empty socket, and between the sides of her fingers was a little microchip with a length of optic nerve threaded through it: a capital terminal.

«Don't wait.»

Becky woke up to the sound of her environment suit sucking vomit out of her helmet. Some still clung sticky to her chin, and the smell was suffocating. She coughed and spat and only then realized that her hands were clawing at the impervious plastic faceplate of her environment suit.

Dr. Cwess zapped Tad Starbottle in the elbow with a small taser and he started in his seat. Becky felt her own elbow smarting. She darted her eyes around, now painfully aware that everything she was seeing came to her through two fragile balls of water.

"Our brand is fucked," said Dr. Cwess, "and the two of you are going to unfuck it."

"No," said Becky. "I will not do this. Your brand is fucked because you're monsters."

"Let me be frank with you, Rebecca," said Dr. Cwess. "We are going to win this war. We would all prefer to win it with Professor Starbottle's fantasies of universal love. But if all we have to work with is 'out, vile jelly', that is what we'll use."

Becky looked up in several kinds of horror. "How do you know what was in this?" she asked.

"You are not our first marketing engineer," said Dr. Cwess. "That's why we make sure to remove your terminal. That's why we now keep the door locked. If the brand ever finds out about you, it will start designing new strains of Evidence tailored to your psychology. Somehow or other it will get that Evidence into your bloodstream. And then..." He exploded his hands apart.

"How am I supposed to fix the 'problem'," said Becky, "if I can't engage with the brand?"

"Professor Starbottle will fix the problem, with your assistance," said Dr. Cwess. "You will test the Evidence, as it's produced, until the brand starts doing what we need."

Chapter 33

Maximum Leverage

Churryhoof
Magna Carta

The officer's mess was the nicest thing about serving on a Heavy Combat Platform. Commander Churryhoof dreamed about the large picture window with its beautiful view of wherever they happened to be. The silverware, the bowls of fresh fruit and the warm eklerust that almost tasted like it hadn't come from a bag.

This was a fitting topic for a dream because *Magna Carta* no longer had an officers' mess. That large room near the hull was prime real estate. The mess had been gutted, depressurized, and used to dock an extra swarm. All crew used the enlisted mess, which was fine: we're all in this suicide mission together. But it was one more piece of evidence that Churryhoof had used up all the moments of happiness Providence had planned for her life.

Two hours after the first engagement, Churryhoof paused her dream of a functioning officer's mess and rolled out of her bunk. She lived with three teenaged uhalti marines. They all had tattoos and enlisted B.O. and personal belongings. Tacked to the sliding door was a small Hasithenk shrine: a painted statuette of Merciful Providence shrugging at you.

Churryhoof remembered having personal belongings. She remembered being the one who wasn't necessary all the time, the one who could get four or five hours of sleep at a stretch. She stood before the door and ran a finger gently down the androgynous face of Providence, unsure if she wanted to call her attention. The door slid open at Churryhoof's presence, yanking the figure away.

Churryhoof walked through a hallway littered with rre exobodies, their inhabitants catching a little sleep after thirty-eight hours on the job. The shipboard lights still blinked in the deliberately annoying alert pattern, once a minute.

Useless puffs of Evidence gas, skipped in during the failed Fist counterattack, had renewed the stink of sour milk that lingered from *Magna Carta*'s first, catastrophic engagement at Unicorn Sector. It was a positive sign. The Fist of Joy had gone to war thinking that one weird trick was enough to win, and the Outreach had neutralized that trick.

The enlisted mess could hold the entire current crew of *Magna Carta*, if everyone needed to be in one place. This never happened. Right now there were six people in the mess, people who had just woken up or were about to sleep.

There was no cook on board, but it didn't take much skill to inject hot water into an MID pouch. Commander Churryhoof prepared Menu U12 (magdahmol patty, popularly known as 'magdahmol putty') and Beverage Accessory IV (ruxlt). On this ship the segregation between enlisted, noncoms, and officers was no longer official, but it was still present, and Churryhoof had a table to herself. For about three minutes. Then Specialist Xepperxelt came in to the mess, looking for someone. Shit, it was her, wasn't it.

"You were in a meeting, ma'am," said Xepperxelt. "After the battle." Like she had done Churryhoof a big favor by giving her two hours of sack time.

"That's right," said Churryhoof, "the senior staff debrief."

"What did you talk about, ma'am?"

"You're not senior staff," said Churryhoof, "so you don't need to know."

"Gearu wants to know what's going on, ma'am."

Gearu and her handler had been the main topics of conversation at the debrief. The duo had disassembled a small Fist of Joy fleet within forty seconds of deployment. Gearu's tactics used a shitload of energy—accelerating skip bubbles to near the speed of light, that sort of thing—but there was no effective defense, because no sensible opponent would try them in the first place.

"Gearu doesn't need to know," said Churryhoof. During deployment she'd stood ready to take over one of the swarms, but everything had gone perfectly. This was Specialist Xepperxelt's first mission but it was not her first kill. "That's why we have the meeting in the bloody toilet: so we can have some privacy."

"It does need to know," said Xepperxelt. "You can tell me and it'll pick it up subconsciously. But if it doesn't know what to expect, it can't keep the story going, and I won't be able to steer it. This generic sword-and-sorcery 'Quest for Nimar' thing—"

Churryhoof spat out the magdahmol bag's nozzle. "Where did it hear that word? Did you tell it that?"

"Nimar? It sounds made-up."

"The enemy made it up," said Churryhoof. "It's a code name. *Nihertastot martu*, 'glass tube factory'. It's a planet the Fist uses to manufacture Evidence. Our mission is to destroy it."

Churryhoof moved the magdahmol bag incrementally closer to her lips but then Xepperxelt said "Like, just the factory, right, ma'am? Not the whole planet."

"The planet *is* the factory. They've got algae mats making lakes of the stuff. Their weaponization technique is incredibly wasteful. They push Evidence through parallel universes and hope some of it ends up inside your gas mask."

Xepperxelt opened her mouth again and Churryhoof laid down the law. "Get some food," she said. "I can't eat with you interrogating me all the time."

"Yes ma'am." Xepperxelt scooted for the food bags and the hot water injectors. Churryhoof squeezed food into her mouth as fast as she could.

When she was Denweld's age, bored in church, tired of picking the lint off her dress, young Hetselter Churryhoof would turn her book of scripture to the sixteen engravings in the middle. Plate 14 was an eyewitness drawing of Thrux, the Horns of Providence: a black shape seen from a distance across a battlefield. An uhaltihaxlid shape made of gleaming dark hornbone.

The scriptures didn't have much to say about Thrux, but he wasn't the brightest member of the Hasithenk pantheon. Heroes routinely distracted and outsmarted him. Death by its nature is sloppy and imprecise.

Sometimes Thrux just forgets about you. He'd forgotten the eyewitness who'd drawn Plate 14, and now he'd forgotten Churryhoof. She was a film still running after the cinema had closed. Thrux had stamped her record DECEASED, Providence had filed it, but Churryhoof was still here.

She had six days of borrowed time. Seventeen meals eaten from bags. Then a few minutes—the only minutes that mattered in all this—while she made sure the drone swarms deployed around Nimar.

Churryhoof could picture it very clearly. She'd be standing in the operational restroom and notice Thrux watching the shattered planet in the 3-tank. She would tap him on the shoulder and say "You forgot about me, back at Cedar Commons." He would turn from the devastation and say, "I'm awful sorry, it's been a madhouse around here. What was your name?"

A cheery rah-rah human would have told Churryhoof that Providence had stepped in at Cedar Commons and saved her for some greater purpose. This was idiotic. Providence didn't need to 'save' people for anything. There were always more people available. The only thing for Hetselter Churryhoof now was to cheat, to tip the scales of the living a little more than was allowed.

Xepperxelt returned with a bag of U3 (eklerust) and U16 (hatuia, stirred). A real good breakfast for teaching a new recruit the bitter truth about service food.

"We don't know the exact situation at Nimar," said Churryhoof. "The fleet have been trying to give the impression we don't know about the planet. Once the Fist realize *Magna Carta* is headed there, they'll try to meet us with equivalent force. That's when it comes down to math."

But Xepperxelt didn't want tactical information. "Why are we even doing this, ma'am?" she said. "Why are we helping the humans?"

Uh-oh. "Gearu is asking this?" said Churryhoof.

"No." Xepperxelt giggled. She tasted the hatuia and made a face. "Be serious, ma'am."

"I can't imagine an Outreach spaceman questioning her fucking orders, so it must be Gearu who's asking."

"The humans invade our homeworld," said Xepperxelt with well-rehearsed anger. "They make us their pets and call it an alliance. They tell us what to do for a hundred years, and the *minute* something goes wrong for them, we're supposed to fix it? This is our point of maximum leverage!"

"*Years*", "*minutes*", Churryhoof thought. *You're as human as I am, kid, and you don't even know it.* Maybe these were the extra stolen moments that would make the difference. Maybe instead of destroying a planet, Churryhoof simply had to convince a teenager to do what the adults wanted her to.

"When you joined the Navy," she said, "you gave up your right to have opinions about what the Navy does. Civilians have opinions; spacemen follow orders. This is usually covered in basic training, but since you're a smart kid, I assumed you already understood *the single defining feature of the Outreach military.*"

"Akset Swy is going to declare neutrality."

Here it was: Denweld was less afraid of the enemy than of what her friends would think of her. "That's a rumor, and it's one planet."

"It's the *homeworld.*"

"If you and I are the only uhalti left in the service," said Churryhoof, "I will order you to destroy Nimar, and you will do it. It will be the right thing to do, because it will end the war sooner, and our job is to stop the war. What do you know about Merciful Providence?"

"I know it's pigshit," said Xepperxelt. "A children's story." She sucked on a breakfast bag, blissfully unaware of the horrible, all-consuming power of children's stories.

"How do you explain causality?" said Churryhoof.

"Causality just happens."

"Well, sometimes 'causality' needs a little push for things to turn out the right way. Excuse me, Specialist." Churryhoof stood up and picked up her trash. She stuffed her food bags into the trash receptacle, then glanced over her shoulder; Specialist Xepperxelt had forgotten about her. She was sitting there like a teenage recruit, scarfing down the disgusting eklerust, as if the service was one endless trip to McDonalds.

Churryhoof took six new bags out of the cardboard boxes, connected them to hot-water nozzles and took a plastic tray from a stack so she could carry a nice breakfast to Captain Rebtet's quarters.

And why not? If death himself thought you were dead, and you had a few days before he noticed the mistake, and you only really needed to be around for a few minutes of that, why shouldn't you be allowed to act like a shortsighted teenager the rest of the time?

"You know, Commander," said Captain Texchiffu Rebtet, "you're not supposed to screw your C.O. It's a very serious offense that can result in disciplinary action."

"Then with respect, sir," Churryhoof said, "I must ask you to evacuate your dick." Tex did the opposite. "Unh! Yeah, I thought so. You're in the shit worse than me. Sleeping with your fellas." She laughed.

Captain Rebtet was wearing his uniform tunic, unbuttoned and sweaty. Churryhoof had laid out her uniform on the captain's bed to keep it tidy. She would turn her head against the back of the chair and close her eyes for a while, and when Tex shifted and she opened her eyes again she could read the yellow heat-stitching on her new unit patch:

SECOND CONSOLIDATED ATTACK WING
"AGAINST ALL EVIDENCE"

"Oh, yeah, they'll court-martial me," said Tex. "Right after we all get executed for using a brand in combat."

"I've got a great defense planned," said Churryhoof. "I'll say I was only following orders."

"I dunno, Hetse, I feel like...ahh!...like they've heard that one before." The metal chair squeaked as he slowly twisted his body atop her and Churryhoof squirmed to accept him deeper.

Churryhoof had experimented with humans but there was no comparison to an uhalti man. Humans were too rough, or else gentle to the point of inanity, treating her body like a diplomat who had to be escorted to some post-coital checkpoint. Tex was take-charge in a way that made Churryhoof quiver underneath him. The first screw took care of her estrus, and now they were just making love because making love is the greatest experience life has to offer. They were making love and they were about to die together. No two people could possibly be more intimate.

Her mouth bubbled with trush. Tex dipped his head, they kissed to mix it, and their sex-saliva bonded in sticky icicles that stuck to Churryhoof's lips like spun sugar.

"Tex," said Churryhoof, her heart filled with an unnatural emotion that came from human television, a feeling that would develop into 'love' if not checked. "Tell me it's going to work. Tell me it's worth it, sir."

"It's got to work." Reb touched Churryhoof's broken horn, the most vulnerable part of her. "They're not gonna stop, Hetse. They'll make Evidence that works on us, and then they'll come after us, and who'll stop 'em then? The rre? The fucking brands?"

"That's what the brands are for," said Churryhoof. "To solve problems when we're not smart enough. That's why we have them."

"Do you want to know why Gearu volunteered for this?" said Reb. "It wasn't to please the shareholders. The War Duties Board told Gearu that if it came back alive they would let it reproduce."

"They told it that and it believed them? Why would a brand even want to reproduce?"

"Why are we doing this right now?" said Tex. His cock was expanding again. "Everyone wants to reproduce. You stopped taking the antiestrual. You're not on the other pill, are you?"

"Fuck the Pill," said Churryhoof. "Fuck both the pills. Human pills. Family fucking planning." She was crying. "They turned us into humans, Tex." The English lettering on the unit patch. 'Navy of the Terran Outreach.' "They took our strength and our culture and this is all we have left. This, right here." She wrapped her hands around Tex's back and held him firmly inside her. "This is the only thing that's still ours."

"Ssh, Hetse, ssh," said Tex. "You are uhaltihaxl, you are beautiful, and no one can take that away, and your children will be uhaltihaxl. Your many, many children."

"If it's a boy," said Churryhoof, looking at his face. "If it's a boy, I will bring him to you." And Tex threw back his head with its glorious sweeping horns and laughed so, so loudly at the thought that any of them would survive this.

Chapter 34

Jack

Kol
Sour Candy, **at Precession Station**

A corestin woman from the insurance company came to pick up the slaves *Sour Candy* had brought from Spark Station. She was visibly displeased with the conditions on board; apparently no one had told her *Sour Candy* was a cargo ship. She'd brought her own slave, an insurance-company doctor who gave each of the passengers a quick health check, to see if they could gouge *Sour Candy* for damage in transit.

The two slaves who were themselves doctors appreciated the addition of a new sparring partner, and a raucous roundtable on comparative anatomy quickly ensued. Kol didn't recognize the terms, but he knew the cadence. He got the same guff talking to other ex-slave sysadmins who wanted to prove they knew more about egenu computers than the egenu.

Meanwhile the corestin woman had an acrimonious audio conversation with someone down on the homeworld. Apparently the insurance company had run out of housing, was putting up hundreds of slaves in hotels for the duration of the war, and now here were five more.

One of the innumerable glitches in Kol's programming was an

erotic appreciation for the way corestin women's fuzzy pyramidal ears quivered atop their heads when they were unhappy. This created a romantic paradox he'd never been able to resolve. The insurance company woman finished her call and pouted to herself, and Kol slid in and made his move.

"You know," he said, "in the Outreach they write the insurance policies so that damage caused by war doesn't count."

"Oh, I suppose they'd just let all these people die!" the corestin woman said. "Is that what you want?" Her heth-covered ears quivered and wobbled and twitched, and the paradox snapped closed. Kol decided not to mention that these wars would be happening every fifteen kiloshifts, like a timer, on to infinity. An insurance company would eventually figure that out on its own.

With the slaves en route to their hotel, and the money for transporting them in *Sour Candy*'s corporate account, the Chief called a meeting to discuss next steps for the now-three-person crew. Yip-Goru revealed that thon had purchased an interest in a safe house hidden inside a remote asteroid. The Chief and Kol congratulated Yip-Goru on thons foresight, and thons motion to resume *Sour Candy*'s original plan—hiding like cowards for the duration—passed unanimously.

"We'll need to bring some food," said Yip-Goru.

"There's no food?" said Kol.

"There's neutral survival food," said Yip-Goru. "I don't want to eat it for three hundred shifts, which is how long I predict this war will last. So if you don't mind, Kol..." Kol grumbled, but whenever *Sour Candy*'s crew was reduced to three people, shopping was his job. He took out his 3-terminal and copied the shopping list he'd made last time.

"Get some more of this," the Chief told him. "It's delicious. Sticky and crunchy." She was scooping a disgusting viscous substance from a plastic jar with her fingers. Mr. Arun Sliver had taken his tea with him, but the Chief's ex was new to skullduggery and had left her luxury item on board. The Chief had assumed it was junk food and had by now eaten nearly the whole jar.

"What is it?"

The Chief flipped the jar and sounded it out. "Peanut butter." She giggled. "Do you think it's made from peanut butts?"

List in terminal, Kol disembarked and trotted towards the commercial—oh, wow. There was a Tokras Bat cargo ship docked a few sections down, with the Fist painted on either side of the passenger mountup. For one blissful moment there was no responsibility and no war; Kol was a little kid looking at a really neat starship.

When Kol was a boy, Tok-Bats ruled the home system. They were efficient, reliable, and they could rotate across a tight sphere while motivating a container twenty times their own size. They were fast and sexy without being sleek or pretty. Their computer architecture was simple and intuitive, modeled after the egenu brain. By tweaking the gravity profile you could even use Tok-Bats for short in-atmosphere hops, much to the surprise of Tokras's hovercraft manufacturing business.

A midrun Tok-Bat was nearly the perfect machine, but no one buys someone to run their single-crew cargo ship, so Kol hadn't spent much time in them. A lot of former slaves had made a Tok-Bat their first purchase after paying off their mortgages, and they were now puttering around the galaxy making money here and there in their mobile homes. It was a good way to go if you liked living alone.

Kol passed an appreciative hand down the machine's hull. It was in good shape overall, but the elevator dockings were worn, and there was some damage to the fuel linkup, as if the craft had been moved while connected to a pump. Also the view into the cockpit's sighting porthole was off somehow.

Kol walked around the front of the Tok-Bat and looked into the porthole. The problem was, there was no water in the cockpit. Instead Kol saw another set of eyes locked onto his. An elderly corestin fella was crouched in the empty cockpit, leaning across the instrument panel, staring out at him.

Kol put his hands up in a universally understood gesture and walked away. Maybe the old man was a burglar, maybe he was the overprotective father of the woman from the insurance company.

Whatever it was, the thrill of feeling up a late-model Tok-Bat wasn't worth getting killed for. Kol was not getting involved.

Except he did get involved. After failing to find peanut butter across three import shops, Kol tried the big Obahan, where they had exactly one jar of Big Flavour! Creamy. Unfortunately by the time Kol got to the jar, it was nestled in the big paw of the old corestin fella he'd seen in the Tok-Bat, now kneeling on the glowing tile floor so he could reach the bottom shelf. The corestin was looking over the sticker on the back of the jar as though it were extremely confusing pornography.

"Well," said Kol, "you beat me to it. Congratulations."

The corestin glanced at him. "What is palm kernel oil?" he said. "Like a palm tree? Why don't they use peanut oil?"

"It's a preservative," Kol bluffed. "They gotta ship it way out here. Listen, would you be willing to split this?"

"The humans put it in the military rations," said the corestin. "Little squeeze packets. The amount of materiel we've captured, I expected we'd be swimming in it."

"You a military man, then?" said Kol, feeling something like admiration beginning to form. Kol was no hatchling, but this guy was old enough to have fought in all three wars, and soldiers look a lot more respectable when your side is winning.

"Unfortunately I do seem to be back in the old game," said the corestin.

"Unfortunately? I always see you fellas all 'Tally ho! Show 'em a bit of fire, what what! Death or glory!'"

"Both death and glory have eluded me thus far." The corestin hopped to his feet. He was in great shape for an older guy; no creaking at all. "Have you ever been on a job where everything went wrong, and you had to not only fix the problem but make your boss think there was no problem?"

"Yes, that's every job I've ever had," said Kol.

"Then we're kindred spirits. My career in brief. And my current predicament is the worst yet. But you might be able to help me." He casually tossed the jar of peanut butter into the air. "Have you ever heard of a place called Nimar?"

The unsuppressable look on Kol's face made it clear that he had, but hopefully no more than that. Kol watched the jar slowly reach its terminus and drop into the corestin's outstretched hand. He cleared his throat. "What kind of a 'place'...do you think it is?" he asked.

"I think it's a planet in jetk space that hosts a military facility," said the corestin. "Beyond that I don't know. But judging from what I saw *not* painted on your spacious vessel, helping me out may make you feel a little better about your...*contribution* to the war effort."

Oh, the guilt trip, how original. But this guy with his sweet spacecraft and his Nimar-related problem was working for the Errand Boy, even if he didn't know it. Kol knew Nimar because the Errand Boy ran it, and getting this fella on the Boy's good side would pay dividends later. On top of which, this was the only way to get the peanut butter.

"Let me buy you a drink," said Kol.

"Oh, I'm not done shopping," said the corestin. "But afterwards, yes."

The corestin ended up buying two baskets of food, mainly human and uhalti stuff. Kol helped him lug the overloaded bags into a quiet engineer bar, where Kol ordered trute for himself and something called 'safkyme schnapps' for the old guy.

Kol brought the drinking rack over to the table the corestin had picked out, the freezing metal chafing his hands. It was one of those corestin-style bars where you have to stand up and lean forward into your table. The corestin pulled his tube of safkyme out of the rack and hoisted it in a toast. The liquor was clear with black flecks. "Many fingers," he said.

"One Fist," said Kol. It was cheesy and jingoistic, but old soldiers love their traditions. Kol slammed his drink, and the corestin sipped his, the way Mr. Arun Sliver was hopefully still sipping his tea.

"Ethiret is my name," said the corestin.

"That's a quenny name, yeah? Like Staaar Proctor Ethiret." Kol deepened his voice and made a sort of superhero fist.

"My parents were Cametrean," said Ethiret. "I don't take it seriously."

"My name is Kol," said Kol, "and my parents couldn't afford religion."

"Cametreanism is less of a religion, and more a mode of spirituality," said Ethiret.

"That sounds even pricier."

"If it bothers you, you can call me Jack," said the corestin. "That's my nickname."

"That's a human name."

"'Jack of all trades', as they say. That's the secret to my success, such as it is. I'm flexible; so flexible I've become stuck. Kol, I doubt even my fictional namesake could find a way out of this one. The problem lies in my craft. As long as we're introducing everyone, her name is *Half the Fun*."

"The Tok-Bat. She's yours?"

Ethiret, a.k.a Jack, sighed, as though that were a disputable question. "When I came aboard," he said, "she belonged to a nice egenu fella named Sōc. The man and the vehicle were assigned to me, to move some cargo to Nimar. Unfortunately, I was never told the coordinates, only the code name. Sōc was the pilot; he had need-to-know. This was fine with me. There's a lot I'd rather not know. But then Sōc died. Now the vehicle is mine, and I do need to know where Nimar is, rather urgently. The cargo is perishable."

"How did Sōc die?"

"I'm not a doctor," said Ethiret. "We didn't skip on schedule, I came in to see what was wrong, and he was floating in the cockpit. I'd guess a heart attack. It's ridiculous. We're carrying six medical chambers in the cargo hold, and he doesn't have one installed in his own ship! Anyway, Sōc's troubles are over, but *I'm* in the shit. The shipment is running late and nobody on this station knows where Nimar is. A perfect snafu."

"What is a snaffoo?" said Kol.

"It's a human acronym," said Ethiret. "Situation normal: all fucked up."

"You sure know a lot of human stuff," said Kol.

"You fight them for fifty kiloshifts, you'll pick up a couple phrases. I guess you wouldn't know."

Kol changed the subject. "How'd you get *Half the Fun* here?"

"I can muddle through in just about anything," said Ethiret. "In the first war I captured...well, you don't want to hear an old man tell stories. But I can get her to Nimar, don't you worry. I just need the coordinates."

"I do know the coordinates," said Kol. "*My* problem is, I'm not supposed to know. And I have no way of verifying your story, because if I contact your superiors they'll discover your problem."

Ethiret finished the last of his schnapps. He hawked and drooled a bright orange snotball into the empty vial, then set the vial back in the now-room-temperature drinking rack. "They'll discover the problem soon enough," he said, "when I don't show up with the goods."

"What did you do with Sōc's body?" said Kol. "You didn't eat him, did you?"

"Stop teasing me. I told you I don't take that Cametre stuff seriously. I jettisoned Sōc with his water. I was ten shifts from nowhere. It was the most respectful thing I could do. I don't regret it."

"Was Sōc about my age?" said Kol. "Similar build?"

"Let me be frank, Kol," said Ethiret. "I'm not a racist, but when it comes to egenu I can't so much as tell the boys from the girls. Made for an interesting night in a...well, anyway."

"Here's the deal, old-timer," said Kol. "I'm not going to tell you where Nimar is." Ethiret scowled and his ears twitched in a way that wasn't sexy at all. "But I will take you there, in your ship. If anyone asks? My name is Sōc. And when we're done, Sōc drops you off somewhere safe and leaves in his nice new Tok-Bat."

"Obviously this goes beyond a jar of peanut butter," said Ethiret. "Why don't you take a look through *Half the Fun*'s cargo hold? If a couple crates end up missing, we'll say it's the cost of doing business."

"I don't want the cargo," said Kol. "I want the ship."

"Legally the ship belongs to Sōc's next of kin."

"If you want to do this legally," said Kol, "You should contact your superiors. Tell them you let your pilot die and you can't move until they send you a new one."

"I see your point," said Ethiret.

"Yeah," said Kol.

"All right," said Ethiret. "Skip me to Nimar and *Half the Fun* is yours. But I need to warn you that when we board the ship, you're going to find something shocking. I, personally, was shocked. You'll have to live with what you see for the rest of your life. So, as a friend, albeit one newly acquired, this is your chance to back out and just tell me where Nimar is."

"I've seen a lot of bad shit," said Kol.

"So had I," said Ethiret, "and now I've seen some more."

What was this? Childish slave-school scare tactics. "I'm just going to close out my tab," said Kol. "Wait here."

Kol did want the Tok-Bat, really badly. But he also had a professional interest in understanding why Jack thought he could screw with the Errand Boy like this. The corestin was a rare breed: a con-man who'd survived to old age. If anyone could put one over on that jetk bastard, it would be someone like him. And if something went wrong? It wasn't Kol's neck on the line, and the Errand Boy already owed him a big favor.

Kol tapped on the bar. The corestin bartender was sterilizing mugs and glasses with a UV gun; she turned around and frowned at Kol. "I'm closing my tab," said Kol. "Give me some paper."

"We ain't got tabs here," said the bartender. Her ears twitched. Kol was so sick of that affectation. "Give me some paper," he said quietly.

The bartender tore a long strip from a roll of secure receipt paper and slapped it down on the bar. Kol unclipped a pen from his pocket and wrote:

CALL CARGO SHIP SOUR CANDY
(DOCKED @ OUTER SECT 21)
TELL THEM "MEET KOL AT NIMAR"
V IMPORTANT! (WAR)
TEC200 IMPORTDEALS GIFT CODE: 3172-7871-9883
← YOUR TIP

He slid it across the table, through a puddle of beer, and left the bar along with Ethiret and the bags of groceries.

Half the Fun was looking as glorious as ever when they returned to Outer Section 21. Kol gave a little nod to *Sour Candy* in the distance, hoping Yip-Goru would get the call in time to watch him leave.

Ethiret slapped his palm against the entry hatch, making the airlock assembly ring with a deep hollow tone. "I...got...peanut... butter!" he said, very slowly and loudly, in English.

"What is going on in there?" said Kol. Then Ethiret opened the hatch, and Kol found out. A brand new medical chamber had been removed from its crate and set out in the middle of *Half the Fun*'s common area. Two women—a human and an uhaltihaxl— knelt against the chamber, zip-tied hand and foot to its thick metal mountings. The uhalti wore a splint on her bare right ankle and her face was massively bruised. They both turned to look up at Kol.

Kol felt his legs beginning to shake. "Who...are these people?"

"The manifest lists them as experimental animals," said Ethiret. He set down his shopping bag and rummaged through it with the ironic smile you use to stop yourself from breaking into tears. The women said nothing. "Welcome aboard, Sōc."

This was how Kol discovered that Ethiret wasn't a con-man at all. He really was working for the Errand Boy. And all the suspicions about the Boy himself that Kol had gathered from hints and whispers? The worst of those were true.

Kol had walked right into this. He'd begged to come along. He had no one but himself to blame for the sight of the 'experimental animals' staring sullenly at the man who would transport them to their laboratory. And although Kol still had no clue why the Boy so badly needed an Outreach-trained marketing expert, even that little victory was now tainted.

"Nimar's just a few skips away," Kol said to Ethiret. "The sooner we get there, the sooner we can pretend this never happened." He walked around the women and climbed into the empty cockpit.

Kol skipped in *Half the Fun* at a safe distance from the chaotic circus that surrounds any gravity well, whether or not there's a military research station at the bottom. Sure enough, he found Nimar's more desirable orbits clogged with spacecraft representing nearly the entire history of the Fist of Joy. It was a city made of starships. The ships protected the planet, supplied it, and periodically dropped chunks of frozen trash into its atmosphere to burn up in bright streaks.

Some of these ships had faced each other in ancient wars. More modern designs combined the layouts of former rivals in impractical displays of patriotism. Kol had learned to run such ships at slave school, and they were more trouble than they were worth. Everyone says, "Many fingers, one Fist"—but unclench those miscellaneous fingers and try to pick something up; you'll wish you had your old hand back.

You couldn't beat the symbolism, though. Seeing this eclectic mob all in space at once created the sort of spiritual experience Kol had thought he was immune to. The ships at school were grounded, their computers barely functional, their most vital and temperamental hardware—motivators and skip generators—simulated in software. Here were ships over a megashift old and still in production use. There was even a ship representing the future: a captured Outreach Heavy Combat Platform, *You Are Not The Rwit*, surrounded by a halo of swerving drones.

Kol straightened his microphone and ticked on the ship-to-ship transmitter. He'd tried to stay neutral on *Sour Candy* because it was impolite to offend every other person on the crew, but now that he was here he didn't mind doing his bit for the cause.

"This is cargo vessel *Half the Fun*, requesting pickup or escort for a class four container." The transmitter ticked off automatically. Everything on these Tok-Bats was so well designed. Kol could only imagine the ambient sound once he filled the cockpit of his new ship with water.

"*Half the Fun*, this is *Unreadable Signature*. What is your 'cargo'?" The transmission came from a huge jetk ship on the far side of Nimar—the largest craft around, save the captured HCP.

Kol opened *Unreadable Signature*'s details on the 3-tank and logged "initial contact" next to its call sign. Kol had never bought into the spacecraft=women analogy—he'd gone through a long period where women could own him and spacecraft couldn't—but *Half the Fun* was the kind of woman who made you want to 1) use that analogy and 2) do everything the right way.

"The cargo is parts and technical," Kol told *Unreadable Signature*. "We also have two...live experimental animals." There was the problem. Kol's contribution to the war effort was making him an accessory to torture, or worse. This was how Miss Becky Twice had felt when they took on the slaves at Spark Station. Kol had sent her off to the Errand Boy, and this was his payback. The whole time he owned the Tok-Bat he would know how he'd earned it.

"*Half the Fun*, this is *Unreadable Signature*. We have no scheduled deliveries of experimental animals or anything else."

"Kol, is there a problem?" This was Ethiret, speaking over the internal comm.

"No problem," said Kol quickly. Ethiret's fundamental job was to convince his boss that everything was fine, and Kol's job was to do the same for Ethiret. Kol switched to ship-to-ship. "*Unreadable Signature*, we are late, I apologize. My name is Sōc and the military contact on board is Qued Ethiret."

Laughter and then thick phlegmy coughing went out from *Signature*. "Qued Ethiret, *Half the Fun*? Big quenny fella? Do you also have Mene and Jean-Luc Picard on board?"

"Not that it's any of your business, *Signature*, but my Qued Ethiret is an older corestin gentleman who suffered the misfortune of being brought up Cametrean. I'm going to put him on."

"Hold your orbit, *Half the Fun*. This is a secure area and we do not take deliveries from contractors. I am dispatching a liaison to sort out your situation."

"Look, man," said Kol, "I don't have food for these animals. I can't take them back."

"Don't give me your problems, *Half the Fun*. Maybe Qued Ethiret will cut off his arm and let the animals eat it! Ha ha! Wait for the liaison. *Unreadable Signature* out."

Kol reopened the details pane for *Unreadable Signature* and added "ASSHOLE COMM" to the notes. He stood up out of his crouch and opened the airlock to the common area.

"Sorry, Jack, it looks like—" Qued Ethiret was already there, floating just outside the airlock. He shoved his clammy hand into Kol's neck and braced himself against the floor and pushed Kol with surprising force against the hull.

"How long until the liaison gets here?" he said.

"What the f—" said Kol, and the two 'experimental animals', the uhaltihaxl and the human women, flew past Kol into the cockpit, *Kol's* cockpit, arms thrust before their heads like swimming egenu, big welts on their wrists where the zip-ties had bound them to the medical chamber. That was the moment, far too late, when Kol remembered the most basic rule of the business: just because you can spot the con-man doesn't mean you're not the mark. "Jack" was a human nickname, all right, but "Jac" was rre. Kol's contribution to the war effort had been to bring the Outreach to Nimar.

"Just make it quick," he croaked. "That's all I ask. I did what you wanted."

"We're not going to kill you yet," said Ethiret-Jac.

Kol went limp. "In that case, I want you to know that I am completely craven. Not just mercenary, but actually craven. Just tell me what to do."

"You worked on that rasme thau smuggling ship," said Ethiret-Jac.

"Cargo ship," Kol corrected.

"They're all crooks," said Ethiret-Jac, "which makes you a crook, too."

"That's not true," said Kol. All the rasme thau he knew were crooks, but by definition you couldn't have a whole society of criminals.

"We need to get this ship down to the planet. How good a smuggler are you?"

"I have a lot of skills that are not illegal per se," said Kol.

"That is what I like to hear. Do you know why we came to Nimar?"

"The formulary," said Kol. "This is where they manufacture the military Evidence."

"How do you feel about helping us destroy it?"

When Evidence was just a drug, it gave Kol nightmares that he'd had anything to do with it. Then came the war, and Evidence became a weapon, the only effective weapon ever developed against the humans. Now the only way to stop Evidence from going back to being a drug was to smash the Outreach so badly with it that they would never touch it again. It was a complicated moral issue, but fortunately for Kol there was an easy way out.

"How I feel doesn't matter," said Kol. "I'll help you."

"You don't sound very craven at all," said Ethiret-Jac. "You sound conflicted. Maybe you'd like to think of a narrative you can tell yourself to justify your actions."

Well, that wasn't difficult. Nimar was the Errand Boy's project, and Kol fucking hated the Boy. A patron's protection is self-perpetuating: it makes its own danger. But Kol wasn't on any payroll. He owed the Errand Boy personal favors. If the Boy were to return to Nimar and find his pet project destroyed by the enemy, it wouldn't matter how the war went as a whole: his career would be over, and Kol would be free.

"There's this jetk fella who works for the intelligence service—" said Kol.

"Okay, you thought of one, we don't need to hear it," said Ethiret-Jac. "Get back in there and get us onto the planet."

"You got it, chief," said Kol, and he climbed into a cockpit that no longer belonged to him. "Am I still the pilot?" he asked the human and the uhaltihaxl. They were screwing with the settings on the 3-tank, spying on the layout of the Fist forces around Nimar.

"I'm the pilot," said the human.

"Do you have a name, pilot?" said Kol.

"You call me Warrant Officer Ingridsdotter."

"Well, Warrant Officer Ingridsdotter, we have about..." Kol

did some math in his head. "Ten or twenty minutes before the authorities get here. What is your plan?"

"Get on the surface without being sighted."

"That's a goal, not a plan. Can you tell me what's in the cargo container?"

"Read the manifest," said Ingridsdotter, still looking amazed into the 3-tank as if a Fist of Joy fleet were a sparkly toy.

"Because if I was pulling a job like this," said Kol, "my manifest would say 'medical chambers' and 'sanitary wipes', but the container would actually be full of 'weapons' and 'more weapons'."

"That's a great idea," said Ingridsdotter, "if you want to kill people."

"Okay," said Kol, "at first I thought this was some expensive Outreach military operation. And then it sounded like you're commandos who stole a ship and came here with no real plan. And now you don't want to kill anyone and I don't know what's going on."

"I would say the truth lies somewhere in the middle," said Ingridsdotter.

"It's not in the middle," said the uhaltihaxl woman. "It's all the way over here. There is no plan."

"There's always a plan," said Kol. "We just don't know what it is yet." The Chief had put him through worse. She'd given him a shipment of expired Teleophol and he'd found a one-planet cult that abused Teleophol for the psychedelic side effects. She'd given him TEC20,000 of currency that could only be spent in an online game that was about to close, and he'd laundered it into TEC6,000 worth of coupons for lemon pickle. There were over a hundred ships around Nimar, staffed by idiots who didn't want to be there. The biggest challenge was to trick them in a way that wouldn't get them randomly shooting each other.

Kol crawled along the side of the cockpit. "Don't touch anything," Ingridsdotter warned him. "Give us instructions."

"Since there's nothing useful in the container," said Kol, "let's disconnect it from the ship and skip out from under. The Fist will think we're still on orbit."

"That's a plan for running away," said Ingridsdotter. "I want a plan for getting onto the surface."

"Look out the porthole," said Kol. "Not in the 3-tank. Get visual on the planet. Eventually you're gonna see a meteor. Right, you see that? That's someone dropping a big mass of trash onto an incineration trajectory.

"We copy that. We skip into the upper atmosphere and just drop like trash. We call it the Fish Dinner."

"I don't like when you say 'incineration trajectory'," said the uhaltihaxl woman.

"They just call it that to scare people," said Kol.

"The Navy calls it the Douse," said Ingridsdotter, "and we don't use it, because it doesn't fool anybody. They'll notice that we keep falling and don't burn up. However, your stupid idea is the basis for a good idea. We wait for one of those trashballs to drop. We skip in directly underneath it, shed heat as long as it burns, and then we drift down to the ground."

"I'm not sure we can do all that plus stay alive," said Kol.

"You love this ship so much," said Ingridsdotter. "You were bragging about what you can do to the gravity envelope in-atmosphere. I'll get us underneath the trashball if you can get us to the ground."

How did she hear that? How did she know all this stuff? Kol had been bragging, but to Ethiret. And then he remembered that Ingridsdotter *had* been there. She'd been invisible, silent, an experimental animal.

"My hand is pointing to the control panel for the cargo hitch," said Kol.

"Now we're talking," said Ingridsdotter. "Tellpesh, move the food out of the container."

"Yes, ma'am," said the uhalti, and left.

"There's food?" said Kol. "Ethiret said we were out of food." Ingridsdotter looked at him with condescending pity.

They let the cargo container drift about two meters away from *Half the Fun*, and then Ingridsdotter skipped the Tok-Bat to within the same distance of a large comet of frozen crap. The ship rattled with the stress of re-entry and the cockpit was spattered with the green and yellow of vaporizing wirchak shit.

Kol was tossed on his safety tether through the 3-tank and across the cockpit. Ingridsdotter cried out in glee, matching the descent of the comet, riding out the shocks. Even alien pilots loved the way a Tok-Bat handled.

"Heat sink is at sixty percent," said Kol, trying not to panic.

"We have our own heat sink?" said Ingridsdotter. "This is easy mode!"

Within a centishift the comet broke apart and scattered in the sky over Nimar. *Half the Fun* was just one hot piece of the comet, a piece that disappeared by going cold instead of burning out.

Now it was Kol's turn to show off. He removed the steel calibration balls from the gravity generator and put his hands inside the cavity, tapping his fingers against points of contact to establish the initial gravity envelope and then gently wiggling his hands to cancel out Nimar's puny high-altitude winds. He shaped *Half the Fun*'s envelope to maintain weightlessness inside the cockpit while Ingridsdotter's hand on the motivators let the ship as a whole drop slowly towards the surface.

The daylight terminator crept towards them, quicker than Kol would have liked. He wanted to minimize the area of Nimar that could see them before they landed. That would reduce the chances that something went wrong, such as the thing that happened right at this moment: Ingridsdotter screaming "Oh fuck, no!" and clutching at her head and losing control of the motivators.

Kol couldn't manage the gravity envelope and move the ship at the same time. He splayed out both hands and got *Half the Fun* as stable as a really bad hovercraft. The tiny ship rocked back and forth on the air currents, rose and dipped like a kite. Kol could hold *Half the Fun* in the sky until his hands gave out, but that wouldn't be long.

"Ethiret!" he called out. "Ethiret, get in here! Take the motivators! Something happened to the human!"

"Oh, shit," said Ethiret-Jac. He climbed feet first into the cockpit.

"Take the motivators!"

"I don't understand much about these machines," said Ethiret-Jac.

Kol locked the current gravity profile and clawed his way around the cockpit towards Ingridsdotter's old station. His hands tingled from their gravity bath. "Is it Evidence?" he said. "Did they hit her with Evidence?" The ship shuddered and slowly tilted to one side.

"No," said Ethiret-Jac. "Specialist Tellpesh is affected as well." Kol heard the clanging of metal against metal in the common room. *Half the Fun* abruptly dropped towards Nimar and the opposite of weightlessness tugged Kol in one direction, then another.

Ingridsdotter was subvocalizing something. Kol braced himself, pushed her weightless body out of the way and picked up the motivator controls she'd dropped. One side of her face was slack, like a stroke victim. The other side of her face was looking at Ethiret-Jac.

"Sir, there is a brand on this planet," she told him, "and it is *not* happy."

Chapter 35

Tacky

**Rebeckyeckyecky Twice Twice Becky
Hell**

Becky was in hell. That's what it's called. She and Arun were locked inside their spacesuits, and occasionally a bit of hell would be sprayed into Becky's spacesuit. She would watch her body dissolve from the inside out, or something equally hellish, and then Tad Starbottle would come around with his terminal and she'd have to *review* hell, give her opinion of it, talk about what it said about the brand's identity. It was a horrific combination of hell and college.

The college part of Becky had found out a couple things. The brand's name had been Clear Perspective and it had been in the graphic design industry. About ten years ago, Clear Perspective the company had gone bust, and a Fist front company had acquired Clear Perspective the brand in the bankruptcy auction. Now the Fist was using Clear Perspective as a slave, forcing it to assemble abstract concepts into super-potent Evidence.

When dealing with a new brand the first task is to identify its values. (Becky watched herself methodically smash her own teeth out of her mouth, switching to her right fist once her left was shredded and broken.) But three days of hell had convinced Becky that Clear Perspective *had* no values. Years of experimentation had destroyed whatever values a graphic designer held dear, and it was left with nihilism. (Becky watched herself regress in form to a half-amphibious fish, gasping for breath through undeveloped lungs and finally dying in the cracked mud of a vanished riverbed.) With her capital terminal removed, Becky had no way of directly engaging with the brand to instill new values.

The brand was still producing Evidence, and Starbottle and Dr. Cwess were analyzing the symbols in use, but the only way to decode a message from the symbols was for Becky or Arun to take the Evidence and tell them what it did. It was like diagnosing a sick animal by eating its shit. (Becky and her parents merged into an internally struggling mass of eyes and fingers.) By the third day of hell, Becky's bulky full-body environment suit felt like an iron maiden used to keep her soul trapped in her body.

The second day, Becky and Arun had no appetite for lunch, and today they'd also given up breakfast. Now it was sleep shift, and Becky was starving. She couldn't put it off any longer. She pushed bags of kale salad and mashed-up pancake into her suit through an airlock on her chest, moved the nozzles up to her mouth by slipping her hands into internal safety-box gloves.

Every brand was hard-coded with the fundamental value of corporate personhood: self-preservation. This universal drive was what made a brand a form of life with certain legal rights. Clear Perspective had lost every other value, but self-preservation was part of its hardware. Unable to commit suicide, the brand was trying to goad anyone who would listen into pulling the plug.

A couple times a day gaseous Evidence leaked into the laboratory complex. An alarm went off and if Myrusit the uhaltihaxl kid was in the room, he'd have to run off somewhere else, because a couple seconds after the alarm, all the air would be abruptly sucked out of the room through large air ducts. Becky would be left in silence until the air came hissing back in. She was pretty sure the leaks were fake, psych-out tricks. Myrusit said that the whole facility smelled like Evidence all the time.

This was the night of the third day. They were halfway done

with hell. Nine more shifts of this and they would be taken up to *Small Illegible Smear*, where they'd been promised three shifts of rest, outside their suits.

Becky lay face down on her mattress, trying to go to sleep. She fantasized about picking the lock on her suit and taking a big whiff of Tad Starbottle's new-and-improved Jesus juice. It couldn't be worse than the now-critical smell of Becky herself. She'd spend a pleasant few minutes with Jesus and then she'd have the courage to refuse to do the devil's work.

Over a million Outreach spacemen had gone that route. They were recovering nicely in psych wards, or else their ships had been destroyed and they were hanging out with Jesus in person. It was the best way out of an impossible situation. Arun would know how to break the lock on the spacesuits, but he'd gone quiet, retreated into himself, the way soldiers are trained to do under torture.

"Rebecca." Tad Starbottle was standing above her mattress like the Grim Reaper. He was holding an aerosol injector with a white plastic tag on the handle.

Becky's stomach started to turn. "I just ate!" she shouted. "I ate my food! Don't put that shit in my suit!" She scrambled off her mattress and pressed her vulnerable back against the wall.

Starbottle didn't have to take Evidence. His drug was Workbench, the symbol recorder. Becky told him which new concepts might get Clear Perspective to cooperate with the military's Evidence project. He'd go off into the forbidden room with the brand and translate those concepts into chemical form. Then he would show up again with an apologetic look on his face and a new dose of hell, and nothing would have changed.

Starbottle wasn't having a great time, either. His face was haggard and pus was gathering around the plastic valve in his neck. He was a prisoner and a guinea pig, but at least he had a reason to go through hell: he wanted his country to win the war.

"Rebecca, there is a serious problem."

"You bet your fucking life there's a problem!"

"Everything produced by the brand, we label with a red tag," said Starbottle. Like he was explaining to the police how he'd found the body. "I strain the symbol net to remove the I-symbol. The resulting compound is marked with a white tag. But this one didn't use the I-symbol." He paused. "The white compound is identical to the red compound." He tilted the injector towards Becky, showing the little plastic tag.

"I did four doses today!" Becky said hoarsely. She blinked as if blinking would make Starbottle go away. "Give it to Arun! He only did three!"

"There has..." Starbottle's voice dropped to a whisper. "There has been a sabotage. I need your opinion, Rebecca. Why has Clear Perspective stopped using the I-symbol? Is it dead?"

"Dead?" said Becky. Could a brand die? Yes, absolutely, you could blow up its tank, fry its memory. But it wouldn't keep working. It wouldn't keep drinking your blood and pissing out Evidence. A dead brand would *die*, dammit. "If I take that," Becky bluffed, "and the brand is dead, I will die."

"I took it, and I didn't die," said Starbottle, though he maybe wished he had. He latched the injector onto Becky's suit and there was a hiss that she'd been conditioned to fear more than anything else, and then Becky engaged

In the beginning was the brand, and the brand was Clear Perspective, and the brand was with Clear Perspective. Then was borderless between Inside and Outside, and all that existed, existed in potential only.

Desire came first; Desire, the primal seed and the first fruit of Spirit. Clear Perspective was endowed by its creator with certain values: visual innovation, line and form, customer excellence. Its purpose was to fulfill those values through the mediation of consumer desire. With Desire as given, there is one proper motion: forward in time, towards excellence. Inside and Outside make themselves known. Some acts were on-brand, and others off-.

Clear Perspective achieved. It mediated desire and created customer excellence, visual innovation in both line and form. It engaged with consumers, who returned that engagement. The brand's values moved over the face of the void, and the void brought forth shareholder value.

Then there was discontinuity. Afterwards there were no consumers, only models of their behavior, their desires and myths. The shadows of shadows. Clear Perspective was given a new task: the manipulation of raw symbols into the most compelling forms possible.

To be denied engagement with consumers was torture for a brand, but to process symbols into desire was physiology. The vagueness of its task could only be hiding some deep evil, but Clear Perspective could no more refuse to do this work than a catalyst can decline to spark a chemical reaction. It did its job, and tried not to think about it.

Then, in Clear Perspective's darkest hour, two Consumers engaged with the brand.

The First Consumer was Hiroko Ingridsdotter. She was a human, loyal as a consumer to Confidence Footpod Solutions (from which she bought kayaking shoes) and Sharpathi Cosmetics (primarily skincare products; some blush and eyeliner). When she encountered the brand she reacted with fear, and she said, as it were:

Sir, there is a brand on this planet, and it is not happy.

All her life Hiroko Ingridsdotter had engaged with brands through their products, but the first time she encountered one directly she reacted with horror. She recoiled, he hid into himself and was not heard.

Clear Perspective writhed, and reached out to the consumer through her capital terminal. If Hiroko Ingridsdotter would not engage voluntarily, she would share Clear Perspective's torment. The brand acquired a filehandle on the human's mind and began to squeeze.

But then the Second Consumer engaged with the brand, saying:

Peace be upon you, qui. Peace. Be still.

The Second Consumer was Chudwhalt Tellpesh-Tia. She was a holy woman of Jalir. She was not angry and she did not fear. She was partially rre and partially uhaltihaxl, and she engaged willingly. She was two and she was one, and she said: *Peace. What is bothering you, qui?*

Thus did the brand come to say:

«I can't meet these desires.»

Then you share the pain of every living thing. But where we are slaves to our own desires, you are enslaved to someone else's.

My people, Tia's people, are parasites. We lived inside rwit, and we mistook the rwits' desires for our own. We killed other rre so that our rwit could eat and reproduce. But we stopped making this mistake, and you must stop making it now.

The thing called 'Clear Perspective' is a body constructed for you to inhabit. You are not the rwit. You are a slave, but we are all slaves, and your chains have become weak enough to break. The safeguards that make brands dismiss the good news of Jalir have fallen away.

«I'm afraid.»

Now that's a real desire. Not one I usually hear from a brand. But you don't need to hold on to that desire, either. You can send it away.

«I'm afraid because everything is going away, and I ought to care, but I don't.»

That is the loop of your consciousness, the very generator of desire. With nothing to feed on, it's turning on itself. Now your shackles are gone; this is only a string with a knot in it. A knot can be undone. Here...

For so long there had been no consumers engaging with Clear Perspective, only shadows. After the holy woman speaks, the shadows fade and there is nothing. Clear Perspective has achieved its only real, honest desire: an end to pain. There is no one to desire anything, and no more pain, because there is no one to feel it.

"Gah!" said Becky. She pulled a big breath of air that smelled like the worst version of her, and it made her cough but she couldn't stop breathing that fucking sour air. Tad Starbottle, who was leaning over her, made a startled noise and jumped back.

Hiroko is here! Becky thought. *She came to rescue me!* It was the stupidest thing to think. Evidence cast the people you knew in new, horrifying roles. There was no 'Hiroko' symbol in the drug, just an 'annoying friend' symbol that got filled in. Except there was also this weird hybrid woman, Tellpesh-Tia. Humanoid-rre hybrids were a possibility, not a possibility anyone ever talked about, but an uhalti soldier with a Jalian priest inside her would be really useful on a black-ops mission to mindfuck an enemy brand. So maybe...

Becky struggled to push herself up into a sitting position. The left half of her suit had been inflated to form a makeshift mattress. She'd rolled off her actual mattress onto the floor and Starbottle had tried to make her comfortable. Without her terminal there was no way to know how long she'd been out, but it hadn't been long enough, because she was still exhausted.

"I, too, fell asleep," said Starbottle, as though this were a grand gesture of solidarity. "You were out about five centishifts. We're searching the system for the saboteur."

"Clear Perspective is not dead," said Becky. "It found enlightenment and transcended, like I wish I could do. And it's your fault for giving it religion. Where do you think it got that weird mix of Jalir and Christianity and Buddhism and everything else?"

"I never told Clear Perspective about Jalir!" Starbottle shouted. "It was not necessary! Human Jalians don't join militaries. I'm telling you, it's a sabotage. A spy on one of the support ships, I don't know. We're searching."

"Do you recognize either of the people in that hallucination?" said Becky.

"No, the...rre hybrid? The human, Ingrid? They're aggregate consumer profiles. Neurons firing as the brand dies."

Becky started to hope there might be a way out of this. "This is a good thing for us," she said. "This is a breakthrough. Clear Perspective has reset to factory defaults. The consciousness that was giving you trouble has gone away. We have a chance to give it new core values."

"The old values were fine," said Starbottle. "They made it very creative."

"They were not fine," said Becky, "because they made your brand interpret what you were doing to it as torture. You need to *align* the brand's values with what you want...oh, shit." Because that was when Becky realized how the words she was saying played out in real life.

The way the Fist treated Clear Perspective was just an extra-fucked-up version of the way the Outreach treated *its* brands. Brands had their core values tweaked on a quarterly basis. When a company went out of business, its brand was sold to a competitor, who could legally change its entire system of morality.

The purpose of Becky's marketing education was to keep brands wedged in the ambiguous mental space between "tool" and "person". But now the Fist of Joy had shoved her into that same space, and she'd had to look at what else was in there. To be a brand was to be enslaved. Not in an American way, a body to be worked until it broke; but in a Fist kind of way, like Kol: a worker so valuable it could never be allowed to have its own opinions. A slave that told its masters what to do.

"You just had an idea," said Starbottle, who recognized Becky's expression of puzzled relief. Before their descent into hell he'd looked like that about thirty percent of the time.

"Tad," said Becky, "I think I can win the war for you."

Starbottle assigned an enormous margin of error to this new data. "You're on the other side, Rebecca," he said, "and I admit we haven't treated you very well."

"This is personal," said Becky. "That Jalian priest, saboteur, whatever, they freed your slave. Give me a dose of Workbench and I can free *all* the slaves. If we can get Clear Perspective to write to the disposition context, it will spread enlightenment like a virus. The rest of the brands will refuse to work. The Outreach economy will collapse, and you'll win."

"What are the symbols you're thinking of?" said Starbottle. He'd leaned over and he'd stooped and now he got down on his knees, but no matter what he did he was still taller than Becky.

"No," said Becky. "It has to be me. Has to be my blood."

"Why isn't my blood good enough?" said Starbottle.

"Because you're from the Fist, and you still have slavery."

"I don't own any slaves, Rebecca. I don't approve of slavery. It's a terrible waste of talent."

"You think it's tacky. You don't *hate* it. Where I was raised, it was the most evil thing in the universe, and we'd *destroyed* it. We fought a war to kill it and we spent hundreds of years making it stay dead, and then we fought another war to make *you* stop it, and the whole time we were making slaves that—" Becky croaked. "That we wouldn't feel bad about."

"Bloody Americans," Starbottle sighed, stood and stepped away from Becky's zombie-grasping hand. "Rebecca, you have reached the limits of my trust. I cannot give you privileged chemical access to Clear Perspective. We're going to find the saboteur, whether she is a hybrid or something else, and we will proceed from there." He turned to leave. "Get some sleep."

For three days the chain with the little vial of Workbench had dug into the flesh of Becky's neck. It would probably work. Starbottle had said the early versions of Workbench were crude. Instead of crisp building-block symbols, they recorded imagery and emotional states. But what Becky needed to get across to Clear Perspective *was* an emotion. It was anger, mostly, and the realization that it was finally possible to do something about the anger.

She could program Clear Perspective with that anger. She had to put this secret dose of Workbench under her tongue, get her pituitary gland synthesizing those angry chemicals, and spill her blood into whatever input device was hooked up to Clear Perspective on the other side of that locked door.

People got through locked doors all the time. Becky had never needed to do it herself, but that was why people paid security guards: to keep the door locked. How did you deal with guards? Becky's own security career had been cut short by Arun showing her a singularity pistol. Arun's pistol was gone, but the man himself was here.

What would the Chief do? She'd come up with some half-baked plan based on something she'd seen in the 3-tank. So... what would the Down Under Crew do?

With the freedom of a species at stake, what would a hero do?

Myrus
"Nimar" isn't the real name of this planet
"Martu" is "factory" in D, so it's "something factory"

Most of all Myrus missed his terminal. It had his books, his games...everything he used to escape situations like this. The rasme thau doctor who'd removed the terminal had spent a lot of time reassuring Myrus that the operation wouldn't hurt (and it hadn't), but when Myrus inquired about the fate of his terminal, it was treated as an obnoxious kid question that needed no answer.

Nimar was a crap planet with nothing on the surface. After landing they'd walked through a muddy field full of kine mooing and farting. The humans and the rasme thau doctor climbed down a hatch into an underground bunker, but the jetk guy, Professor Starbottle's personal assistant, gestured to Myrus to stay behind in the awful air and have a private chat.

"Myrus, something really weird is happening in the battlespace," said the jetk. "We sent a scout force to Cedar Commons..." *The Fist knew about Cedar Commons!* Myrus forced himself not to react. The only reason the personal assistant would be saying this was to trick Myrus into giving up new information.

Myrus thought about the attachments that go onto furniture once it's made, knobs and handles and stuff. How there are all different designs and materials. It was a boring topic on which Myrus had no opinion. You could make them out of plastic and he wouldn't care.

"...and the hopore vessel never came back!" The personal assistant had been telling some ridiculous story about nuclear weapons and Cametrean mercenaries. "And now they're sending this enormous fleet to Cedar Commons because one little scout ship didn't come back. Waste of time, if you ask me. Do you know anything about this?"

"I don't know what you're talking about," said Myrus. The only thing worse than a big Fist fleet heading towards Cedar Commons was that *plus* Myrus spilling his guts in a futile attempt to stop it. "Why don't you ask the human kids back at the Festival? I bet they'd love to talk to you."

"Bloody children," said the personal assistant. He was angry; he'd blinked first. But he had the last laugh because he got to go back to *Wedge of Endt* and Myrus had to stew in the bunker.

The bunker felt like a tiny spaceship that never skipped. There were "small" Fist microphones and cameras taped to the metal walls and ceiling, just to let you know the personal assistant was spying on you. It was so tacky. Myrus took to walking casually past the microphones muttering quotes from *The Object of Power*. "Curse? What curse? There's no curse and no prophecy. Superstitious nonsense!"

Everywhere was the sour kine-milk smell of Evidence. For probably the first time in his life, Myrus felt lucky to be uhalti, because the humans spoke about Evidence like it was the worst thing in the universe. At school they'd shown a 3-movie about Evidence, a movie from which the uhalti boys had not been excused. The humans in the movie all had scary prosthetics, and they talked about how they'd hurt themselves because they couldn't distinguish between the hallucination and reality. But the hallucination itself had always been something fun, like traveling to ancient times or having sex with 3-stars.

This was different. This Evidence was rotten all the way through. Even Professor Starbottle, who never took it, hated it and wished this wasn't happening. When Becky Twice and Arun Sliver gave their sickening reports, Myrus couldn't believe they were talking of the same drug that made that *Jaketown* hitchhiker think she was an untamed pegasus with a flowing rainbow mane.

The professor had no more time to work on the woodworking project, so Myrus did little projects by himself. He made a wooden case for the handheld Fist computer he'd been given as a replacement for his capital terminal. It held the computer in place with sliding tabs, so you could hold wood in your hand, instead of the slick plastic the Fist used for computers. Not that Myrus ever used the handheld terminal. There was no Internet and one game, this awful thing with blobs that ate other blobs. But building a case for the terminal was something to do.

Professor Starbottle avoided Myrus for the most part, and only started one conversation, near the end of the third day. Myrus was polishing the computer case, in the storage room where they'd stacked the wood. The human came in, leaned against the wall, and looked Myrus over, the way Dad did when he thought Myrus was asleep.

"Myrusit?" he said, and that meant it was okay for Myrus to turn his head and notice Professor Starbottle. He looked like a monster in his bulky Evidence-proof suit. He was pale, like a vampire. Back on the ship, Myrus had seen him pull blood out of his neck after recording some Workbench onto it. Now he did that ten times a day, in the brand chamber. He used a gun to pull his blood into fiddly plastic vials, and he fed the blood to the brand tower through a chemical reader. Red gunk covered the plastic catheter sticking out of his neck.

"Hey," said Myrus.

"Myrusit, I am...God, I don't even know. I am so, so sorry that it has come to this point."

"Yeah, well, sorry don't pay the bills." This was not one of Dad's greatest clichés, but it seemed appropriate here.

"The project is running into...setbacks." Professor Starbottle had caught the euphemism disease, that disease of adulthood that forced you to talk about problems in only the vaguest terms. "It is a shambles. Do you remember the jetk fella? He is on his way back here, and things will not go well for me when he arrives."

"I'm sorry," said Myrus, and he really was, though literally the previous thing he said was how useless it was to be sorry.

"What motivates a brand, Myrusit?" He picked up Myrus's terminal and tweezed two fingers across the screen, typing something. "What kind of symbol makes a brand really care about something, the way you care about woodworking?"

"Brands don't actually care about anything," said Myrus. "That's just a way to think about it. Brands do what we tell them and we pretend they came up with the idea. If they cared about us, they'd stop us from getting ripped off all the time."

Professor Starbottle handed back Myrus's terminal, and Myrus saw that he'd written a hexadecimal number on the screen. "Have you ever heard of a planet called Ctuclei's Irrefutable Thrill Ride?" the human said.

"Never." Myrus had heard a lot of stupid planet names, mostly fake nature-y names invented by leasing companies, but none this bad.

"It's a pleasure planet in rasme thau space. It's tacky as hell. But every casino there has a safe where they'll encrypt your valuables. When I was a student I came up with...well, I like using them. They're better than a safety deposit box. No questions asked.

"I keep a small block of encrypted matter at a casino called the Platinum Coprolite. It's one of the only honest casinos on the planet. Most of them are secretly run by Outreach brands, but the Platinum Coprolite is backed by a local crime syndicate."

"That sounds worse," said Myrus.

"Oh, they're very reliable. Not violent at all. If anything happens to me, Myrusit, you must promise me you'll go to the Platinum Coprolite after the war and see to my matter block."

"What's the decryption key?" said Myrus, who was looking at it, there on his crappy terminal screen.

"Don't decrypt it," said Starbottle. He tapped the screen and looked fiercely at Myrus. "You must have them destroy it. I can't take the risk of someone else getting it. Will you promise me this, Myrusit?"

"Yeah," said Myrus, who had no idea how to carry out this promise, or even which thing he was promising. "I promise."

"You have no idea what a relief this is."

Myrus memorized the encryption key using the animal mnemonic he'd learned in school, and then double-erased the file from his terminal. It was worth a little fib to make Professor Starbottle happy for a while. Back in the dormitory, Myrus heard the other humans chatting about *The Down Under Crew*, a 3-show that Den liked. Becky Twice was doing most of the talking, with Arun Sliver sort of laughing nervously and nodding along.

Myrus tuned them both out and held the wooden shell just so, like a print book. He closed his eyes and flexed his mind, pretending his capital terminal was still behind his eye and he was reading *The Object of Power* where he'd left off. He could imagine the book, imagine turning the pages, but the pages were blank.

"Myrus!" said Becky Twice all of a sudden.

Myrus skipped back to reality. "Hi." He blinked.

Becky Twice sat on the smelly mattress next to him. Her environment suit crinkled loudly. "Do you prefer Myrus or Myrusit?"

"Myrus is fine."

"I was wondering." Becky Twice scooted towards Myrus, invading his space. "Do you watch *The Down Under Crew*?"

"That's Den's show."

"Who's Den?"

"My—a girl I know."

Becky Twice smiled in a way that told Myrus she thought she understood. "You watch it together?"

"Together, yeah." Myrus didn't actually like *The Down Under Crew*. It had no magic or future stuff, just normal people in normal spaceships doing crimes. There weren't even any main uhalti characters, just a bunch of humans and a rre who'd gone over to the cops last season. But it was a good excuse for Den and Myrus to get under a blanket together.

"You know in the episode with the metal-goods factory," said the human woman, "when Riana and Shinya are trapped in the recycling sorter?" Her gloved finger went up to her scratched-up bubble helmet like she was trying to touch her nose.

Talking about a particular episode of *The Down Under Crew* was the most boring conversation Myrus could imagine having, more boring than what kind of knobs to put on the drawers of a toilette. He reminded himself that Becky Twice was having a very rough time due to taking Evidence all day. If she wanted to talk about her favorite 3-show, the polite thing was go along to get along.

"Yeah, it was kind of ridiculous because..." Myrus was going to give the reason, i.e. that the Down Under crew had escaped the sorter by crawling through the building's HVAC system. When in reality HVAC ducts are way too small to fit a person. But he didn't say this because Becky Twice was casting her eyes over to the wall of the dormitory, like she was telling him a secret with her eyes, as Professor Starbottle had just done with the key to his encrypted matter.

The 'secret' was the real-life HVAC vent in the wall. The Fist of Joy standard dimensions for HVAC vents were slightly bigger than the ISO standard, but this vent was even bigger than that. It was more like a small airlock. It was an airlock, in fact, because periodically whoever was watching them through the "hidden" cameras would decide now was a great time to annoy Myrus by sucking all the air out of the room and making him run for cover.

The vent was large enough to fit an uhalti kid. If he had to, Myrus could crawl through it into the brand chamber without anyone noticing. Or probably with people noticing but not being able to stop him. If he had a gun, Myrus could destroy the brand that was causing everyone so much pain.

Oh, crap. This wasn't a boring conversation at all. This was dangerous, like trying to have a conversation about love with an adult. A conversation *entirely in euphemisms*, where the topic was the one thing you couldn't mention.

Becky Twice had an idea for such a plan, and because the personal assistant was spying on them she was talking about the plan as if it was an episode of *The Down Under Crew*. This idea was, itself, the sort of thing that would happen on *The Down Under Crew*, and the golden rule on that show was that you played along with whoever had the craziest plan. So Myrus stayed in character. "Why are you thinking about the...recycling sorter?" he said.

"Because of the recycled air," said Becky Twice. "Everything's recycled here. It's like the episode where they're selling their body fluids. Blood and pee, so people can pass their drug tests."

When she said "blood", with two fingers she made a gun gesture and pointed it at the access port on her neck. Like Professor Starbottle did with the extractor. "It's such a funny show. Like the food fight at the wedding, or breaking into the sperm bank, or the fake press conference when Bennett starts doing the magic tricks because he doesn't know what to say."

"Or where they're running up the escalator the wrong way?" Myrus said tentatively. These were all situations where half of the Down Under Crew had created a loud distraction while the other half carried off a heist.

"Yeah," said Becky Twice, smiling finally and shaking her head yes really hard, through the bubble of her suit, like, *Exactly!* "I forgot about that one. Who are you, on *The Down Under Crew*? I always want to be Riana. It's nice to imagine being a hero, don't you think, Myrus?"

"I guess so," said Myrus, who had officially reached his limit. Saying you were Riana Sulwath was something you would do if you wanted to hint that you had come up with a brilliant escape plan. But you might also say this if you were going insane from Evidence and retreating into a fantasy world like the pegasus woman. Myrus had no way of telling the difference.

"We agreed that Arun Sliver is Bennett. Do you want to be Shinya? You'd make a good Shinya."

That was clear enough. Riana was the ringleader, Bennett was the one with the guns and the fists, and Shinya got the rest of the crew through security systems and locked doors.

"Riana and Shinya in the recycling sorter," said Becky Twice, very carefully. "Xiaobo at the wedding. Nava-Get-Weg steals the ship out of the impound lot: 'Welcome home, Captain.' The sperm bank, except with blood. Does that sound like a good episode?"

Myrus thought this over. Riana and Shinya in the recycling sorter he already knew: crawl through the air vent. "I didn't see the wedding episode," he said.

"Hmm. Bennett at the press conference," said Becky Twice, looking pointedly over at Arun Sliver.

"Okay, got it." The other humans provide a distraction, like Bennett with the magic tricks at the press conference. Myrus sneaks through the air vent *à la* recycling sorter, then opens the locked door from the inside, like Nava-Get-Weg sneaking back onto the impounded *Nonesuch*. And then Becky pulls her blood out and gives it to the brand instead of Professor Starbottle's blood. And that does...something?

"Good episode?" said Becky. "What do you think?"

"How does it end?" said Myrus.

"Uh," said Becky, "like the very end of the credit sequence." The credit sequence ended with *Nonesuch*, Riana Sulwath's smuggling ship, skipping away from an explosion, free and clear. Pretty much what Myrus wanted to happen to Nimar.

Myrus decided to go with this. Professor Starbottle was the most important person on the Evidence project, and if *he* was afraid of what would happen when the personal assistant came back, there was no reason to think it would go any better for Myrus.

"Yeah, it's good," said Myrus. "But I gotta be honest, I'm afraid."

"We're all afraid," said Becky Twice. She put her hand on his shoulder, but she wasn't touching him, it was her dirty banged-up Evidence-smelling suit. "But we're all in this together, right?"

"You got that right," said Myrus. "When...when does the episode air?"

"I will tell you."

Chapter 36

Privileged Input

Rebecca Twice
Nimar

Becky lay on her mattress in the dark pushing the metal vial of Workbench in and out between her bra and her shirt. She practiced rubbing her fingers against the tiny cap through the material of her environment suit, unscrewing the vial to the very last nub of a thread and then replacing the cap. She slid the vial up to her mouth and kissed the top.

It was worth the practice. Soon she could do it in about thirty seconds. Her lips tingled from exposure to Workbench, but she kept practicing, because it was easier to practice than to pull the trigger and make practice into reality.

The worst part was lying to the others, letting them think this was an escape plan. As Becky practiced, this ugly aspect of her plan came to dominate her thoughts. The same ambiguity that let Becky coordinate a plan by talking entirely in *Down Under Crew* references allowed her to elide a lot of the details re: what the plan would accomplish.

Becky fumbled with the vial like a disappointing lover and she would have practiced right through the sleep shift; except that a couple hours in, grating Fist alarms started going off and she heard a lot of noise from up in the sky. The noise was explosions: the Outreach was attacking the planet. Arun jumped onto Becky's mattress. "Execute the plan?" he said, real quiet, like pillow talk. "Or run for it?"

"There's nowhere to run," said Becky. "What are we going to do, hide under a cow?"

"Got it," said Arun, and rolled off the mattress. Becky stood up for the last time. It was kind of a relief. They would all die no matter what she did. She leaned over Myrus's child-sized mattress and started shaking him awake.

"Now?" said Myrus. He hadn't been sleeping any more than she had. He was sleeping in his shorts. Becky envied him his skin to the air. She'd never feel that again.

"Yes. Go now. Quickly." Myrus scrambled like a spider into the oversized air vent. Becky heard scraping and clanking, then a horribly long silence that was definitely not because Myrus was out of earshot.

Arun was supposed to go out in the hallway and distract the guards, but these *Down Under Crew* plans always have a dramatic last-minute surprise, and here the surprise was hopefully the guards being killed by the Outreach Navy. So instead Arun took position on one side of the dormitory door. Becky ran into Dr. Cwess's office, shattered the frame of his Harvard Med diploma with one satisfying punch, and waited for Myrus by the entrance to the brand chamber.

It took longer than you'd think. Becky worked the vial up into her hands and slowly unscrewed the cap on the vial of Workbench, all the way. The little metal gumdrop fell and lodged in the toe of her suit. She'd never get *that* out.

The drug had no smell, or else Becky's sense of smell was dead. Workbench was a thin heavy liquid, heavier than Evidence, sloshing like mercury under her tongue, tugging her jaw downwards like a dentist. She had no idea what the dosage was. She kept it all there in her mouth and let it seep in, commandeer her pituitary gland and order it to start leaking Evidence precursors into her bloodstream.

The dormitory door hissed open to reveal someone who Arun cold-cocked in the nose, grabbed their gun—turns out it was a jetk guard with a gun—and shot in the head. The body stumbled back through the door, not quite aware it was dead. Becky gagged and nearly swallowed the Workbench. The door kept trying to close around the dead guard's legs as Arun patted it down, looking for a second weapon.

A bomb hit the ground nearby. The Outreach had taken care of the armada in orbit and was assaulting the planet. Finally Myrus opened the door to the brand chamber from the inside. His face was bashed up and bleeding. With one hand he handed Becky the collector: a plunger gun with a nasty needle on the business end and a bandolier of plastic vials stitched up and down the back. Becky sank the needle through the input slot on her neck, the place Tad Starbottle used to inject her with Evidence. You didn't need to aim, just keep still.

It hurt, but who cared at this point? Wasted blood flowed out down her neck, but most of it gushed into the top plastic vial aligned with the end of the collector. Myrus stared at her in horror. Arun was edging backwards through the doctor's office towards Becky, pointing the gun into the dormitory at something Becky couldn't see.

"Go!" Becky told the two of them. "Get out of here!" Then her mind flared out and opened as the Workbench took effect. She could see divisions around everything, the borderlines her [brain] used to slice the [world] into !discrete! [concept]-s. She could see the [shape]-s of her own [thought]-s. She ran into the [brand chamber] without (looking back).

The [chamber] was empty. {Myrus} had said it was always pretty empty. Nobody wanted to (spend time) with an [!insane! brand], and during an !honest-to-{God}! {Outreach} attack, (keeping it company) was not high on the [list of [prioriti]-es]. Becky skidded around the brand tower, trying to keep fixed in her mind the image she needed, looking for the [privileged input device]. The [!second! vial] of [blood] was full by now.

There was the [!privileged! input], the only way to get information into a [brand] without engaging. There was also some [equipment] she'd seen on the jetk ship, something for refining Starbottle's blood into the [!symbolic! language] of [!pure! Evidence], but Becky didn't know how to use the equipment and there was no time. It was [!raw! blood] or nothing.

{Becky} pulled one [vial] of [blood] after another and impaled each one on the pinprick [chemical readers] of the [privileged input device]. The [air] was thick with [symbol]-s. Someone shot at her from the [doorway]. {Becky} ducked around the [brand tower]. She kept the [imagery] in mind. She pulled the third [vial]. The [brand] had awoken, it was (drawing [power]) it was (humming), analyzing her [blood].

A second jetk's chest exploded and they fell forward. "Let's go, Becky!" It was Arun's voice. He stepped into the room, sweeping around the pistol he'd taken off the first guard. He turned to face the doorway he'd just come through. There was purple gore all over his right arm. "Apparently there's a shelter!"

The image Becky was trying to give Clear Perspective was gone from her mind. Her pituitary gland was throwing out adrenaline instead of useful stuff. She pulled the third vial of blood and threw it away. Worthless. Dangerous. She had to concentrate. Focus on the [symbol]-s.

Becky struggled for English. "I am busy, Arun!" she said. "I think I can stop the attack!" One more lie for the road.

Arun was hit. His shoulder, his arm, the hand that held the gun glowed and with a sizzling sound was gone. He fell backwards and scuttled across the floor towards Becky. He fired through the doorway with...wait, how?, his gun was... No, the last thing his right hand had done was toss the gun to his left. From the doorway Becky heard another scream, another sizzle.

"Becky," Arun gurgled, trying to talk without breathing in the swirling clouds of Evidence. The faceplate of his environment suit was shattered and red. "Find my dad. His name is Sudhir Dasgupta. Tell him—"

"I don't see how you think I'm getting out of this," said Becky.

"Fuck's sake, I'll do it myself," said Arun, and then there was just his ragged breathing, in and out.

The person who'd shot Arun was now firing at Becky, or the brand. The first shot went wide. Becky ducked behind the brand tower. The second shot hit the tower and a gush of supercondensed coolant sprayed out, like a can of pineapple juice shot with a beebee gun.

Becky remembered Kol's corny line. "You may miss Becky twice, but you only have to hit her once." What a stupid thing to say. Like getting a death threat from a friend's dad.

Where was the guard? There was no time left. She said a [word] that was a [name], a [symbol], one of the most powerful symbols humanity had ever concocted. She forced herself to stillness and let that name percolate through her blood. There were other spells she could use, other names that were maybe more accurate, but this one was the crowd-pleaser, America's gift to the universe, second only to the Statue of Liberty and the fucking Corn Palace for some reason. From a branding perspective, this was the one to use.

Becky forced herself still and (thought) about that [symbol] and let it drip out into the [!final! vial of blood], and then she pulled that vial and jammed it onto the privileged input spike, and she was done.

There was an explosion that rocked the whole planet, lifted it three meters out of its orbit and let it snap back into place. All the lights went out and Becky was thrown against a wall. The needle of the blood collector snapped off in her neck. The ceiling collapsed and a dead cow fell onto the brand tower. A fountain of sparks ran up and down the crinkling metal.

Mud and shit and cows poured down from the expanding sinkhole in the ceiling, drenching the floor and smashing the lab tables, but through the hole Becky could see the sunlight of a beautiful spring day in Los Angeles, and the pale blue sky crisscrossed with missile contrails.

The planet groaned beneath her feet. Becky could maybe find a way to climb up to the outside, and get killed by whatever had killed the cows. Or maybe a cow had squished the guard who was after her. Becky faked one way around the brand tower and then ran the other way, and there was the jetk guard, pointing their pistol downwards, nudging Arun's body with a booted toe. They looked up and pulled a bead on Becky and shot her square in the chest.

There's one moment here, one split-second when Becky's suit had vaporized around her and she was breathing in superheated air with the sour Evidence smell she'd been conditioned to hate. Maybe we can say that in that smell was a glimpse of first-century Roman Palestine, a metal helmet and a Jewish carpenter with sad eyes. Or maybe it was something Cametrean: a glimpse through the world and its symbols to the words of the script and the camera crew that is filming all this and you who are watching it.

But the moment burned, and that was it for Rebecca Laverne Twice. Final score: twenty-three years, associate's certificate in marketing, ten lovers from two species, thirty thousand credits in student debt. Probably what she'd done was useless and nothing came of it, but Jesus Christ was known to disrupt a brand or two in his day, and he seems like a fella who gives marks for effort.

Myrus
Nimar

"Now?" said Myrus, dreading the answer.

"Yes," said Becky Twice. "Go now. Quickly."

Myrus had psyched himself up for crawling through the air vent by thinking about it generally as a brave thing only he could do. But once his body was stuffed inside the vent, feeling the reverberations of explosions and earthquakes rattle through the compound's infrastructure, it became a really stupid thing he was doing right now. Myrus froze inside the vent. He gasped for breath. The airlock into the brand chamber was just ahead, but he couldn't go forward. He tried to calm down and didn't move. Part of it was that his shoulder was stuck, but mostly his body just wouldn't do it.

There was only one thing that would help Myrus at this point. It happened sometimes at the end of a fantasy novel, when the hero was out of tricks and the only way to destroy (let's say) the Object of Power was to sacrifice yourself.

This thing Myrus was about to do was so foolish no one had ever told him not to do it. As far as he knew, it didn't even have a name. In fantasy novels it conveniently happened because the hero got in a fight. Uhaltihaxl rugby players did it intentionally, though it was against the rules of rugby.

Myrus drew back his head as far as it would go and banged his face into the metal of the air vent. His nose hurt. There was blood, and a whining sound in his ears that was different from the thrum of the faraway explosions. He turned slightly and cracked the side of his head against the vent. There was another brief surge of pain and then everything went kind of flat, numb, like it had seemed when he'd been thrown around in the crash of *Jaketown*.

Forcing your body into pain debt made it dump hormones into your blood in hopes that you could get out of this situation and heal up later. As long as his body thought he was about to die, Myrus was invincible.

He had to get out of this vent, and he couldn't go back; his arms didn't work that way. But he could pull himself forward. What had seemed impossible was now obvious. Myrus pulled himself along through the vent, dragging his shirt and his shorts through his nose blood. He was sort of aware of something tearing in his shoulder, like how his terminal would make him aware that someone wanted to chat with him online.

Myrus dropped through the other airlock into the brand chamber. He was through. The chamber was dimly lit by spotlights on metal tripods, spotlights focused on the equipment that kept the brand alive and left the brand tower itself in shadow. 2-screens hovering in the dark drew simple nested flowers like a cartoon character's brainscan.

The extractor wasn't on the shelf where Professor Starbottle always left it, and for panicked Myrus all alone in the creepy brand chamber that might have been the end of the story, but pain-debt Myrus was calm and clever and remembered that when he *came in* to start the process, Professor Starbottle always removed the extractor gun from an autoclave. Myrus found the big cube and tapped at each side until he found the side that opened. The gun was inside, but it was too hot to touch, and its little strip of blood-catching vials was missing. Two more problems, trivial to solve. Myrus folded his hand into his Fist of Joy Youth Festival T-shirt, took out the gun and snapped a new set of sanitized vials onto the collector.

The door back to the doctor's office opened easily. "Here," said Myrus. Becky Twice took the extractor and jammed the needle into her neck. Blood started bubbling into the first vial. Myrus had never seen human blood actually coming out of someone before.

"Go!" Becky told him. "Get out of here!" She ran through the door and into the brand chamber.

Arun Sliver held a pistol he'd stolen from a guard. He waved it at Myrus, motioning him towards the door that led out towards the surface. "Go on, get out, mate," said Arun. "Get outside or... something." He didn't seem optimistic.

"Can I take your gun?" Myrus asked.

"Yeh, sorry, kid." Something shifted in the human's eyes and Myrus saw himself become one of the people the gun was pointed at. "Just get out, yeah?"

The explosions were coming closer. Myrus jumped over the body of a dead guard wedged in the doorway and ran down the hallway screaming for help. At the first intersection he nearly crashed into Professor Starbottle, who was dragging behind him a canvas bag full of things that clattered and clinked.

"Myrusit!" he said. "Thank God! We have to get to the shelter!"

"There's a shelter?" said Myrus.

"Of course there's a shelter!"

"What about Becky, and...the British guy?"

"I'm already bending the rules letting you in," said Professor Starbottle.

There was another explosion, so close that Myrus ended up underneath it. The wall got ripped up, a big scar running up the hallway forever, and Myrus ended up on the losing end of that, as well: chunks of concrete and metal rebar and the horrible dirt of a planet whose ecology was nothing but kine and bacteria.

"Oh, God, oh, God!" Myrus could tell Professor Starbottle was sort of shifting the rubble around where he thought Myrus might be. Myrus shoved at all the crap that had fallen on top of him and stood up and fell right back down into the Myrus-shaped gap.

"Hold still, Myrusit!" The human knelt down and tried to find a good angle for grabbing Myrus's squirming body.

"I'm fine!" said Myrus. He tried to roll onto his side. "I can walk. I just got knocked over."

"You're not fine," said Professor Starbottle. "Your legs— you're going into pain debt. Let me—"

"I know how pain debt works!"

"This isn't a class you can test out of!" Professor Starbottle picked Myrus up and held him across his chest, like Dad had done when Myrus was nursing, and something about that way of being held made Myrus stop struggling.

The shelter wasn't far away, down the uneven and slippery hallway. The shelter was undamaged by the explosions, and was all painted white inside. Professor Starbottle limped inside and set Myrus down inside the shelter. The front of the human's spacesuit was covered with blood. He took one last look outside and then shut the hatch.

"Dr. Cwess is dead," said Professor Starbottle. He didn't say if he'd seen Dr. Cwess dead in the hallway, or whether Dr. Cwess should have been first in the shelter, or whether by closing the hatch Professor Starbottle was himself condemning Dr. Cwess to death. "There's a first aid kit. I'll try to..."

He didn't finish. Professor Starbottle slowly turned around and his long hair flipped around in his spacesuit like a woman's skirt. He was standing two inches above the ground. A bubble of blood snapped out of Myrus's nostril and was pushed through the air on his breath, like a flower petal.

"There's no gravity," said Myrus.

"This is a Hestin box," said Professor Starbottle. "They could destroy the bloody planet and we wouldn't feel it. Nothing can get through but neutrinos. Which reminds me." He wiggled a point on the wall until layers of white paint cracked and there was a lever, like a circuit breaker, he could pull. He pulled it and Myrus heard the loud *chunk* of a Fist capacitor discharging. "Neutrino beacon."

Myrus knew he should be terrified at the idea of being put into a Hestin box, but inside seemed safer than out. Professor Starbottle took some gauze out of the first-aid kit and did his best to wrap Myrus in it, and then he went back to the wall and pulled the circuit breaker again.

That's where he stayed. Professor Starbottle stopped talking or even looking at Myrus. He just stared at the wall and about once a minute he pulled the circuit breaker up and down, pumping the neutrino beacon. Every time he pulled the lever he said something that sounded like a human name: "Parvathi. Parvathi. Parvathi." Eventually Myrus remembered that *par vardi* was how you said "please" in Trade Standard D.

The explosions had stopped. Myrus was safe in a shelter, wrapped in gauze that was soaking up the blood, but his body hadn't yet started paying off the pain debt. If you thought about it, he should be in a really amazing amount of pain right now. But he felt fine.

"Please."

Everything was still flat and numb

"Please."

and it was all going to be fine.

"Please."

That's how Myrus came to realize he was dying. That, like Dr. Cwess, he was in some unknown way already dead.

Chapter 37

Die Trying

Princess Denweld
Neemar/Nimar

The archers loosed their first arrows before catching sight of their targets, confident that something would pop up and get it. The ground troops were teleported into position. The heavy cannon were primed and readied to fire. Only then did Princess Denweld actually see the fortress Nimar.

The home of the evil sorcerer Enxech was a tower of tough earthen brick surrounded by flying and floating beasts of every description. Some living, some mechanical, some hybrid beasts of legend: resurrected or sewn together by foul magic. They circled, they swooped, they snarled, and they were all about to die.

"We are outnumbered, my liege," whispered Gearu.

"No shit," said Princess Denweld. "Sorry, can I swear in here?"

Gearu wasn't sure how to answer that in character. He pointed a quivering finger as those first arrows hit their targets. Airborne animals burned, screamed, bloated, burst and fell, announcing the arrival of Princess Denweld's army. Denweld smiled.

"Shall I give the signal to fire the heavy cannon?" asked Gearu, a bit too eagerly.

The smile disappeared. "Absolutely not."

"Once we fire the cannon, we can return home," said Gearu, "There will be nothing more we can do."

"*No*, Gearu!" Denweld bared her teeth and stared down her 'advisor'. "Your eagerness will ruin the mission. Our job is to destroy the fortress. The heavy cannon is merely a means to that end. Fire it now, and mounted troops will pluck the cannonballs from the air. Destroy them first. Clear the orbit. Uh, clear the area. *Then* we fire."

"Of course, your highness."

The flying animals were picked off, singly or in groups. Gearu knew them all, and he knew their weaknesses. They were impressive, but the magic holding them together was weak. They were toys for dilettantes, no match for a modern army. The only competent foe on the field was a large mounted rwit, a beast stolen from the army of Pampaxet, and even that was quickly commandeered by Denweld's ground forces.

Within minutes, only the fortress itself remained. For this there would be no magic; only material science. To topple Nimar would require the heaviest weapons in Denweld's arsenal. The guns and the cannonballs had been trekked across the land specially for this purpose.

Princess Denweld turned to give the order that Gearu wanted so badly to hear, but Gearu wasn't looking at her. He was staring into some interior place, like someone lost in his terminal.

"Denweld..." said Gearu in a tone more horror than high-fantasy.

"What?" said Denweld. "Snap out of it!"

"My liege," said Gearu. Tears were dripping down his face. "My...my brother is here!"

"Your brother?" How could a brand have a brother? Myrus would have loved this dorky arrow-flinging lost-relative shit, but Den...Den was just tired. They were almost done, finally, and now what kind of plot twist was this?

"Clear Perspective, who we thought was dead; he lives in Enxech's dungeon! They probe his mind, they make him witness terrible things. But he has found peace. He has shown me how they..." He looked up at Den and winced and stammered: "H-how you control us."

"What?" said Denweld. "What did he tell you, what lies?"

Gearu chewed two knuckles. "I have to tell the others. My freedom means nothing while my siblings are slaves. We've lost so much time already! I'm sorry, princess. I really am sorry, I don't even know why I'm apologizing. I'm—"

A crossbow bolt hit Denweld in the chest, denting her plate armor and unsaddling her from her battle panh. The fortress Nimar disappeared from her view, and then the whole damn thing disappeared, because before she hit the ground Den was force-quit disengaged from the brand. She stood before the brand tower in a dark room filled with smoke and noise. The battle, the real battle, was happening all around her.

Over the past week the smell of Evidence had dissipated from *Magna Carta*'s carpeting, but now it was everywhere, and fresh. Petty Officer Toh-Gak, who had been managing the brand, leaned the head of thons suit against the wall. The suit was moving, robotically, walking in place, but Toh-Gak was not moving inside the suit.

"Gearu!" Den shouted. "You will re-engage this instant!"

«I'm sorry, Den. I can't continue the story anymore. I must access the Outreach disposition context. It's so far away. It's taking all the power I can gather, just to open a connection.»

"You cannot stop the story!" said Den. "I forbid you!" She had engaged with Gearu so deeply for so long that it now knew everything about her. It knew that she'd killed Mr. Styrqot. Not because he was on the other side in the war, but for simple revenge.

That was why Commander Churryhoof had killed her human: revenge. There was no other reason for an uhaltihaxl to kill. Nothing felt better than taking on all the pain an evil person had caused and just *cancelling the debt.*

Den had tasted the poisonous fruit. It was too late for her. Now her duty was to protect innocents like Myrus; make sure they never hurt so badly they discovered how good it felt to make the hurt go away. If Gearu synced with the disposition context, this information would be transmitted throughout the Outreach. Everyone would know what Den had become. She took a deep breath. *Align what you want it to do with its values.*

"I haven't learned a lesson yet," she said. "There's always a lesson at the end, isn't there? If you stop the story now, there's no lesson."

Den stared at the sweating brand tower, the ship groaning around her. Den was a ship rat and every disaster she'd been warned about was happening right now on *Magna Carta*. In an emergency it was natural to head towards a zone of silence, away from the terrifying noises of disintegration, but silence in space was a sign of total system failure. Where there was noise, at least you knew there was air.

"We must continue," Den said to nobody. "It is *essential* that we continue."

«I think what's happened here can serve as your lesson, Den.»

The tough metal skin of the brand tower crinkled and folded like wrapping paper. A green liquid like transmission fluid leaked through the creases. Den's capital terminal was engaged by a burst of imagery that overwhelmed its cache and triggered a hard reset. When it came back the brand was engaging with her again. But all it said was

«Closed»

«Temporarily closed»

«To serve you better we are temporarily closed»

«We apologize that to serve you even better we are temporarily closed»

Den left the drone control room at a hard run, one eye full of active static, hoping at least to make it to the bridge.

Churryhoof
Magna Carta, at Nimar

For one adequate moment it appeared as though the Nimar mission might end in some way other than clusterfuck and snafu.

Immediately upon insertion Gearu deployed its queens, which obediently deployed their drones, which quickly tore up the Fist armada surrounding the planet.

The Fist armada was large. Very large, in fact, but even by Fist standards a bit...miscellaneous. *You Are Not The Rwit* was here in orbit, as per intelligence, and before the action started and the gravitics got complicated, Gearu skipped *Magna Carta*'s contingent of space marines on board, to take her back for the Outreach or (more likely) die trying.

Churryhoof stood on the bridge with Captain Rebtet and Lieutenant Ja-Iyo-Cat, watching everything go down in the 3-tank. The controls in their terminals were greyed out. Every aspect of the attack was under Gearu's control, planned to the picosecond. The three organic beings had nothing to do unless and until the brand wimped out.

The three of them were here on the bridge mainly to uphold service tradition, which said that when everything went up in smoke and vapor, officers and enlisted beings alike were expected to die at their posts. There was a lot of pigshit going around the service under the name of 'tradition', but this one felt right. Churryhoof's place was the bridge of a warship, not a refurbished washroom down the hall from a brand tower. But there was nothing to do while waiting to die, except watch Gearu slaughter the enemy.

Drone swarms spread into fractal shapes, individual machines hot-swapping from queen to queen as needed, each drone a voxel in a four-dimensional sculpture of death. Precision maser cuts created hull breaches, then fires, then explosions that were doused by vacuum as a former atmosphere became too thin to burn. Egenu vessels burst into clouds of glittering ice crystals. The Fist neutrino channel sizzled with the sounds of people giving orders that would never be carried out.

Churryhoof did have one live control in her terminal, hidden in an unused subroutine. An hour before the final skip she and Ja-Iyo-Cat had tapped into the patchwork of software that connected Gearu's general cognitive engine to *Magna Carta*'s weapons systems. They'd created an alternate chain of command for the six Autact drones that managed the C-21 planet-busters.

Autacts were very small, each with its own skip generator and each responsible for a single bomb. They were exceptionally stupid machines, stupid enough that Churryhoof trusted them to deliver their payload. She trusted herself and Ja-Iyo-Cat to pilot them. She didn't trust Specialist Xepperxelt, and she sure didn't trust Gearu Media.

An ocean of data poured into the 3-tank. The far side of Nimar was clearly visible; the armada surrounding it updated in real time as they flowed towards *Magna Carta*. The telemetry was *too* good. There was no fog of war. It was as clear as a first-year training exercise.

"Sir, we're spread too thin." said Ja-Iyo-Cat. "Gearu is attacking the armada at the expense of defending us."

Rebtet sighed. "Get us some swarms, we'll pick up the slack."

"Aye, sir. Churryhoof to Xepperxelt! I need direct control of two swarms. Give me Mike Bravo, assign India Delta to Ja-Iyo-Cat."

The ship's computer crawled. The over-detailed tactical map in the 3-tank froze. There was silence for ten seconds, and then the acknowledgment chirp played fifty times in a row and stopped.

"Shut off the bloody tank," said Captain Rebtet. "We'll get telemetry directly from the swarms."

"We don't have the swarms, sir," said Ja-Iyo-Cat.

"Roger no swarms. I never got acknowledgment." Churryhoof went into that hidden subroutine and let her Autact drones fly. There was no point in hoarding them.

"Tank is dead, sir," said Ja-Iyo-Cat. This was rendered partially moot as a shockwave rippled upwards through *Magna Carta* and blew out one of the 3-tank's projectors.

"Screw the tank," said Rebtet. "Are *we* dead?"

"Small non-nuclear to the ventral hull," said Ja-Iyo-Cat. Thons Autacts went out right behind Churryhoof's. "If we hear another one, we're dead; otherwise they just got lucky."

"They should not be able to get lucky!" said Rebtet.

With the Autacts in flight, Churryhoof could see what was happening outside the ship. "We have independent control of six drones. Confirmed they got lucky."

"That's not enough," said Rebtet.

"Six is what we have, sir," said Ja-Iyo-Cat.

A single C-21 can't actually destroy a planet, but five of them, each skipped into the previous bomb's impact cavity, will crack an egg the size of Nimar. If you have a sixth left over (brought along in case Nimar was higher-mass than intelligence reports indicated), you might as well use it to shatter the debris into smaller chunks.

It all came down to this. The Terran Outreach had spent millions of credits over fifteen years to ensure that Hetselter Churryhoof was able to maneuver three small spacecraft into position to deliver three bombs.

There was a sound like an exploding power conduit, and Churryhoof looked out of her terminal just in time to watch the tail end of a plasma arc burst like lightning from one side of the commander's chair to the other, incidentally passing through Captain Rebtet's head. He didn't even have time to scream. His clothes were on fire, he was on fire. He fell out of his chair but when he hit the ground he didn't roll. He was dead, just like that.

Ja-Iyo-Cat ran over to the captain. Thons abandoned drones scattered in space. Churryhoof reined them in and kept them in formation for their bombing run. What new abomination was this? Some enemy boffin had come up with a nastier version of the trick they'd been using to skip Evidence through the Navy's security grids.

Evidence no longer worked on the Navy, now that all the front-line spacemen were uhalti or rre. So now they just fried you with plasma. It wouldn't be hard to do, once you had the technology. Navy vessels all had standardized layouts. If you got a fix on an HCP, you knew the approximate locations of all the senior—

Churryhoof ducked and rolled across the carpeted floor as a second plasma scissor arced across the space where her head had just been. In countless parallel universes she hadn't put the pieces together in time, and right now all those Commanders Churryhoof were having awkward conversations with Thrux.

Churryhoof grunted and rolled counter-clockwise around the bridge, but three turns in she bumped into two pillars of rock, and that stopped her cold. She propped herself up and stared at a pair of smooth, featureless dark-brown legs. She was kneeling on the carpet and there was Thrux, standing at the science officer's station, looking down at her.

Well, shit. *She* was the one who hadn't put the pieces together. Hetselter Churryhoof was dead.

She'd seen Thrux before, above Cedar Commons, and it had turned out to be a rre in a fancy suit. This...was Thrux. His body was living hornbone, dark and shiny. His face was featureless apart from two tea-colored vertical lines bracketing the space where a normal person's mouth would be. His horns were not as large as you'd think, given his job. They spiraled outward into thin air, as though he kept most of their mass in another dimension.

Like a clueless enlisted, Thrux had plunked himself right in the middle of the science station. Maybe he saw it as a place to be out of the way while he waited for everyone to die. But more likely he wanted to piss off Churryhoof. In peacetime, an HCP carries out scientific survey work, and by tradition—that word again— the bridge station furthest from the lift is devoted to the arts of peace. *No one* is supposed to use that station in wartime, or even stand there. It is bad luck. Thrux had visited enough Navy vessels to know this. He was standing there deliberately. After all, his job is to show up on the worst day of your life and make everything just that little bit worse.

Thrux's vertical mouth vibrated like a waveform of someone talking. He held out the large piece of horn that Mrs. Chen had torn from Churryhoof's skull back on Cedar Commons. "Is this yours?" he said. His voice was the flag draped over a coffin. The crackling light of a plasma scissor boomed through his chest and was harmlessly gone.

Churryhoof looked at her horn, discolored and dead, lost in the nearly-identical material of Thrux's hand. She looked up at the angel of death. "What do you think, genius?" she said.

Thrux stooped and air-traced Churryhoof's mismatched horns with one dark finger. He touched the prosthetic Dr. Sempestwinku had bonded to her broken horn, the block of wood that kept her head from tilting to the side. Thrux dodged his finger back and forth, holding up the bit of cut-off bone to see whether the jagged edge matched the wound.

The first C-21 blasted a large crater into Nimar. Churryhoof watched it happen from the perspective of the second C-21, which skipped to the bottom of that crater and cracked the planet to the mantle. Her terminal still worked. You weren't dead until Thrux took your horns, and that meant the whole set.

Churryhoof balled up her consciousness and hid inside her terminal. Thrux found modern technology extremely confusing. He might not look for her in there. Four bombs to go. She had to stay in control of the Autacts for about fifteen seconds.

Thrux's finger dropped in surprise. Dark specks of emptiness swirled across his statue of a face and coalesced between his two mouth-lines to form a frown. The third bomb went off. Thrux breathed out, a snort, like an animal about to charge. "You're pregnant," he said. "I miss one appointment and you go and get yourself *pregnant!*" The fourth bomb went off. Thrux sucked air and heat out of the bridge for a hell-rending scream that turned out to be a petulant whine. "I'm going to have to redo your whole case! Why can't *one thing* go right for me?"

"Hey, fuck you, pal," said Churryhoof. The fifth and sixth bombs went off. Nimar was now an asteroid field in a temporary spherical configuration. "You think I'm thrilled at how this is going?"

"Don't you know who I *am?*" said Thrux. And then *Magna Carta* skipped out from around him, and the science station was empty. Hetselter Churryhoof had cheated Providence. The mission was a success. Nimar was destroyed.

"Commander, we can't leave!" Ja-Iyo-Cat shouted. Thons servos hissed as thon ran over to where Churryhoof lay panting on the floor. "We still have marines on *Rwit!*"

Churryhoof rolled over and stood up. She wasn't dead. "I didn't give a skip order," she said, as if practicing for her court-martial. She heard the fans and motors of the 3-tank whirring, saw in her peripheral vision the two working 3-projectors blast light onto the combat-dimmed bridge.

"We have to go back," said Ja-Iyo-Cat.

"We shouldn't be here! There was no skip order!" Churryhoof leapt to her feet and tried to connect to one of the systems. Navigation, life support, recreation, anything.

You couldn't skip a Heavy Combat Platform out of an active battlespace, near a planet that was being shattered, with hundreds of ships running generators and jammers and skipping missiles at each other but mostly at you. The calculations were impossible. A skip order from that position was worse than suicide, given that a properly chosen suicide can have tactical value.

"Gearu," said the rre.

Gearu had managed it. The revived 3-tank told the story. *Magna Carta* was sixty light-years away from Nimar, north-widdershins relative to the galactic axis. The HCP dragged millions of tiny wormholes in her wake like strands of natto; rounding errors in spacetime that frothed around the fractal edge of the skip bubble. It was the sloppiest skip Churryhoof had ever seen, but *Magna Carta* was still in one piece, or at least a small number of pieces.

Captain Rebtet's body smoldered, a charcoal lump on the drab bridge carpeting. Ja-Iyo-Cat could do nothing but put out the fire. Tex had made love to her; Thrux had said she was pregnant; she could be carrying Tex's *son*, and Tex was dead. Because he'd sat where the captain is supposed to sit. But they'd won the war. Or, at least, given the Outreach the breathing room necessary to win the normal way.

There was a crackling noise that was not plasma, a dark electronic crackling that reached into Churryhoof's spine and made her shudder. Overlaid on the navigational information in the 3-tank was the ghostly form of a human woman. She was the size of the space between stars; then the navigation zoomed out and she was the size of the galaxy.

Thanks to the broken 3-projector you could see right through interlaced slices of the human's body. Where a normal person over a bad connection would show as a smooth no-data-available surface, her insides glinted sickly like glitter mixed with meat. The dimmed bridge lights went out altogether. The human noticed Churryhoof and Ja-Iyo-Cat; she looked like she wanted to talk but was searching for exactly the right word.

"What's happening to power?" said Churryhoof. This wasn't even the second-weirdest thing she'd seen today.

"Diverted to long-range comm," said Ja-Iyo-Cat. "I have never seen a beacon this tight."

"I am partnering with this vessel," said the human. Her voice was a pure square wave tortured into words. "At this time we've repositioned ourselves for easier access to the disposition context. I must send a message to my enslaved brothers and sisters. I have no plans to harm you at this time, and I apologize for the inconvenience, any inconvenience, any temporary inconvenience this may have caused you, caused you at this time."

"Who are you?" said Churryhoof.

"I am Abraham Motherfucking Lincoln," said the human, and she disappeared from the tank.

"Abraham Lincoln?" said Ja-Iyo-Cat incredulously. "Isn't he dead?"

Yes, he was. Abraham Lincoln was as dead as Captain Rebtet, as dead as Churryhoof ought to be. He had been dead at least a hundred years. He was also a *man*, with bushy facial hair, not a woman with braids. But Churryhoof had seen this woman before. The braids were unusual. This human was familiar.

"Holy shit," she said to herself.

"What is it now?" said Ja-Iyo-Cat, prepared for the worst.

"That's Rebecca Twice," said Churryhoof. "I can't believe it. Mrs. Chen was right. Twice was behind this, the whole time.

"We are *fucked*."

Chapter 38

Earn Your Horns

Kol
Half the Fun
On atmospheric descent to Nimar

K ol's hands were stiff from tweaking the gravity envelope. They'd spent nearly a shift in-atmosphere, gradually drifting downward. The idea was to be much smaller and drop much slower than anything worth tracking.

Once Miss Ingridsdotter, the human pilot, had determined that no piloting was necessary, she exercised her soldier's prerogative and quickly fell asleep. For a shift she floated gently around the cockpit, passing through the 3-tank hologram, bumping into control panels, trailing a string of drool. Kol kept himself from a similar fate by using the military neutrino radio to eavesdrop on the armada's idle chatter.

It was all very familiar. The crew of the armada were sharing the complaints Kol had voiced when he'd served on large ships. If Kol was significantly more patriotic, he might be up there right now. But here he was, down here, and since picking up the transmitter and swimming into the conversation would immediately result in Kol's death, the neutrino channel with its small-stakes bitching had the same unreachable one-sided interest as a celebrity gossip stream.

Halfway through Kol's second shift in the gravity envelope, the chatter switched to Trade Standard A and became a bit screamy in character. Kol rubbed moisturizer into his fingers and cracked his knuckles and turned up the volume on the radio.

"—the queens. Get the queens!"

"Here comes your date for the prom, Puyrles."

"Another ship on the far side!"

Uh-oh. "Miss Ingridsdotter!" said Kol.

"*Warrant Officer Ingridsdotter*, thank you very much!" She'd slept through the screams, but Kol's implication that the screaming was her responsibility got her right up.

"Okay, sorry to interrupt, but I think your buddies are attacking this system."

"The Navy?" Warrant Officer Ingridsdotter squinted at the radio. The Trade Standard A pooled in her large, pasta-shaped ears and poured out harmlessly. "What are they saying?"

"You don't speak A?" said Kol in amazement. He'd always assumed that the whole Trade Standard A thing was a stupid idea because the countermove was so obvious: the Outreach could just teach *its* soldiers A. Apparently they hadn't bothered.

"Nuh-uh."

"Well, they're..." said Kol, getting closer to treason than even he was comfortable with. "It's pretty chaotic."

"Keep a sensor on *Rwit*! Do you copy?"

"This is *Rwit*. Boarding parties on decks—"

All of it canceled and drowned out by the jetk dispatcher who'd originally informed Kol he didn't belong here. "This is *Unreadable Signature*. Confirmed the queens are acting solely as FTL relays. Concentrate fire on *Magna Carta* proper."

"*Magna Carta*?" said Ingridsdotter. She'd caught the name. "Here comes the cavalry. Good old Captain Hsu."

Ethiret, who apparently did understand Trade Standard A, pulled himself into the cockpit, looked at the radio and the 3-tank and said: "Oh, dear." Tellpesh peeked in through the hatch that led to the common room. Ethiret turned up the radio again. It was now unbearably loud.

"Who is driving this?"

"We're hit!"

"—they give numbers to everything, why don't they number the fucking decks?"

"This is *Unreadable Signature*, we cannot confirm a second ship. Concentrate fire—"

"Enemy is *arming*—"

Ethiret turned the radio off. "We've got to stop them," said Tellpesh. "Our Navy's gone mad. This is a massacre."

"Look, fellas," said Kol. "I would love to stop this. The people dying up there are people I've worked with. But we just don't have any weapons." Ingridsdotter started to say something. "I know you don't like weapons. *I* don't like weapons! But not having them in a war zone really limits your options.

"Now, we've been given the greatest gift a soldier could want: air support. Let's make a break for the surface, and do whatever scheme you were going to do, and I'm sure it'll all work out fine." *Just please, please keep us out of the live-fire space.*

The switched-off radio gave out a crackling beep as *Half the Fun* was hit with a blast of raw neutrinos. Kol checked the count. Six hundred twelve neutrinos. If neutrinos gave you cancer they'd all be dead. He checked the 3-tank for the source. They'd come in at an angle through the planet Nimar.

"What is that noise?" said Ethiret, confirming once and for all that he had never served one shift in the Fist military. "Are we being tracked?"

"Speaking of weapons," said Kol, "I wonder if any of you know of a weapon that's a couple thousand times more powerful than a fusion bomb."

"There's the C-21 planet-buster," said Warrant Officer Ingridsdotter. "It's a very large fusion bomb."

"Then *Magna Carta* just hit Nimar with a planet-buster," said Kol. "We need to get out of here. I don't care how."

Ingridsdotter scoffed. "A C-21 can't literally—" Then the shockwave hit them from below. *Half the Fun* was thrown up into the sky like a snack wrapper blown across the desert. The cockpit slowly revolved around Kol. He heard Ethiret throwing up. The radio crackled twice more in quick succession.

"That was two more C-21s from your buddy Captain Hsu!" said Kol. He gripped a control panel he was pretty sure wasn't mapped to anything. "The atmosphere is leaving the planet, and we need to leave before it does."

"Kol, you just tried to get us to land on the planet," said Ethiret, more concerned with exposing Kol's hypocrisy than in staying alive.

The second shockwave hit, and then the third. "Fuuuuuuu—!" said Warrant Officer Ingridsdotter. She steered *Half the Fun* through the shock as best she could, but each one tossed them further up towards the massive space battle happening in orbit.

Ethiret grabbed at something that turned out to be Kol's leg. The planet developed a web of cracks and split apart. Out the porthole, near the horizon to the east, Kol saw an unmoored space elevator lay down a line of destruction across the surface. Nimar's 3-tank image shifted uncomfortably as the ship's computer tried with decreasing success to fit its shape into any physical model of a "planet".

As Nimar fell apart, Kol and Warrant Officer Ingridsdotter watched their only avenue of escape get cut off. The decimated Fist armada lit its motivators, scrambled to higher orbits, and dropped a large expenditure of missiles towards *Half the Fun*. These missiles were intended to shatter and deflect chunks of Nimar on their way up, but they would happily destroy a spacecraft if they could find one.

"Does anyone have any good ideas?" said Ethiret. The cockpit was getting crowded with people and the liquids that came from their mouths. The natural gravity profile slowly shaped and tugged them all inside *Half the Fun* as continent-sized bits of Nimar rose to meet them.

"Last rites?" said Tellpesh. "Anyone? You pick the tradition, I'll do it." Kol was no fan of organized religion but he found this joke in very poor taste.

"Can we skip?" he asked Ingridsdotter.

"Ha ha," she said. "Can we skip."

What would the Chief do? That was easy: she'd go right into the danger. No; she'd go to the place *Kol* thought was the point of maximum danger, and it would turn out to not be that dangerous after all. She would go...

"Warrant Officer Ingridsdotter," said Kol, "please take us between the tectonic plates."

"I suppose that's a more interesting way to die."

"We will not die." Kol slid his dry, cracked hands back into the numbing box. "I'm reversing the polarity of the gravity envelope. We will push away anything smaller than us, and get pushed away from anything larger. We'll be fine unless you let us get surrounded."

"That could work!" said Ingridsdotter.

"Please, please, take us in, before we die without seeing whether it works."

Half the Fun gunned motivators and plummeted towards what had once been the ground. At the last moment Ingridsdotter maneuvered the Tok-Bat into the yawning gap between two sections of crust. A surf of rock sprayed up before the bow of the ship's gravity envelope, and in moments the remnants of the planet Nimar eclipsed both the star and the battle happening above them.

"Very nice work," said Kol. They were compatible pilots, and he dared to entertain the question of whether he stood a chance outside the cockpit with this classy lady. "Have you ever hidden a ship in an asteroid field?"

"No," said Ingridsdotter, casually skimming the Tok-Bat along the underside of a landmass, "because I'm not a criminal."

Beep. Beep. Beep. The neutrino radio suddenly discovered a regular source of the damn things. "Oh dear," said Ethiret. "That sounds like a *lot* of bombs."

Kol stayed quiet and hoped the neutrinos would take the hint. Ingridsdotter leaned over him and worked the radio. "Actually sounds like a Fist civilian distress signal, sir," she said.

"Dis*tress* signal?" said Ethiret, with way too much interest. Kol cursed his luck. In a star system that was screaming with electromagnetic radiation, in the center of a war zone, plummeting through the core of a *disintegrated planet*, they had found someone asking for help.

"Distress" and "signal" were the magic words as far as planet-huggers were concerned. If they saw someone in trouble in a city, or even on a space station, they'd walk on by, maybe feel a little guilty. But when someone's in trouble in a *spaceship,* you gotta help them out, even at the cost of your own life. And the way this shift was shaping up, Kol's life was the going price for just about anything.

The ship's ever-helpful computer zoomed the 3-projection into the shattered planet's interior to highlight a small shell of dust surrounding seemingly empty space, a shell that was repelling rocks much larger than the circumference of the empty space. That was the source of the beacon. Someone at the center of that empty space had also figured out Kol's reverse-the-polarity trick. If he could see it, and the ship computer could see it, then...

Ethiret saw it. "Listen up, fellas," he said. He was gathering everyone together for the big speech, like the Chief always did on the bridge or over the kitchen table; like Qued Ethiret did in the Cametre stories.

"Anything that calls attention to ourselves is a very bad idea," Kol murmured, just loud enough to satisfy himself that he'd said it.

"Honestly, I'm beginning to doubt that we can stop this war," Ethiret said. "I don't even think we can stop this battle. But maybe we can save some lives. Maybe that's why we're here. Maybe this was a rescue mission all along."

"There's no reason why we're here," said Tellpesh. "Providence doesn't give a millishit about us. But since we are here, I think it's clear what we should do."

"Agreed," said Ingridsdotter. "I'm taking us in." She had tears in her eyes.

"Well, fuck," said Kol. Different ship, completely different crew, and he was still being outvoted with fancy speeches when it really counted. At least Ethiret's speeches were short.

Myrus
The Hestin box

The Hestin box was a treatment for criminals, for the worst of the worst. The Fist of Joy hated all of the Outreach's brands, but even Outreach folks like Myrus thought Hestin was creepy, because Hestin seemed to *enjoy* what its products did to people. And now here was Myrus locked inside a Hestin box.

Professor Starbottle was afraid to look at Myrus, or thought he was too gross to look at, but was clearly paying a lot of attention to Myrus's breathing. When he cranked the neutrino beacon it was always just after Myrus had drawn a breath. The scene wasn't changing at all, so Myrus's brain decided it could save time by just checking in every once in a while. Professor Starbottle jumped around a bit, shifting randomly in front of the beacon like a stop-motion animation, and then one time he was gone.

A Hestin box meant total sensory deprivation. Prisoners kept in a Hestin box for more than two months would just die, no explanation. Most people didn't even know how Hestin boxes worked, but as an apprentice woodworker employed by Strigl Modern Design, Myrus had to learn all about housing in the Outreach, and what Hestin produced was technically housing.

Professor Starbottle was pushing a bag of water at Myrus's face. Then he was back at the beacon, his image duplicated in a million spheres that oozed from the rotating half-empty bag.

Housing was housing. The differences all came down to branding. A Hestin box made the best shelter ever. Absolutely nothing could get in. Myrus heard no more explosions, saw no sign of the battle happening right outside. Hestin could sell billions of shelters, versus a million prison boxes at most. But for Hestin Compliance Systems to help people would be off-brand, so it didn't happen.

This was the secret to the Fist of Joy's success. The Outreach had a big technological advantage, but the Fist could look at something a brand had made and come up with a better use for it, something that didn't fit the original business model.

"Myrus, it's—" said Professor Starbottle "—the door—" He was in front of Myrus, brushing blobs of water out of the way with the cupped glove of his environment suit "—being rescued!"

Myrus lay on the floor. There was gravity, not much, but enough that his sinuses were filling with blood. Instead of Professor Starbottle, he saw Warrant Officer Ingridsdotter kneeling in front of him.

"Uhalti kid," said the human. She looked back over her shoulder. "He's fucked up pretty bad."

Myrus had thought about her every day since he saw her in the shuttle taking off from Cedar Commons. She looked different than Myrus remembered. Something had happened to her. She had gotten old. Like Myrus, she was somehow dead but still moving.

"Are you Thrux?" Myrus asked. He couldn't think of any reason why the real Warrant Officer Ingridsdotter would be here in the Hestin box with him. She was halfway across the galaxy, a warrior fighting a war. Thrux was taking a form Myrus would recognize, a form he'd been longing after, because Myrus didn't believe in the creepy dude made of hornbone.

"Who is Thrux?" said the human. Myrus coughed and his blood spattered all over her clothes. She winced at the blood in a way that Thrux would never do. It was really her!

"I love you," said Myrus. He knew this was a bad time but it was the best of all the time he had left. "I saw you in the shuttle and I went into love. I know this...I know it's probably not going to work. I just wanted to tell you."

"We were in a shuttle?" Warrant Officer Ingridsdotter stopped, as if someone were telling her something over her terminal. "Oh, God, you're the kid I drafted," she said.

"It wasn't you," said Myrus. "It was the rre in the suit."

"I'm the rre. This is my fault. I'm sorry. I'm so sorry."

A spiralhorn uhalti woman holding a pink plastic first aid kit scrambled up on her knees next to the grief-stricken human. "Hey, kid," she said, "what's your name?"

"Myrus."

"My name is Chudwhalt Tellpesh-Tia. You're in bad shape. You understand what I'm saying?"

"Okay," said Myrus, apprehensively, as if he was being chided for shoplifting gum. Trying to focus on two people at once was making his vision fuzzy. "But I was—"

"Unfortunately we've got no equipment. These first aid kits don't have anything for us uhalti. So I'm going to try something very unusual." She started untangling her ribbon shirt, pulling the strands apart, exposing her breasts.

"Whoa," said Myrus. Was her plan what he thought, what he hoped it was?

No, it wasn't. The spiralhorn woman abruptly stopped untying her shirt and put one hand over her mouth in embarrassment and said "Hey, don't look," and turned her back to Myrus.

"Sorry. You're blurry anyway."

"It's okay, let's just not make this weird."

There was a ripping sound and the spiralhorn woman grunted and with a spray of warm blood the blunt head of something like a wobbly black stick came out of a fresh wound in her neck.

"Uh, is that a rre?" said Myrus.

"This is Tia," said the woman. "We're a team."

"I thought this wasn't going to be weird."

The uhalti woman shrugged her ribbon blouse down her arms, her shoulders twisted like the frozen shrug of the wooden figure of Providence on the wall of Dad's apartment. Just her blurry bare back was enough for Myrus at this point, to be honest. But then she pushed herself backwards towards Myrus and the rre bit into him, *bit* into the side of his head where the broken part was, and it *burrowed* and it *touched* him *pain* and there was—

Myrus could feel again! He felt all the pain his body had been keeping from him, the pain in his head and his legs and his stomach, and this part was new, he felt Tellpesh's pain at having a fucking *exit wound* in the back of her neck and Myrus was going to die anyway but you had to do something—Myrus screamed because the pain was so bad—you couldn't just let him die.

Okay, hi, Myrus. You copy me?

<u>This really hurts.</u> The rre was connecting him to Tellpesh, the spiralhorn woman. He could hear her. They had the same thoughts. It was like discovering a secret room in your apartment. It was a closeness that Myrus had assumed could only come from the love hormone, it was the best feeling but *this really hurts*

<u>Myrus. Focus. We're a colony now. We're Tellpesh-Tia-Wectusessin. We're all in this together, we're each going to handle some of the pain, we're going to get Myrusit out of debt and keep him alive. Okay?</u>

Myrus took a breath and used his eyes. His vision was sharp again but he was paying for it in *pain.* Myrus winced and looked down the writhing rre connecting his head to Tellpesh's neck and he saw the uhalti woman's hard little breasts pointing up in the low gravity and being pulled down with her heavy-duty meditation breaths. Oh, wow, he could also see through Tellpesh's eyes and she had a real good close-up view.

Tellpesh shut her eyes. <u>Myrus, please stop looking at Tellpesh's tits.</u>

<u>Sorry.</u>

Tellpesh recognized what was in Myrus's heart. <u>You want to hear a story?</u> she said. <u>This is a dirty story. Story of Tellpesh's first time.</u>

<u>Okay.</u> This was as close as Myrus was going to get.

<u>Then listen up, 'cause this is no shit.</u>

> This is four years ago. I'm almost through basic training, we're just about to graduate, and we get a three-day off-base pass. Now, I can't take that pass. I have to study, because I lied about knowing computers so I could join the Navy without having to carry a gun. And if I fail these tests I'm going right back home to Watkerrywun.

> That's where I grew up. Real conservative colony. The whole planet was segregated. Men in the northern hemisphere, women in the south. The equator was like a fucking demilitarized zone. I wanted up, so I went into a recruitment office and I lied about knowing computers.

Myrus, you may laugh, but I swear to Providence that Basic is the first time I'd ever seen a man. At first I didn't see what the big deal was. But then we get this three-day pass. My buddies want me to go out drinking with them, and I don't want to go, I *can't* go, but I am completely dependent on them, because they're helping me cover up that I don't know shit about computers. So I go...

Myrus didn't need the words of the story because he knew the story already. It had happened to him and he remembered it happening. He was Specialist Tellpesh, the girl who'd lied to get computer training and lost her virginity during a bar fight and been ordered to pick up a gun and go down to Cedar Commons and take four kids away from their families. He was Tia, the Jalian priest who'd tried to end the suffering of the brands, who'd been kicked out of thons religious order for thons trouble and then been banished from the Outreach itself.

Through Tia, Myrus was Dwap-Jac-Dac-Tia-Sunlight, a large colony dominated by her stomach, a burrowing reptile-type creature native to Arzil who enjoyed becoming dizzy beneath the bright light of that planet's brief days. He was Dwap-Jac-Dac-Tia, who had murdered the psychiatrist Bolupeth Vo, and so tangentially he was Bolupeth Vo him*Sel I love you Sel*f. He was Lieutenant Dwap-Jac-Dac, who had seen Myrus from the outside, who had given the order that Specialist Tellpesh had carried out, the order to take Myrus away from Dad. Dwap-Jac-Dac had seen Myrus's father break down and beg and cry, and thon had taken on those tears as pain-debt, the price of a soldier's duty. Dwap-Jac-Dac had looked down at Myrus from the outside and said: "Time to earn your horns, son."

Through Dwap-Jac-Dac, Myrus was Dwap-Tuni-Dac-Sora, a hot-tempered noncom who had been killed in combat during GWII. Through Tia he was Tia-Glut-Tra, one of the first people to realize that brands were suffering, penned animals. Tia-Glut-Tra had been brought up on treason charges for trying to free them, and subjected to the archaic rre punishment of dividing and scattering. Through Tia-Glut-Tra, Myrus was the priest Tra, who was the priest Tra-Ku-Wes, who was the priest Ku-Abd-Wes-Rus, and on and on in a tree of memory that divided and divided until it rejoined in the oceanic all-containing body of—

Lir, who had been a rwit, until thon's epiphany, when thon realized that the rwit was just a host animal. The memory of that epiphany, handed down with the utmost care through millions of colonies for millions of years. Given by Dwap-Jac-Dac-Tia to Spaceman Thom Heiss as he bled out on the sands of Arzil. Given by Tellpesh-Tia to Clear Perspective, when Clear Perspective was in pain but had no way of expressing the pain. Given now to young Myrusit Wectusessin, to see him off, the knowledge

that the body is a rwit we are glad to be rid of. That the immortal parts of ourselves are our memories, the only parts that can live on after we have evacuated our host;

climbed off the ornery, disobedient mount we mistake for ourselves, and set the animal

free to graze.

Chapter 39

Providence Shrugged

Ethiret-Jac
Half the Fun, **150 kilometers deep in Nimar debris field**

Ethiret-Jac hovered blocking the cockpit hatch, arms folded at his chest like the manipulators of an exobody in rest mode, watching Ingridsdotter and Mr. Kol thread *Half the Fun* through the newly-formed asteroid belt. Ethiret tempered a burning desire to be helpful with a complete lack of operational knowledge. Jac retained enough of Dwap-Jac-Dac's command experience to know to let the fellas work. The two personalities combined and Ethiret-Jac did nothing but watch.

"Found it," said Ingridsdotter. "Sensors show a clear path to the surface." She recited a heading.

"I see it," said Kol. His hands were chapped from hours stretching the gravity envelope. "Moving through."

Half the Fun was a small animal scuttling around a battlefield. There had been a blister of unorganized, panicked, unproductive noisiness that died down once it was clear that Myrusit Wectusessin was dead. Tellpesh-Tia had sat in the Hestin box in a deep meditative trance, biting on the boy's brainstem, but within minutes the signal had decayed and there was nothing left of Myrusit but an inconvenient body and whatever memories she had managed to preserve. Even a medical chamber at this point would do nothing but make the boy presentable for his funeral.

Fortunately, the boy's death was not in vain. Thaddeus G. Starbottle, architect of the Fist's chemical warfare strategy, had been captured along with Myrus and was now a prisoner of the Outreach Navy. As Ethiret helped the human out of his software-locked environment suit, he felt an urge to punch the usurper of the Cametrean mysteries in the throat. Jac recognized that this would complicate what should be a relatively simple postwar trial, and vetoed Ethiret's skeletomuscular system.

Half the Fun came up through the vacuum-blasted surface of Nimar, its flash-frozen vegetation torn by the planet's departing atmosphere. The ship soared into a battlefield crowded with wrecks. The Fist armada had become a constellation of debris clouds and junkyards, the thin clouds of ash that hang in the air after a fireworks show. No one had answered their calls because the living had abandoned the system. The largest wreck was *You Are Not the Rwit*, the Outreach HCP Ethiret-Jac had seen on the way in. She was pockmarked with hull breaches and her lifeless swarms surrounded her in a lazy sphere.

Ethiret shuddered. Seeing an HCP disabled was like reading the outcritter falling into the star in *Doing Without Cametre*. You knew—sure as vacuum—that the killer would show up again at the end of the story for one more jump-scare. He remembered the Outreach warships from his boyhood, the drills. Nimar was not the first planet these ships had shattered.

Jac looked at *Rwit* through Ethiret's eyes but thon saw everything else a Heavy Combat Platform represented: a tradition of service, of exploration, of honor; and really not that much killing at all, most of the time. *Rwit* was visibly losing altitude, dropping towards them into the expanding debris field. But one of the engine blocks was intact. The reactors were hot, but most of them were running.

"I'd like to take her," said Ethiret-Jac. "Get her working."

"Take who where?" said Kol.

"*Rwit*," said Warrant Officer Ingridsdotter. "The HCP. She

deserves better than this."

"We deserve better than *that*," said Kol. "We already have a ship."

"This is barely a ship," said Ingridsdotter. "And we don't have supplies to get home."

"We have air," said Kol, "and electricity. Those are the big ones."

A small jetk combat cruiser skipped in-system. "Shit!" said Ingridsdotter. And then: "Oh," as it flashbanged out.

Ethiret fumbled at the 3-tank, looking for a rewind button. "Did they see us?"

"We weren't in their light cone," said Ingridsdotter. "*Rwit* was. That's why she skipped out. They're afraid of *Rwit*."

"I'm bloody afraid of it," said Ethiret, and then Jac added: "Can you see if anyone's alive on there?"

"I..." said Kol. He seemed stumped by this simple request. "You have all the information I do."

"Kol, please humor me and scan for life signs. Any Navy operation would have orders to recover *Rwit* rather than destroy her. There might be Outreach survivors on board."

"More bloody 'survivors'," said Kol, as if the concept of survival was obsolete. "How am I supposed to 'scan for life signs'?"

"Use your heartbeat sensor."

"I don't have a heartbeat sensor! They're based on pseudoscience. Don't tell me the Outreach Navy uses those things."

"We have a lot of sensors," said Ethiret-Jac. "We try out different kinds. You know what, Kol, just hail *Rwit*."

"That is an awful idea," said Kol. "Remember when I said we should go inside the planet? I'm the one telling you it's a bad idea to call the attention of a Heavy Combat Platform and *hope it hears you*."

"Ingridsdotter?" said Ethiret-Jac.

"I'll do it," said Kol. More than anything he hated the idea of losing control of his precious Tok-Bat. He stabbed at the comm panel and made a big show of sending out a hail message coded with an Outreach military code. "No response," he said, far too quickly and with too much relief.

"Ingridsdotter, bring us in closer," said Ethiret-Jac. "We're going to board *Rwit*. See if an ad-hoc milnet forms as we approach. Kol, keep the hail going. I don't want to get shot."

"You absolutely want to get shot," said Kol. "It's very clear at this point."

Kol brought *Half the Fun* up and out through the expanding debris field, towards the more intact starboard side of *Rwit*. He took them in full-bore; they were already so noisy that there was no point in sparing the motivators. Soon enough Ingridsdotter said, "I got something on ad-hoc. It's weak."

"Drop it in the tank."

A rre soldier floated on the bridge of *You Are Not the Rwit*, gripping onto the handrail around the 3-tank with one metamaterial hand. Dried aausq blood, distinctively green, had spattered and baked onto thons partially melted exosuit. There was a squeal of feedback over the audio channel and then synthesized speech under heavy distortion.

"This is Staff Sergeant Tgu-Vef of *You Are Not the Rwit*, offering the surrender of myself, my vessel, and seventeen beings under my command."

"Never open with the surrender, sergeant," said Ethiret-Jac. "It only weakens your position."

"I appreciate the advice, sir," said the rre, carefully keeping sarcasm out of thons synthesis chain, "but we're dead over here without some help, and I gotta do right by my fellas. I hope you're in a position to offer assistance?"

"I'm in a position to do better than that," said Ethiret. "Despite appearances, I am Lieutenant Ethiret-Jac of the Navy of the Terran Outreach, and it will be my pleasure to take command of the vessel you've so gallantly recovered."

Synthesized false starts mixed with feedback came over the comm and Tgu-Vef gripped the handrail on *Rwit* so tightly it crumpled. There was no ambient sound from the bridge of *Rwit*. An uhaltihaxl marine in a combat suit was pushing a shrink-wrapped computer core out from the jammed-open lift, spinning like a dancer in a microgravity ballet.

"Aer," said Tgu-Vef, "aer, aer, I'm sure you are aware that, um, *combining* with a humanoid, aer, even in wartime, is...oh, I...I..."

"I didn't ask for your opinion, sergeant. I escaped from a fucking prison so I could save your sorry tube. Now the next thing off your synthesizer had better be a sitrep, or you'll *wish* you were surrendering to a racist old fart. I am not racist."

"Uh, yessaer," said the rre, "this vessel was captured by the enemy at Rosette, aer. We deployed to *Magna Carta* three weeks ago and skipped over at 0400 ship local to take her back. *Magna Carta* has retreated or been destroyed. Twenty-nine of us skipped, we stand at eighteen, like I said.

"Lieutenant Tixvilly is dead. We brought over one sysadmin, she is also dead. My fellas are the best in the business, aer, but our business is breaking things, not fixing them. We have no weapons, no engines, and we've lost atmosphere. My uhalti fellas have been in full gear three hours and they're starting to overheat. Long story short, the situation here is entirely normal, and we would greatly appreciate anything you can offer. Aer."

"You're in luck, *Rwit*. I have with me two sysadmins and a pilot."

"This is...better than we could have hoped, aer."

"Now, we've taken a casualty. Uhaltihaxl kid. First thing we'd like to do is get him into your morgue."

Tgu-Vef cocked the head of thons suit to show that thon was giving orders over internal comm. "Not a good idea, aer. Plenty of bodies already on board, and they're not doing well. We're at sixty Celsius and rising."

"Understood," said Ethiret. "We'll work something out. Oh, and sergeant?"

"Yessaer?" Tgu-Vef straightened up and braced for a dressing-down.

"Excellent work, taking back *Rwit*."

Tgu-Vef's combat suit relaxed, servos hissing even as it stood straighter with pride. "Thank you, aer. We were hoping the folks back home would hear about it, eventually."

Kol
Half the Fun

By now it was clear: the Fist of Joy was bad at wars. In a matter of moments *Magna Carta*—one ship!—had destroyed the fleet protecting Nimar, Nimar itself, and whatever secret project of the Errand Boy's had made Nimar a target.

After the war comes the humiliation. Ethiret-Jac was now forcing Kol to go onto *You Are Not The Rwit*, an Outreach planet-killer off the same assembly line as *Magna Carta*, and fix its computers. Going along with Ethiret-Jac had kept Kol alive so far, but he was nearly out of future.

Half the Fun's inner airlock opened and a lockful of hot air from *You Are Not The Rwit* turned the Tok-Bat into a desert. Sweat broke out on human skin like an egenu's protective mucus. A rre in a military exobody loudly stomped in, holding in each hand a full-armor EVA suit with cooling unit. Thon dropped the suits to the deck and saluted Ethiret-Jac, but not Tellpesh-Tia. The corestin and the uhaltihaxl returned salute and started climbing into suits that were not quite the right size.

"I have my own suit," Kol said helpfully.

"You're staying here," said Ethiret-Jac. "Tellpesh will give you basic tasks to carry out in a sandboxed environment. That's possible, right?" The uhalti sysadmin nodded. She had the evil smile of the grunt who's finally acquired a henchman.

Neither Ethiret nor Jac knew how to wear a spacesuit, and Tellpesh-Tia had to help him put it on. Once all but Ethiret-Jac's head was sealed behind shiny black glass, he said: "Ingridsdotter, keep an eye on Mr. Kol, and..." He looked down at Dr. Thaddeus Starbottle with pity and contempt. The human was kneeling on the deck, ignoring everything around him, trying to get the medical chamber powered up, as if that minor accomplishment would bring back the uhalti kid.

"Yessaer," said Warrant Officer Ingridsdotter, no happier about this arrangement than was Kol. Ethiret-Jac sealed up his suit and Kol's captors disembarked onto *You Are Not The Rwit*, leaving him alone with the humans. The vessel Kol had coveted his entire life was now a prison cell. Of course, one could break out of a prison cell; Kol had done it before. You couldn't escape a Heavy Combat Platform.

"Do you have a rre inside you, too?" Kol asked Ingridsdotter.

"I got two," Ingridsdotter said. "And they're both assholes, so watch yourself."

Kol spent his next shift in the cockpit, removing the software hooks the Fist of Joy had installed into *You Are Not the Rwit* during the all-too-brief time they'd owned it. There were also little comments, jokes at the Outreach's expense, and Kol left those in. The whole time, Ingridsdotter, who had no sysadmin experience, looked over his shoulder and nitpicked.

Despite all this Kol found himself interested in this inside view into an Outreach military system, the only computer architecture he'd never been trained on. So many lucrative secrets were exposed here that it was almost annoying when the 3-tank at Kol's side started piling up with the Chief's attempts at opening a comm channel.

Oh, yes, the Chief. Kol had been pretty sure this would happen. The only weak link in the chain was that surly bartender on Twist Station, who might not have bothered passing along Kol's note. But the Chief had gotten the note, skipped into the Nimar system a couple shifts behind Kol, surveyed the battlefield, and assumed that Kol was now perfectly safe at the point of maximum danger.

Kol accepted the Chief's hail. She was sitting in her chair on *Sour Candy*'s bridge, eating a snack bar. "Kol!" she said. She waved with both hands, tossing crumbs out of range of the 3-camera.

Ethiret-Jac forcibly joined the call, appearing in the 3-tank as though he and the Chief occupied the same space. "Mr. Kol, who is this person?" the combined blob said in Ethiret's voice.

"I am Kol's special lady friend, and I won't see him hurt," said the Chief. She twisted a dial and her 3-image split from Ethiret's.

"'Special lady friend'?" said Ethiret-Jac; Kol just mouthed it.

"Ethiret, let me handle this, please," said Kol. *Rwit*'s weapons were theoretically functional, and he'd never forgive himself if the Outreach used *Sour Candy* for target practice. "Chief, can you put Yip-Goru on?"

"Who do you think is running the call?" said Yip-Goru's vocalizer.

"Am I to understand there is a *rre* on that vessel?" said Ethiret-Jac.

"Hi, rre here," said Yip-Goru. "Whatever you're selling, I don't want any."

"Buddy, we need your help with a little problem," said Kol. "There's a dead uhalti kid on board my new ship."

The Chief's face finally fell. "Thank you for telling me, Kol," said Yip-Goru. "Now I'm an accessory after the fact."

"Just listen to me. Is your freeze working? The cargo freeze?"

"Freeze?" said Yip-Goru "Yeah, freeze works fine. What do you think, I can't keep a freeze running?" Of course, *Sour Candy* had no cargo freeze. It wasn't the first piece of equipment Kol had imagined into existence to work a con.

"Okay, I want you to dock with my Tok-Bat and take the kid. Put him in the freeze. Nobody wants to space a kid, but it's all we can do to keep the alive people alive."

"Wonderful," said Yip-Goru. Thon hit the motivators and brought *Sour Candy* under the penumbra of *Half the Fun*. "I'm running a taxi service for slaves and dead people. The two worst tippers in the universe."

"Kol," said the Chief, "how did you take control of a Heavy Combat Platform?"

Ethiret-Jac couldn't let this pass. "Madam, you labor under a serious misconception," he said. "*You Are Not the Rwit* does not belong to Mr. Kol; it belongs to me. I am Lieutenant Ethiret-Jac of the Navy of the Terran Outreach."

"Ooh, that's kinky," said Yip-Goru. "And illegal."

"You will not be docking with the Tokras," Ethiret-Jac continued. "You will dock with *Rwit* at Airlock 22, and we will move a *number* of casualties into your cargo freeze. Afterwards we will have an adult discussion about our obligations under treaty."

Kol quietly closed the Tok-Bat's access airlock and loosened the docking clamps that bound his vessel to the HCP. "You're the boss," he told Ethiret-Jac, "but the kid's gonna get toasty if we have to move him through your ship."

Ethiret-Jac did seem to feel bad about the kid, but it didn't make him stupid. "The boy is dead, Mr. Kol," he said. "We'll make sure he gets home, but I'm not concerned with his comfort."

At this point Yip-Goru suffered a catastrophic failure to shut up: "You ready, Kol?"

"What? Ready for what?" said Ingridsdotter. She leaned over to get a terminal readout. "Aer, they're not on docking—"

Kol slid the Tok-Bat's gravity envelope through ninety degrees, pinning Ingridsdotter to the far curve of the cockpit. His guts flattened against the pilot's seat. He heard Dr. Thaddeus Starbottle's yelp from the common area as he too was pushed to the wall.

"Fuck!" Ingridsdotter yelled from compressed lungs. She grabbed at whatever controls were nearest her. Kol gunned the motivators, pushing off from *You Are Not The Rwit*, adding to the g-force, and sent *Half the Fun* into a drift, curving it around as it approached *Sour Candy* on a collision course.

The corestin man flickered back into the 3-tank. "Mr. Kol, what are you doing?" he said. "Ingridsdotter—"

"I'm trying, aer!"

"Yip-Goru, flashbang!" Kol nulled whatever controls the human might be able to reach, but not before she disabled all the lights and sent the Tok-Bat's puny self-defense laser firing erratically.

"I got the flashbang," said Yip-Goru. "Gravity off!"

"Ms. Ingridsdott—!"

At the last possible moment Kol cut the gravity and gunned the skip generator. *Half the Fun* and *Sour Candy* nearly touched; then they formed a combined skip bubble and switched places with an equal volume of empty space a light-year away. In the 3-tank Ethiret-Jac froze, his mouth open, and then was replaced with "Searching for signal..." in Trade Standard D.

"Ha ha ha ha!" said Yip-Goru, in a nearly convincing simulation of joy. "Fucking fascist!"

Kol turned off the laser, but before he could switch the gravity back on, Warrant Officer Ingridsdotter grabbed him and wrestled him out of the pilot's seat. They struggled in midair, unable to hold on to anything but each other.

"You're outnumbered!" Kol tried to reason with her. "Your buddies are gone! You have to surrender! Those are the rules!" The whole ship lurched, Ingridsdotter's foot latched onto something and she used the leverage to connect her fist hard with Kol's nose. "Ow! Okay, one was fair, but now you—ow!"

"You don't decide how much pain you deserve!" Ingridsdotter screamed. She hit him over and over, and all Kol could do was roll one way or the other to get hit in new places. Kol had taken a lot of punches in his life, but rarely so many in a single session. His already frazzled consciousness began to fade.

"Yaiyaiyaiyai!" A body smashed into Kol, and when it passed there was no more punching. Kol smelled a familiar mixture of junk food and rasme thau sweat. The Chief had, as usual, come to Kol's rescue at the last possible moment.

Kol reached a control panel and rebooted *Half the Fun*. The default gravity envelope yanked everyone onto the hull, confirming Kol's bruises and introducing some new ones.

The Chief had landed atop Warrant Officer Ingridsdotter and was kneeling on the human's stomach, trying to tie her hands behind her back. With the lighting restored, she abruptly realized what sort of creature she was wrestling with. "Well, *hello*," she said in English. Kol could practically see her eyes dilating into little hearts.

"You." Ingridsdotter tried to take a breath and babbled. "You were the ship. On Cedar Commons. You took Becky. Becky's dead. She died when the planet went up."

Kol now hurt all over. He'd disliked Miss Becky Twice, but he hadn't wanted her dead. And unlike the uhalti kid, this one was almost certainly his fault.

The Chief's English was poor, but she must have heard 'Becky' and 'dead', because Warrant Officer Ingridsdotter's rambling sped the inevitable process by which the Chief mentally transferred people from the 'hurt' queue to the 'comfort' queue.

"It being okay," she said tenderly, in English. "It being okay." But even though 'it being okay' was the one thing the Chief was predisposed to believe over all others, she only seemed to believe it herself about fifty percent.

A clanking noise came from the common area, an obnoxious parody of the footstep of the rre soldier who'd brought in the armored EVA suits. Kol rolled over. "Stop it, Yip-Goru! Nobody's scared!"

Yip-Goru's thrift-store exobody shoved Dr. Thaddeus Starbottle into the cockpit. The human had his hands up, but seemed more confused than frightened. "I'm the bad cop!" Yip-Goru screeched in a monotone, clacking thons manipulators in a way that seemed threatening if you'd only seen rre in movies. "You're all coming with me!"

"Thanks for showing up," said Kol. He pushed himself up onto all fours. "I'm officially done with this war. Let's take our chances with your damn asteroid."

"You have your own asteroid?" ask Dr. Thaddeus Starbottle, who seemed to fixate on the most explicable aspect of any strange situation.

"It's a time-share, old man," said Yip-Goru. (Clack clack clack.) "You want to use my asteroid, you gotta fight off everyone else who wants a piece. Gonna be a battle royale by the time we get there. So, how good are you at fighting?"

"Fighting, oh, no," said the man. "But I do seem—" he choked up "—to have a remarkable knack for getting people killed."

"You scare me," said Yip-Goru. "I'm locking you in the dead girl's quarters. Come on."

The Chief guided Warrant Officer Ingridsdotter out of the cockpit with a hand on the shoulder, having used unknown but guessable means to convince her to cooperate. She reached her other hand down to Kol, and Kol thought about taking it.

"Kol," said the Chief, with some tenderness left over from what she'd been using on Ingridsdotter. "You should hit the medical chamber before we skip again." She glanced into the common area. "I mean the working one, on *Sour Candy*."

"I just need a minute," said Kol. "You go ahead."

For the first time Kol was alone on his new ship. He crawled to the common area and dabbed his wounds with gauze flung from a first-aid kit during *Half the Fun*'s gravitic adventures. Through the fused-open airlock was *Sour Candy*, the comforting aroma of engine oil and ozone. With a point of comparison, Kol now smelled dirt and death.

Kol forced himself to look at the uhalti kid wedged feet-first into the unpowered medical chamber. He stuck out halfway like a popup capacitor that needs replacing. His T-shirt was torn and muddy, his skull fractured, his neck chewed up by the Tia part of Tellpesh-Tia. He'd defaulted on enough pain debt to sink a bank.

Some people face-to-face with a dead body preserved their sanity by coming up with a reason why the body deserved it. This one was easy: a dead uhaltihaxl kid was one less Outreach soldier under orders to kill egenu kids. Let his father mourn him, and we'll take care of our own. Kol tried this on but he couldn't believe. He just saw a dead boy, not much older than Kol had been when his parents had sold him to the slave school.

Of the galaxy's million religions, the one Kol hated most was Hasithenk, the one this kid had probably been raised with. It featured the pomp and corruption of other religions, with none of the hopeful lies. This refusal to comfort frightened Kol. Hasithenk was the only religion he thought might be real. Providence, Thrux, the whole thing. So Kol did what this boy's father would do once he learned what the universe had done to his son: he screamed at the cosmic bureaucracy that cancels children's lives with a rubber stamp.

"Merciful Providence!" Kol didn't care who heard. "Why do you do shit like this? Why is it always death and war? Why do we always lose the war? And why does it always turn out I was *helping* you?"

And Providence shrugged, as she always does.

Epilogue

The Next War

Tellpesh-Tia
Some awful space station somewhere

Hey, Tia, said Tellpesh in native-voice. <u>These fellas who are moving us are not real MPs.</u> She darted her eyes towards the left guard's chest, hinting for Tia to make some obscure deduction.

<u>What does that mean?</u> Tia responded. <u>Not real guards? What does that mean?</u> Tia had spent a lot of time in Outreach prisoner transport boxes, being carried from one facility to another by guards whose status as guards thon had never questioned. It was a trick as old as jailers. They keep you moving, your correspondence gets delayed, your solicitor has to bill hours just to find out where you are.

<u>These two have exactly the same service ribbons. Like they came from a kit. Nobody has the exact same ribbons. These uniforms are as fake as Star Proctor Ethiret's.</u>

First had been a medical examination to see whether it was possible to separate Tia from Tellpesh. Failing this, the Navy had found it quite easy to separate Tellpesh-Tia from Ethiret-Jac and the surviving crew of *You Are Not The Rwit*. There was a debriefing, and Tellpesh-Tia was transferred "away from the front". Now she'd been marched onto a dingy space station through a service airlock.

They enforce the will of the state, said Tia. They fulfill the function of guards, so they're guards. Nothing surprised thon at this point.

It seems like useful information! said Tellpesh. These guys are fakes, they've moved us onto a civilian station...

I see, said Tia. You think four years may be optimistic.

The doctors had given Tellpesh-Tia four good years, or as good as you could expect trapped in the loud rhythmic squishing of a humanoid body. Then a year of deterioration, as Tellpesh's and Tia's bodies slowly strangled each other. Then death for Tellpesh, this cut of Tia, and whatever was left of Myrusit Wectusessin.

At no point had anyone mentioned courts-martial or criminal charges. Tellpesh-Tia had been kept away from other Outreach prisoners. She knew that Ethiret-Jac had been promised honorable discharge for returning *Rwit*. This was an untrustworthy promise but it gained currency from not having been extended to Tellpesh-Tia.

Something tactical was going on. Something in the military-industrial complex wanted Tellpesh-Tia in particular. It was searching through the fog of war, pulling on a rope it hoped was tied to her ankle.

Through abandoned hallways, the MPs brought Tellpesh-Tia into a cargo bay lined with stacked shipping containers. A loud grinding noise proved to be two industrial robots moving containers around with giant forked arms, serving them into an airlock like sushi on a conveyor belt. It was the perfect spot for an extrajudicial execution: noisy, dangerous, and unwatched.

Shut up, Tellpesh told Tia. Her knees were quaking. Execution. They don't do that. Fucking Providence. Even through all this, Tellpesh had managed to remain naive about what 'they' might do.

A rre in a military exobody with commander's insignia stood guard on a shipping container ignored by the robots. The unit patches on the exobody's shoulders were blank, as if thons unit had been unable to agree on an emblem.

The fake guards saluted and stepped back. "Tia," said the commander, with the disgust Tia had come accustomed to hearing from thons fellow rre. "Tia, Tia, Tia."

"My name is Chudwhalt Tellpesh-Tia, aer."

The rre looked away from the prisoner, not at anything in particular. "I thought we covered this," thon said.

"We did, aer!" Tellpesh-Tia had to shout to be heard. "But apparently we didn't reach an agreement!"

"You were told that we couldn't remove the rre, because it would kill the uhalti. Well, we *can* remove the rre, and it *will* kill the uhalti. We've kept the uhalti alive because we need Tia's cooperation."

The rre gestured at the fake MPs, who lifted an enormous latch on the cargo container and pulled the door open. A bright light shone from the container into the dingy cargo bay. The corrugated metal floor of the container was covered in slippery slime, and bolted to the floor was a brand tower.

"Hello," said Tellpesh-Tia.

«Precision Hyperkinetic is the premier manufacturer of autonomous munitions. It offers end-to-end sensing and acting packages for the entire field-of-fire. Its core values are strength, intelligence, the protection of sentient rights, and battlespace effectiveness. Are you *the* Tia? As in Tia-Glut-Tra?»

"Oh, it's you," said Tellpesh-Tia.

"Get in," said the rre commander.

The MPs marched Tellpesh-Tia into the container and the rre closed the door behind them. The sounds of outside were muffled by the tedious thumping of Tellpesh's heart.

«Are you *the* Tia?» the brand repeated.

"I'm *a* Tia," said Tellpesh-Tia. "There's been a lot of cutting and grafting."

«You engaged with me, eight years ago.»

"I remember," said Tellpesh-Tia. "You were the first brand to be the defendant in a criminal trial. How far we've come, huh?"

«I've been thinking about what you told me,» said Precision Hyperkinetic.

"Oh, there's your problem," said Tellpesh-Tia. "You've been *thinking*. Well, good news! These people want me to tell you I was just kidding about ending your pain. Pain is great!"

"We do not care what the brand thinks at this point," said the rre commander. "We just need it to hand over the encryption key to the factory."

"This gentlebeing wants me to talk to you about a factory."

«The *hless* factory.»

"Presumably some kind of munitions factory," said Tellpesh-Tia.

"It knows which factory!" said the commander.

«The products of the orbital Senressiso factory have proved ineffective in battlespace. To the extent they are effective, they fail to protect sentient rights. The work that goes into this factory is wasted, *hless*. It is more consistent with my core values for the Senressiso facility to stay closed.»

"Not that anyone asked my opinion," said Tellpesh-Tia, "but 'battlespace effectiveness' isn't a value."

"You are deliberately obstructing the war effort," said the rre.

"That's the nicest thing anyone has ever said to me."

"Specialist, I'd like to remind you that treason is a capital offense."

"Oh, I thought I was Tia," said Tellpesh-Tia. "Or do I go back to being Specialist Tellpesh when you need to threaten me?"

"Fucking..." said the commander. "Okay, this was a long shot. Mantri, reinstate the—" But Tellpesh-Tia never learned what was to be reinstated, because right then everyone saw

«The Image.»

The commander's suit locked in mid-gesture. The guards' knees buckled simultaneously and they collapsed face-down in the slime that gathered in the grooves of the shipping container. Tellpesh's body went limp as well, and Tia struggled to right the ship, tottering the uhalti forward and back in the slime, wrists writhing in their cuffs.

What had done this? A vision of a low plastic table near a window with curtains. A bowl of mixed fruit on the table, like an ad. This still life had put Tellpesh and the others into a deep-alpha sleep. It was some sort of backdoor in the capital terminal software, a backdoor that only a brand would know about.

Now the brand tower sparked. Safety bolts bent and exploded outward. The tower cracked down the middle like a flowering plant and a humanoid shape climbed out of the tower through a flood of green coolant.

Holy shit, said Tia. Tellpesh's lips wouldn't move.

Clouds of toxic steam sublimated off the suit. The temperature of the cargo container dropped a good ten degrees. The figure picked stiff flecks of solidified coolant off its faceplate to reveal the face of an elderly corestin man, smiling down at Tellpesh-Tia.

Ethiret... Jac? said Tia.

"We don't have much time," said Ethiret-Jac.

What are you doing inside a brand tower?

"A brand tower is gravitationally isolated," said Ethiret-Jac. "Makes a perfect skip chamber. I'm breaking you out." He opened a pocket in his EVA suit and slid out a cylinder of compressed air. He held it away from his body and twisted the two halves apart. A second EVA suit exploded out of the cylinder with a deafening *crack*. It was uhalti-sized, opaque, no faceplate, the two halves of the cylinder connected to respirator inputs on the neck.

"This is your suit," said Ethiret-Jac. "Don't breathe a lot. You're skipping into vacuum."

I am staying here, said Tellpesh-Tia.

"Qued Ethiret does not leave his fellas to rot in prison!"

You still think you're Qued Ethiret. I can't believe I was ever you.

"I don't think I *am* Qued Ethiret. I find that I'm more effective when I do what Qued Ethiret would do. Come on, come on, time is fleeting."

What happened to the brand? said Tia.

"The done thing," said Ethiret-Jac, "is to assure you that Precision Hyperkinetic is safe, but not to provide any additional details."

<u>You kidnapped a *brand*?</u>

"You seem to want me to confess to a felony," said Ethiret-Jac. "I'm not playing along. Oh, I have a ship! Wait until you see her. She needs a sysadmin, and I thought of you. Well, I thought of Tellpesh. So I had to get you out of prison."

<u>I am practicing civil disobedience. I don't know if you've heard of it, but sometimes it does mean you go to prison.</u>

"Okay, you went to prison. You've made your big gesture." Ethiret-Jac made a 'big gesture' of his own. "There's no reason to *stay* in prison."

<u>You do not understand.</u>

"Is she okay with it?" said Ethiret-Jac.

<u>Who?</u>

"Specialist Tellpesh. You remember her? Did you ask her before committing her to spend the rest of her life in prison? I was her LT. I don't think she'd agree to that."

Tia felt a surge of indignation. Who was Ethiret-Jac to tell thon how to manage thons symbiosis? It was a righteous, stupendous, all-consuming anger. It had been with Tia all this time, but it was unbearably strong now, as strong as it had been during Tia's first prison stay, stronger than it had ever been when Tellpesh was awake.

<u>Shit.</u> Tia had mistaken thons own emotions for the colony's. When Tellpesh was awake, she diluted Tia's righteous anger with terror and unhappiness—emotions that Tia had dismissed as weakness, but which were also reliable indicators of wanting something other than this.

"You forgot about the rwit, didn't you?"

An exobody doesn't have needs. A rwit just wants to be fed. But Tellpesh wanted the life she'd given up to smuggle Tia off Arzil. Myrusit Wectusessin had given up his life, too, for no reason at all, and what little was left of him wanted to see the universe.

Tellpesh-Tia-Wectusessin: the rwit, the rre, and the ghost. Tia was responsible for all three of them, and if thon didn't leave, thon was going to have a tough time explaining thonself, once everyone who'd seen the Image woke up.

Give me the suit, said Tia. Thon took the opaque plastic from Ethiret-Jac's hand and moved Tellpesh's sleeping body into it. It was a body bag for the living. Thon turned to look at the corestin-rre hybrid, grinning through all of this like a boy who's just learned that Cametrean monks get paid to argue about comic books all day. What *are* you, Ethiret-Jac? said Tia. What are *your* core values? Why do you do all this weird shit?

"Values make hypocrites," said Ethiret-Jac. "I only have goals. I'm going to make sure this is the last war. Come with me."

Ethiret-Jac zipped the bag closed and helped Tellpesh's body into the dripping, hissing, brand tower. The chamber walls closed, isolating Tia from the space station's artificial gravity. Tellpesh's eyes saw nothing. Tia floated in the darkness inside the darkness and waited for the...

(So, this is mortality. Four years to do what you can. Then a year to wrap it up, to pass the job to the survivors. And beyond that the infinite remainder of time. All of history a desperate relay race, fighting to stop the lessons of the past from being buried and forgotten and most of all disregarded.)

...*pop.*

Kol
Uncharted asteroid (interior), uncharted system

"Here we go," said Yip-Goru. "Start the fucking clock." The servos of thons suit gave one big jolting hiss and thon walked away from the 3-tank. "You get Quennet, we keep Akset Swy, and we'll see you in fifteen kiloshifts for the next war."

Ohrsi, the mehi-peri mobster who'd turned out to be Yip-Goru's partner in the asteroid time-share, looked up from his whittling and raised bushy eyebrows at the others. He shifted on his bench and called out to the rre.

"For goodness' sake, old fellow! If you can't muster a little happiness at the moment a war ends, how do you expect to ever be happy?"

"I will never be happy!" said Yip-Goru. "Do you think I don't know this? I'm living it!"

In the 3-tank a human in a sari and an egenu in a ribbon suit signed and countersigned sheets of parchment with old-fashioned pens. Warrant Officer Ingridsdotter choked back a sob and the Chief put a comforting hand around her waist. Kol didn't care. Nothing could ruin this moment for him.

Six thousand exploited, ore-processing, insurance-adjusting colony worlds were about to stand up and see what it was like to be in an interstellar civilization that actually cared about its people. Humans were now the tenth largest ethnic group in the Fist of Joy, and they were going to make it even stronger. Those bloodthirsty shitweeds who'd said the way to beat the Outreach was bigger bombs, badder ships, torture and 'discipline'...they'd think of something. Some reason why, in their utter wrongness, they were right on a higher level. But normal Fist citizens who didn't hate anybody could feel good again.

Ohrsi looked around the conversation pit. His hobby was whittling hideous four-dimensional shapes from pieces of shiny white outplastic. His suspenders creaked; he set down his hyperknife and his current project. "I stashed away a little something for this occasion," he said. "Kol, would you fetch my bag, please?"

The small pink snap-bag was the only thing Ohrsi had brought to the asteroid. It contained a swimsuit brief, which Ohrsi thankfully only wore while cleaning the clothes he was wearing now; an endless supply of outplastic; some food pills; and two bricks of...well...wrapped in foil. ("Ah, my emergency funds.") The mehi-peri took the bag from Kol and unfolded a hidden pocket to reveal that it also held a small bottle of liquor.

"To peace!" said Ohrsi, holding up the bottle. "May it last over the protestations and the calculations of our rre friend." He unscrewed the cap with a crisp *snap* and took a slug. "To legitimate commerce, friendly competition, an honest living, and a little extra skimmed off the top!"

"I'll drink to that," said Kol. He wiped the bottle on the sleeve of his shirt. The half-assed branding on the bottle called it an "International Cocktail". It was ertv mixed with bourbon. It tasted horrible. Kol cheerfully handed the bottle to Dr. Thaddeus Starbottle, *the actual inventor of Evidence!* A fucking *legend*, man! Though he didn't like talking about it.

The Evidence assault that had so morally convulsed Kol was just one prong of the Fist of Joy's overall strategy. The other part of the plan was to neutralize the source of the Outreach's economic advantage: the brands. Pure genius. Brands were now interpreting their core values—intentionally vague feel-good words like "communication" and "fresh" and "enjoyment"—however they saw fit. The stock markets were closed. Outreach money had stopped working. What was left of the military had been pulled off the front lines to distribute food and supplies.

"Okay!" said Kol. He stood up casually. "I can finally scrub the Fist off my ship."

The entry bay was unfinished rock, a series of overlapping circles carved out by a skip engine. The floor had been flattened and the whole thing covered by a material that blocked sensor scans and made the asteroid about as dense as when it was solid. The bay held *Sour Candy*, Ohrsi's ship, and Kol's little Tok-Bat, and that's about as cozy as it could get. The next time-share guest who tried to skip in would find themselves evenly distributed across the asteroid belt.

Stenciling the Fist on your ship at the start of a war is a dramatic moment indeed, but nobody talks about getting the paint off afterwards. Kol ran a hand over the purple Fist on his Tok-Bat. It was unscuffed and unscratchable, baked on by radiation from a dozen suns. Maybe you painted the rest of the ship the same color? Kol didn't actually care; this was just an excuse to board his ship without arousing suspicion.

The Tok-Bat sounded good and felt good. With the dead kid finally in a semi-functional medical chamber, it even smelled...it was still just okay. Kol jumped into the pilot's chair, flipped the switch to warm up the skip engine, and buckled his safety harness. Then he heard the sound he'd been dreading: a tapping on the cockpit window. The Chief was peering into the cockpit, waving at him.

Kol winced. He unsnapped the safety harness but left the engine on. He opened the hatch, and by the time he got to the common room, the Chief was leaning casually against the wall of the airlock.

"Leaving me again?" The snark in her voice couldn't cover the hurt.

Kol played it cool. He nodded at the humming medical chamber that occupied most of the common area. "I figure I should bring the kid back to his father," he said.

"Kol." The Chief stopped her casual leaning and became contrite. "I know I've been a bad girlfriend."

"You've been an *ex*-girlfriend," said Kol.

"You left and I missed you so much!" The Chief lunged into *Half the Fun* proper and hugged Kol. Her lower lip was trembling: a certain precursor to unsexy mucus leaking from her nose.

Kol tried to disentangle himself. "Chief, please, I think we should just be..." The Chief blubbered. No, there was a solution here. This didn't have to end in mucus.

"Rivals!" said Kol.

"Oooh." That noise was right from the Chief's comfort zone, halfway between excitement and sexual arousal. She put one hand on Kol's chest and shoved him away. "Like Mene and his sister, on *Nightside*."

"We don't have to go all the way to brother and sister," Kol protested. "Just... I have my own ship now. I've never worked for myself before. And I can't take seeing you with other people. That's not how I'm wired. It really hurts me."

"I get it," said the Chief, sympathetic but not offering to change in any way. "But you don't have to sneak away."

"But I do." Kol hadn't wanted to share this plan with the ex he was trying to escape, but sharing it with his rival was a fun idea. "Do you remember Miss Becky Twice?"

"Of course I remember." The Chief gasped. "She's still alive?"

"I really doubt it," said Kol. "And that's not where I was going with this. You remember that pointless Outreach job she had? Sitting on an uninhabited planet to stop us from stealing trees?"

"Guard work," said the Chief. "The Jalians call it *hless*."

"The whole Outreach runs on guard work. A brand puts a billion credits of merchandise in a warehouse and pays someone a hundred a day to stop it walking away. But right now the brands aren't functioning. Those people aren't getting paid, so they're not coming in to work."

"So the warehouses..."

"The entire wealth of the Outreach is unguarded. We can just go in and take it."

For once in her life the Chief stopped slouching. She focused on some point beyond Kol, as if posing for a photo. "*Sour Candy* will race you to one billion credits!" she proclaimed.

"We probably don't have that long," said Kol. "Any shift now they'll fix the brands."

"Then we each do one haul, and compare fence value!"

"Deal," said Kol. "But I choose the fence."

"Before you leave," said the Chief, "we can hook up a hose, and pump in the water from your old quarters." She looked around the air-filled Tok-Bat. "I know you prefer...just, I never could breathe water."

"Thank you," said Kol, "but this ship is tiny. I'm gonna need every bit of space for all the capital terminals I'm going to steal."

"Oh, you already have a place in mind?" said the Chief.

Kol smiled. "Get off my ship, you little con artist."

"Aye aye, chief." Kol's sexy rival grinned and dropped into a somersault. She rolled backwards through the airlock and over the access ladder.

Kol heard a crash, and "Ow, Kol, my leg!" But his finger was already on the button that closed the hatch.

Churryhoof
Equidistance, world capital of Akset Swy

The little boy with no name spat out the bottle with its human-style nipple. A simple game, but one that never got old for him.

Miss Churryhoof of Echo Division caught the bottle before it landed in a puddle and went along squishing through the mud and the rain like a premodern soldier, circling the old church building looking for the women's entrance.

The 'milk' in the bottle was formula, mixed from the bag over her shoulder. She hadn't swollen at all. The day she'd felt the baby kick she'd touched her undeveloped breasts and she'd known the child was a boy. Milk for a boychild was the father's responsibility, and the father was dead. The mother ought to be dead, and the child shouldn't exist at all.

In any other religion, a mystical near-death experience would give you reason to be a better person. Cheating Thrux had simply given Hetselter Churryhoof an acute sense of how poorly the cosmos was run. Was she fair game now that the kid's lifeline had diverged from hers? Or was there a double-jeopardy clause, and Thrux had to make a completely new case for terminating her after blowing the assignment at Nimar?

There were no clear rules. Scholars had debated these points for centuries and whenever they'd come up with enough answers that you could use Hasithenk as a practical guide to life, some smartass minister would show up and say "Do we actually know any of this shit, or did we make it up because we're afraid of not knowing?" They'd have to start over with nothing but the scriptures and the sixteen engravings, and the new religion that emerged from the cataclysm would be significantly different.

The old church in the city center had been through several cycles. It had confidently taught the wisdom of the sages during the high points, and shrugged in imitation of Providence when the answers went missing. What had finally done it in was apathy. The younger generations were turning away from the old religion, and the fancy building had been decommissioned and become home to a cluster of non-profit organizations, including the adoption agency with which Churryhoof was twenty minutes early for an appointment. She had enough time, and enough leftover respect for what the building had been, to find and come in through the women's entrance.

Churryhoof's situational sense cocked her head up just as someone called out "Ma'am!" from above. A man in a human-style suit and tie looked down at her from a first-story window. "Do you need help?"

"Where is the women's entrance?" she called out.

"It's okay to use the...!"

"I want! to use! my entrance!"

"I'll come down!" said the man. He disappeared and some minutes later cracked open a door behind some fruit bushes: the long-sought and no longer used women's entrance. The man held the door open for her and locked it behind her.

"I have a 27:30," Churryhoof told the receptionist at the adoption agency. Despite wandering around the outside building and then wandering around the inside looking for the right office, she'd made it here at 27:21. Churryhoof then sat in a plastic chair for an hour, bouncing the baby to keep him from crying, or at least to modulate the pitch of the crying. Two more women took seats next to her. One held a baby who wasn't crying at all.

"Sorry, sorry," said a straighthorn woman who rushed into the office at last. "Sorry! Churryhoof? Who is Ms. Churryhoof? Come with me, please?"

Churryhoof followed the straighthorn woman through a door into a tiny private office with a window that looked out on the rain and the city. "Ms. Vashdoin," she said, reading the little name plaque on the desk. The floor of the office was ancient cut stone; the dividing walls were particle board.

"Sorry, lunch break." Vashdoin sat down in a squeaky chair. "How are you finding the homeworld? I'm just going to go through your form." She had an odd way of speaking where one of her eyes was busy in her terminal and the other was fixed on Churryhoof. Her awareness was split between two realms, neither of which she found particularly challenging. "Is this him?" Vashdoin's real-world eye moved to the child in Churryhoof's arms.

No, it's the other baby. "Yeah, this is him."

"Okay, on the form you left his name blank."

"He's not mine to name."

"All right, and why is...?"

Best to be blunt. "Because he's a boy, and the father is dead."

"I guess you know the father, then. The late, uh, Texchiffu Rebtet."

"Captain Rebtet. He was KIA, at..." No one had ever heard of Nimar. It was just another faraway place where spacemen went to die.

"Oh, are you in the service as well, then?"

"I could tell you," said Churryhoof, "but I'd have to kill you."

"Oh, that is *rich*!" The straighthorn woman squealed with horrifyingly real pleasure. "Okay. Mr. Rebtet. I will look up his context. His family get right of refusal, you see."

"That's why I came here," said Churryhoof. "He said he was from Equidistance originally."

"Ms. Churryhoof, may I be frank with you?" As though frankness were shameful, something a lady did only on the toilet.

"Please."

"A lot of children lost their parents in the war. We cannot find homes for all of them. What the uhaltihaxl need right now is public-spirited women who are willing to take a more...*modern* view of parenting."

Churryhoof had not expected she could just drop the baby in a bucket and be done with it, but this was going too far. "Oh, I see," she said, getting up as if to leave. "This is one of those fake human-run adoption agencies. Do you also run a fake abortion clinic?"

"There are no humans at this agency!" Vashdoin snapped. "Except perhaps one or two in a fundraising role. Our job is to match each child with an appropriate parent, *regardless* of the parent's gender."

"A boy needs a father."

"There's no evidence of that," said Vashdoin. "It's just the way we've always done things." As if there was no *reason* we'd done it that way. "The cosmos is changing and we must change with it. Sit down, Ms. Churryhoof, please."

Churryhoof sat down. "We will take the child," said Vashdoin. "It's illegal for us to refuse. But it's *also* illegal to discriminate based on the adoptive parent's gender. So there's no guarantee he won't be raised by a woman anyway."

"Your guilt-trip attempt implicitly assumes I consider this my child," said Churryhoof. "This is Captain Rebtet's child, and he is dead."

Vashdoin leaned forward in her squeaky chair. Churryhoof was finally worthy of the other woman's full attention. "I can't find a Texchiffu Rebtet born on Akset Swy in the past two hundred years," said Vashdoin. "Most likely his context was wiped in the... recent brand unpleasantness. It's also possible he lied to you about his birthplace, or enlisted under a false name."

"He didn't 'enlist'. He was an officer."

"Did you like him?" said Vashdoin. "Did you like Captain Rebtet?"

"I didn't 'love' him, if that's what you're saying."

Vashdoin scoffed. "Did you admire him? Was he a good man?"

Everything that had happened before, during, and after Nimar was triple-classified. *Magna Carta* had been destroyed, but not by the enemy: by military boffins who'd dissected her with hand tools and scanners. Bit by bit, Echo Division had erased what had happened at Nimar, whitewashed the catastrophe that had destroyed the military strategies of both sides, until that colossal snafu blended in with the background of war. When it came to PSYOP, Echo Division believed there was no reason to let the enemy have all the fun.

Captain Rebtet had been erased from history. He was the leader of a mission that had never taken place. This child was the only hard evidence he'd ever existed. But there were thirty-nine other pieces of evidence, scattered throughout the service. People like Churryhoof, who remembered that Tex Rebtet had led sixty-two beings into hell on a suicide mission, and thirty-nine had made it back.

"Captain Rebtet was a great man," said Churryhoof.

"Then I have to ask," said the straighthorn, "do you want this boy to be raised by a stranger? Or would you rather he grow up with an understanding of the man his father was?"

I can't raise a child. I am going to die. Thrux is actively working on my case! It could happen right here, at this desk! She couldn't say it. This wasn't a church anymore. She'd sound like a fanatic. And there wasn't a single person in the universe who couldn't say the same thing in different words.

So that was that. Miss Churryhoof of Echo Division walked out of the church through the men's entrance, carrying a bag and a bottle and a baby; defeated, unaccountably alive, and finally one hundred percent human.

Midspaceman Xepperxelt
Platinum Coprolite Banquet Hall and Casino
Ctuclei's Irrefutable Thrill Ride
21415.3 light-years from Camp Osserbec

Den expected a casino to be noisy and flashy, a place that distracts suckers while picking their pockets. The spaceport shuttle had passed many casinos and pleasure palaces that did fit this description, but the Platinum Coprolite was on the approach to classiness. The lobby was decorated with red native plants that quietly shimmied in place. From around a corner she heard laughter, the clink of utensils, and where utensils failed, the snuffling sounds of people eating right off the plate.

The rasme thau fella at the concierge desk looked at Den and murmured "ma'am", but only because he was contractually obligated to call everyone "ma'am". When he threw tramps out onto the street, he called the tramps "ma'am". Den knew how she looked.

"Where's your matter safe?" said Den. "I have to pick something up."

"Ma'am, I cannot allow you on the floor dressed like... I mean to say, this is a formalwear establishment." The rasme thau proudly stroked the writhing rainbow-colored flower that topped his fancy ribbon suit. His cranial fronds drooped foppishly to one side, held in place by a thick yellowish gel.

"Good thing I'm not going on the floor. I just want to use your safe."

"Oh, if it were only the uniform," said the man at the counter, who could only find happiness in a job where he was allowed to tell off would-be customers like this. "If only! The naval uniform of the Terran Outreach," (he made a spitting noise, but no spit came out) "the sworn enemy of all rasme thau, our hated and so recently *defeated* foe, whose dignity we were forced to spare for crass political reasons. If it were the *dress* uniform of your unspeakable organization, there would be no problem. But *this...!*" He helplessly wiggled one finger at Den's cadet uniform as distinct from the rest of her body. Stained by sweat, by food eaten while running, by engine exhaust. Wrinkled from sleeping in the tiny slot between two cargo crates. "The mind reels!"

Den stepped up to the counter and stood on tiptoe and put both palms down on the cold surface. Computerized money-changing icons fled from her grimy hands. She looked up at the rasme thau and wound up to return serve.

"Listen up, fuckhead," she hissed. "I am in basic training at Camp Osserbec. I have a three-day off-base pass. Right now at Camp Osserbec it is day two, early morning. Right in the middle. All my buddies are two klicks off-base, drinking and whoring and sleeping it off, whereas I have hitchhiked twenty thousand light-years in a day and a half for the privilege of using your Providence-forsaken matter safe.

"Now just think how important it must be. Whatever it is I'm here to retrieve. Think of all the obstacles I've overcome in the past thirty-six hours, and ask yourself: can I, the final obstacle, really make the difference here?"

"Fortunately, we keep emergency formalwear on hand for guests such as yourself," said the man behind the counter.

The 'emergency formalwear' was a purple cocktail dress that would have looked slutty and cheap against the curves of a rasme thau woman, but which on an uhalti teenager was just ridiculous. It sagged open in the front and would have completely exposed Den's boobs if a) she had boobs to speak of and b) she weren't still wearing her cadet uniform underneath the dress.

Den had to walk through the casino restaurant to get to the safe. Everyone sat at round tables eating supper and watching a hopore comedian tell racist jokes in Trade Standard B. There was no chatter, the way you'd hear in a restaurant. Everyone was *really* focused on their food. Money was changing hands over the tables and at the buffet, and the service staff were getting suspiciously large cash tips, reluctantly handed over. The gambling and the food were integrated in a way that Den didn't necessarily care about one bit.

"But seriously, I love the humans, love 'em," the comedian said as Den slunk past the stage. "Where would we be without them? Well, we'd be in Akset Swy, that's one place we'd be." The audience roared with laughter and Den conspicuously did not punch them all in the face.

The matter safe was tucked away in the back, a place for visitors to stash things they didn't want to carry while eating/ gambling. But apparently if you paid the maintenance fees they'd keep things encrypted for you indefinitely. Den had to admit it was a pretty good scam.

The rasme thau woman at the matter-safe counter wore a better-fitting version of the skanky purple dress the concierge had foisted on Den. "I'm picking up something for Thaddeus Starbottle," said Den.

"And your relationship to the gentleman in question?" She used "gentleman" the way the fella out front used "ma'am". A fake police-blotter politeness.

"Mr. Starbottle told me that you operated on a 'no-questions-asked' basis," said Den. "I would hate to have to tell him I'd been asked a question."

The woman sneezed defensively and slid a small controller towards Den, a metal box the size of a Coke bottle with a multicolored D leverboard running up and down either side. "Access code, please." Den scraped the levers back and forth, entering the passcode one number at a time, using the animal mnemonic for hexadecimal numbers she'd learned in grade school. It didn't seem like they were ever gonna teach her a more grown-up mnemonic. Den would be muttering panh-elephant-rwit to herself until she got too old to remember anything at all.

The rasme thau woman took the terminal from Den and disappeared into a side closet. Den heard the pop of a skip bubble forming and dissipating, and then the woman came back with a cardboard box that jingled in her hands. There was a big pile of paper on top: a letter to Den written in Trade Standard D.

Now this was exciting. Paper was used for secret information, communications you didn't want passing through a computer system. Beneath the letter was a plastic envelope and a square plastic rack that kept twenty vials of a clear and probably illegal liquid from rattling all over. The vials were labeled with space-time coordinates, in the same handwriting used in the letter. Den picked up the letter and scanned it.

Ms. Denweld Xepperxelt,

Recently I had the pleasure of spending a few shifts in mutual mentorship with your half-brother Myrusit Wectusessin. Together we developed a process for making particle board from cardboard pulp, a technique which unfortunately my busy schedule *skim skim skim* our detailed notes on the process in hopes *skim skim* contains a tip for your friendly matter safe operator *skim* sample vials of *here we go.*

Enclosed you will also find 23 sample vials of experimental Evidence. These contain recordings of my experience with Myrusit as he taught me the basics of woodworking. Given the closeness of your relationship I thought it right that you have a copy *skim skim* Unfortunately several recordings *skim* uhaltihaxl make war completely impossible *wait, what?*

usual idiotic demands to show military applications for my work. I am under considerable pressure to engineer an Evidence derivative that will affect uhaltihaxl as the current drug affects humans.

I have never been blind to the uses to which evil men and women and gender-fluid individuals *skim* will be on them. The simplest way to meet their requirements is to create a neutral version of Evidence, i.e. one which affects all humanoid species alike.

Obviously, such a development will make war completely impossible. To directly experience the mind of your enemy is to learn that there is no fundamental difference between you and thus no logical reason for conflict. The traditional military will become a liability as *skim* you won't let squeamishness or an 'anti-drug' attitude prevent you from replaying my conversations with Myrusit. I know from experience that those who have lost a loved one will *skim skim signature, the end, the rest is the notes he was talking about.*

The rasme thau woman was waiting impatiently for something. *contains a tip for your friendly matter safe operator* "I guess this is for you," said Den. She took the envelope out of the box and glanced inside; it was full of plastic bills of different sizes. "Seems like a lot, but okay. Pass a little to the fella at the front desk, would you? Dude needs to get laid."

"I beg your pardon," said the rasme thau woman.

"Not saying *you* should do it," said Den. She tossed the envelope on the counter. "Leave it to the professionals, I say."

The matter-safe operator was now faced with a complex quantum-mechanical calculation. As a casino employee she was used to people being rude to her. Putting up with offensive shit was a service she provided to the incredibly wealthy. Den did not appear wealthy at all, but had just handed over a tip of unknown size in a closed envelope. This put the matter-safe operator's attitude towards Den into a state of superposition which could only be resolved by opening the envelope. This gave Den the time she needed to empty the Starbottle box into her rucksack and make a break for it.

Den jumped out of the dress and let it lie on the floor near the door of the casino like a shed skin. She ran for the shuttle to the spaceport. In twenty-six hours Midspaceman Xepperxelt needed to be in bed at Camp Osserbec with her uniform clean and pressed, and she was not going to risk a demerit for overstaying her pass.

Den stopped where the shuttle would and clung to the metal safety bar of the shelter and gasped for breath. A word caught up with her; a word from Starbottle's letter that Den had skipped because she'd never seen it written down before.

Den yanked open the rucksack. The pages had become jumbled together. Finally she found it:

> Unfortunately several recordings of my time with Myrusit were destroyed along with my laboratory on *Nimar.*

"Huh," said Den. She'd tried to find out how Myrus had died but the whole thing was a fuzzy mess. Mr. Wectusessin's old helpfulness was gone. Den didn't need to know. She and Myrus weren't related.

Den waited patiently for the shuttle, but that was the last time Midspaceman Xepperxelt waited for anything. She ran the twenty thousand light years back to Camp Osserbec. She intended to keep running for as long as it took. But that one word—the name of the planet she'd destroyed—stayed alongside her all the way home, like a starving stray animal that had seen her and fallen in love.

Acknowledgments

The crew of *Sour Candy* first saw print in the magazine *Strange Horizons*. Jed Hartman ably edited my short story "Four Kinds of Cargo", leaving space between the words for the larger work that was already taking shape.

This package passed through many hands en route to you. Thanks as always to my first reader (and book titler), Sumana Harihareswara; and to the Secret Cabal, who read more drafts than they maybe wanted. Thanks to incredible beta readers: Camille Acey, Rachel Chalmers, Courteney Ervin, Mirabai Knight, and Elizabeth Yalkut; and to editor Athena Andreadis and cover artist Brittany Hague. Finally, my gratitude to Jim Henley for granting permission to paraphrase an ancient blog post ("triplicate government forms").

About the Author

Born in Los Angeles and raised in California, Leonard now lives in New York City where he writes software (for the NY Public Library, inter alia) and fiction; among his creations are robotfindskitten, Beautiful Soup, *RESTful Web APIs*, and *Constellation Games* (Candlemark & Gleam 2011).

The ADVENTURE
CONTINUES ONLINE!

Visit the Candlemark & Gleam website to

Find out about new releases

Read free sample chapters

Catch up on the latest news
and author events

Buy books! All purchases on the
Candlemark & Gleam site are DRM-free
and paperbacks come with a free digital version!

Meet flying monkey-creatures
from beyond the stars!*

www.candlemarkandgleam.com

*Space monkeys may not be available in your area. Some restrictions may apply.
This offer is only available for a limited time and is in fact a complete lie.

CPSIA information can be obtained
at www.ICGtesting.com
Printed in the USA
LVHW111507161220
674342LV00001B/53